FAMINE

BOOK ONE OF THE APOCALYPTICS

MONICA ENDERLE PIERCE

§

MONICA ENDERLE PIERCE

FAMINE

BOOK ONE OF
THE APOCALYPTICS

Editorial: Maia Driver
Cover Design: Jennifer Munswami/J.M. Rising Horse Creations
Photography: Ric Colgan, ByteStudio Photography
Book Design: Monica Enderle Pierce

Published in the United States by Stalking Fiction
ISBN-10: 0985976128
ISBN-13: 978-0-9859761-2-5

For Dad
Thank you

ALSO BY MONICA ENDERLE PIERCE

Novels

Girl Under Glass

The Mother Element

The Shadow & The Sun

A Castle to Keep

The Bones Beneath

Short Stories

A Sad Jar of Atoms

Rust and Ruin

To Give Her Heart

Love Lies Bleeding

Anthologies

The Dragon Chronicles

Prep for Doom

The Doomsday Chronicles

Once Upon a Time in Gravity City

PART ONE

1

WESTERN UNION TELEGRAM
April 6, 1895
C. Vernon, P.O. Gen'l Delivery

Have arrived Ogden. No sign of trouble.
Susanna

CAUGHT IN A MAELSTROM OF BLACK FEATHERS AND BEADY
eyes, Bartholomew tugged down his top hat and turned up his
coat collar to a murder of crows' sharp talons and beaks.

Black-winged bastards, he thought, ducking the raucous
birds and continuing along the murky Mulberry Bend as
evening's growing shadows reached for him.

The fabric shop's squat proprietress leaned from its doorway. "I have some lovely calico for your lady, sir."

Lady? A sneer curled Bartholomew's upper lip as he
continued past. Though she bore a feminine and striking form,
Famine, his unwanted mistress, was far from ladylike.

Indeed, her presence impelled Bartholomew to spend as much time as possible in New York City's infamous Sixth Ward—the Five Points. Famine found its poverty pathetic, and her disinterest provided him some small measure of escape. So it was that Bartholomew Etienne Pelletier had a strange affection for the Bend's wretches and crooks.

"A fat duck for your dinner tonight, sir?"

Bartholomew skirted the butcher and the pale, plucked carcass the man thrust into his path.

Crows minced along the rooflines and plucked trash from the streets. They watched his passage from perches upon the gas lamps. Doubtless they were haunting him for a reason. But, after fifteen hundred years of searching, it seemed too much to trust they were leading him to freedom.

"You look like a gentleman who appreciates fine tobacco, sir."

Bartholomew glanced down at the tobacconist. Indeed, he was one to appreciate the finer, and coarser, activities the Five Points offered an Edwardian gentleman—he'd already been entertained by one of its ladies that afternoon. But a practiced sniff brought the bitter stench of tar across his palate, so Bartholomew strode onward. The rickety shop was a charlatan's abode.

The crows on his path winged up en masse, wheeled about, and disappeared into a narrow alley. Bartholomew scowled and stepped into the dank corridor but saw only broken bricks, crumpled paper, and stagnant water—until he followed the rustle of wings. The black sentinels stared down from the ledge of a four-story, red brick tenement. His displeasure deepened. He disliked the creatures; among them were spies. But he knew not to ignore them. They were the Catcher's inhuman eyes and, clearly, there was something she wanted him to see.

"By any means necessary," he murmured, pocketed his gray kidskin gloves, and scaled the wall, finding handholds few men could grip.

Once atop the roof, Bartholomew straightened his black frock coat and brushed dust from its folds. Exacting in appearance, manners, and most particularly, revenge, he wore clothing the color of ashes and coal and bore the semblance of a man not yet bent by middle life but beyond the follies of youth. Truth be told, he still recalled his boyhood on the banks of the Rhine, though fifteen centuries had passed.

The crows skittered from his path as he prowled the roof's perimeter and surveyed the cesspool that was New York's Sixth Ward. Built on reclaimed swampland, the ward hosted impoverished immigrants, thieves, murderers, whores, and all manner of slumgullion. It also sustained mosquitoes, lice, bedbugs, cholera, consumption, and an ongoing turf war. Only the latter puzzled him; Bartholomew saw nothing worth fighting for in the streets below.

He removed a silver cigarette case and a box of matches from his coat pocket, extracted a cigarette, and struck a match off the roof tiles. The acrid woodiness of fine tobacco obliterated the sulfuric tang of the match as he inhaled the flame into the tip of his cigarette. He held a lungful of smoke, enjoying the warmth it spread through his body, and flicked the match over the ledge to land in a puddle. He turned the case, running his fingers over the lines and leaves etched into its silver surface.

Taller than the average man, Bartholomew's wiry muscularity belied his physical power. He wore his light brown hair short, sported a trim beard, and didn't care a whit for current fashion. He smoked and drank, though he was incapable of getting drunk, and Bartholomew cursed—in many languages. He was, by many accounts, a remarkable character bearing a compelling, indefinable quality.

As one, the crows peered over the ledge and up the Bend. He followed their gaze and spied a small figure flitting between horse carts, tradesmen, and sluggards. A young girl, her blonde braids flying and blue shawl clutched to her chest, sprinted his way with a larger girl and two boys in pursuit. Bartholomew slipped the case into his pocket and crouched at the ledge. He dragged on his cigarette and watched.

With her pursuers gaining ground, the urchin found her path blocked by an overturned market cart. She ducked between two men and scuttled around the corner into the dead-end alley below Bartholomew's perch. She ran to a door at the rear of the building and tugged on its handle. It didn't give. With a little, high-pitched noise and a kick to the door, she whirled, and found her escape blocked again.

"Gimme that." The larger girl's voice bounced off the grimy alley walls as she shoved past the two boys.

Bartholomew surveyed the aggressor's black eye and ratty, calico dress. A sneer curled her lips back from her broken front teeth. He glanced at the crows. The Catcher wanted *her*? But the birds squabbled, preened, and minced about the roof. They called insults at him, arched and flapped their wings, and chortled as if sharing a good laugh at his expense.

"No!"

The word was clear and strong. Bartholomew looked down, surprised by its power.

The older girl stalked toward her defiant prey, hand outstretched. "Gimme that or we'll smash yer face."

"No!" the little girl repeated. "This is fer Samuel. Get yer own, *Catherine*."

Bartholomew leaned out over the roofline like a gargoyle as smoke swirled around him and away. A small smile tugged up the corner of his lips. He hadn't missed how the little girl had twisted Catherine's name into an insult.

Neither had Catherine, evidently. Her fist smashed into the little girl's cheek. The child crashed into the building wall and landed in a slimy puddle. Her head struck the bricks with a *crack*.

Catherine smirked as she yanked the bundled shawl from her victim's arms. "Now it's fer me. *Matilde*." She spat on the little girl then marched back to the waiting boys.

Bartholomew's fists clenched as Catherine unwrapped a small heel of bread from the ragged fabric and doled out shares to her lackeys. Her back to the little girl, the bully draped the stolen shawl over her shoulder and shoveled bread into her mouth.

Matilde rolled over. She rose to her knees and looked around. She hefted a chunk of red brick, and the smile returned to Bartholomew's lips. Her palm barely fit around the flat side, and the jagged, broken edge jutted past her fingers. His smile became a wicked grin as Matilde stood, clutched the wall for a breath, and turned to her attackers. She stumbled toward them, her hand down and behind as she came upon her assailant.

"Hey, Catherine."

The bully turned and the little girl leaped forward. Her rock-filled fist whipped around to smash Catherine's cheek and nose. The bully's head snapped to the side. She staggered into one of the boys and they both hit the ground as the second boy stared at Matilde, open-mouthed like a fish. He wore a swath of bright red blood across his chest and face.

"Nobody steals from me!" Matilde fell upon her attacker, fist cocked for the next strike. Somehow, Catherine dodged the brunt of the blow. Matilde's fist glanced off her cheek and smashed into the ground. But the pain of crushed, bloodied knuckles didn't stop her. Nor did the older girl's sobs and pleas. As one boy stood staring and the other bolted, Matilde raised the brick again.

A burly man pushed past a gathering crowd and captured Matilde. She kicked, cursed, and twisted. "Settle, child," he said. "She got yer message."

The girl grew still. She looked from the watching adults to her prone assailant.

Two women bent over Catherine, who sat broken and stunned, her face unrecognizable and her calico dress covered in blood and breadcrumbs. And the remaining boy still stared at Matilde with wide, reverent eyes.

Matilde. Bartholomew rocked back on his heels, twisted, and stood. He slunk along the roofline, his focus on the retreating man and child. The girl sobbed as the man carried her along the Bend, turned the corner into a narrower space between two tenements, and ascended a set of rickety wooden stairs.

Bartholomew stuck his cigarette between his lips, trotted toward the edge of the building, and leaped to Matilde's tenement. He moved away from the roofline, crouched, and closed his light brown eyes. He focused on locating the girl within the building. When he was certain of her whereabouts, he crossed the roof, dropped to a rusty balcony outside the child's apartment and, melding with the shadows, beheld a wretched home.

A gaunt woman stooped at a wooden washbasin, scrubbing clothes like she was skinning a live cat. Her face, so similar to the girl's delicate countenance, had been beautiful but now bore the pockmarks of disappointment and drink. "Where's the bread?" she demanded.

The man put Matilde down.

The child scurried to put a table between herself and the woman. "Catherine Connelly stole it from me, Mama."

The mother jerked around to glare at her daughter. Water dripped from the shirt in her hands, darkening her faded red dress and pooling at her feet. The weight of her judgment slowed time. "I suppose that's yer excuse for losing yer shawl and soiling yer dress?"

"Yes, Mama."

She pinned the man with a withering glare. "I thought you showed her how to fight, Pieter."

"I did, and Tilde gave the Connolly girl a sound beating."

The woman grunted. "Clean that blood outta yer hair then bring Samuel for supper. You'll eat last, since you've lost the babe his bread." She returned to the wash. "Maybe hunger'll make you run faster next time."

"Yes, Mama." Matilde disappeared into an adjoining room and Bartholomew moved to peer through the grimy bedroom window. The girl paused at a basin in the corner of the room. She scrubbed blood from her cheek and blotted it from her scalp and knuckles. Her body trembled and she swallowed sobs as she cast an evil glare toward the door while her mother lit into her father to get their bread money back.

A toddler boy sat on the bedroom floor, his leg tied to a bed frame with a length of rope. He wielded a wooden spoon like a cudgel and Matilde endured several blows as she freed him, changed his diaper and clothes, and cuddled him.

"I'm sorry I lost yer bread, Samuel," she said as the babe chanted, "Bed, bed, bed."

Night came and Bartholomew held to the shadows watching the stars brighten and a waxing moon on the rise. Back pressed to the cold brick wall, he turned a matchstick over and over, itching to light a cigarette. But he dared not lest he draw unwelcome attention. Famine's soulless cadavers haunted the Ward's midnight alleys and rooftops. Her unnatural brood would love nothing more than to report his interest in a certain small girl.

When all had been long still within the apartment, he returned the match to its box and slipped into the tenement through the open kitchen window. He grimaced. The place stank of whiskey, cheap tobacco, rot, and shit. Two mangy, orange cats cowered and hissed from atop the kitchen table as he passed. Mice and cockroaches scattered. He entered the bedroom and stole across the room.

In the only bed, Matilde's inebriated parents snored and slept like the dead. In the corner by the window, the sleeping girl curled around Samuel on a mattress and pallet.

Bartholomew halted an arm's length from her.

Matilde's honey-colored curls framed her elfin face. Her features were delicate, doll-like, and marred by the purple bruise darkening her fair cheek.

The children breathed slowly, deeply. Tiny mice feet scritch-scritched beneath the floor, and the sounds of singing, fighting, and fornicating drifted in from neighboring rooms. Cold night air whistled through the gaping wallboards. Matilde shivered and pulled her baby brother closer.

Bartholomew, whose haunted past made him shun the company of children, looked upon the girl before him and was drawn not to her seraphic countenance but to the dark determination that had driven her to seek swift and brutal revenge. He crouched and rested his arms upon his knees. He sensed the rhythm of the girl's heart, watched the rise and fall of her body, and went to war with himself.

Administer the smallest infusion of his soul and he would have his freedom. A child. So easily hidden. So unexpected, so malleable. But was it true? Could this girl with her delicate, little bird bones possibly be the next Apocalyptic?

He closed his eyes and pinched the bridge of his nose. It was madness, an absurd notion borne of desperation—*his* desperation.

She can't be more than eight years old.

He opened his eyes and sighed. Matilde echoed his sigh in her sleep. Her breath caressed his face. Something stirred within him.

"Breath of life," he whispered.

He stood and stared at her. Finally, he reached out, hesitated, then feathered his fingers over her bruised cheek. The light caress was more than enough to reveal her powerful soul to him. His fingers became a fist as a shudder spread through him. His nerves flared, burning bright with the strength of the child's spirit. The immeasurable power of the Catcher's soul, so long dormant within him, stretched, surged, and demanded to be free.

"I've found you." Bartholomew's exhaled words were as much a cry of horror as a sigh of relief. He'd found the Catcher's next body. But knowing what that meant for this innocent child made him feel monstrous. He paced the room as one thought circled his mind: *By any means necessary.*

After many turns around the small space, he stopped and crouched before the pallet. He removed a narrow leather sheath from his coat pocket. From that he slid a thin, sharp blade. He reached for the girl. His fingers hovered. The blade waited.

Bartholomew spied the Roman eagle tattooed upon the back of his right hand. It signified he was a soldier, a *guardian.* The scars and marks upon his shoulders, chest, and back attested to his commitment. "Not a child," he whispered. He sat back on his heels and sheathed the knife. To condemn Matilde without her consent would be to embrace the black hole that threatened to swallow his soul each day.

Bartholomew stood and slipped the blade into his coat. He lifted his pocket watch and turned it between his fingers, feeling the movement as time slipped. He gazed down upon the girl until tapping drew his attention to the window. A crow clung to the sill in the moonlight. The bird cocked its head as if considering Matilde then looked back at Bartholomew and tapped the glass with its sharp, black beak.

Bartholomew shook his head.

I will not consign someone so young to this fate.

He'd searched fifteen centuries for her. He could wait one more decade. He could protect her and ready her for war. But he could not sacrifice a child, no matter how many souls hung in the balance.

Once more the crow tapped the glass. It bobbed its head then dropped away from the sill. The bird swooped around and up and joined the rest of its murder to form a black-winged cloud that made the stars wink as it soared over and away from the Sixth Ward.

2

Back in his Fifth Avenue home, Bartholomew stripped off his hat, gloves, and coat. He crossed the white marble foyer and strode down the hall to pause outside the salon. Conversation came from behind the closed pocket doors, Famine with several of her cadavers.

"There's nothing quite so effective as starvation and disease to start a war," she said, sounding smug. "I left the Chinese well on their way to a sizable rebellion."

Her throaty laughter grated on Bartholomew's nerves. His mistress was pestilence, suffering, and a slow, wasting death.

As she was wont to do, Famine had recently appeared upon his doorstep, unannounced, with a group of cadavers. She'd sashayed into the foyer and smiled like she'd eaten a puppy. She'd surveyed the chandeliers and artwork, caressed the mahogany and marble.

"Lovely. What's Bartholomeus's is mine. What's mine is yours. Welcome home, gentlemen."

After a blissful, twenty-seven-month holiday from her

bloody appetite and dominating spirit, Bartholomew had not celebrated their reunion. And he most certainly hadn't welcomed her undead entourage.

"Any sign of the other Horsemen there?" The voice was masculine; the words were Russian.

Famine replied, "That's not your affair, Stassi. Inquire again and I'll cut out your tongue."

Merda. Koorva. Derr'mo. Latin, Polish, Russian—in any language the word perfectly conveyed Bartholomew's mood. *Shit.*

Death and bones haunted his house.

He drew a deep breath and held it, then exhaled irritation and entered the room. Two half-dressed Poles and a Russian played cards at the table with Famine. A particularly irritating American cowboy, who smelled like cattle and old blood, had his feet on the new chaise. Rubbish occupied the Chippendale library chairs, filthy dishes littered Bartholomew's black baby grand piano, and discarded clothing hid the elegant curves of the mahogany settee.

Famine called herself Lady Claire Staniak. The name was a deliberate irritant and Bartholomew never used it. She wore blush-hued silk and lace, sequins and pearls. Her wavy, auburn hair was twisted into elaborate curls and displayed more pearls and silk flowers. Diamonds winked from her ears and twined about her pale throat. Creamy silk stockings bearing golden, hand-embroidered birds and white roses peeped from beneath her gown, and her satin slippers were tied with wide, blush bows. Famine was a beautiful lie from head to toe.

"Bartholomeus." She wrinkled her nose. "You've been rolling with the pigs again."

Her cadavers laughed. Neither living nor dead, they were Famine's creation, men whose souls she'd consumed. She fed them morsels of her flesh and thimbles of her blood to keep their bodies whole, but a subtle scent of must and decay wafted off them. With each innocent soul consumed, she gained strength, yet every cadaver she maintained depleted that power.

"All afternoon," Bartholomew replied as he went to the bar and filled the last clean glass with Scotch. "With luck I'll give you syphilis." He frowned at the first sip, displeased by the pinchbeck blend. The damnable cadavers lacked discernment as clearly demonstrated by their inferior choice of Scotch.

Famine glowered at him with ice-green eyes.

The cadavers' amusement had ended, leaving only the ticking of the mantle clock and the brush of fabric upon fabric as the strapping, young cowboy, Mr. Nash Barnes, sat upright. "You seem to forget you're talkin' to a lady. You shouldn't be speakin' like a blackguard in her presence, Centurion."

Bartholomew set down the glass. "You seem to forget that this is my house." He jabbed his finger toward Famine. "That bony bitch I am forced to tolerate." He kicked Barnes's legs. "You bastards are another story." Famine's boy sprawled across the floor as the chaise tipped. Bartholomew seized his coat collar and dragged him from the room. He hauled Barnes to his feet and propelled the cadaver down the long hallway and into the foyer. He stopped when Barnes's face met the mahogany front door.

"Bonjour, Mr. Barnes." Bartholomew yanked the cadaver back, opened the door, and shoved him into early morning light in full view of mortal pedestrians. He slammed the door and grinned at the shout and the snap of branches as the cowboy dodged the sun's exposure by diving behind the dense flowering viburnums that edged the mansion.

In darkness the cadavers appeared as ordinary as the mortals upon whom they fed. But daylight revealed their true nature—sunken flesh hanging from desiccated bones. They rattled when they walked and the removal of their heads released the most offensive odor, decay that Famine's power hid but never could overcome completely.

Since the Catcher's demise, Famine had assembled an army of her monstrosities, while Bartholomew and his associates had worked to dismantle it one head at a time.

"Bartholomeus." He turned at her call. "Go bathe," she said. "You reek of poverty and whores."

SMOKE MINGLED with the steam of Bartholomew's bath. He closed his eyes and dragged on his cigarette. He missed his butler Mr. Vernon and his housekeeper Mrs. Henderson. But he wouldn't entrust their welfare to a horde of filthy, flesh-hungry cadavers. So, with Famine's arrival, Bartholomew had dispatched his mortal house staff to his country home in Rye.

The bathroom door creaked.

Without souls, Famine's cadavers stood apart from the vitality of the world's creatures and their nothingness announced their presence like a beacon. They could hide from him only if they remained still. Their mistress, however, had a powerful soul that shielded her from his notice. She could come upon Bartholomew undetected, much to his discontent.

Floorboards squeaked.

Famine's hand slipped between his legs.

Warm bath water rippled across his skin. Bartholomew took the cigarette from his lips. "I am uninterested." He opened his eyes.

Her hand tightened. "I am not." Famine snatched the cigarette, stuck it between her lips, and took a deep drag. Then she plunged the butt into the water and blew smoke in his face. "Do you plan to defy me, Aesir?"

Aesir. Bartholomew's jaw set. The ancient title meant "halfling." From Famine it sounded like "weakling."

He stood, ignoring her hand though her grip hadn't loosened. "Leave me be, moecha." His power stemmed from his connection to the Catcher and the outer darkness, but Famine's touch drained it.

Her eyes narrowed. "You may call me 'lover,' 'sister,'" she smirked, "or 'mother.'" Then her voice took on a dangerous edge. "But don't call me 'whore.'"

Like a stone mantle, her will settled upon his shoulders and pulled him down. Famine would grind him into the ground before she'd give him free will. She wielded malice like a sinister goddess and thrived on death and suffering. She relished Bartholomew's flesh, blood, and loathing. He'd never overcome her will without the Catcher's aid.

He wanted to push Famine away, twist her hand off his flesh and keep twisting until her bones broke. Tonight, freedom felt so close. The mere breath of the child had started the Catcher's soul singing within him. It was a song he'd neither heard nor felt for fifteen centuries and it gave him strength.

He caught Famine's wrist but paused. If he showed his increased might, if he pushed her back with renewed force, she would haunt his steps more surely than did the Catcher's crows. Famine knew him all too well to miss any change in his power, no matter how subtle.

His grip eased and he lifted his other hand. He slid his fingers along her jaw and through her thick hair to cup the nape of her neck.

By any means necessary.

He pulled his oldest enemy close and kissed her.

"Is there any part of you that loves me still?" Famine asked.

"I've never loved you." Bartholomew lay in his broad bed, naked but for the sheen of perspiration that fornication had left behind to chill him. He was studying the dentil molding that crowned the fireplace, counting its carved notches—and the moments—until she released him.

"Liar." She rolled over. "Is there any part of you that loves me still?"

Trente-huit. "Non." *Trente-neuf. Quarante.*

"What remains?"

"Revulsion. Pity. And even the pity soon will be spent."

She sighed, and her sigh became a sob. "I'm only ever warm when I'm in your arms."

He said nothing. He'd heard this plea before. Yet he pulled her cold body against his, holding his enemy as she cried, because he hadn't lied about the small amount of compassion that remained within him for the creature that sought to destroy the world.

Famine nestled into his arms. "When you are inside me, I can almost conceive of what it is to be human. Almost."

Bartholomew shivered as her cold breath caressed his neck. He hated that his body responded to her touch as her fingers crawled across his skin. They lingered on the red Kali yantra tattooed on his right biceps. They traced its five inverted triangles, its lotus, and the odd geometric shape that delineated the symbol of the Hindu goddess Kali, the Destroyer of Time.

Famine straddled him. She touched his cheekbones, his nose, and his lips. "You have the face of a god—the kind mortals cut from marble." Bartholomew grimaced at her mockery. Famine laughed. No trace of her vulnerability remained. "With the glare of Michelangelo's *David*. Will you slay me with a stone, my dear Gaul?"

"I'll remove your head with steel."

"Oh, I do enjoy your abhorrence," she purred and leaned down. Her breath brushed his face. "Kiss me, Bartholomeus."

"Non."

"Yes. You will."

He turned his head and their lips met. She moaned and moved, pushed her tongue into his mouth, and ground her hips against him.

There had been a time—before the Catcher had made him an aesir, before Famine had forced him to sunder the Catcher, before Bartholomew had known anything about the Apocalyptics and the perilous decision that had released the Four Horsemen to threaten the world—a time when he'd been grateful for Famine's protection and companionship. He'd come to love her, even as she'd fed off his flesh and blood. She'd taught him how to touch a woman. She'd instilled in him a belief in his power. And she'd tended each new wound she'd inflicted, carefully, lovingly, like a mother doting over a newborn babe.

It was those memories of Famine from his boyhood that Bartholomew now recollected as he gripped her hips and lifted her so that he could slide into her and try to warm the cold-blooded monster that held nothing but misery and enmity for all the world. He tried to see past her jutting bones and angular beauty, tried to find the feminine form that Famine preferred, tried to imagine a woman's softness. Then, failing at that, Bartholomew recalled fair-haired Aemelia who'd loved him, married him, and given him a son.

He closed his eyes and remembered returning to his wife after a long campaign in Barbaricum. She bared her body to him, opened herself to his need, and took all of his longing. She never asked about his scars. He was a Roman soldier, a Gaul, a warrior. Scars were part of his history and she said they warned of his strength to any man who would question his power.

There was their small house, always dim and smoky from the hearth fire. Aemelia's rough fingers snagging his tunic, the creak of leather as she undressed him.

"This is new, and this one," she murmured as she inspected his skin for scabs and bruises. There was the saltiness of her lips and the sweetness of her tongue.

Lost in memory, Bartholomew groaned and gripped Famine. He pushed into her harder, deeper, wishing for all the world to resurrect his lost wife, if only for a moment, if only in his dreams.

Aemelia.

Famine moaned and Bartholomew looked up at the green-eyed, auburn-haired form she'd chosen. He wanted to control her, but as he came she arched back, laughing and riding the waves of his release, luminous with the power that she gained from him. His relief turned black and moldering, like fruit rotting upon the vine. Famine would not allow him pleasure. Her will dominated him in all things, even this.

He shoved her off his hips and rolled away, disgusted with her and himself.

Moecha.

He would have prayed to God to save him from this fate, but he'd stopped praying centuries ago; it did no good. God had assigned him a task and would be unsatisfied until the work was done.

Or God loathed him and took great delight in this torment.

"Only three?" Famine's tongue snaked up his spine. Her hands slid over his hips. "You cannot expect me to believe you are slowing in your old age, Bartholomeus."

He willed his flesh to be still. He thought of ice, death, and the countless victims of her ravenous hunger. His revulsion held and his loins did not respond to her.

"Roll over." She sat up. "Now, Aesir."

The weight of her will garroted him. Bartholomew was forced to obey. In that moment he yearned to smash her skull against the white marble fireplace. He held that image—her blood staining the walls and puddling beneath his feet—as Famine lapped sweat from his skin, as her hands, tongue, and mouth encouraged him to perform once more and surrender another morsel of his strength to her endless hunger.

3

SCREAMS ROSE OVER THE ROAR AND CRACKLE OF BURNING huts. Men shouted. Steel clashed with steel as warriors fought.

"Boy!"

Bartholomeus slipped and slid down into the dim gully. Spindly branches snagged his tunic, scratched his face and arms. Slush and mud sucked at his boots as he lunged behind a beech tree. He rasped in the frigid March air. A stitch stabbed his side. He dug his fingers into it.

Above and behind him a horse whinnied and snorted. Metal clattered. Bartholomeus peered around the trunk. Two mounted soldiers reined in their horses at the lip of the gully. Their swords glistened in the early morning light, slick with his family's blood.

"Where'd that boy go?"

"Down there."

The soldiers' armor was stained with the blood of everyone Bartholomeus knew.

"Boy, come out and die like a man."

Metal clattered as a horse champed its bit. Hooves scraped stone.

"I'm not going into that pit," one soldier snarled to his companion.

"No one walks away. Those are our orders."

"The horse'll get mired."

"Do you want to tell the king one of the Gauls escaped to warn the Romans?"

A chill crawled across Bartholomeus's scalp as a high-pitched wail rose and was cut off. He squinted toward the gully's shadowy opposite slope. Frost dusted the brush and lichen around him. Icicles fringed the tree branches, and an icy stream burbled between him and the rise. Could he make it across? Did he want to? A witch lived in those black woods.

A muttered curse and a saddle creaked. Boots crunched in the snow. "I'll gut you when I catch you, boy!"

Better the witch than the Germanii. Bartholomeus lunged away from the tree.

"There! There he goes!"

Bartholomeus hit the edge of the creek, leaped, and sprawled face down on the other side as his foot slipped on ice. A figure loomed over him. He cringed and closed his eyes, expecting death. But pain never came. Instead there were shouts, thuds, snapping branches and cracking wood. A fight?

A woman's voice made him look up. "Gag them, Ewan," she said.

A man, tall and broad as the oldest oak, was binding Bartholomeus's pursuers. The men were muddy, bloody, and laying upon the opposite stream bank. Like frightened bucks, they strained against their tethers, their eyes wide and rolling. Bartholomeus scrambled to his feet, turned to run, and was *blocked by the woman. She had auburn hair, fair skin, and hard, green eyes. She circled him, studied him. She touched his tunic and his hands. She seized his shaggy, brown hair, leaned close, and sniffed him. "What are you called?"*

"Bartholomeus," he mumbled and watched her hands. She wore bones and iron crosses. She carried a blackened dagger at her waist.

"What is your age?"

He swallowed and glanced at her face. "Eleven years."

She stopped before him. "You're tall." Her scraggly nails bit into his flesh as she gripped his arm. "And strong." She shoved him back and seized the dagger hilt. "Are you a coward, Bartholomeus?"

"I—"

"Who died when you ran away?"

He looked down again. "Everyone."

She laughed. "Slaughtered like spring lambs." She strode across the creek to the bound men, pulled the short, black dagger from her belt, and turned to Bartholomeus. "Are you a Christian, boy?"

He shook his head.

"Of course not," she murmured. Louder she asked, "Do you believe in revenge?"

The men stared at him, fear twisting their faces. Their eyes begged for his mercy.

Bartholomeus nodded.

The woman smiled. "Good." She crouched. Flesh and fabric tore. Bones cracked. She stabbed and stabbed. Blood splattered the frosted brush and icy stones. A man groaned and sobbed as the witch bent over him.

Bartholomeus stumbled back from the muffled screams and

frenzied violence. An eerie, pallid light illuminated the gully. It revealed bones and carcasses littering the ground. Scuttling rats and squirming maggots feasted upon them and grew fat. He slipped and fell on the muddy stream bank. His hands sank into black, stinking mire.

Behind him the witch growled and spoke, her language unfamiliar but her rage unmistakable. Bartholomeus looked back and stared. The pallid light emanated from her hands. She straightened and turned. He got to his knees. He had to escape. He searched the opposite rise, searched the creek bed. He saw only steep, slick walls and carnage in all directions.

Bones crunched beneath her feet as the woman crossed the gully once more. "Look at me." She loomed over him. Cold crept up his spine and the hair stood on the nape of his neck. The eerie glow encased her hands and cast a sickly light upon her face. Gore darkened her skin and stained her dress. It dripped from her hair.

"Witch," he whispered.

"I'm no witch, stupid boy." She spat on the ground. "I am the first Horseman of the Apocalypse. I am called Famine." She crouched over him and raised the dagger.

Bartholomeus's heart thundered. He stared as she reached toward his chest. The pallid substance slipped and stretched between her spidery fingers like warm pine pitch. Fresh blood slicked the blade and left a smear as she slit his tunic from his sternum to his throat. Famine touched his skin. Blinding, burning pain radiated throughout his chest. He arched and grit his teeth, shaking and staring as the amorphous glow wormed into his skin.

Then it was over.

He was alive.

Famine withdrew the burning light and removed her hand from him. Through tears he squinted at her outstretched palm. Nestled upon it was a beautiful, nebulous blue substance, an orb of liquid fire.

She tilted her hand to let the orb slide down to her bloody fingertips. She captured it, held it to her lips, and looked past it to him as she sucked it into her mouth. Eyes half-lidded, she savored it, then swallowed. She parted her lips to show Bartholomeus that it was gone. They curved into a satisfied smile.

"Penumbra," she murmured. She gestured to the hulking man who moved to stand behind her. "Bring the boy. He belongs with me."

Bartholomeus rubbed his aching chest. A jagged web of silver scars branched outward from the spot over his heart where she'd touched him.

The giant man grabbed his arm, jerked him up, and shoved him. "Move, boy."

BARTHOLOMEW AWOKE from the foul memory and rubbed his chest. Beside him, Famine lay as still as death. Regrettably, she was merely asleep. He sat up, swung his feet to the floor, and stood.

Nightmares were the Catcher's punishment for defiance. Though trapped between worlds, she could twist his mind in a relentless drive to be given form.

"Penumbra," Bartholomew murmured. *Almost shadow.* "*Skurwysyn.*" That word meant son of a bitch in Polish.

He pulled on his white union suit up to his waist, leaving

the top and sleeves to dangle like tails as he splashed his face at the washbasin and rinsed his mouth. The rancid taste of Famine lingered on his tongue to mix with the bitter nightmare. One last swig of water, then Bartholomew spat regret.

He wiped his face and hands on a towel, moved to the bedroom's tall windows, and pulled back a heavy blue curtain. It was early morning. The sky was at its darkest and much of the world still slumbered, ignorant of the evil that moved among them and the struggles of a small few to capture and contain it.

He considered returning to his abandoned bath. Even old, cold water was better than wearing Famine's stink. She smelled like a walking mausoleum. Letting the curtain fall, he turned, but his nemesis was awake. She mirrored his turn. And she held his sheathed knife.

Merda.

She eyed his scarred right forearm like a child considering a cake. The blade whispered against leather as she slid it from its home. "I'm not sated."

Stifling the urge to smack her, Bartholomew crossed his arms. "You cut me yesterday."

"And I will have more today. Give me your arm."

He looked down at her. How he yearned to break her. It would bring such pleasure. But he was only an aesir, an incomplete Apocalyptic. Her will far outweighed his.

She lunged forward and pressed the knife to his chest. "Give me your arm or I will carve out this creature's eye." She was threatening the winged bull tattoo that rampaged across his skin and hid the bloom of ancient scars.

"*Très bien.*" He proffered his arm and looked at nothing as she perused his ladder of scars like a merchant in search of the perfect silk. He didn't flinch as she filleted his skin. He'd had centuries to grow numb to his mistress savoring his flesh. She chewed, swallowed, and lapped up his blood, humming all the while. Within minutes, Bartholomew's wound would heal.

She straightened. "So you still can't watch?" She snatched his white linen shirt from a chair and wiped her lips. "Too painful to see yourself in a monster like me?" She smirked and dropped the shirt. "Just remember, an Apocalyptic's soul isn't so pleasing as you believe, Bartholomeus. It will make you *weak*." She went to the door, paused, and said over her shoulder, "That's why the Horsemen exist. We're the only ones from the outer darkness with enough spine to do God's dirty work."

He retrieved the shirt. "You're no more than parasites."

She faced him, a scowl ruining her beauty. "Wrong. We're population control." She cocked her head. A wicked light returned to her face as she smiled. "Halfling flesh is a poor substitute for the Catcher's full-proof soul. Hasten to summon her, Aesir. I tire of your dilute stew."

"And I tire of you. I will take great pleasure in ridding the world of you and your cadavers."

Famine's smile became a snarl. "Your Catcher's first breath will be her last. I'll suck her soul and consume her flesh, and you will be with me forever." She strode to the door, her fiery hair cascading about her shoulders. "God's Apocalyptics cannot stop my reunion with Death, War, and Conquest. The End of Days will come, Bartholomeus. And you will herald it." She stomped from the room, leaving her clothing behind.

He picked up her gown. He fingered the fine blush silk, the delicate gold embroidery, and tossed it into the cold, black fireplace ashes. She was right though; he did loath seeing himself reflected in her bloody smile.

He stared at the filthy, wadded dress.

Conquest. Not Righteousness. Not Pestilence.

Famine intended to summon the fourth Horseman in his most powerful form—a warrior who would conquer every mortal, every soul, and even God above. Only the three Apocalyptics—the Catcher, the Guardian, and the Beacon—could stop this apocalypse.

He scratched his forearm. The scars itched. He eyed the ladder of symmetrical lines climbing from his wrist to the crook of his elbow. Each had been carved and recarved by Famine. Bartholomew turned his hand and stared at the Roman eagle tattooed on the back of it.

Long ago he was a hero.

AFTER BATHING AND DRESSING, Bartholomew stood in his study, surrounded by blissful quiet as Famine and her monsters slept.

Open before him was a plain teak cabinet from which he had extracted tobacco and white rolling papers. He measured a precise portion of tobacco onto each paper, then rolled and sealed the cigarettes. He replenished his silver pocket case, stowed his supplies, and closed the cabinet, then stuck a cigarette between his lips and placed the case in his coat pocket.

He settled into a black leather wing chair facing the study's tall, bare windows. He smoked and watched New York City turn purple, rose, and gold with the sunrise.

A smile curved his lips.

You are one day older, Matilde. And I am one day closer to freedom.

When his cigarette was spent, Bartholomew went to his desk. There were arrangements to be made with his banker and attorney. Messages to be sent. Papers to be signed and exchanged. Best to do business while the cadavers were inactive.

He sat and amended his will. He drew up a trust, as well as a directive delineating a stipend for Matilde. Letters were written and signed. A new birth certificate was created for *Matilde Anne Royce*. Father: *Unknown*. Mother: *Deceased*. There was the matter of her living parents, but Bartholomew knew everyone had a price, and for some it was abhorrently low.

When all was done, he placed the letters in white envelopes. On the bank's envelope, he wrote *A Contribution*. Upon the attorney's envelope was written *Against Tribulation*. He placed money in a third unmarked envelope. He removed two white calling cards from his desk and notched their corners. Donning his top hat, coat, and gloves, he pocketed the envelopes and cards and left the house.

4

BARTHOLOMEW REVELED IN THE CHILL SPRING AIR AND soft sunshine as he headed for Columbus Circle. New York City awakened around him. Paperboys hawked the news from every corner. Small gray birds flitted from tree to tree, flirting and chirping. Spring presented her budding greenery: the purples and whites of emerging crocuses, brilliant yellow daffodils, and the riotous colors of primroses lining the side-walks and spilling over window boxes.

Bartholomew strolled several blocks to the Circle and the shoeshine who made his living selling news, providing simple tailoring, and giving shoes a high gloss in the lush, green shadow of Central Park. He sat to have his shoes polished and caught the attention of the shoeshine's two young sons. They watched with expectant, brown eyes as his shoes were made glossy. The dollar he handed the man was a generous payment and held the calling cards in its fold. Bartholomew nodded his thanks and left knowing the boys would retrieve the cards and scamper off to their respective destinations.

The shoeshine's sons had been delivering Bartholomew's calling cards to his New York associates for four years. They knew if his cards reached their destinations, he would return later to purchase a newspaper and leave a dollar for each boy.

He consulted his pocket watch then set off on a brisk stroll through Central Park. There was time yet to enjoy the day before heading to St. Patrick's Cathedral. The morning held fine, though a chill clung to the air. He smiled at gray squirrels playing chase around the tree trunks and through the flowerbeds. He glimpsed red, yellow, and blue among the trees' budding branches, proof the birds were shedding their winter drab for spring's showy plumage.

Early morning strollers tipped their hats and nodded as they passed. Bartholomew joined the parade, a smile playing across his lips for the ladies. He'd grown accustomed to their first and second glances, but his pleasure was no less diminished for that familiarity. Their attention made him feel alive.

He inhaled the morning's cold, sweet air. After spending a long night with a corpse, strolling beneath the blue March sky among the awakening plants, animals, and mortals was invigorating.

Bartholomew crossed the path of the morning riders on their way to exercise their mounts and emerged onto Sixth Avenue. Dodging horses, carriages, and trolleys he walked the few blocks to the church and paused to take in the cathedral's imposing stone edifice. Once again, he consulted his watch as churchgoers walked past him and through the wide, bronze doors on their way to morning Mass. He glanced up the street and spied a small, well-dressed gentleman striding toward him.

Bartholomew snapped his watch shut, removed his top hat and gloves, and entered the church.

Silence enveloped him. Quiet voices, the reverberations of the organ, and the musky scent of candles and incense filled him with ease.

At the font, his fingers hovered over the holy water for a moment before rippling the surface. He made the sign of the cross—forehead, heart, left shoulder, right—as he settled into the far end of the last empty pew on the right. He placed his top hat and gloves over two empty places beside him and waited.

A few moments later, a gentleman asked, "May I?"

Bartholomew knew his attorney's deep voice. "Of course." He shifted his items and the gentleman sat. As the choir began and the shuffle and chatter of the parishioners hushed, his banker took the last empty seat beside the attorney.

The three gentlemen sang with the congregation. They repeated the priest's invocations. They bowed their heads when they were told to repent. And when the donation basket reached their row, Bartholomew deposited three envelopes into it. The two men in the pew beside him each exchanged a blank envelope for a marked one.

After Mass the banker took his leave immediately. The attorney joined the line to thank the priest for his service. Bartholomew remained seated, his eyes closed and head bowed until the church was quiet and empty of all but a few of the neediest and most penitent.

His route back to Columbus Circle took Bartholomew past a small toy store. He'd seen it more times than he could remember, but he'd never crossed its threshold.

For the first time, he paused to take in the shop's window display where wooden guns, shiny metal trains, toy animals, and baby dolls with real hair and staring, painted eyes enticed tiny shoppers. He turned away, paused again, then entered the store.

"How may I help you, sir?" The bespectacled shopkeeper emerged from behind a small counter at the back of the cramped store. Dust motes swirled around him.

Bartholomew peered about.

Toys covered every surface and climbed shelves to the ceiling. Red, blue, and green alphabet blocks, monkeys with shiny cymbals, dolls' dresses, flowery tea sets, roller skates, drums and horns. He never knew so many toys existed.

He turned his attention to the proprietor. "How much is the cat in the display window?"

The man smiled and tottered past him. "The little, gray velveteen kitten? Her name is Bettina. She's lovely, sir, a perfect pet." He lifted the toy from her perch in a little wicker basket. "Ninety-nine cents, sir." He handed the cat to Bartholomew.

Bettina wore a blue collar with a silver bell and sat upon his palm, upright and expectant. Her shiny black eyes brought a small smile to Bartholomew's lips.

"Will you wrap it? I'll pay now but will retrieve the package in a few days. If that is acceptable?"

"Of course, of course. Glad to see her going to a nice home, sir."

Bartholomew left the toy store and headed for the Circle. There he purchased a newspaper from the shoeshine and left two dollars for his messengers.

He settled upon a bench beneath a budding black willow

in the park and waited. He needed to replenish what Famine had stolen from him—the power of the outer darkness—or the hole she'd created in his spirit would fester and grow. The only source for that power on earth was a soul.

He smiled at passing beleaguered governesses and young mothers with their rambunctious charges and rocking baby carriages. He ignored the crows in the trees around him, even when they squawked and flew close enough to be swatted.

Finally, as the afternoon waned and the trees' shadows crept across the grass to reach for him like bony fingers, a hunched man trudged past the bench scowling at the women and children. When a young, tottering boy sent a red ball rolling into the man's path, the fellow kicked it into a stand of thick bushes and sneered at the child's squalling protest.

The boy's caretaker said, "Sir, that was unkind."

He responded, "Children and their toys belong behind closed doors," and tromped onward.

Bartholomew stood and followed the rancid vapor of the man's bitter soul.

As an aesir, he could tear spirits from their bodies, or he could siphon their power, leaving body and soul intact. The malevolence of the target determined the severity of his attack. It was an ability that had taken decades to learn and centuries to master.

When the fellow stopped for a trolley amid a crowd, Bartholomew touched his wrist. He sensed self-loathing and desperation over a life misspent and lonely. The brief exchange left behind the daze of a daydream and a silver band of scars that outlined the man's nerves and blood vessels, a permanent lightning flower upon his skin.

Bartholomew stepped out of the crowd and trudged along Forty-third Street. Consumed with the man's misery and no longer aware of the ladies' notice, he scowled past the tall buildings into twilight. Famine would be preparing for her evening constitutional in Central Park. She required he join her.

"Defy our enemy." The Catcher's whisper filled his mind as she offered more encouragement than he needed. It had been centuries since he'd heard her voice so clearly.

He swallowed the jaundiced pill of the desperate soul he'd subsumed and turned his back on Fifth Avenue and his unpleasant mistress. Accompanied by the Catcher's carrion crows, he headed for the Five Points.

THE GLOAMING WAS UNUSUALLY STILL.

Bartholomew sat upon the roof of Matilde's tenement, smoking and observing the streets as evening's shadows swallowed the Ward. The stolen soul's malaise had eased, leaving an ache behind his eyes and irritation that he'd come to the Five Points at day's end.

Stupide.

He'd been swayed by the spirit's desperation, as well as his own. It was a hazard when Bartholomew robbed souls; memories and emotions came with their energy.

He blew smoke rings at a handful of crows perched just beyond his reach. Seemingly serene with their ebon feathers fluffed against the evening chill, the birds' beady eyes remained fixed upon him. Theirs was a mutually held distrust.

Bartholomew scanned the roof. The Catcher had sent a growing number of crows to his side. The tiles were black and undulating with their wings and more arrived as he turned away. He couldn't recall the last time he'd seen so large a murder. The Catcher had encouraged him back here against his better judgment, too. He wondered why.

The screech and scrape of wood against wood drew his attention to the apartment below. He peeked over the ledge. Matilde slipped through her bedroom window to the iron balcony and crouched behind the ragged sheets draped across it to dry. She made a hollow clicking sound with her tongue, waited, and repeated the noise.

The crows around him rustled and arched their wings then echoed her call. A handful hopped to the edge of the roof and, one-by-one, dropped over the ledge.

Bartholomew eased forward another inch, risking discovery as he peered down upon the little girl.

She'd pulled a cracker from her apron pocket and offered crumbs to the black birds, extending the food on her palm. "Hello, sweet souls," she murmured as the crows ducked and bowed, gently plucking the morsels from her hand and crooning their pleasure.

Forgetting secrecy for astonishment, Bartholomew leaned further out from the roofline. He'd never known the black sentinels to exhibit such civility.

One of the birds hopped forward, crowding its companions and ruffling feathers. "Now you," Matilde said, "wait yer turn. There's another cracker in my pocket. Don't make a rumpus or Momma will hear."

Ash from Bartholomew's forgotten cigarette gave way to gravity. It drifted down in a fine powder to dust coal wings.

Matilde looked up and froze. Her eyes widened.

"*Bonsoir,*" he said.

"Hello, sir. Why are you on our roof?"

He brought the traitorous cigarette to his lips and took a long drag. The smoke escaped him in gentle puffs as he replied, "I was conversing with the crows."

Her attention returned to her impatient pets as they squawked and squabbled. She distributed more crumbs then peered back at her unexpected visitor. "But why are you doing so on our rooftop, sir?"

"Do you feed them often?"

She shook her head. "No. Momma will beat me if she sees me wasting food."

"I understand. Hers is a valid point."

Matilde shrugged. "They're my friends."

Stubbing out his cigarette, Bartholomew shifted to dangle his feet over the precipice. "Generosity is an admirable quality, unless it is a detriment to yourself or your loved ones."

She met and held his gaze for a surprisingly long moment before answering. "There's always money for *grog.*" She returned to the crows and said, "The crackers are gone. I hope all you got some." She stood and brushed her hands on her apron. "Excuse me, sir. I gotta go in before I'm missed. Good evening."

Bartholomew didn't answer. The distinct, cold void of a cadaver had captured his attention.

Matilde shrugged and climbed into the apartment.

The cold void resolved into three individuals.

Bartholomew dropped to the balcony and yanked up the window. Matilde stood at her bedroom door, looking at him wide-eyed as she turned the doorknob. He slipped into the room, his hands raised, palms facing her. "I won't harm you."

The apartment's front door crashed inward. Matilde jerked around at her mother's scream. Bartholomew reached her as her father's life was splattered across the floor and the ceiling. He clapped his hand over her mouth and eased the bedroom door shut. "Not a sound if you wish to live," he whispered. A baby's cry rose from the kitchen. Matilde tore at his iron grip.

Bartholomew lifted the girl. He retreated back through the window. He leaped to the adjacent apartment's balcony. Ignoring sharp pain as Matilde's teeth sank into the fleshy part of his ring finger, he yanked up the sash on the closest window and tumbled backwards into an empty room. Her teeth met bone. His grip didn't lessen. With the child pinned to his chest, he pressed his back to the wall and peered through the window toward her family's balcony.

Instinct had served him well. Ewan stepped into the night and leaned over the balcony rail. He looked left and right, frowned, then straightened. Famine's oldest and most dangerous cadaver, the Celtic brute had cropped chestnut hair and a scar running from ear to ear across his face—a gift from Bartholomew. Ewan shrugged out of his black frock coat. It left red streaks on the clean laundry. The cadaver swiped both sides of a knife clean with his tongue, returned it to its sheath, and hopped over the rail to the alley four stories below.

A moment later, Nash Barnes appeared, backlit by a fire's wicked, orange glow and followed by screams and panic. He shed a pair of kid gloves and tossed them back into the apartment. The cadaver wiped his face on one of the sheets, leaped up to catch the roof, and disappeared over the edge.

Acrid smoke stung Bartholomew's sinuses and throat, the stench of burning hair and flesh roiled his gut. The crackle and snap of wood afire accompanied the sounds of mortal fear as people fled the burning building. Moving unnoticed among them was a third cadaver.

Black smoke oozed between cracks in the wallboards and the ceiling. The cadavers had set a thorough blaze and the overcrowded building soon would become an inferno. When its gas lines ruptured, the whole structure would go.

Bartholomew could jump off the balcony, but the cadavers circled the chaotic scene like hounds. Their presence rang out, and he couldn't risk revealing Matilde's location. They couldn't sense him, but he didn't doubt they were watching and waiting.

Matilde coughed and gasped, her struggles waning with exposure to the noxious smoke. He yanked a shirt from a nearby chair, covered her mouth and nose, and tied it at the back of her neck. "Keep your eyes shut, child."

Wrapping a blanket about the weakening girl, he gathered her into his arms and charged into the tenement's burning central hall.

Black smoke and orange flame climbed the walls and undulated across the ceiling like liquid, like damned souls. With no doors or water to slow it, the conflagration was racing through the wooden structure's thin walls, consuming the meager possessions of its dispossessed inhabitants.

Bartholomew dodged falling, flaming debris. He ignored the pain and stench of his own singed skin and hair and the sting of cinders in his eyes. Upon the second floor landing, he took the brunt of a fall as the stairwell caved beneath his feet with a mighty *crack* and sent him plunging two stories. He curled around Matilde to protect her tiny body from the impact and scrambled away from burning wood as the upper floors crumbled.

Like a train thundering down from above, the building roared and gnashed at his heels as he charged down a bisecting hall on the first floor and crashed through a boarded door as the tenement's interior collapsed.

Derr'mo.

He'd emerged into the smoke- and ash-filled storage room of an adjacent, street-level laundry. Lying upon his back, the girl still clutched to his chest, Bartholomew groaned. He was bruised and singed from head to toe, inside and out.

"Roasted alive. Those rotten bastards."

Matilde was unconscious but breathing. Bartholomew quickly traded his burned wool frock coat for a loose-fitting sack coat, donned a brown bowler, and wrapped a cloak around the girl. With her safely cradled in his arms, he slipped into the bedlam that had consumed the Bend.

Onlookers gawked as the dying building, like some long-suffering behemoth, collapsed upon itself with a groaning, splintering death cry. The Ward's denizens cheered as the fire carriages, their bells clanging and wide-eyed horses snorting, thundered up Mulberry and shed firemen.

Bartholomew didn't hurry. He kept to the shadows, tracking the circling cadavers as he made his way toward the Bowery. When he was well away from the Bend's chaos, he hailed a hansom cab.

The driver asked, "Where to, sir?"

"Washington Square."

Matilde stirred, wheezed, and was wracked by a fit of

harsh coughing. Bartholomew held her tightly. She accepted his handkerchief, wiped her eyes and blew black mucus from her nose.

"Where's Samuel?" Her voice rasped, ragged from screaming behind Bartholomew's hand, parched from inhaling smoke and terror. "I heard him crying. We gotta go back fer him."

"He's dead."

"Dead?" She struggled away from Bartholomew. "You don't know that! You don't!"

"Monsters murdered your parents. Do you think they'll coddle your brother?"

"That's not fair! Samuel was a baby! He didn't do nothin' to 'em!" She kicked the cab's closed doors again and again and pounded the black bench padding. "He didn't do nothin'!" She closed her eyes, grabbed fistfuls of her hair, and screamed until coughing doubled her over and left her weak.

She was like some small wild animal and her wrath, once harnessed, would be a marvelous weapon.

The fit subsided, replaced by a tenuous faith that lifted her expression. "Maybe he crawled under the bed. Can't we go back, sir?" She leaned forward. "Please? Maybe the firemen saved him."

"Non, child. The building collapsed. It's not safe to return. You haven't considered the possibility that you were a target, as well."

She straightened. "Me? Why? What did I do?"

He shrugged. "Have you made enemies?"

The girl's mouth turned down. Her hope crumbled. Tears welled in her eyes and spilled, creating white streaks through the soot marring her fair cheeks. A sob escaped her, lifting her whole body with the emotion. But no more than that, and as quickly as the tears had come, so too did she stop them, a door slamming shut on a loss too painful to contemplate. Matilde wiped her eyes and nose again, gulped long, deep breaths, and stared at the floor. "All right," she whispered. She asked no more of Samuel's fate.

Bartholomew offered neither comfort nor explanation. When the carriage let them out, he crossed the square— Matilde's hand firmly held within his—and hailed another livery. Thus, in stages, they made their way from Lower Manhattan to his country house in Rye.

Soft peach light heralded the new morning as they finally arrived at their destination. Matilde slept in his arms as Bartholomew stepped from the carriage.

Mr. Vernon welcomed them into the boxy white mansion. "Good morning, Monsieur. Who is this girl?" The butler was dark complexioned, hard as mahogany, and bald as a newborn's bottom. He had a ready smile, a keen mind, and a broad, crooked nose. The epitome of refinement, he buttoned a light blue waistcoat over his starched, white shirt and donned a morning coat that matched his dark gray trousers.

Mrs. Henderson appeared in the foyer. "What circum- stance brings you to us in such dreadful condition?" She produced a blue, cotton handkerchief from her sleeve and wiped soot from Matilde's pale cheeks.

"Miss Matilde Anne Royce." Bartholomew's employees followed him up the stairs. "Cadavers orphaned her. I have made her my ward." He entered a guest room at the end of a long hall and stood patiently as Mrs. Henderson removed the child's worn shoes.

Mr. Vernon lit and turned up the gas lamp until the room was filled with a soft, warm glow. "Is she injured, Monsieur?"

"She inhaled a great deal of smoke, but she will recover." Bartholomew settled the girl on the bed and turned to the housekeeper as Matilde curled into a tight ball and whimpered in her sleep. "The child is your responsibility, Mrs. Henderson. You will be her governess."

"Yes, sir," Mrs. Henderson said as Bartholomew left the room.

Mr. Vernon trailed him downstairs. "What are we to tell enquirers?"

"Only that her family perished in a fire." Bartholomew paused on the last stair. "It was set by my enemies, Mr. Vernon. Matilde witnessed her parents' deaths."

The butler shook his head. "A child of tragedy. That will haunt her."

"Oui. But she is strong. Her young brother's death troubles her more than the parents' demise. The child has been ill treated."

"We'll do our best to help her overcome her troubles." The butler's gaze went to the window and sharpened. "I've never seen the likes of that," he muttered.

A gathering of crows had settled in the trees and upon the white fence bordering the near end of the property, painting all black with their glossy wings.

"They soon will disperse, though some will linger," Bartholomew said. "They are not to be harassed, Mr. Vernon."

"Understood." The butler, who had aided him for more than twenty years, nodded. "I'd best make arrangements to protect the gardens."

"Of course."

BARTHOLOMEW SCRUBBED the stench of smoke from his skin and hair, dressed in fresh clothing, and found his butler in the kitchen. "I must return to Manhattan. Doubtless, already I am missed." Accepting a cup of coffee, he sat at the table. "However, I will not remain long. The girl," he gestured upward, "is the one I have long sought."

Mr. Vernon turned from the stove where he was cooking eggs. "A *child*, Monsieur?"

Bartholomew lowered his coffee cup. "You needn't fret." He paused as Mrs. Henderson appeared in the kitchen doorway.

"If I may interrupt your breakfast, Monsieur?" She spoke with a careful, cultured accent acquired during a childhood spent among Boston's political elite.

Bartholomew waved her toward the table. "Oui, Mrs. Henderson?"

Her dark green skirt and layered petticoats rustled as she approached. "What are your expectations for the girl?"

"I expect Matilde to become a refined and educated woman under your expert tutelage. She will learn the language arts, arithmetic, politics, history, strategy, and the sciences. Do not waste her time with word games, recitations, and the fine art of simpering."

"May I speak plainly?"

Bartholomew regarded her from beneath his brows. "You always do."

Mrs. Henderson wore her brunette hair shorter than her employer wore his own and she spoke more bluntly than was acceptable in a normal household. Bartholomew, who was not a normal master, welcomed her frankness.

"The child is filthy and infested with lice; clearly a street urchin. I can only surmise that she has long lacked care and guidance. Certainly there is no refinement. I must question your decision to take this girl into your home."

"Are you incapable of fulfilling the duties of a governess?" There was no animosity behind Bartholomew's question.

"No, Monsieur."

"Are you unwilling to teach a guttersnipe? Are you unwilling to address her as you would a child of privilege and opportunity?"

The woman's chin lifted and a flash of indignity flushed her face. "I am quite willing to teach this girl. And I believe our familiarity after my seventeen years of service in your household should preclude any question of my capabilities and my devotion to your cause."

Satisfied, Bartholomew turned to the plate of fried eggs Mr. Vernon set before him. "Indeed, Mrs. Henderson. However, know this: Matilde may have been born a guttersnipe, but she was not born a victim. She has the strength to hold the Catcher."

That brought the housekeeper to the table. Her knuckles whitened her skin as she gripped the back of a chair. "You would consign a child to this fate?"

"It is well that you and Mr. Vernon are already concerned for the girl. However, I am not so monstrous as that. Matilde has become my ward so that I may protect her. You will tutor the girl until she attains the age of consent. Only then will I summon the Catcher."

The governess placed her hand to her chest. "That is a

relief. My mind and heart would not believe you could do something so wicked."

Bartholomew sipped his coffee. As the salty scent of frying ham filled the kitchen, he explained his intention to leave New York with all of them. "Distance is the only measure of safety. Once I'm free of Famine's influence, I'll have the liberty to ready that child for war."

5

THE FOLLOWING EVENING, BARTHOLOMEW TRAILED
Famine and Nash Barnes as they strolled over the graceful
arch of Central Park's Bow Bridge. He made all attempts to
ignore her and her lapdog as the cowboy paraded her about.
The dullard enjoyed the attention she garnered from the
mortal passersby. Famine knew how to play the part; after all
she'd had even longer than Bartholomew to practice being
mortal.

"Do you see how the older men adore me?" She paused to
smooth the front of her burgundy gown, her fingers making a
languorous trek down her bust. "They are my favorites." She
looked past Barnes to Bartholomew. "Do you know why,
Nash?"

"No, ma'am."

She smiled. "Because their droopy, old wives despise me.
Jealousy is delicious, like sweet cream and berries."

Bartholomew turned away as she laughed. He was
required to be available and protective, but Famine knew

better than to expect attentiveness. He leaned against the bridge's elegant, gold-and-white iron balustrade and took in the slate-colored sky. It threatened rain.

A sizable murder of crows circled the lake to find a roost in a tree above the boat landing. The branches bent with their weight and appeared as black gossamer with the movement of their wings. It was an unnatural number of the birds and Bartholomew saw it for what it was—a message from the Catcher. She wanted to be summoned. Now.

The shadow of Famine's jaundiced energy fell upon him. He looked away from the tree as she approached with the cowboy.

"Why do your Catcher's pets follow us this evening, Bartholomeus?"

He dragged on his cigarette. "They're seeking an opportunity to soil your fine chapeau." He gestured with his cigarette toward the spray of blue and cream feathers that arched over her broad hat.

She cocked her brow at him and waved her gloved hand toward the tree. "If they come near me, I'll have Nash shoot each one through the heart. And you will pluck their feathers. I'll have a fine feather collar made and dine on their bloody corpses for days."

Bartholomew shrugged and strolled across the bridge.

Famine and her cadaver followed.

"The Gaul was too interested in that whore and her family," Barnes said loudly enough for Bartholomew—and passersby—to overhear.

The cowboy was more irritating than customary this evening. Bartholomew thought his agreeableness would be

48

greatly improved with the removal of his tongue. He inhaled; the air smelled of sweet rain.

"Oh?" Famine asked.

"Yes, ma'am. He was loitering in the Ward, trying to hide from the Celt and myself."

Raindrops fell, darkening the park's paths and Bartholomew's already-black mood. People hustled past them, hats and umbrellas firmly gripped against the rising wind.

Famine put up her umbrella as she came abreast of him. "Is there something special about the slut, Bartholomeus?"

"Aside from being freshly murdered by your fools? Non."

"No?" She picked a stray leaf from his lapel and smoothed down his cravat. "So why do you care that she's dead? Yearning for a *family*, again?"

He brushed her hand aside. "I was interested in the gentleman of the house—a street brawler I was considering sponsoring. Now he's ashes thanks to your cadavers' stupidity."

"Good," she murmured. "Because I'm the only family you need." She laughed, showing her little predatory teeth. "Lovely work, Nash. You brought death and carnage to the Ward and irritated Bartholomeus."

Barnes smiled like a schoolboy in love. But his pleased expression quickly dimmed as Ewan appeared on the path leading to the Bethesda Fountain. Bartholomew smirked. If a cadaver fell into disfavor, Famine would withhold her vitality. He'd seen many a monster wither and decay from neglect and starvation. Ewan was an expert at holding his mistress's interest. Barnes faced a gross disadvantage.

Famine made a breathy little sound and strode forward to meet the Celt. Ewan doffed his bowler and inclined his head as she gestured for him to come closer. She rose on tiptoe to whisper into his ear. He nodded, straightened, and approached Bartholomew.

"Centurion. Lady Staniak expects you to provide the evening meal and requests your presence at her table tonight."

Bartholomew's amusement crumbled and his gaze slid across the Celt to Famine. "Why?"

She touched her hair, cocked her head, and smiled as a gentleman slowed to take her in. He stopped, blinked, then hurried to catch his wife and young daughters as they crossed the bridge. Famine watched the man's boisterous girls then turned hard eyes on Bartholomew. "Because I gain such pleasure from your exhilarating conversation."

He dragged on his cigarette, considered her answer, and blew smoke toward Ewan. "I must strive to be less winsome."

Her lips tightened. "I expect dinner to be waiting when I return in an hour." Bartholomew intended to ignore her until she added, "A little child, Bartholomeus, fair and sweet. I find I've developed a taste for them." With a twitch of her skirt, she pivoted and crossed the bridge, the Celtic brute and the American lickspittle at her heels.

"How about a lunatic from Bellevue for your dining pleasure? Alive and armed," Bartholomew muttered as he marched through the park, smoking his cigarette down to a stump. He reached Fifty-eighth Street and raised his hand to hail a hansom cab but lowered it just as quickly. He had a better idea than hunting the Bowery for that bitch's meal. Why go out when there was food rotting at home?

BARTHOLOMEW SET out his finest blue-and-white china, the polished silver, and crystal glasses. He served his mistress's meal upon a beautiful Wedgwood platter. He seated her cadavers—the Poles and the Russian—around the table, so she could admire them and they could amuse her.

The cadavers' vitality came from Famine's energy. But they were corpses no less, and just as the sun's illumination exposed their hidden nature, thus did their bodies begin to rot when Bartholomew relieved them of her power.

"You bastard!" Famine's screech when she entered the dining room brought a smile to his face.

What had greeted her were the bodies of her three soldiers seated at the table and dressed impeccably for dinner. However, their heads, rather than balanced upon their shoulders, had been removed and placed in the center of the table upon Bartholomew's lovely platter. He had opened the windows, not to reduce the stench of death, but to invite more dinner guests, and the room buzzed with sleepy flies. The bodies already had begun to swell and a greenish puddle filled the platter and spilled over upon the ivory tablecloth.

"Whoreson!" Famine whirled and slapped him hard enough to draw blood from his nose and make his eyes water. She screamed something unintelligible and raised her hand again, but he seized her wrist and pushed her back against her cowboy.

"I'll deal you a blow you won't soon forget, Centurion." Barnes sounded like a child. He pulled a Derringer from his coat pocket and aimed at Bartholomew's face.

Bartholomew took a step toward Famine and her little boy. "Put that away or you'll be eating it."

"Don't be an idiot, Nash." Famine swatted the cadaver's hand.

Barnes fired.

The shot struck Bartholomew's right shoulder and heat radiated through his torso as he staggered back from the close impact of the bullet. He stopped, exhaled pain, and looked at the cadaver. "That was unwise." He shoved his mistress aside and punched Barnes. The fool's front teeth skittered across the table. Ignoring Famine as she screamed and pounded upon his back, Bartholomew beat the cadaver until he stopped moving.

"You will not destroy him, Aesir. I forbid it!" Famine's iron will denied Bartholomew the satisfaction of beheading the bastard even as his knife pressed into the cowboy's Adam's apple.

Bartholomew bared his teeth at her. He straightened and kicked the limp Texan in the gut. He seized her arm and shoved her into the chair at the head of the table.

She looked from the rotting corpses to Barnes's crumpled figure to Bartholomew. Tears spilled down her cheeks and her voice cracked as she cried, "You are determined for me to be alone."

Bartholomew stabbed his finger at her. "*Wrong.* I am determined for you to be gone."

Her body shaking and her hands like claws on the chair arms, Famine sobbed, "You only want to see me suffer."

"You only want to see *everyone* suffer!" He slammed his fists on the table. The silverware jumped. A water glass tipped. It shattered against a china plate.

A smirk replaced the sorrow on her face. Her voice turned to stone. "You believe you've hidden your house and your servants and that little girl from me, don't you, Bartholomeus?"

His face froze in a snarl.

She laughed. "I smelled her on your breath and tasted the change in you. I'm going to kill them. I'm going to make that child scream. I'll flay her alive while you watch. When Ewan returns—"

Bartholomew stuffed a white napkin into her mouth and bound her to the chair. He retrieved his large boning knife from the kitchen sink, cut out Barnes's tongue, and slapped in onto the plate before her.

"Bon appétit."

As BARTHOLOMEW REACHED his Rye house, the explosive concussion of a shot greeted him. His white horse skittered sideways off the long cobblestone driveway. "Holà, Riga," he reassured the mare as he pulled her up, dismounted, and led her across the lawn to the side of the house. "Shhh, fille." He tied her to the stair rail then eased open the kitchen door.

"—send you back to hell." Mrs. Henderson's voice carried to him as calm, firm, and cultured as ever.

Quiet as a shadow, Bartholomew slipped through the kitchen and down the hall toward the great, curving staircase. He peered around the corner. Ewan stood at the first stair, a gaping hole aerating his back.

The governess occupied the second floor landing, a steady rifle aimed at the Celt. Mr. Vernon, his nose bloodied and lower lip swelling, stood mid-stairs, his fists up and ready.

Ewan replied, "I'm from Inverness, woman, not hell."

Glass crunched beneath his feet as Bartholomew stepped

into the foyer behind the cadaver. "Doubtless, they're pleased to be rid of you."

Ewan eased around to face him. "So the master of the house is home."

"Forgive my tardiness. I wasn't expecting an unwelcome guest."

The cadaver sneered. "Your housekeeper's manners leave something to be desired." He gestured at his chest where the shot had ripped through. "You can expect my bill for a new coat and shirt."

Bartholomew jerked his head toward the wall where the bullet that had pierced the cadaver had also shattered a massive, framed mirror and lodged in the wall plaster. "And you can anticipate mine for a new mirror and plaster repairs."

Ewan squinted. "It was my understanding that you were expected at dinner in Manhattan."

"Your mistress disliked my menu." Bartholomew stepped forward. "I failed to realize her dislike for tongue." He pulled his sheathed knife from his pocket. "And I grew tired of hearing hers wag."

Ewan's fists clenched. "Whatever you've done, you'll come to regret it."

"I'll add it to my growing list of regrets." The unsheathed blade glinted in the soft gaslight glow as Bartholomew pointed it at the cadaver. "You can't have the child."

With a roar, Ewan launched at him, arms wide and swinging, brute force and sheer size his advantages.

But Bartholomew knew this enemy and had been trained by Rome. He dodged at the last moment and wielded his knife with precision. It snagged his opponent's abdomen and carried through as Bartholomew pivoted, opening a gash from Ewan's belly to his back.

The cadaver stopped. "Damn you, Aesir," he muttered and touched the wound. His fingers came away coated with a glaucous ooze. Then he pivoted, a revolver in hand from his coat pocket and aimed at Mr. Vernon.

A shot rang in the stairwell.

Ewan cursed and dropped his gun.

Mrs. Henderson's aim had been true.

"We're not finished, Bartholomeus." Nursing his bleeding hand, the cadaver backed through the front door. "I'll bring you and your Catcher to Famine. I swear it." He jumped off the porch, ran, and was swallowed by the night.

When Bartholomew was certain Ewan was gone, he turned to his house staff. "Are your injuries serious, Mr. Vernon?"

"No, Monsieur."

"Good. Tend those wounds then get ready to travel." He squeezed his butler's shoulder as he passed the man on the staircase. "Mrs. Henderson, pack what you and the girl cannot be without."

"Of course." She gave her rifle to Mr. Vernon and followed her employer.

Matilde was not abed when Bartholomew opened her door. Dropping to his knees, he lifted the blankets and found her beneath the bed. "Come, child. The threat has run away. But you must dress and be ready to leave by morning light." She made no move to obey him until Mrs. Henderson entered the room and lit the gas lamps, then she crawled from beneath the bed.

Bartholomew retrieved a black-and-tan travel trunk from

the attic, left it in the governess's bedroom, then headed for his own rooms. He shed his bloodied clothes and cursed to realize the cowboy's bullet hadn't passed through his body. He cleaned dried blood from his chest and donned clean clothes.

Mr. Vernon appeared with a black travel trunk and began packing his employer's spare clothes and toiletries.

"I'll require your services to remove a bullet from my shoulder, Mr. Vernon." Bartholomew's ability to swiftly heal sometimes created unique problems—the extraction of an intractable bullet from an inconvenient location, for instance. So, in addition to his duties as butler, valet, and business representative Mr. Vernon was Bartholomew's personal physician. The man held several university degrees—something the aesir lacked. In a society where Negro men and women were denied basic liberties, Mr. Vernon's accomplishments made him a marvel and Bartholomew held him in the highest esteem.

Mr. Vernon nodded. "It will wait?"

"Oui. It appears to be lodged behind the right shoulder blade. A nuisance, but not worthy of the trouble now." Bowler in hand, Bartholomew returned to the hall.

He found Matilde dressed in blue and white, neat, and waiting upon the top stair.

"Will they return?" she asked as he started down the stairway past her.

"Not before we have departed."

"Gimme a knife."

He paused on the stairs and turned, eye-to-eye with the girl. What he'd thought was fear driving her to hide beneath her bed, he now recognized as a fierce determination to survive. "After you have had lessons in their use."

"When?"

"Soon."

She scowled. "That's a no-good answer."

His chin lifted. "Are you in the habit of speaking back to your elders, child?"

"I'm used to gettin' beaten, whether I speak my mind or not."

"Give respect and you shall receive the same. I'm not in the habit of beating those who don't earn my fists. And my answer remains unchanged. I will teach you to wield a knife —soon."

Mr. Vernon appeared in the hall with Bartholomew's black trunk. Matilde followed him and her guardian down the stairs.

"Watch your step around the broken glass, Miss Matilde," the butler remarked as they reached the foyer.

"What's that rotten smell?" she asked.

Mr. Vernon set the trunk down on the porch and looked at her, a quizzical expression tugging down his brow. "Smell, Miss?"

She covered her nose and mouth with her hand. "Like some dead thing, sir."

Mrs. Henderson joined her charge in the foyer. "That sounds dreadful."

Matilde's voice was muffled as she asked, "Did it come from that empty man?"

"Oui. He's a cadaver," Bartholomew replied as he headed for the kitchen. He glanced back at her. She'd noticed Ewan's stench and hollowness. He'd never known a mortal who could sense Famine's offspring.

He fetched Riga from the side yard. "I'm sorry to disturb your sleep, once again, fille." He stroked her dappled gray nose. She nuzzled his palm and he smiled at the tickle of her velvet lips. "I shall miss you, as well, but Mr. Ross will care for you. He owns that bay gelding whose company you so enjoy." After one last pat, he removed his saddlebag and led the Hanoverian to the front of the house. "Mr. Vernon, please ride to the inn and hire a coach. Leave Riga with Mr. Ross as payment."

"Of course, sir." Mr. Vernon mounted and headed out at a fair trot, a lantern held aloft to light the way.

Bartholomew retrieved the black-and-tan trunk from his housekeeper's room. Matilde gaped at him as he carried it down the stairs upon his shoulder. "Why the astonished look, child?" he asked.

Her eyes narrowed. "That's yer butler's work."

He set the trunk atop the black one. "I'm doing what must be done. There are only four of us in this household. Too few to afford the illusion of supremacy."

Mrs. Henderson swept broken glass into a dustpan. "Not that it would set well with you even if there were forty of us, Monsieur."

Bartholomew went to his study. When he'd sent Mrs. Henderson and Mr. Vernon away from his Fifth Avenue home, all of his ledgers and contracts had gone with the butler. These, along with a palm-sized, tin box, he now retrieved from his office safe and secured in a black leather case. He closed the safe, went to his desk, and added wax, his seal, pens and ink, stamps, envelopes, and writing paper to the case. His hand lingered on the marble blotter. He touched the teak desk and slowly closed the drawer.

He went to the library and pulled a few books from the underutilized shelves—Plato's *Symposium*, a book of Shakespeare's sonnets, *The Iliad* and *The Odyssey*. Then, thinking

Mrs. Henderson would want to read to Matilde, he added *Le Morte d'Arthur*, *The Canterbury Tales*, and *Beowulf*. He paused in the doorway as his ward's and governess's voices echoed down the hallway.

"What's a cadaver, Mrs. Henderson?"

"That is a question for Monsieur to answer, but not now."

"Yes, ma'am."

Bartholomew found them sitting on the stairs. He added the books to his trunk and left his case and saddlebag with the luggage. Then he went about the house securing windows and doors and verifying the gas was off.

"Monsieur?" Mrs. Henderson beckoned him.

"Oui?"

She bent over Matilde. "Show him your forearm, child."

Matilde looked down and shook her head.

The governess put her arm around her shoulders. "You need not be ashamed, Miss. Monsieur needs to see what has been done. He will not be angry with you."

Angry? Bartholomew settled onto his heels before the child. "Show me."

She scrutinized him before slowly extending her right arm.

He eased up her sleeve to reveal white bandaging. When he unwound it, what he saw made him more than angry. Pink and scabbed skin in the clear shape of a fork's tines marred the inside of her forearm—a burn that would leave scars deeper than flesh. He rewrapped Matilde's bandage and gently tugged her sleeve into place. "Merci for showing me." He stood. "Mrs. Henderson, keep the wound clean, dry, and loosely bandaged. It appears to be healing well." He fetched a box from his saddlebag and offered it to the girl. She stared at it but didn't seem to understand that it was for her. "Open it, Matilde," he said.

She looked from the box to him then did as directed. She lifted the stuffed cat from inside, her eyes wide but wary.

"The shopkeeper named her Bettina."

Her eyes widened even more and she murmured, "She's soft." She glanced up at him, dropped the toy into the box, and clasped her hands behind her back. "No thank you, Monsieur."

"You don't want her?" He wasn't surprised by her rejection. Gifts given could become weapons when they were taken away. The more they were loved, the more grievous the wound.

She shook her head though she hadn't looked away from the box.

He considered her and sighed. "Well, this is a conundrum. I assured the shopkeeper that Bettina would have a good home, but I haven't the time to attend to my business affairs, oversee our household, raise a child, *and* care for a cat. I may have to leave her behind."

Matilde's head jerked up. "Oh, no! You can't do that."

Bartholomew shrugged. "What choice do I have? I can't ask Mrs. Henderson or Mr. Vernon to take on more responsibility."

Matilde grabbed for the box, but he held it back.

"Lemme care for her," she said.

He cocked an eyebrow at his ward. "You're certain?"

She nodded. "Yes, sir. I can do it." She reached for the box again. "Please?"

There was desperation in her eyes, a need to save what couldn't be saved in the past. "Very well, Matilde." He passed her the gift. "You are responsible for Bettina. Thank you for taking this burden from me."

She sank back to the stairs, the box open upon her lap, and stroked the cat's ears.

Bartholomew left the foyer and stood beneath the portico, smoking and staring at the stars.

Four parallel scars and so much distrust.

He fingered the link on his right cuff and ignored the urge to scratch his scarred forearm. He couldn't imagine any act the child could have done to warrant such cruelty. And what kind of damage had been done to her that he couldn't see? How deep were those wounds?

The sky changed from black to dark blue with the coming day. The clip-clop of horses and the creak of a carriage broke the morning's sleepy silence.

Bartholomew ground his cigarette beneath his heel and went inside.

A covered coach appeared upon the driveway. When it stopped, Mr. Vernon swung down from the carriage door and retrieved the trunks from the porch.

Bartholomew donned gloves and his black coat.

"Here is your coat, Miss Matilde." Mrs. Henderson held open a dark blue, wool garment. "Remember to remain with Monsieur, Mr. Vernon, or me at all times. You may not wander unaccompanied."

"Yes, ma'am." Matilde slipped her arms into it and secured the buttons. She put on the white gloves that her governess proffered, picked up the box that held Bettina, and took Mrs. Henderson's hand.

Bartholomew led them to the carriage and instructed the

driver to take them back to the city. "To Grand Central, please."

When their party reached Grand Central, they'd charter a Pullman Palace car on a Pennsy train to Chicago. From there they'd change stations, board a private Pullman hotel car, and continue in luxury to San Francisco.

After that?

Bartholomew didn't know. The Pacific Coast was the end of the country. Going further west took him back to where his downfall began. It took him full circle.

Bartholomew despised going in circles.

6

BARTHOLOMEW LOOKED OVER THE TOP OF *THE NEW YORK Times*. Matilde lurked at the far end of the Pullman Palace car. Dressed in her nightgown, she appeared as a small ghost left behind by Death to haunt the train.

"Why are you out of bed?" he asked. She remained unmoving and watchful. "You should know, Matilde, that you cannot hide from me. Ever." He folded the paper, leaned forward, and gestured for her to approach.

"I feel sick." She swallowed and touched her stomach.

"Nauseated?" Her brow furrowed. Bartholomew clarified. "Do you feel that you will vomit? That is the meaning of the word."

"Mrs. Henderson gave me tea, but it ain't helping."

"*Isn't* helping. The motion of the train is making you ill. You'll grow accustomed to it. Come here."

She padded forward, her bare feet tripping a light rhythm that played upon Bartholomew's nerves. He curbed a smile. It had been many centuries since the Guardian's instincts to protect had sung this way. A quiet song now, should the girl be endangered the beat of war would thunder through him. His need to safeguard Matilde grew stronger with each passing hour. Better still, Famine's grip upon him stretched thinner with every mile that rolled away beneath the train's steel wheels. Proximity to the girl and distance from Famine was strengthening Bartholomew's will.

She stopped before him, her velveteen cat clutched to her chest. He proffered a plate upon which perched several small salted crackers. "Take one, but do not eat it." The girl glanced from the food to him and slowly did as instructed. He set down the platter and said, "Now."

Matilde dropped the cracker and stepped back, anxiety twisting her brow.

Bartholomew schooled his expression to remain neutral. He retrieved the cracker and held it out. When she took it again, he continued. "Inhale a slow, deep breath through your nose and exhale, also slowly, through your mouth."

She contemplated the cracker for a moment, then did as he instructed. After a few breaths, her face relaxed, though her eyes didn't lose their distrust. "I feel better, Monsieur."

He gestured toward the cracker. "Eat. If it doesn't increase your nausea, you may have one more then go to your berth." He sat back and returned to reading. Nibbling the cracker, she studied his face. He tried to ignore her. She finished eating. She took a second cracker from the plate and, like a mouse, held it with both hands, slowly turning it, rounding its corners and whittling its edges. But when the tidbit was gone, the child remained.

Once again, Bartholomew looked over the edge of the paper. "Your bed awaits, Matilde."

She held her ground. "Are you from France?"

"Non."

"So why are you called *Monsieur*?"

Bartholomew turned a page.

"Don't you have a name?" she asked.

"Of course I do."

"Is it Monsieur Royce?"

The child was damnably resolute. "It is *Monsieur*."

Her head tilted. "Is it odd?"

He glanced at her. "Non. But you are."

She squinted at him and her mouth tightened. "That's what the other children said."

"Why?"

"'Cause crows like me."

"Hmm." He refolded his newspaper. "I keep my name private to protect others."

"Oh. From the monsters?" she asked.

"Oui."

"But why is mine now Royce?"

"To protect you. And I like the sound of it."

Her face screwed up and she shrugged. "All right."

He unfolded his paper.

Matilde ventured a step closer. "Who were they?"

He grimaced and slapped the newspaper onto the table, steepled his long fingers, and leaned toward her. "The question is not *who* but *what*, Matilde."

She was destined to become the Catcher. This information was imperative. Now or later, she needed to know what hunted her and that which she would hunt in return. If she relayed it to anyone, her youthfulness would lead to the story's dismissal as the fancies of a child's mind.

"The creatures responsible for your family's demise are cadavers."

"Like the man at yer house."

"Oui. Do you believe in good and evil, Matilde?"

She nodded, her blonde braid bouncing around her shoulders. "I believe in heaven and God and hell and Satan. Are the cadavers demons?"

"They are bodies without souls."

She was silent for a few moments as emotions—fear, anger, guilt—played across her face. "I hit Catherine Connelly. She pushed me down and I was mad." She chewed her lower lip. "Do you think God sent the cadavers to punish me?"

Bartholomew shook his head. "They enjoy suffering, but they know nothing of your quarrel."

She plucked at a lace ruffle on her pink nightgown, and her voice was quiet when she asked, "Why did God take Samuel? Momma and Papa was sinners. But Samuel was a baby."

"God had no hand in the cadavers' act. Despite the claims of the Church, God does not interfere in the realm of man."

She stepped back. "That's blasphemy."

"It is the truth." It was interesting that she feared superstition more than cadavers.

She returned his steady regard. "Why did you save me?"

The heart of the matter. "Heaven, hell, sinners, and saints— that is all stuff of books and rich old men. Don't be led by the nose, child. The truth is much simpler than the mythology you've learned from the Church and the *Bible*."

"I don't understand."

He rested his elbows upon his knees and knit his fingers together. God and the afterlife were simpler than the Church would have her believe. "There are no angels or seraphim.

There is no heavenly host or throne of God or purgatory. There is no hell. There is no Satan. There is God and there are souls. There is the realm of man and animals," he gestured around, "and there is the outer darkness." He pointed upward. "Nothing more."

She gaped at him. "How can you say those things don't exist?"

"Hmm. Your soul gives your thoughts flight and animates your body, oui? Yes?"

She nodded, her expression a mixture of puzzlement and skepticism.

"When a body dies, the soul does not die with it. Do you agree?"

She nodded again.

"Here is where the Church and the good book are wrong. Most souls remain in the realm of man and are reborn into new bodies. But some become damaged. Those souls are captured and imprisoned in the outer darkness."

Her brow wrinkled. "But what about heaven?"

"Hell and heaven are concepts created by men to frighten parishioners."

"Why would they do that?" Matilde's puzzlement had given way to skepticism.

"Because fear is profitable and faith has become a business. Frightened people will pay to have their sins absolved." He'd found deterioration in all of God's houses.

She opened her mouth to reply but paused when he raised his hand.

"The Four Horsemen of the Apocalypse were among the most dangerous of the souls imprisoned within the outer darkness. They should not have been released. Their influence corrodes the faithful, destroys trust, and poisons humanity. One of them, Famine, I have known for many years. The cadavers are her creation."

"One of the Four Horsemen is a woman? And you *know* her?" Matilde stared at him and her expression clouded. "You think 'cause I'm from the Sixth Ward I'm stupid. Well, I know the *Bible*." She stepped forward and her little hands curled into cudgels. "And I know yer lying."

Such conviction. Bartholomew smiled at her fierceness.

"And now you smile and mock me!"

He shook his head. "I do not, Matilde."

"You do!" She stomped her foot and bared her teeth, an angry, little lion with a wispy blonde mane. "You *do* mock me!"

"Miss Matilde, moderate your tone. You should not be out of bed." Mrs. Henderson hurried toward them, her pale-blue tea gown pulled tight around her thin frame. "I am sorry, Monsieur. She was asleep when I retired."

Bartholomew raised his hand. The governess halted. "Return to your berth, Mrs. Henderson. This conversation must be had. I will send Matilde to bed when I'm certain she understands her circumstances." The woman turned, hesitated, and turned back, but was stopped once more by her master. "Good night, Mrs. Henderson."

"Yes, all right. Good night. Miss Matilde, come straight to bed when you are dismissed. I will be watching for you."

The child just glared at her guardian.

When Mrs. Henderson was gone, Bartholomew said, "I do not make a habit of mocking children. I understand your dismay, but what I tell you is true. You and I know that what was done to your family was the work of soulless men."

Anger warped into suspicion upon her face. Then her eyes

widened with some dawning realization until she whispered, "The blame is yers, isn't it?" Her words barely carried over the clack of the train upon its tracks.

"Oui."

Her fist came at his face, but he caught and held it.

"It was never my intention to involve a child in this war, but you have been placed upon my path. I promise you this. I will protect you from Famine and her cadavers or be destroyed if I fail. My associates and I have long sought her banishment to the outer darkness." He let her yank her fist away. "I neither ask for, nor expect, your forgiveness."

"Good! Because you won't get it! I hate you and I will forever!" She ran to the sleeping berth.

Mrs. Henderson's voice carried through the curtains. "Child, hush. What has upset you?"

"I hate him! It's all his fault, Missus!"

"Quiet, now, Miss Matilde. Control yourself and tell me what has happened."

"Samuel's dead 'cause of him!"

Their conversation grew muffled as the governess calmed her. But Bartholomew couldn't escape the sound of Matilde's sadness or Mrs. Henderson's whispered words as the woman attempted to comfort a child who now knew the man responsible for her keep was also responsible for her family's annihilation.

He considered his pocket watch. Was there time for a trip to the smoking compartment before Mr. Vernon arrived to extract the cowboy's bullet? He snapped the watch shut and removed his cigarette case from his coat, but instead of rising he grew still and his focus strayed to the far end of the Palace car.

She is not my child. Her contentment is Mrs. Henderson's responsibility.

Bartholomew didn't need to care. He only needed to get the girl to the distant safety of the Pacific Coast. She was merely a vessel and he had no reason to concern himself with her happiness. He needed to summon the Catcher, become the Guardian, and stop the Horsemen. This was the duty he had accepted. Nothing more.

He studied the Roman eagle adorning his right hand. He closed his fist and the bird stretched its wings with the movement. He recalled a windswept cliff and the previous Catcher's words:

"I am not your *Catcher. She must be of your making and she must willingly bind you to her, Bartholomeus."*

In him the Catcher had seen a champion—for good or evil. The fate of all souls rested upon his broad shoulders, and his fate rested in the hands of a troubled little girl.

"Merda."

Mr. Vernon entered the coach with several white towels over his arm, a basin of water in one hand, and a small, leather kit in the other. "She'll not trust you easily."

Bartholomew tossed his paper and cigarette case on the bench and stood. "It's no matter."

Mr. Vernon deposited his items on the opposite bench and accepted his employer's frock coat, waistcoat, tie, and shirt. Bartholomew unbuttoned his union suit and shrugged the top down to his waist.

After some inspection and manipulation of his shoulder, the butler located the bullet. He unrolled the kit to reveal a scalpel, retractor, and forceps.

Bartholomew accepted a leather bite strip from Mr.

Vernon. He could endure a great deal of pain, but it was suffering nonetheless and he had no love for it. *I will make a soup bowl of Barnes's skull*, he thought as Mr. Vernon's scalpel made the first sharp cut.

"If her trust was unimportant, you would have made her the Catcher, not your ward."

The leather creaked between Bartholomew's teeth. The butler had him at a disadvantage and would have his say.

"It's not a good precedent, Monsieur. You have only a decade to make her your ally. That little girl needs someone to believe in." Mr. Vernon reached past him for the retractor and murmured, "It is unhelpful that you heal faster when you're angry."

"Koorva." Bartholomew cursed as his butler's blade recut flesh, muscle, and nerves that persisted in healing almost as quickly as they were severed. Mr. Vernon was fast, but the nature of Bartholomew's immortal body meant that any wound needing to remain open provided a continuous feed of burning pain as the nerves were severed, healed, and severed again and again until the procedure was completed.

Adding to his discomfort was the pulling that came with the retractor as Mr. Vernon leveraged Bartholomew's muscles away from his scapula. And the persistent rocking of the train amplified the movement of each pull and cut as the men, the train, and the surgical instruments moved at odds with each other.

"That bullet's being uncooperative. It's found a tricky spot —to— No. There, I've got it."

The pressure of the retractor eased. Bartholomew's grip on the back of the seat bench loosened. He glanced down and frowned. He'd created a hairline crack that ran the length of the polished wood. He blew out a long, slow breath. "Merci."

Mr. Vernon washed blood from his employer's back, as well as the instruments, and stowed the tools. "All's well."

Bartholomew looked at nothing as his body healed. The train rumbled and swayed. "I will consider your advice."

Mr. Vernon helped him dress, handing over his white shirt and crimson tie, his black waistcoat, his black frock coat. Bartholomew retrieved his cigarette case and newspaper. "I'll be in the smoking compartment if I am needed."

"Yes, Monsieur."

THE TRAIN'S rhythmic clack and sway had lulled Bartholomew to sleep, but not so deeply that he missed Matilde's furtive movements. Once again, the girl was out of bed. He peered past the heavy curtain enclosing his berth as he pulled on trousers and donned a shirt and waistcoat. The car's parlor section was dark, but he discerned that the child wore her coat as she crossed the aisle to pull up the window shade above a small desk. Silvery moonlight flickered upon her face and cast distorted shadows about the car. His leather case rested upon a chair. She opened it, fished about its compartments, and withdrew something. There was a flash of metal in the moonlight—Bartholomew's letter opener. It disappeared into her coat pocket along with the few remaining crackers from his evening repast.

She looked toward his berth and left her toy cat on the desk. "You'll be all right, Bettina," she whispered. Matilde took several steps toward the women's berths, hesitated, then turned back and snatched up the stuffed gray kitten. As she scuttled to the Palace car's door, Bartholomew slipped from his berth and followed on bare feet.

Looking neither left nor right, Matilde passed through several cars without notice from sleeping passengers and without spying her follower. When she reached the empty observation car, she glanced up at its large windows and saw his reflection. She gasped and jerked around.

He clasped his hands behind his back. "Where are you heading, Matilde?"

She hugged the cat to her chest. "Away."

"I see. Away is an enormous place. Have you family there?"

She shook her head. "No. No kin nowhere."

"Hmm. It will be hard for you and Bettina to survive in Away without relations to help you." He sat in one of the barrel-shaped chairs that lined both sides of the car. "But Here you have a guardian, a butler, and a governess. That's something like kin."

She didn't respond.

He sat back. "Well, it's your decision, but Here doesn't seem so dreadful to me."

She crossed her arms and glared at the night passing beyond the wide observation windows. "I ain't getting away, am I? I'm stuck with you."

"I'm not your warden." He rested his forearms upon his knees and interlaced his fingers. "But I can't help you if you run away from me."

She went to a window. "I think the monsters want you, not me."

"Ah." He dug his toes into the plush green carpet. "I would

73

agree with you, if I didn't know that you can sense souls." Her sharp inhalation confirmed his assertion. "That's why the other children scorned you, and why your mother hurt you." He watched her from beneath his brows.

Her blonde braid bounced across her back as she shook her head. "I don't know what you mean."

"Non?" He scratched his chin. His beard was getting unkempt. He would have Mr. Vernon trim it in the morning. "I sense them, too, child." Her eyes widened, but she maintained her composure. *Marvelous creature.* "And you were right that the cadaver in Rye was missing something." Bartholomew watched her expression carefully as he added, "Famine ate his soul."

"*Ate* it?"

"Oui." He stood and gestured for her to precede him. She clutched the toy cat tighter and headed back toward their private car. When they reached the darkened Palace car, Bartholomew took her coat and boots, retrieved his letter opener with nary a comment, and watched her return to her berth. He touched her hand as her eyes closed. "Will you permit me to protect you, Matilde?"

"You can try," she murmured and rolled away from him. "But I think they're gonna get us." Her breathing slowed and she slept.

7

The next afternoon found Matilde perched at one of the windows watching Mr. Vernon. He sat opposite her buffing one of Bartholomew's tan shoes. A table separated them. Her elbows rested upon it and her chin was propped upon her clasped hands. "How did your ear get mangled, sir? It looks like a fighter's lobe."

"Before becoming Monsieur's butler I was a pugilist, Miss," Mr. Vernon replied. "They called me the Gentleman Giant when I stepped into the boxing ring." He rotated the shoe and set to work on its heel.

She straightened. "I heard of you. Papa said you was the best fighter he ever saw."

"Your father had a keen eye," Mrs. Henderson said. "Mr. Vernon went six years without a loss." The governess's chin lifted. "Please remove your elbows from the table and sit like a proper young lady."

"Yes, ma'am." Matilde sat back and folded her hands in her

lap. Her attention remained on the butler. "Why'd you stop fighting, sir?"

"After my last bout, I came up against an enemy I couldn't defeat." He glanced at Bartholomew.

She followed his gaze. "Monsieur beat you?"

Mr. Vernon smiled. "No, Miss Matilde. My last opponent in the ring was Gerald McCreedy."

"Never heard the name." Her attention returned to the butler. "He was the winner?"

He shook his head. "The fight was fairly won." He glanced at her, a smile quirking his lips. "If you consider a thirty-pound advantage fair." He swiped his rag over the shoe, frowned, and went to work on its tapered toe.

She asked, "The advantage was yours, sir?"

"Yes, Miss. And the fight was my opponent's doing. I wouldn't have taken him on with such a disparity, but he kept at me about it. I knocked him down three times before the referee called it in my favor."

"On a technicality," Bartholomew said from the small desk where he was drafting a letter. "They gave more consideration to the darkness of Mr. Vernon's complexion than to the power of his fists."

Bitterness filled the butler's voice as he added, "A *technicality*. As if the man could've risen after that last blow."

"Shameful, Mr. Vernon," Matilde said. "My Papa wouldn't've gone for that. He said all men was equal in the ring, until one of them was on the ground. But it was all fair where fists was concerned, no matter the color of your skin."

"*Were* concerned, Miss," Mr. Vernon replied.

Matilde stood and meandered about the car, the silver bell tinkling on her toy cat's collar as she hopped Bettina from seat to seat. "Papa would be green to know I'm on a train with the Gentleman Giant."

Mr. Vernon asked, "He was a betting man, Miss?"

"Naw, sir. A fighting one. He said you was akin to Goliath and so big no man could best you."

The butler nodded toward Bartholomew. "The only man who's ever beaten me is sitting at that desk."

She studied her guardian then peered up at the butler. "Why'd you fight? Papa said you had a finer education than any Negro he'd ever heard of."

"I do. Two degrees from Yale. But a man who fights for his meals is a man with motivation, and I believe all men should comprehend such incentive."

Mrs. Henderson added, "And know how to fight."

Bartholomew rolled his blotter over the finished letter. "It was the men outside the ring at Mr. Vernon's last bout who brought an end to his boxing career. Too many fools disagree with your father's assessment of equality, child."

"And even those men could be overcome." Mr. Vernon held the shoe into the flickering sunlight streaming through the railcar's windows. "Gave me a sound thumping, that crowd, but they had the decency to leave me alive. The cadaver who next came calling had no such courteous intentions." He looked back at Matilde. "Only by the grace of God and Monsieur's sharp blade did I survive *that* fight."

She stared at Bartholomew. "You saved Mr. Vernon? Was he threatened because of you, as well?"

Bartholomew shook his head as he pressed his seal into a dollop of wax to secure the envelope. He ignored the bitterness in her tone. The girl was welcome to nurse her resentment. There was no advantage in denying her the pleasure.

Mr. Vernon answered. "Cadavers are drawn to violence. They're often found where blood is shed."

"Much like sharks, Mr. Vernon," said Mrs. Henderson, who was hemming a new pale-blue pinafore for Matilde.

The butler sat back. "I didn't know that, Mrs. Henderson."

"Sharks?" Matilde looked at her governess.

"Fascinating and frightening creatures, Miss. It has been discovered they have special receptors in their skin that act as an additional sense, allowing them to hunt more effectively. Sharks smell blood in water from a distance of many miles."

Matilde's nose wrinkled. "Do they eat people?"

"The largest sharks will," Mrs. Henderson said.

Bartholomew added, "Blood and the struggle to survive draw predators."

Matilde watched him through narrowed eyes. "Mrs. Henderson, how did you come to be with Monsieur? Did he get your family killed, too?"

The governess's expression hardened as her focus went to the girl. "Matilde Anne Royce, restrain your voice, your manners, and your thoughts. Monsieur has removed you from an unfortunate existence and certain death. Gratitude will take you further than bitterness."

Matilde cuddled Bettina. "I'm sorry."

"I am not the one to whom you should apologize."

Quiet fell over the car but for the rhythmic click-clack-click-clack of the train's wheels and the rattle of the cars.

Matilde wandered closer to Bartholomew and studied him as he replaced his papers and closed his leather case. She gestured toward his letter seal. "Can I see it?"

"You *may*," he said. "*Can* implies the ability to accomplish something. Use *may* when you seek permission."

She huffed a breath and shot him a look that would have choked a goat. He suppressed a smile. Mrs. Henderson's reprimand wouldn't bear fruit so easily.

"*May* I?" She stepped closer and he handed her the seal. She turned the dark wooden handle to study its brass matrix. It depicted the same Roman eagle he bore upon his hand and a banner beneath that read, *Deo Volente Surgam.* "What's this mean?"

"God willing, I shall rise."

She looked up. "Rise to do what?"

He took the seal from her, returned it to its case, and stood, the letter in hand. He gazed down upon her for a long, heavy moment. "Evidently, mail a letter to London." She scurried out of his path as he shooed her away with a gesture.

She meandered down the aisle, tossing and catching Bettina, then climbed upon one of the last seats beside a window and began to play. Beyond the glass, countryside had turned to houses as the train neared Chicago.

Mr. Vernon stood—polished shoes in hand—and accepted the envelope. "I'll post this before we leave Union Station."

"Merci." Bartholomew moved toward the rear of the car. His aides-de-camp needed to be apprised of his separation from Famine. It would have her cadavers on the move and he wanted them watched even more closely than was customary.

At that moment a great *crack* was heard. Bartholomew lunged forward and yanked Matilde from the window seat. She shrieked. He pivoted, protecting her with his body. Wood splintered. Glass shattered inward and downward, falling in daggered shards to shred the fine, velvet seat and lodge in its padding.

"Mercy! What has happened?" Mrs. Henderson shouted

over the whistling wind invading their moving sanctuary. She snatched papers from the air as Bartholomew's stationery flew up and about in a train-made tornado.

Mr. Vernon pulled on the bell rope. Presently, their porter appeared in the car. His eyes widened as he took in the scene and, complaining about "fools with guns and no sense," he set off in the direction from which he'd come.

Bartholomew carried Matilde to her berth and set her down. "Are you injured?"

"No, Monsieur. Why did it break?"

"Gunshot," Mr. Vernon called over the wind and the thundering train as the porter reappeared with the conductor and another trainman. Bartholomew joined them beside the window.

The conductor grimaced and shoved up his cap. "Everyone all right?"

"Oui." Bartholomew glared at the gutted velvet seat as bits of cotton stuffing flapped and tore away with the biting wind. Had he reacted a second later his ward would have been disemboweled. "Who fired that shot?"

The conductor pushed his cap even higher and shouted, "I suspect it was one of the drunks riding in the observation car. We lost several windows, sir. But they managed to stash the gun before my fellows got there, so I have no proof." The wind caught his cap and he snugged it down as it threatened to fly away. He nodded at the porters. "My men will take care of the glass and help gather your belongings. We'll make certain you get transferred to Wells Street Station and onto the *Overland Flyer*, sir." Still holding his cap, he proffered his hand and Bartholomew shook it. "I sure am sorry about this mess. Relieved that none of your party was injured."

"As am I."

The conductor left and the porters went to fetch work gloves and buckets for the shattered glass.

"We can only hope that those troublesome gentlemen are not going on to Omaha," Mrs. Henderson called over the squeal of metal as the train slowed.

Bartholomew lit a cigarette beside the gaping window. "The imbeciles would be wise not to cross my path." Smoke billowed from him with each word.

Mr. Vernon straightened from retrieving papers and books from beneath the desk. "If they need something to shoot, we've got much more worthy targets than windows and wood."

"Cadavers?" Mrs. Henderson righted her sewing basket and gathered runaway spools.

Matilde watched her, then crossed the car and tugged Bartholomew's coat sleeve. "Teach me how to kill them, Monsieur."

Bartholomew paused in lifting the cigarette to his lips. "The hooligans or the cadavers?"

"The cadavers."

He dragged on his cigarette and considered her. When he spoke, vapors escaped his lips like he was a dragon. "A good notion, but there is much that you must understand about their nature before you go into battle." He watched the passing cityscape and nodded. "I will teach you this, Matilde." He focused upon her. "It will be long and tedious, and you must not surrender to despair."

"I give you my word that I will not stop. I want revenge."

"Oui," he said as the shadow of Chicago's Union Station swallowed the train. "When the time comes, you will have it."

SOMETHING WAS AMISS.

After transferring from Union Station to Wells Street Station, Mr. Vernon had chartered a hotel car on the *Overland Flyer*, and their trunks had been loaded. Their party had boarded and, at the behest of Matilde, whom he found himself reluctant to part with, Bartholomew stood upon the open rear platform of the car.

But something was amiss.

"Do you think those are the shooters?" Matilde pointed toward a boisterous group of men who were hanging from a car halfway down the length of the *Flyer*. Deep night was upon them and the girl should have been in bed, but the hustle and fuss of changing stations had her too excited to sleep.

"I hope not." Bartholomew glanced past the men as he scanned the bustling platform. Danger was near. Something tugged at the back of his skull. Something prickled his skin and raised the hair upon the nape of his neck. Something. Or someone.

Women pulling children. Men walking and talking. Lovers in a last embrace. Porters directing, helping, pushing luggage while dodging passengers.

The train jolted forward and Matilde squealed. A cloud of crows dropped from the depot's wide rafters, wheeling, diving, and calling a raucous farewell. She tugged his coat sleeve. "Look at all the beautiful crows!"

He paid no attention to her. He knew what troubled his mind and pricked his skin—the approach of some wicked thing.

He turned and time slowed to a crawl.

Famine strode through the soft shadows of the gaslit platform, her lush, burgundy skirt and black lace petticoat swirling about her. She gestured toward the *Flyer*. Ewan and Barnes pushed through the milling crowd.

Bartholomew felt a sharp tug on the tie that bound him to his enemy.

Gunfire split the cold night air.

Once again, the hooligans were aiming for the wrong prey. But this time, the shooter hit his target and a bird plunged toward the ground.

Matilde's shriek echoed the pain and rage coming from the wounded crow. As the shooter took aim again, the girl leaped from the train and charged across the tracks to rescue the floundering bird.

"Damnation!" the man shouted. His next shot went wild. It struck metal and ricocheted over the heads of the people crowding the depot. Screams filled the air. Passengers and trainmen scurried and ducked. Amidst overturned luggage carts and scattered baggage, the crows wheeled, dived, and threatened anything that moved. Except Matilde.

Bartholomew's foolish ward stumbled over the tracks toward the wounded black bird.

He could leave her. The cadavers didn't know her. The Catcher did not possess her body. Yet.

Non. He shook his head. Of course he couldn't.

Spurred by the sickly, sinuous energy of Famine emanating from the platform behind him, he, too, leaped from the train, risking everything as an inbound locomotive bore down upon Matilde. Its warning whistle rang through the depot, adding to the bedlam as Bartholomew scooped her up and dodged the behemoth. The train passed so close the air stole his top hat and nearly knocked him off his feet.

As one, the cadavers moved toward him.

Simultaneously, the *Overland Flyer* squealed, roared, and hissed into action, grinding away from Chicago and leaving Matilde and him in its wake.

He wove between boxcars and over tracks, racing for the freedom of the departing transcontinental train and away from Famine's shackling will. Her enraged scream could not draw him back this time. He could slip free of the garrote that so long had bound him to his enemy because the Catcher was spurring him to protect the vessel she favored above all others.

As Bartholomew came abreast of the departing *Overland Flyer*, Mr. Vernon leaned from the train. The butler hung precariously over the blurring tracks and reached for the girl. "Give her to me, Monsieur!" Bartholomew, cadavers rattling at his heels, passed the child to Mr. Vernon. She was captured and handed to Mrs. Henderson.

With one great effort, Bartholomew lunged for the step. But it was not a success as Ewan and Barnes leaped upon him, taking him to the ground. He rolled to his back and kicked out. He caught Barnes in the chest and sent the cowboy tumbling away.

Bartholomew scrambled to his feet. Ewan regained his own footing and lunged toward him, arms wide and meaty fists swinging. Bartholomew blinded his opponent with a handful of oily dirt. He followed through with a right hook. His knuckles cracked, but the blow left the Celt's jaw hanging.

He pivoted as Barnes thrust a knife at his stomach. Bartholomew grabbed the cowboy's wrist. He delivered three vicious jabs to the American's face and a kick to his crotch. He yanked the staggering cadaver off balance. He kicked him in the gut and wrenched the knife away. Another kick to the side of his knee sent the cowboy to the ground. Bartholomew turned and left the knife in Ewan's skull. Then he was off at full speed.

Another train—this one towing box cars—pulled away from the station, its shrill whistle warning all living things away. Bartholomew sprinted toward its black bulk, crossing the tracks with only a hair's breadth of safety and close enough to see fear in the conductor's wide eyes. He put all effort into this one chance to escape Famine's allure. Bartholomew leaped and caught a door pull, cursing as the train's force nearly removed his arms from his body. Asserting all of his inhuman strength, he clung to the car like a spider, pulled up and onto the boxcar's roof, and sprinted toward the engine.

A shadowy beast retreating into the night, the *Overland Flyer* was ahead on a parallel track, gaining speed. Soon she would be diverted. He had only one brief chance to catch her.

With a final push of speed and determination, he leaped to the transcontinental train. Pouring every effort into the jump, he sprawled across the *Flyer's* roof. He slid over the sleek body. He tumbled into the dark gap between two cars.

By the grace of the Catcher, or perhaps genuine fortune, his fingers snagged the edge of the roof and his feet found purchase upon a strut.

Mon Dieu.

He pressed his forehead against the thunderous beast and regained his breath.

8

BARTHOLOMEW STRODE THE TRAIN'S ROCKING PASSAGES. Murmurs filled his wake. What had these mortals witnessed? What would they relate to others? Was it of any consequence? From his centuries of experience, he knew the answer was no.

"Sir?"

He stopped. He straightened his frock coat, slapped black dust off the tattered, dark gray vicuña, and patted his breast pocket, relieved to find his cigarette case still in its place. He faced the man who had spoken behind him. "Oui, Mr. Conductor?"

"I, ah, require a ticket from you, sir."

"Of course. If you will direct me to the hotel car? My butler purchased the fare and holds my ticket."

The conductor's tight expression reflected puzzlement rather than annoyance as he led Bartholomew to the private car that had been hooked up to the *Overland Flyer*. He was presented with a ticket, touched the brim of his cap, and left with more questions than answers.

"Leave us," Bartholomew ordered his butler and governess as he shed his ruined coat. He scowled at his filthy waistcoat and tie. His hat was a part of his past and his gloves were beyond redemption.

Matilde cradled the damnable bird in her lap. Tears streaked her dirty face. Tar, blood, and feathers marred her pink pinafore. Her chin trembled, yet her eyes revealed her defiance.

He looked at the crow, expecting to see nothing more than bloody bones and feathers, but the creature glared at him with as much recalcitrance as the child.

"Matilde Anne Royce, if you act so foolishly again, I shall abandon you to the cadavers."

Her steely reserve collapsed. "You hate me." She sobbed. "You don't care what becomes of me."

He clenched his fists and looked away from her tearful face.

"I gotta save this bird, but I don't know how. What am I gonna do?"

Bartholomew ground his teeth, but it was no use; he couldn't block Matilde's suffering no matter how much he willed it. He exhaled a long, slow, irritated breath and said, "Stop your self-pity and let me see the damnable creature."

"What?" She swallowed her sobs, hope and doubt at war behind her expression.

He retrieved a handkerchief from his waistcoat pocket, leaned over her, and wiped the tears and filth from her face. "Let me see what help I can offer the insufferable bird that's the root of our present ills."

She held up the crow for inspection. Its right wing was

shattered; irreparable shards of bone and feathers were all that remained.

He took the bird, holding it firmly as the creature attempted to gouge his flesh with its talons and beak. If he did nothing, the beast wouldn't last the night, and the girl would mourn.

He sat opposite his ward and studied her from beneath his brows. She trembled as she knit her fingers together and leaned toward him. Tears shimmered in her eyes. She wiped them away with her open palm.

Bartholomew realized Mr. Vernon was right. He needed Matilde's faith and she needed someone to trust.

He nodded. "It will survive."

She sniffed again and hope now lifted her voice as she said, "It will? Truly?"

"Oui. But you may not make it a pet. The bird will fly again and must be released back into the wild."

She nodded. "Crows shouldn't be caged."

"You won't be upset to see it leave?"

"No, Monsieur."

"All right. Go to Mr. Vernon and ask for a towel and one of my blue glass vials. He will know what medicine I seek. Take care not to come into contact with its contents. The vapors are poisonous for you."

"You're going to poison my crow?" She grabbed for the creature.

"Non, Matilde. You must trust me. Do you wish for me to save this bird?"

"Yes, but I don't want you to poison it!"

"I said the ampoule's contents are perilous for *you*. Now do as I said."

She hurried to fulfill his request, though her movements were furtive and anxiety twisted her bow lips and fair brow.

When Bartholomew had the thin, finger-length vial, he returned the crow to the girl. "Hold the creature steady. I must stretch its wing." She nodded and gripped the struggling bird as Bartholomew wrapped the towel around its body and her hands then extended the remainder of its tattered pinion. He snapped the long, narrow neck from the ampoule and poured its nebulous blue contents over the leading edge of the bird's splintered wing.

The crow grew still at the first drop and remained docile as Bartholomew bound its wing against its body with a strip of his ruined shirt.

"What sort of medicine is that?" Matilde asked.

"A preparation of my own making." He tore away another portion of his shirt and wrapped it around the broken glass vial. "It's both rare and powerful. I don't spare it without careful consideration of the need."

"Are you a physician?"

He shook his head. "Merely a soldier. This is one of my few weapons in the war against the cadavers, but it comes with a price, as all weapons do. Will you keep your knowledge of its effectiveness secret?"

"I will. You have my word."

"Good. Make a bed for your friend and give him some water. Then wash up. You're a mess. And for my sake and sanity, go to sleep."

Matilde scuttled to her berth. She returned with another towel, which she fashioned into a nest. She settled the crow within its confines, put Bettina beside the bird, and extracted a piece of bread for it from her pocket. "Monsieur?"

"What?" Bartholomew frowned. She was hoarding food. He wasn't surprised.

"Thank you for saving my bird."

He grunted and glowered at her. "Mademoiselle, my mood will be unpleasant as your friend and I convalesce. Knowing your foolhardy act is the cause of my bruises and ill humor, I suggest you avoid garnering my attention for a few days."

"Yes, sir." She scooped up the crow and disappeared into the privacy of the women's sleeping section.

Bartholomew's muscles crackled as he rotated his stiffening neck. A malaise had settled upon him, the result of his exertion to escape Famine and the sudden fierce drive spurred by the Catcher's power within him.

He didn't understand why his soul both healed and destroyed. It was a power he rarely shared, but it had saved his butler, as well as Mrs. Henderson's father. Yet his spirit, tainted by the Catcher's power, was lethal for his ward. It would end Matilde's life and ready her body for the Catcher.

"Of all the foolish things to waste my power upon," he muttered. The whole evening had been calamitous. Famine knew they were traveling west. She couldn't know how far, but he resented her knowledge of him nonetheless.

He yawned and his mood darkened in anticipation of hours spent with the Catcher's nightmares.

"Mr. Vernon?"

The butler appeared in the parlor. "Yes, Monsieur?"

"I need sleep. The girl is to remain in the hotel car."

"Of course. I'll keep watch overnight."

"Merci."

"NOT EVEN A WINCE." *Famine smiled up at him. "That's your strength, Bartholomeus. You endure." She placed the strip of his bloody skin upon her tongue and sighed as she savored it.*

He looked away. Even after seven years, watching her eat made his gorge rise.

"Are you certain you want your little boy to leave?" Ewan still called Bartholomeus little though now they were equal in height and almost in strength.

"He's a man, Ewan." She ran her tongue over the straight wound she'd created on Bartholomeus's forearm—one of many scars she'd inflicted and reopened daily for years. Famine hummed. Like a cat bathing a kitten, she lathed the open cut. Then she dressed the wound with salve and a clean strip of cloth.

"You're certain they'll take me on?" Bartholomeus had no history with the legions and no affiliates in Rome.

She tied the bandage. "Bartholomeus Corona Pellis is expected in Damascus. There is a place for him with the new recruits in the Third Gallic Legion."

"So you've said." He flexed his bandaged arm. "But why am I going so far east?"

"Because that is where the Catcher dwells. You will go east. She will find you. We will follow. And I will consume her soul."

He adjusted the bandage. He loathed the scars and wounds the fabric hid; they were a sign of weakness. "Then what?"

"Then you will stop questioning me and do as you've been instructed." Famine touched his cheek. "We are family. Do not think because you are not at my side I will forget you."

He heard both the affection and the threat behind her words. To avoid his mistress's icy green eyes Bartholomeus watched

Ewan saddle the horse. It was daytime and the towering Celt's hideous form both fascinated and revolted him. He resembled a desiccated corpse—sunken, leathery flesh, ropy tendons, and protruding bones that clattered when he moved.

Famine leaned against Bartholomeus, snaked her fingers up his chest to his neck, and pulled his mouth down to hers. Their tongues touched, stroked, and he exhaled into her mouth. Her lips brushed his as she pulled back and murmured, "Soon we will be together. Again and always, my penumbra."

BARTHOLOMEW AWAKENED to the heady scent of fresh coffee, then grimaced at the clickety-clack of the train's wheels and the clink of silverware on china.

Like the cacophony of Ewan's bones.

He rubbed sleep from his eyes and peered through the heavy curtain at bright, mid-morning light.

Mon Dieu.

How long had he slept? He consulted his pocket watch. Twelve hours with nightmare memories.

Mr. Vernon had laid out clean clothes, soap, and towels. Bartholomew rose and washed the previous day's grime from his face and beard and combed it from his hair. The ache of sore muscles and torn flesh was gone, but his dark mood persisted.

The services of a chef and a porter were theirs with the hotel car and his companions were dining on cheese, fruit, and scones with coffee and tea when he emerged from the gentlemen's dressing room.

Matilde's crow perched upon the back of her seat. It cooed

and bobbed its head as the girl offered up crumbs from her plate. Bartholomew paused to inspect its wing and resisted the urge to swat it off the seat when it grumbled and pecked at him.

"Be polite, Edgar," Matilde scolded.

The crow's pinion was growing new feathers—snow-white ones.

"It's healing well." Bartholomew sat and accepted a cup of coffee but waived away all offered food.

"Yes, he's much better," she replied. Gone was the resentment that had poisoned their recent interactions. She nattered about the bird's unusual white wing, the train, and some strange dream she attributed to the excitement of the previous day.

Bartholomew drank his coffee and exchanged suspicious looks with the crow.

I am an imbecile. How else could he explain the self-sacrifice that had welcomed one of the Catcher's spies into their midst?

Afterward, the girl cajoled him into joining them in the observation car. "Please, Monsieur? I want to see everything. That way when I die and join Samuel, I can tell him all about it."

Bartholomew grimaced but relented. "Very well."

Once there, Mrs. Henderson settled into one of the floral-patterned chairs lining both sides of the car. Matilde, who had left the crow in the hotel car, pressed her nose to the window and peppered her governess with questions as the train sped past the world.

"The *Overland Flyer* passes right through the mountains?"

"Yes, Miss Matilde, in the Sierra Nevadas. Granite was blasted with black powder to create tunnels for the tracks."

Bartholomew surveyed the car. Two women at the coach's far end smiled as they watched Matilde. A gentleman in a gray bowler sat opposite them reading a book.

The girl threw her arms upward. "What a bang that musta been, Mrs. Henderson."

"Must *have* been, please," the governess corrected her charge.

Boisterous voices filled the car as the door opened to admit four children. The eldest, a boy close to Matilde's age, carried a toddler girl. The two middle children—a boy and a girl—ran to the rear door and pressed their faces to the glass.

Noticing Bartholomew's attention upon him, the older boy averted his eyes and snapped his fingers at his companions. "Hush up!"

Matilde slunk behind Mrs. Henderson's chair, her interest riveted on the children.

Hands on her hips, the older girl scowled at her keeper. "You can't snap your fingers at us, Thomas Green. You're not our pa."

The boy crossed the car and sat in the chair closest to the rear door. "No, but I'll tell him you was sassing me, Ulna."

Her chin sank to her chest and her gaze changed from defiant to fearful. "Please don't," she begged.

Thomas shook his head. "Ah, you know I won't." He had green eyes and wavy, chestnut-colored hair. Judging by their matching blue eyes and black hair, the three younger children were siblings. Their patched and ill-fitting clothes identified them as immigrant car passengers.

The younger boy said, "Thomas, see how fast we're going?"

"I told you it was faster than a stagecoach, Perry," Thomas replied while the toddler girl gummed his fingers. Ulna stood at the door, and he toed her foot. "Don't smear the glass." He snuggled the younger girl on his lap and wiped her face with a ragged, yellow handkerchief.

"Sorry." Ulna stuck her hands in her pockets, but her forehead remained pressed to the window.

Matilde's attention had stopped upon Thomas. She chewed her lower lip as she studied him. Even as the other boy and girl slipped between the chairs and the windows closer to her, she continued to watch the eldest of the group.

Scowling at the children, the other adult passengers rose and departed. Their tolerance of Matilde's enthusiasm clearly didn't extend to the lower class children. Bartholomew grimaced. Classism, like racialism, was an ugly mortal trait.

He looked at Thomas. The boy was smiling at Matilde. She glanced at Bartholomew, blushed, and ducked behind her governess.

A party of men, far more boisterous than the children, interrupted the peace as they entered the quiet car, laughing and joking.

"Sit, child." Bartholomew gestured for Matilde to settle beside Mrs. Henderson as he took up guard over her.

"Deal the cards," one of the men said and slumped into a chair. His slurred speech and loud voice attested to too much alcohol consumed.

"Hold your hosses, MacAuliffe," the dealer replied as he shuffled a deck of blue-and-white cards.

Thomas stood, shifted the littlest girl to his hip, and

headed for the door. "Ulna, Perry, come on." The younger children followed with glances at Matilde, but her attention was now on the men.

The fellows played poker and cast sidelong looks at Bartholomew. They elbowed and jostled one another as they spied Matilde. These were her pet's hunters.

Mrs. Henderson passed a workbook and a pencil to Bartholomew's ward. "Both print and cursive. Uppercase and lowercase lettering, Miss." She corrected Matilde's grip upon the pencil and the girl bent to the task of imitating her governess's neat lettering.

The shooters were growing bold and gaining volume as they held a lively discussion about the merits of eating crow. But Bartholomew turned a blind eye to their antics. They were young and foolish, full of bravado and lacking moderation.

Matilde straightened and passed her paper to the governess. She scowled at the men.

Mr. Vernon asked, "Why didn't you greet that boy, Miss Matilde? I believe he wanted to speak with you."

"Me?" She shook her head. "No. Other kids never wanna talk to me."

Mrs. Henderson paused in correcting her work. "Why would you say such a thing?"

"Cause it's true. All of 'em think I'm strange. Except Samuel." Matilde hugged her velveteen cat. "I miss Samuel."

The butler nodded. "Understandable, Miss."

Mrs. Henderson smoothed down the girl's honey- colored curls. She placed the marked sheet before her. "Mind your ascenders and descenders."

"What are those?"

"The parts of letters that go above—ascend—and below—

descend—the middle of each line." She pointed to the paper. "See how this part of the lower *K* rises up and this part of the *J* goes down?"

"Oh."

"Do you understand?"

Matilde nodded.

Mrs. Henderson sat back. "Good. Do another set of letters with that in mind."

The girl bent over her paper, but her attention kept straying to the hooligans, who were cocking their hands like toy guns and making a game of shooting one another. When one of them made a strangled cawing sound, Matilde's pencil lead snapped. She stood, slapped her book down upon the chair, and marched toward the four men. Her beribboned curls bounced with the fierceness of her stride.

Mr. Vernon and Mrs. Henderson made to follow, but Bartholomew stayed them with a gesture.

"Let us see how she manages this." He settled into the seat Matilde had abandoned, leaned back, and crossed his ankles. He fished his sestertius from his pocket and took in the proceedings. The copper Roman coin had been a betrothal gift from Aemelia and he was in the habit of flipping it across his knuckles.

Matilde stopped before the men, who peered at her with amusement. "Which of you gentlemen fired the shot that shattered the window of our car yesterday morning?"

The inebriated fellow, a short, mustachioed man with a brown homburg and a flashy pocket watch, replied. "I'm hard pressed to answer your question, little miss, seeing as neither my companions nor myself know the exact car of which you speak."

She would not be cowed. "Do you talk for yer friends, sir?"

The man glanced around and his companions laughed. He grinned. "It seems that I do."

"Will you come forward?"

The men hooted and jostled him as he pushed up from his seat and approached her.

Matilde gestured for him to lean close. He did so and received a good, hard punch in the nose. He shouted and jerked back. She said, "That's for almost hurting me." She kicked him in the shin. "And that's for shooting a crow."

The man's companions roared and clapped, but his snarl proved he didn't share their glee. As Matilde turned, he reached for her hair but broke off his attack with another shout. He staggered back, his hand over his left eye. He shook his head, straightened, and found the girl had returned to her governess.

Bartholomew now stood in Matilde's place.

"Pardon." The aesir picked up an object at the man's feet. He straightened and added, "I dropped my coin."

Chin jutting forth, eyes and mouth pinched, the drunkard leaned forward and slipped his right hand into his coat. Before he could grasp the small revolver Bartholomew knew was hidden there, the man found a long, angular boning knife pressed to his groin.

Bartholomew loomed over the drunk. "Threatening a child? *Zut.* That's ungentlemanly."

One of the other fellows came forward but was halted by another, thinner boning knife at his throat. He raised his hands. "Whoa. Hey, now, it's all fine, sir. No need for violence."

"She started it," the first man whined.

"That's your defense?" Bartholomew stared at him. Was he an idiot? "My ward is a little girl."

A third man spoke. "He's drunk, sir. Never could hold his liquor too well. Really, we don't want any trouble with you."

"Finally, some intelligence from your group." Bartholomew stepped back and his knives returned to their sheaths as quickly as they'd appeared. He looked at the first man as he addressed the last one to speak. "And you are correct. You do not want trouble from me."

9

Bartholomew had chosen Seattle for their new home, and after several uneventful days the end of their journey neared. They were west of Ogden and had the Sierra Nevada Mountains ahead of them.

He still needed to remain strong and alert, but the mad dash to save the girl and catch the *Overland Flyer* had combined with the Catcher's coercion to deplete him. Neither time nor slumber could fill the breach in his soul. For that he required the power of the outer darkness.

But Bartholomew's actions called for concealment. Should a passenger develop an unexplainable rash and fall into a mysterious stupor, the train could be waylaid and its riders quarantined. That would permit Famine and her kin to catch them. However, alcohol abuse produced a host of strange symptoms, so his late-night stroll through the rocking train had a purpose, to find a certain perpetually inebriated gentleman who'd threatened Matilde a few days prior.

As he walked, Bartholomew turned his pocket watch this way and that, contemplating his long existence.

"While you are bound to me, Famine will be frustrated," the Catcher had told him shortly after she'd made him an aesir.

But Famine wasn't alone in her vexation. He loathed the emptiness and weakness of his halfling state and felt the absence of the Guardian's power like a starving mongrel feels its rumbling gut as it circles a Roman encampment. "How can I protect you in this incomplete form?" he'd said.

"You cannot," the Catcher had replied. She couldn't be convinced to complete him, even though Ewan had destroyed the Beacon, perhaps *because* he had.

Whereas Bartholomew removed souls but only utilized a fraction of their power, the Catcher retained evil souls in their entirety. But without her Beacon's guidance, she'd been unable to deliver those souls to the outer darkness. Thus she'd become congested with their abundant corruption and had struggled against growing paranoia and madness. After the Beacon's sundering, the Catcher trusted no one, including Bartholomew.

As he passed through another car, his fingers brushed the hem of the heavy curtains enclosing the sleeping berths. Behind them spirits slumbered. He paused and felt for dreams. They skimmed his soul, leaving impressions more than pictures. Here was joy, there satisfaction. Worry tainted this one and lust colored a great many others.

He moved on. This wasn't the correct car.

I will miss the train. He'd grown fond of the creak and sway of the iron horse. And something about the trip conspired to make time slip away, just as the miles did. *The endless, undulating brown and green plains are like an ocean,* he mused. *That is the culprit. And the metronomic rhythm of the machine itself.*

Even before he entered the saloon car, Bartholomew heard the caterwauling of the ruffians. Their ability to keep up this level of inebriation was a marvel and, most certainly, a testament to the folly of youth. Unfortunately, the stupidity that accompanied it had robbed him of all amusement.

He made directly for the bar, tipping his hat to the group as they watched him.

The barman asked, "What can I serve you, sir?"

"Your finest Scotch, neat. And a round of the same for this evening's entertainment." He gestured toward the hooligans.

The drinks were served and Bartholomew was savoring the fine, briny Scotch when the fellows let off their wailing and, glasses in hand, approached him. The victim of Matilde's afternoon assault offered his hand.

"Mighty decent of you, sir. My name's Mr. Dougal MacAuliffe."

Bartholomew returned the man's handshake and nodded as the rest of the group was introduced.

"Interesting tattoo you've got there." Mr. MacAuliffe jerked his chin toward Bartholomew's hand. "Military?"

"Oui."

"Never seen one like that associated with the Blue or the Gray."

"It's a continental mark. I didn't fight in your Civil War."

Mr. MacAuliffe stared at him until one of the other fellows said, "Right, you mean French."

Bartholomew brushed his fingers along the rounded edge of the polished mahogany bar. The barkeep's pride showed in its cleanliness. "My ability to speak French doesn't make me a Frenchman, though that is a frequent misperception."

The men's ruddy faces twisted with befuddlement until MacAuliffe shrugged and said, "Join us?"

Bartholomew shook his head. "Non. Merci. I am here for this drink," he lifted his glass and added, "then off to bed."

The group meandered back to the piano and resumed their yowling while Bartholomew remained at the bar, savoring his drink and waiting for Mr. MacAuliffe. He'd made the right choice. From their brief handshake, Bartholomew had perceived the man's thuggish spirit and its love for inflicting pain.

When Mr. MacAuliffe finally staggered off to the observation platform for a piss and a smoke, Bartholomew finished his Scotch and strolled out of the saloon in the opposite direction. But from the open space between that car and the next, he swung up to the roof and continued his stroll to the end of the train, holding his bowler against the wind. He dropped onto the rear observation platform just as the American stepped out.

The man blinked, looked behind himself to the closed door, then swung back, confusion twisting his expression. "Coulda sworn you went the other way."

"I did." Bartholomew removed a cigarette from his case and lit it. He didn't offer one to the fellow, who looked no less stupefied by that answer. Bartholomew inhaled the sharp, acrid smoke of his cigarette, holding it as he considered the puzzled man. He exhaled slowly. The train's draft whipped the vapor into the night.

"Don't be fooled by the drink I purchased for you, Mr.

MacAuliffe. I still require an apology on behalf of my ward. Your antics greatly disquieted her."

Mr. MacAuliffe's muddled expression morphed into annoyance. "I don't make apologies for diverting myself. Nor am I in the habit of expressing regrets to mollycoddled children."

Bartholomew took another long drag, burning the cigarette down by half as he squinted at the man. "Killing defenseless creatures is entertaining?"

"It's a public service. Damnable crows are a nuisance."

"They have souls."

The man snorted. "Not according to the Bible."

"I care nothing for the fabrications of that book. Animals possess souls. They can and do seek revenge."

"What are you blathering about?"

Bartholomew dropped the cigarette, ground it beneath his heel, and stepped close to the man. "Revenge. It is a task at which I excel."

Mr. MacAuliffe froze. His eyes widened as the cold barrel of a revolver pressed against the underside of his jaw. The pearl-handled gun heretofore had been nestled within his own sack coat pocket. "You would commit murder over a damned bird?" he blustered. "You're bluffing. And your jest holds no humor."

"I am neither bluffing nor humorous. Revenge is serious."

"You can't shoot a man on a train. You're mad!"

"Quite." Bartholomew gripped Mr. MacAuliffe's throat and unleashed his own soul, watching with fascination as its glowing blue tendrils reached out, spread up, and burrowed into the man's body. Tremors seized Mr. MacAuliffe's muscles.

His pupils dilated and his eyes rolled back as the luminescence traveled the many branches of his nerves and veins.

Bartholomew's head buzzed. His nerves caught fire as his spirit sought and captured the sacred power within the man's soul. But as quickly as the violation began, he willed his spirit to retreat before Mr. MacAuliffe's soul was purged. The glow receded, returned to its rightful body, and invigorated Bartholomew with the power it had stolen. It left in its wake a spider web choker of silvery scars from the ruffian's shoulder to his jaw.

The man was stupefied but alive.

Bartholomew felt whole. He returned the gun to its holster and let the man slump to the floor of the platform. Mr. MacAuliffe would slowly recover but never recall their exchange.

Bartholomew pulled back up to the roof and sauntered to his private car, revitalized by the man's boorish spirit.

Entering the hotel car, he was greeted with the sight of Matilde's crow perched upon a table edge. The bird stretched its wings and rasped at him.

"Remove that filthy creature from the table, child, or I will knock it off," he snarled.

She scooped the crow into her lap, stroking it as she would a kitten. "They ain't dirty. Crows are fussy about their feathers."

Bartholomew dropped his hat upon a chair, stripped his gloves and coat off, and rounded on her. "They are filthy, irritating nuisances. This one," he jabbed his finger at the beast, "I find particularly offensive. It is a bane I don't wish to see again." The crow snapped at him and Bartholomew's hand became a fist. "Remove it and yourself from my presence or I shall open a window and toss one of you to the wind."

Mouth quivering and tears threatening to spill, Matilde clutched the bird to her chest, hopped down from her seat, and ran to her berth. Her sobs filtered past Mrs. Henderson, who had followed the child but paused in the doorway to the ladies' sleeping area. "Monsieur," the governess said but was interrupted by her employer.

"Tell Matilde to stop wasting her tears." Bartholomew lit a cigarette.

Mr. Vernon stepped forward. "*Monsieur.*"

"But if she insists upon weeping, she should do so quietly. I don't wish to be troubled by the sound." Bartholomew pointed his cigarette at the governess for emphasis. "You can leave my sight, as well. I'm nettled by your laxity with the child. She should have been in bed hours ago. Are you testing the security of your position?"

Mrs. Henderson's chin rose, her lips pinched into a straight, white line. "You are not the only one who is nettled by misbehavior." She looked past him to the butler and added, "Mr. Vernon, please do what you can with the master before he causes too much damage."

As the governess retreated to comfort her charge, the butler's large hand came down upon Bartholomew's shoulder. "You've made an unfortunate choice this evening, sir."

Bartholomew pivoted. "Explain yourself."

Mr. Vernon strode from window to window, drawing the shades. "One of those belligerent fellows?"

"What are you implying, Mr. Vernon?" Bartholomew dragged on his cigarette and glared at the butler as the man added his own coat to his master's upon the chair.

"You left as a gentleman and have returned as a lout." The butler toed off his shoes and shed his waistcoat and linen shirt. He went to the gentlemen's sleeping area of the car and returned moments later with several long strips of dingy white fabric. Two he tossed to his employer, the others he wound about his own knuckles and fingers as Bartholomew smoked and watched. Mr. Vernon nodded at the strips, which had landed upon the floor. "I suggest you don those, Monsieur. I intend to pummel the boor out of you."

Bartholomew sneered. "You can try, but I do hope you packed extra teeth in your trunk." He finished his cigarette, shed his own waistcoat, and wrapped his hands. The fabric creaked as he tightened his fists.

The men faced off, their stances low and their bodies tense.

Mr. Vernon lunged at him. Bartholomew ducked the blow, blocking it with his left hand and punching the butler in the abdomen with a sharp right. But he didn't get away unscathed. Mr. Vernon knew him too well and pivoted away from the strike while landing one of his own on Bartholomew's ear.

The combatants circled and tested. They unleashed blows, recovered, and circled again, two curs seeking weakness. With each punch given and received, the spirit's villainous energy lessened and Bartholomew's mind cleared.

But, becoming aware of an unwanted presence, he stepped back and turned to discover Matilde peering over the high, velvet back of one of the coach seats.

"Girl, was I not clear when I sent you away with your governess?" he snarled.

She slipped off the bench and retreated to stand behind the next seat. "I want to watch."

That she placed furnishings between them irritated him. "This is not for your entertainment."

"I want to learn."

Bartholomew bared his teeth. "Get back to your governess before I scrape you and your insufferable bird off my heel."

Mr. Vernon stepped between them. He scooped Matilde into his arms and strode to where Mrs. Henderson had appeared at the far end of the hotel car. The child was passed off, but not without giving Bartholomew a look that said she'd stab him in his sleep.

The butler returned and sucker-punched Bartholomew in the jaw.

The aesir staggered back, shook his head, and raised his fists. "All right, Mr. Vernon. Let's have at it."

―――――

THEY'D REACHED the Sierra Nevadas. Bartholomew stood upon the open observation platform, smoking and watching the night go by. The mountains, glittering with frost beneath the full moon, resembled silver saw teeth cutting toward the stars. They hewed their way up through the stardust sky to cleave a line between the heavens and earth.

Two worlds and he belonged to neither.

The door behind him opened to release Matilde and Mrs. Henderson. "Goodness, the wind has a bite." The governess pulled her coat collar up. "I am reconsidering this foray, Miss Matilde. It will do none of us any good if you catch a chill."

"I'm not cold, Mrs. Henderson. Please lemme stay."

Bartholomew said, "A few moments of cold air won't harm her."

Mrs. Henderson eyed him. "If she falls ill, I will assign you the task of night duty, Monsieur. And I will sleep soundly knowing she is in your care."

While Matilde clung to her governess's skirt, her regard for him was steely and disconcerting.

Bartholomew looked down his nose at his ward and arched an eyebrow. "You have something to say?"

"Why were you mean to me?"

He dragged on his cigarette, then let the smoke slowly escape his mouth as he turned a little toward her. How to answer that question? "It is difficult to explain."

Her chin jutted up and she gave an angry little jerk of her head. "You should say you're sorry."

Bartholomew met her regard head-on. The girl had more conviction than did most of the adults he'd met. He crouched to her level. "Oui, Matilde. *Mea culpa*—I *am* sorry."

Her head tilted. She assessed him through narrowed eyes, weighing and measuring him. Would she find him adequate or lacking? Her brows rose, her face relaxed, and her attention drifted to the night sky. "How pretty."

He'd been forgiven. Much to his surprise, it mattered.

Bartholomew peered up. "Do you know the constellations?"

"Nuh-uh."

"'No, Monsieur,'" Mrs. Henderson corrected. Bartholomew pointed out Lyra, Cygnus, and Aquila. "Their brightest stars align in the east to form a triangle. Do you see it?" He pointed out the three bright stars that made up the formation—Vega, Deneb, and Altair.

"Oh, yes! I do."

Mrs. Henderson added, "The great swath of stars that

resembles sugar spilled across the sky is called the Milky Way. And that is the name of the galaxy in which our planet resides. There are billions of stars in the Milky Way Galaxy alone."

Matilde turned to her. "Are there other worlds like the earth?"

"No one knows, Miss. But I do not see why there would not be more."

Matilde tugged Bartholomew's sleeve. "What do you think, Monsieur?"

"I believe there's far more mystery in the heavens and earth than we can possibly comprehend."

The girl smiled. "It's a wonder."

It was the first smile he'd evoked from her.

"Indeed," he murmured.

WITH A FIRM GRIP on Matilde's hand, Bartholomew stood upon the train platform in San Francisco and surveyed the depot. Shouts filled the air—greetings between loved ones, tired passengers squabbling over luggage, parents wrangling travel-weary children. No cadavers pushed through the crowd. Nothing pulled on his allegiance to indicate Famine's presence. But after the near-disaster in Chicago, he exercised caution as his party moved away from the *Overland Flyer* and into the city.

"Here comes Mr. Vernon with our porter and the trunks," Mrs. Henderson remarked. Bartholomew glanced in the direction she'd indicated.

His butler had arranged for rooms at the Palace Hotel. They had two days to pass in San Francisco before they boarded a Pacific Mail Company steamship to Seattle. But none of them was discontent with the delay. Once they boarded the steamer, they faced another three-day confinement. So they relished the opportunity to stretch their legs while climbing the city's hills, to revel in the clean ocean air coming off the bay, and to sleep upon properly sized beds. The latter, in particular, pleased Bartholomew; the hotel car's berths hadn't accommodated his height and he had little faith the *Sehome Queen* would offer anything better.

Edgar, whom Matilde held upon her left arm, let out a strident alarm call. The girl scratched the bird's head. "Hush, Edgar. Monsieur won't let them hurt you."

Bartholomew glanced at the girl. "What's troubling your bird?"

"Those hooligan men are coming this way."

Bartholomew followed her gaze and spied the group of men weaving through the crowd toward the depot exit. Mr. MacAuliffe staggered between two of his companions, held steady by their arms around his back.

"The mean one looks ill," Matilde remarked.

Mrs. Henderson picked lint from Matilde's blue coat. "Too much drink."

Mr. Vernon, who'd reached them in time to overhear the exchange, added, "We all must pay for our sins."

Bartholomew nodded. "Have you all of our belongings, Mr. Vernon?"

"Yes, Monsieur, and a carriage awaits to take us to the Palace."

"Bon. Lead the way." As they wove through the crowd, Bartholomew addressed Matilde. "When we reach the hotel, you must release Edgar."

"I know."

They found a waiting carriage and Bartholomew held its door open as Mrs. Henderson and Matilde climbed in. Mr. Vernon helped load the trunks.

Bartholomew glanced toward the station and spied the boy Thomas, younger children in tow, pushing through the exit behind a sullen man and a small, skittish woman.

The man scowled and snarled at the woman. She looked this way and that, as if she'd lost something important. Her eyes met Bartholomew's. She flushed and began fussing over the children.

Mr. Vernon stopped beside him as the driver climbed up to his own seat. Bartholomew and his butler settled into the carriage and it pulled into San Francisco's hubbub.

Once at the hotel, Mr. Vernon and Mrs. Henderson accompanied the baggage up to the suite while Bartholomew stood with Matilde on the sidewalk outside the main entrance.

"Goodbye, Edgar." She stroked the crow's white wing. "Beware of rotten people and cats." She kissed the bird's head then tossed him upward.

The crow took flight, circled the street, and came to rest upon a covered span that connected the Palace with a neighboring hotel. A small family of crows occupied the bridge and after a fuss of cawing and flapping, the congregation of birds settled down, Edgar in its midst.

Bartholomew offered his hand to Matilde. She looked from his face to his open palm, hesitated, then grasped it. They entered the hotel and crossed its elaborate marble-and-wood lobby to one of the elevators. He glanced down at his ward. Her expression was calm. He'd expected tears. The lift's door opened and an operator took them to the fifth floor.

As they reached their room, Matilde asked, "Will you teach me to flip a coin over my knuckles, Monsieur?"

Bartholomew pulled the sestertius from his pocket. He took her hand and turned it palm down and parallel to the floor. He rested the copper coin upon the back of her index finger and showed her how to flip the edge of it over so that the piece came to rest flat upon her middle finger. "Practice is all you need, Matilde." As she struggled to work the large coin, he added, "And bigger hands,"

She looked up at him. "Or a quarter."

PART TWO

10

WESTERN UNION TELEGRAM
June 1, 1898
C. Vernon, Seattle, WA, USA, P.O. Gen'l Delivery

Famine in Bombay plus E and fourteen.
Shravya

FROM HER APRON POCKET MRS. HENDERSON PRODUCED
the worn leather sheath that held Bartholomew's small boning
knife. She placed it upon the desk beside his hand then stacked
a teacup and saucer upon a silver tray and carried them to the
hallway. She returned and began making his bed.

Bartholomew cocked an eyebrow at the weapon. "Where
was it this time?"

What had begun with his letter opener as they traveled
from New York to Seattle had graduated to various knives.
Three years in his household, yet Matilde remained wary of

his ability to safeguard her. Bartholomew frowned. At least she'd stopped hoarding food.

"On the floor at the head of her bed." Mrs. Henderson turned the card from June to July on his bedside calendar and murmured, "Still no sign of your foul mistress."

He nodded. He didn't need the governess to point out what he was keenly aware of—every moment that passed without Famine's disagreeable company.

He stood and walked the length of the room. A hand-drawn map of the world stretched from floor to ceiling, end to end, with each country and all the major cities marked in blue. Bartholomew stopped before India and wrote *Famine (E+14)* beside Bombay with a pencil.

Mr. Vernon stood before Europe. "Seems odd. She was quite eager for a reunion when we left her in Chicago." He was massaging his knuckles.

The governess plumped the bed's goose feather pillows and pulled its white sheets tight. "Do you suppose she knows our location?"

"It's possible." Bartholomew put his finger on India. "Though she's currently in Bombay relishing the famine that's killing millions there."

White blanket in hand, Mrs. Henderson stared at him. "Is she causing that?"

"Non. Not without the power of the other Horsemen. But she couldn't pass the opportunity to grow fat on the suffering." He folded and unfolded the telegram, then tossed it onto his desk with several others and glanced at his butler. "Has Seattle's damp weather aggravated your rheumatism, Mr. Vernon?"

"No more than New York's did." He gave Bartholomew a

wide grin. "Perhaps a reprieve from the ironing would help." Mr. Vernon loathed ironing, but the irksome job had fallen to him when Mrs. Henderson took on her governess duties.

Bartholomew laughed. "Teach Matilde."

"I just might, sir."

"Heartless, both of you." The governess shook her head and she smoothed the blanket over the pillows. "I have a fresh arnica tincture ready for you, Mr. Vernon. It should have you back to ironing in no time."

The butler eyed her, a wry expression twisting his mouth. "How kind of you, Mrs. Henderson." He brightened and added, "Truly, arnica always works wonders on these old, arthritic knuckles."

Bartholomew returned to the map. "Mr. Vernon, please ask our woman in Paris to let slip that we're in Italy." He cocked his head. "And send a cable to Mrs. Sindar offering more aid to her family in Bombay."

"Spread a new rumor?" the butler replied. "With pleasure, sir."

Mrs. Shravya Sindar was a widow from whom Bartholomew received regular reports on his enemy's activities in the Orient. She was one of many mortal associates tracking Famine and her cadavers around the globe, floating rumors to misdirect their search for him. These associates formed a tight-knit group, fostered over generations by Bartholomew, and there were many benefits to their loyalty. Most of them were women; many had been his lovers, including Shravya.

Matilde wandered into the room and slumped into the reading chair beside the bed. She wore a rumpled, pale-green pinafore over a wrinkled lavender blouse that had last occupied the back of the maple rocking chair in her bedroom. Dark circles framed her blue eyes, and though her hair was braided it stood out in wild wisps around her head and looked in danger of escaping the plait.

"Are you unwell?" Bartholomew slipped the pilfered knife into his coat pocket.

Her eyes tracked his hand. "No, Monsieur. Tired. I had ghastly dreams all night."

They never discussed her need to keep a weapon in her bedroom. The knives were always discovered and returned, and they all knew a replacement would be secreted away within a few days. It wasn't theft; it was self-protection against monsters. Sometimes Bartholomew wondered if she considered him one of them.

Mr. Vernon said, "Not the one with the faceless woman, I hope."

Matilde sighed. "The very one. And there was a man with wounds and marks all over his skin," she gestured toward her guardian, "much like the one upon Monsieur's hand, but open and bleeding." Her hands dropped to her lap. "All I could do was circle like a crow and watch him suffer."

Bartholomew asked, "Are you feverish?"

"Illness is not to blame." Mrs. Henderson tugged the white duvet into place on Bartholomew's bed. "These nightmares occur when you do not get enough rest, Miss." She straightened and gripped Matilde's shoulder. "The light coming beneath your bedroom door late into the night told me that you were reading well past eleven o'clock again. Evil dreams will not excuse you from your arithmetic."

In the three years she'd spent under her governess's careful tutelage, Matilde had gained a proper vocabulary, but she wasn't completely tamed. A fact demonstrated by the sour expression twisting her face as Mrs. Henderson added, "Fetch your workbook and pencil."

The girl huffed and pushed up from the chair.

"And fix your appearance, please."

A groan followed that admonishment.

Nightmares. Suffering. Death. Bartholomew's jaw tightened as his ward tromped from the room. *And I a helpless spectator like Matilde in her dreams.* He couldn't ease his ward's nightmares, and he couldn't prevent his butler's rheumatism from worsening. Bartholomew was cursed with too much time. Like a snail upon a wall, he moved inexorably and against reason through the days, while the people around him changed, crumbled, and fell. He glanced at the wall map. *Famine is strengthened by the world's misery, even as Matilde's time runs out.*

His enemy was out there, searching, her cadavers moving in ever-narrowing circles, wolves in the dark. His focus drifted from Bombay to the northwestern corner of the United States. Eventually she would discover him and Matilde. Perhaps she already had.

If so, why was she waiting?

Matilde returned to the room, book and pencil in hand, hair and dress straightened.

The jingling of the front door's bell interrupted Bartholomew's dark thoughts.

"There he is." Mr. Vernon turned away from the map. "Excuse me, ladies, Monsieur." The butler straightened his waistcoat as he disappeared into the hall. His footfalls were heavy upon the wooden stairs. The front door squeaked open and clicked shut. Gravel crunched at the side of the house. Muffled conversation carried through the closed bedroom windows.

Matilde dropped the study book on Bartholomew's desk and looked from her governess to her guardian. "With whom is Mr. Vernon speaking?" She went to the corner window and peered into the rear yard.

"Thomas Green," Mrs. Henderson replied. "The young man has been brought on to help with the horses." The governess opened the tattered book and pointed to a page of unfinished mathematical equations. "You need to mind less what Mr. Vernon is doing and more the task at hand."

Matilde stretched to see the stable. "That was the name of the boy I saw on the *Overland Flyer*. Is he the same one?"

"He is," Bartholomew replied, surprised she recalled Thomas Green. Their encounter had been brief.

The boy had persisted in asking for work over many months. While Bartholomew hadn't doubted that young Mr. Green had a genuine financial need, he hadn't wanted an outsider nosing around his estate, or his ward. However, Thomas Green's tenacity was admirable, and now the boy could be useful.

Matilde said, "That's good of you to employ him."

"Mr. Green asked and it benefits all of us." Bartholomew took the reading chair she'd abandoned. "He lives with his aunt, uncle, and young cousins. The family needs the money. Mr. Vernon and I require freedom from the daily stable chores."

The governess tapped the equations with Matilde's pencil. "Sit, young lady."

The girl returned to the desk and her work. Fabric swished

as Mrs. Henderson bustled about the room, smoothing the curtains, straightening the rugs, and dusting the sills. Matilde's pencil scratched across paper. The mantle clock tick-tick-ticked. Bartholomew crossed his ankle over his knee and read the *Seattle Daily Times*.

"Will he be here daily?"

Bartholomew lowered the newspaper. Curiosity brightened Matilde's eyes. She seemed much restored by the notion of another youngster in their midst.

Mrs. Henderson crossed the room and opened the window above the desk. "Every afternoon except Sunday when he is an altar boy."

"How wonderful," Matilde murmured and twiddled the pencil between her fingers.

"Why?" Bartholomew tossed the paper onto the table, stood, and surveyed the sunny yard from the corner window. "You will be in training."

Matilde's focus snapped to him. "What training?"

"Mr. Vernon will instruct you in grappling. I will teach you how to wield weapons. That is what will take us away from the stables."

"Finally." She exhaled the word.

He faced her. "Matilde, I don't relish the thought of striking you." He cleared his throat. "This will not be easy for any of us. And it can be put off until you are an adult. Are you prepared to experience a great deal of pain?"

Her chin lifted and her expression cooled. "I know how to take a blow. The Sixth Ward saw to that. And I haven't forgotten. Anything."

He spied Mrs. Henderson's tight-lipped expression and

said, "Back to your arithmetic. We'll begin when Mr. Vernon is finished instructing Thomas Green." Matilde bent over her workbook. Bartholomew turned to the governess. "You'd hoped this day wouldn't come, Mrs. Henderson?"

"You know I disagree with this path."

"Nor is it my choice, but time has become my enemy."

"I am aware of that, yet there must be some way of circumventing this situation, sir."

Matilde had stopped writing to listen though she remained bent over her paper, her pencil poised to work the next problem.

"Matilde wishes to have her revenge."

"This has never been about revenge," Mrs. Henderson snapped before she disappeared into the hallway. The rattle of the tea service and the squeak of the floorboards followed.

Matilde spoke without looking up from her work. "Whatever is between you and Mrs. Henderson makes no difference. For me this *is* about vengeance. And if that means Famine and her cadavers are sent to hell or the outer darkness or whatever you wish to call it, we'll be all the better for it."

Bartholomew retrieved a blue ledger from the desk. "You and I are in agreement." He sat in the reading chair and opened the book. "Finish your studies, Matilde."

THREE STUFFED rabbits and two brown bears marched through a valley formed from white pillows. Bartholomew stood over the battlefield, his hands clasped behind his back. "Where would you put your archers?"

Matilde, paper dolls in hand, pointed at the pillows. "On the hills, right?"

"All of them?"

"Yes?" She arrayed her paper figures atop the pillows.

"Keep some to support your other ranks." He circled the scene. "Cavalry and foot soldiers?"

She galloped two small wooden horses around to the back of the valley. "They go here." She placed a trio of porcelain dolls at the other end, facing the stuffed animals. "And I'd use a few of the foot soldiers to draw the enemy in with the appearance of a smaller force."

"You're hiding the majority of your infantry?"

"Yes."

Mr. Vernon appeared in the doorway of the third-floor gymnasium. "Planning an ambush?"

Bartholomew nodded. "The stuffed animals have blundered right into it."

"Shall I return after the massacre is over?" The butler carried a small stack of ragged towels.

"Non. Matilde grasped the lesson immediately." Bartholomew waved him into the room and turned to his ward. "Excellent strategy. Are you comfortable leaving off here?"

"Yes, sir." She picked up a large wicker basket and began gathering the toys and pillows.

Mr. Vernon placed the towels atop a cabinet, one of several that flanked the doorway. Bartholomew unlocked one of the drawers as the butler said, "First lesson, Miss Matilde. When your enemy comes at you, don't run." She deposited the basket by the door and joined them as he added, "Running only excites them and you're not fast enough to escape. But," he raised a finger for emphasis, "wounding them gives you an opportunity to create distance. And distance gives you time to formulate a plan."

"A plan?" She jerked her chin up, filled with the hubris of youth and inexperience. "I *plan* to kill them on the spot."

Bartholomew seized her by the throat, yanked her around, and pinned her against the wall. She trembled beneath his hand and stared at him, a wide-eyed rabbit in a snare.

"Look down," he said.

She did and swallowed against his palm as she spied the boning knife he held to her gut.

"This is not a game with dolls and stuffed toys. If I were a cadaver, you would be dinner."

Her gaze returned to his. All the arrogance had left her and her cheeks were pale.

"You are neither faster nor stronger than cadavers, Matilde. So you must be smarter if you are to survive." Bartholomew lowered the knife then blocked her as she kicked out at his groin. "Good. I see I didn't scare the fight out of you." He yanked her away from the wall. She squeaked as he threw her to the floor. "Now listen and learn, so you don't die." He turned back to Mr. Vernon and awaited his ward's next move.

Would she rise?

Her glare promised him pain in the future, but she gulped a deep breath, stood, and returned to his side. "Please continue your lesson, Mr. Vernon," she said. Her lip was bloody and trembling.

Bartholomew proffered his white handkerchief. She snatched it from him and pressed it to her mouth. He looked past her angry expression and swallowed rue. More than ire glinted in her eyes; distrust flared there, too. But treating her gently would only get her killed.

Mr. Vernon nodded. "Thank you, Miss. As I was saying, don't run from an attack. Move into it with force and purpose. You want to surprise your enemy and wound him as quickly as possible, particularly in the case of multiple assailants. Cadavers prefer to hunt in groups. Correct, Monsieur?"

"Oui. Pairs or trios. One to corner their prey, the other or others to kill."

Matilde frowned. "Like pack animals."

"The victims they kill immediately are the fortunate ones. It's worse for those taken to Famine." Bartholomew held her gaze. "She relishes the taste of fear."

"How horrid." She looked down at his forearm where his sleeve had ridden up to expose the ladder of scars there. She averted her eyes as he tugged the fabric into place.

Bartholomew added, "In a cadaver, you face an enemy that doesn't perceive physical pleasure or pain. A soul is needed for that. It's why they're so fascinated with suffering; they've forgotten how to feel."

Mr. Vernon continued. "What are your advantages?"

She chewed her lower lip. "Advantages, sir?"

He nodded. "You have several."

She squinted. "Determination?"

"It's important but not an advantage." He held up his index finger. "Number One: You're small. That permits you to get into places that most cadavers can't. The majority of them are equal to Monsieur's or my height and weight. Famine chooses her soldiers for their intimidating presence."

Matilde asked, "What else?"

"Once you've learned to fight, you'll be a surprise to them," Mr. Vernon said. "They anticipate fear from their victims, not ferocity."

Bartholomew added, "You have a fierce soul."

Matilde looked at him. "That matters?"

"More than anything. Cadavers yearn to have souls, but spirits elude them. Always. It's why they consume mortals." He touched her chin. "Your soul is the source of your strength."

"But Famine has a soul, right?" Matilde rocked from foot to foot, as if she was a reed in the slightest breeze.

Bartholomew dropped his hand to her arm to calm her. "Correct. She is not a cadaver. What she craves is power. And contained within every soul is the power of the outer darkness. If Famine consumes enough of it, she will be able to summon the other Horsemen from the ether and give them physical form. Separate, Famine, Death, War, and Conquest are impotent, but united they are the end of us all."

Mr. Vernon said, "So you can see the importance of stopping the cadavers from bringing her victims."

Matilde nodded. "That's why Mrs. Henderson said this was never about revenge. Right?"

"Oui." Bartholomew let his hand fall. "This is much greater than you and me."

Mr. Vernon stepped forward. "We'll teach you how to inflict the maximum amount of damage on your opponent as quickly as possible. The more prolonged a fight is, the more injuries you'll sustain and the less likely you are to escape."

Bartholomew added, "You are becoming a soldier, Matilde. Engage in combat, damage or destroy your target, and extract yourself from the situation. You are fighting for survival."

"First you'll learn to kick, punch, escape." Mr. Vernon handed Bartholomew two pairs of the fabric strips that protected their hands when they fought.

Bartholomew reached toward his ward. "Right hand." She extended her palm. He wrapped the fabric from her knuckles to her wrist and around her thumb and fingers. "This keeps the small bones and joints from moving and fracturing when you repeatedly strike something."

"Like a cadaver's thick skull," Mr. Vernon said and grinned.

Bartholomew showed Matilde his calloused and knobby knuckles. "You don't want your hands to resemble mine."

She shrugged. "They look like Papa's did."

"Broken and scarred?"

"A fighter's hands, Monsieur. I won't be troubled if mine look that way."

Bartholomew said, "I will," as he wrapped her left hand.

"You said I'm becoming a soldier. Shouldn't I expect to look the part?"

"Non. I don't want you to become hard."

"Why not?"

He straightened and regarded her. "Because there's a razor's edge between hard and hard-hearted. If you lose your compassion, you'll be no better than our enemy." He began wrapping his own knuckles and added, "I've seen that before and never wish to see it in you."

"I understand." She ran her fingers across her wrapped palms. "It's a good lesson, sir."

Mr. Vernon led her to the center of the room. "Are you ready for more?"

Bartholomew joined them. "Do you remember how to identify a cadaver?"

"Yes, their ghastly stink. Like the smell of a rat rotting in the walls." Matilde's nose wrinkled. "And that strange nothingness."

"Their missing souls." Bartholomew nodded. "If you see them in the sunlight, you will have no doubt about their corrupt nature."

She leaned forward. "Why? How do they appear?"

"Like corpses left to dry in the sun—skeletons encased in leathery, sallow skin."

"Monsters," she murmured.

"All right." Mr. Vernon planted his feet, centered his weight, and raised his fists. "Let's start with proper stance, as well as punching and kicking techniques. I expect you will progress rapidly, Miss."

———

AFTER TWO HOURS OF FIGHTING, Matilde appeared wan and woozy. Bartholomew halted her lesson. "You've had enough pummeling."

She didn't trouble with pushing her damp hair from her face as she sank to the floor and leaned against the wall. She closed her eyes and didn't react as Bartholomew settled cross-legged opposite her and unwrapped her hands.

"Are you well?" he asked as he unwound the fabric from his own palms.

"Yes." Her eyes remained closed.

He surveyed his ward. Her knuckles were bruised and red. Her lower lip was split and swollen. A purple bruise stood out on her fair cheek where she'd failed to block a blow. He frowned. He'd pulled every punch, slowed every strike, had done his best to break her falls, but there was no doubt that his ward had been brawling.

Mr. Vernon wiped sweat and blood from the wooden floor. "You'll have to stay inside until your bruises fade, Miss Matilde."

"I understand." She stood with a low groan. "I'll require your aid to reach my room, Mr. Vernon," she mumbled.

"Yes, Miss."

He offered his elbow. She leaned upon him and tottered to the door. But before leaving, she pulled him to a stop and faced Bartholomew. "I hope we'll continue this tomorrow."

Matilde was bent but unbroken.

"Oui. Tomorrow and the following day and onward until you are a trained warrior."

Her chin lifted, and though her body wavered, her voice did not as she said, "Thank you." She and the butler disappeared into the long hallway.

The wood floor creaked. Mrs. Henderson appeared in the gymnasium doorway. "Monsieur, I hope you will excuse my tone, but I cannot hold my tongue in this matter. What *are* you doing?"

Bartholomew grimaced and kneaded the back of his neck. "Teaching."

She put her hands on her hips. "Miss Matilde is an eleven-year-old girl."

"More than old enough to begin making decisions and accepting their consequences."

"This is going too far. What if you had broken her nose? Or bruised her organs? You are a trained, hardened warrior." She clenched her fists. "How is this possibly a fair match?"

"It's not. And that, *madame*, is the point. Matilde will face cadavers taller, faster, and certainly more intent upon spilling her blood than I am. She will face them in numbers. She mustn't fear pain—neither to receive it nor to deliver it."

"But why now? Why not wait until the Catcher can mend her?"

"It was her choice."

Mrs. Henderson crossed her arms and glared at him. "Certainly not an informed one. You have misled the girl for—"

Menace surged through Bartholomew. "Lower. Your. Voice." The power behind those three words, though they were spoken rather than shouted, filled the room and set the governess back a step. She blinked and looked down. They'd been friends much of her life, but she'd never shown any fear of him. Until now.

"Of course, Monsieur."

"I understand and appreciate your concern but assure you that not one of my blows held anywhere near the full strength of which I am capable. Nor would I *ever* deliberately harm that girl. My every thought is only for her eternal wellness." He stalked toward her. "Do not insinuate that I mean her ill, Mrs. Henderson."

She shook her head but still didn't meet his glare. "No, Monsieur, that is not at all what I meant."

Bartholomew stopped before his housekeeper. "Please do not make me doubt you."

Her head jerked up. "Oh, no. I fully comprehend the weight of your responsibility and Miss Matilde's." She averted her eyes again. "I just fret about her physical health. She is so small compared to you."

The atmosphere of the room eased as Bartholomew touched Mrs. Henderson's elbow. "Stop worrying."

She nodded. "I will help her with a bath. Epsom salts will do much to ease her aches. And arnica to heal the bruises."

"Merci." As the woman backed through the doorway, Bartholomew added, "I appreciate your concern for Matilde's wellness, Mrs. Henderson. Truly I do."

11

WESTERN UNION TELEGRAM
August 26, 1898
C. Vernon, P.O. Gen'l Delivery

22 cdvrs overrun Bangkok—Warn all away.
Josephine A

BARTHOLOMEW LEANED AGAINST THE PORCH POSTS AND watched Matilde as she wandered the yard. She hopped the flowerbeds, zigzagging from one side to the other. His soul harmonized with hers, a warm, late-summer song—slow and sonorous—like waving, golden fields and soaring birds. He smiled. "What is your game, child?" he called as he palmed his pocket watch.

"I'm following the honeybees." She popped out from behind one of the apple trees that marched like soldiers down each side of the yard. She circled it, one hand on its bumpy, gray trunk to hold her upright as she tilted back. Her once-white pinafore had the dappled rainbow appearance of a Monet painting.

Matilde had been training daily for two months and her progress was admirable. She now used her diminutive size to her advantage, dodging her guardian's blows more often than not. Bartholomew no longer needed to confine her to the house to hide fading bruises, which was advantageous; warm days were growing infrequent. They'd come outside to enjoy the fading late-August sunshine following the afternoon fight lesson and low tea.

"You're wearing pollen like a bee," he said.

She stopped and glanced down. She brushed at the bright yellow and orange stains, but only smeared them. "Mrs. Henderson will be vexed," she replied.

"She often is." He slipped the watch into the pocket of his dark blue waistcoat.

The thud and scrape of a pitchfork carried from the stable. Thomas Green was changing the horses' straw. A small family of crows took wing from the trees and swooped the length of the yard to land upon the white building's pitched roof. They'd made a permanent home in the towering pines surrounding Bartholomew's property.

Matilde fished two chunks of bread crust from her front pockets and skipped toward the crows' perch. She stopped below the eaves and clucked to the birds. They answered her in kind. "Come down," she called. "I've a treat."

The crows ducked and bowed, but they didn't join her. She trotted to the corner of the building and climbed the straw bales Bartholomew and Mr. Vernon had stacked there, but she couldn't reach the eaves. Bartholomew had seen to that. He didn't want her following her feathered friends up to the roof.

Thomas emerged from the white building. "Who're you talking to, Miss?" He removed his brown cap.

She turned and stared at him long enough to make the lanky, adolescent boy look down and scuff a worn heel in the gravel. "The crows," she finally replied.

Though they'd been introduced, Matilde had never conversed with him. Instead, like a wary dog that's received too many kicks, she'd studied Thomas from the house, the porch, or the distant corners of the walled yard. Mrs. Henderson had encouraged her to interact with him. "He's an altar boy, Miss," she'd said, "with fine manners." But Matilde had held back, watched, and waited. For what, Bartholomew didn't know.

Thomas grinned. "Do they answer back?"

Her eyes narrowed. She stood still and suspicious, like a cat assessing a threat.

Bartholomew watched closely. Was the boy teasing her? Hopefully, this wouldn't end with Thomas on the ground nursing a bloody nose. Bartholomew had seen enough bruises on the stable boy to know he received blows often; whether from school or home was unclear.

Matilde answered slowly. "Sometimes."

"They're the smartest birds, you know. Don'tcha, Miss?"

She nodded. "As intelligent as some humans."

"That's why I like 'em, too." He put forth his hand. "I'm Thomas Green."

Matilde didn't shake it. "I know who you are."

He lowered his hand and shrugged. "I figured you'd forgotten, Miss."

"You may call me 'Miss Matilde.'"

His grin returned and the boy brushed thick, brown hair away from his green eyes. "Sure." He leaned on the pitchfork and gestured at the crows gathered along the edge of the roof. "They remember fields where farmers've been mean to 'em. You know that?"

"Yes. Crows recognize faces and teach their offspring whom to avoid."

"You don't say?"

She sat upon the straw and faced the darkening yard as the sun dipped below the trees. "Night's coming. You should return to your chores, Thomas Green."

He glanced around the yard and plopped the cap back on his head. "So it is, Miss."

"Maybe we can speak again tomorrow."

"We can?"

"Yes." She looked back at him, her gaze intense and unblinking. "Please go back into the barn, so I can feed the crows. They don't trust you yet."

"Oh. All right, Miss."

Thomas retreated into the stable. The crows hopped down to join Matilde upon the straw and enjoy the bread she'd pilfered from the kitchen.

Bartholomew contemplated the exchange. *Interesting.* Perhaps Thomas Green would prove to be more helpful than he'd anticipated.

Mrs. Henderson appeared at the French doors with her brown sewing basket and a mauve garment draped over her arm. "Supper is ready, Monsieur." She fished in her basket and extracted a collapsible knife. "Under her pillow this morning. Is it not the one you keep in your study desk?"

"It is. Merci."

She squinted at Matilde as the girl climbed off the hay bales. "What has that child done to her pinafore?"

"Pollinated it." Bartholomew turned the knife between his hands. How had Matilde gained entry to his locked office?

The governess sighed. "Bad enough that she outgrows every dress before I finish it. Does she have to destroy those that *do* fit?"

He rested his forearms on the white porch rail. "Apparently."

Mrs. Henderson called to her charge. "Miss Matilde, please come wash up for supper."

"Yes, ma'am." Matilde skipped across the yard and trotted up the steps, her blonde curls bouncing around her shoulders.

Bartholomew smiled. His ward was like the little sparrows that hopped and scratched around the yard, refusing to be intimidated by the crows. She, too, was a little bird—*un petit oiseau*—with a fondness for knives and sneaking. "Matilde." He held up the knife. "You know you have no business in my study."

She bit her lip and looked down. "Yes, Monsieur." She slipped past them into the house.

Mrs. Henderson asked, "Will we stay in Seattle through the winter?"

"Oui." Bartholomew slipped the knife into his pocket as he surveyed the yard. The trees showed the slightest orange and yellow tints.

The governess smoothed a wrinkle on the front of her green dress. "Is it dangerous for us to remain in one place for so long?"

Bangkok overrun. Twenty-two where once there were only two.

"Nowhere is safe for us, Mrs. Henderson." He pushed away from the porch rail and gestured for her to precede him into the drawing room. "But Matilde is happy here." Hands clasped behind his back, he followed with measured steps. "I want to give her as much peace as I can, while I can."

"You still intend to go through with this?"

"It's the Catcher's will."

Mrs. Henderson, paused, met his gaze, touched his sleeve. "But is it yours?"

12

WESTERN UNION TELEGRAM
May 18, 1900
C. Vernon, Seattle, WA USA, Gen'l Delivery

OExprss Istanbul to Budapest—F and eighteen.
M. Istanbul

PERNICIOUS BASTARDS, BARTHOLOMEW THOUGHT AS HE SAT
in the first-floor library, a book of Homeric hymns open upon
his lap. Rather than reading, however, he was mentally cursing
crows as they minced about his muddy yard.

It was a wet May and the size of the spring roost far
exceeded those seen in the previous five years. Thousands of
the black sentinels had made the woods surrounding his house
their winter home and stayed on into the spring. The regulars
were noisy enough when their young hatched, but the sunset
ruckus of the itinerant crow populace inspired Bartholomew to
murderous thoughts every evening.

Mrs. Henderson was giving Matilde a biology lesson. "According to Haeckel, there are three kingdoms: protista, plantae, and animalia. Protista are unicellular organisms." The governess pointed to an illustrated book. "What differentiates them from the plantae and the animalia?"

Matilde studied the picture for a moment as she flipped a fifty-cent piece over her knuckles. "They're simpler in their structure." She'd outgrown pinafores, traded her blonde braids for a Gibson Girl updo, and lost much of the little-girl softness that had made Bartholomew think of her as doll-like. She was lean and strong, developing a woman's curves...and an adolescent's capriciousness.

Mrs. Henderson nodded. "Yes, more primitive. Slime molds, bacteria—these are protista." She tapped the page.

Bartholomew had given the governess a wall of shelves and tables for her growing collection of predatory creatures. He often gleaned interesting tidbits of information from her fascinating hobby. The leather armchair creaked as he leaned forward to better contemplate her most recent passion: predatory birds. His gaze roamed the illustrations she'd pinned to a board and came to rest upon two puzzling drawings. Among the eagles, hawks, and falcons, were a green heron and a hooded crow. He pushed up from the chair and went to the pictures.

"Monsieur?" Mrs. Henderson asked as she and Matilde watched him.

He glanced at them. "Don't let me disturb your lesson." He returned to the illustrations. Why were these birds on the board?

He read the governess's notes:

*Green heron (Butorides virescens): One of the few species
known to utilize tools for hunting. Observed dropping bait—
bread, insects, leaves—onto the surface of water in order to
lure fish.*

*Hooded crow (Corvus cornix): Known to utilize tools for
problem solving and hunting. Has been observed on rare
occasions dropping bait (primarily bread) onto the surface of
water in order to lure fish. Not a hereditary behavior;
appears to be isolated and learned from observation and
deduction.*

Mrs. Henderson said, "Monsieur is studying examples of animalia, the most complex forms among the kingdoms. Humans belong in that classification."

Bartholomew's gaze traveled over the display of serrated shark teeth and past the preserved pit viper with its gaping jaws and needle-sharp fangs. His attention settled upon a small, brown insect speared to a board with a long stickpin. He turned the board to study the creature. It had spindly legs and a long, curved snout.

"What is that?" Matilde came to his side.

The governess joined them. "*Reduviidae.* An assassin bug. This specimen came to me from Australia."

"Assassin? Why's it called that?" Matilde cocked her head to scrutinize the insect.

"They're highly effective hunters of other insects. This one is a spider-catching assassin bug. They've been observed plucking the strands of spider webs, like struggling prey, to lure the spiders to within striking range. It's an aggressive form of mimicry."

Matilde leaned closer to the insect. "So they use themselves as bait?"

"Precisely."

"Clever," Matilde said.

Bartholomew returned the board to its table. "Do they ever fall victim to their own prey?"

The governess nodded. "Yes. Not all spiders are fooled. But assassin bugs are remarkably successful."

Matilde leaned over the board. "Are they poisonous, Mrs. Henderson?"

"I understand that the members of the *Triatominae* subfamily—kissing bugs—leave a bite that can cause illness and possibly death, but they are primarily found in South America."

Bartholomew considered the birds and the bug. "Interesting, Mrs. Henderson."

The governess asked Matilde, "Are insects animalia or protista?"

"Animalia, though it seems strange to include them in the same group as humans."

"Indeed." Mrs. Henderson straightened the board holding the assassin bug. "I sometimes wonder that they have not further broken out the categories."

Bartholomew turned from the display. "Matilde, meet me in the rear garden dressed for a fight lesson after you're finished with Mrs. Henderson."

"In the garden?" she asked.

"Oui. And wear layers."

"Yes, Monsieur."

He slipped from the room as his ward and her governess continued their discussion.

Let Famine come. This time I'll bait the trap.

He went to his bedroom and changed from his gray morning coat, waistcoat, and striped trousers into a black sweater, britches, and boots.

Thomas tipped his hat as Bartholomew entered the wide, white stable. "Afternoon, Monsieur. Shall I saddle one of the horses for you?"

"Non. Merci." He studied the stable boy as the youngster returned to cleaning Obietnica's black leather bridle. Though still thin as a whippet, Thomas had shed the slight frame of a boy and gained the deep, sonorous voice of a man. Bartholomew frowned. The adolescent tumbled him through a looking glass of memories to recall a boyhood corrupted by Famine. He averted his eyes and found the butler watching him from the doorway of the feed room. "Will you be available soon for a task that may take you away until nightfall, Mr. Vernon?"

"Of course."

"Walk with me, please." Bartholomew gestured for Mr. Vernon to accompany him as he turned away from the stable and Thomas Green.

Mud squelched beneath their boots as they crossed the courtyard and entered the rose garden. Two crows glided over their heads and landed in one of the budding fruit trees. Bartholomew considered throwing stones at them, but music carried from the house—Matilde at the piano—and he changed his mind.

Mr. Vernon asked, "How can I be of service to you?"

"It's time to take Matilde away from the security of the gymnasium for her lessons."

Mr. Vernon nodded. "An excellent notion."

"I want her see her surroundings as weapons."

"I'll send the feed order with Thomas, then I'll be available to you for the remainder of the day."

"Merci."

The butler returned to the stable and Bartholomew walked the garden. He strolled amid the flowerbeds, admiring the purple hyacinths and white tulips. He paused to smell the yellow roses that Matilde and Mrs. Henderson had espaliered along the yard's rear wall during the previous summer. The sweet, heady scent lifted his mood.

They were tough those rose bushes, showing great determination by blooming early and beautifully despite the rain. The flowers shouldn't have thrived in the shade of the towering pines and maples, but they'd resisted black spot and some blight that had killed two of the established rose bushes by the carriage house.

Somewhere in the deep woods beyond the wall, a thrush called—a haunting, exquisite minor chord that spoke of solitude and secrecy. Bartholomew waited for the bird to call out again, but there was only the rustle of leaves in the trees. He turned and the eerie note repeated quieter, farther, softer but still there.

He followed the yard's perimeter, cut through the middle, and stopped to tip a bucket. The rhubarb beneath it was ripe. He snapped off a crimson stem. Nodding to Mr. Vernon as the butler returned to the house, Bartholomew stripped away the rhubarb's toxic, green leaves. He reached the back porch, leaned against the stair rail, and savored the bitter stalk. It would be a good crop and he smiled at the thought of Mrs. Henderson's strawberry rhubarb sauce.

Perhaps there'll be enough for a few bottles of fruit wine, too.

Finished with his snack, he lit a cigarette, closed his eyes, and enjoyed the soft breeze on his face. After a few quiet minutes, the drawing room's French doors opened behind him. He peered down at Matilde as she said, "Pardon me, Monsieur," and trotted past.

She crossed the courtyard, a blue sack in hand, and disappeared into the stable. Behind her, Mrs. Henderson appeared in the doorway.

"A word with you, please, Monsieur?"

He turned. The governess proffered a square, white envelope. He accepted it with a glance at the elegant script upon its face. He didn't recognize the handwriting or the Seattle return address. This wasn't a letter from one of his associates or business partners.

"An invitation for Miss Matilde to attend a garden party." The governess smiled and pleasure brightened her voice. "She'll need a new dress. I'd like permission to order some Irish lace—"

"Does she know of this?"

"No, I thought she should receive it from you."

"Send her regrets."

Mrs. Henderson's smile faded. "But she should be introduced to some of her peers. Thomas Green is her only acquaintance. She will be fourteen years old come August. It is not too soon to foster prospects for a good marriage."

"Send her regrets, Mrs. Henderson."

"What is the harm in one garden party?"

Bartholomew removed the cigarette from between his lips and pressed it to the white envelope. He strode past his housekeeper to the drawing room fireplace. Mrs. Henderson said nothing as he rotated the paper to be certain it was well afire before tossing it upon the banked ashes in the firebox.

He faced the governess. "The harm is in establishing false expectations for a normal life. Matilde is not a normal girl. She will not be a normal woman. And she will never have need for the trappings of society. I do not wish to see her simpering and fawning before a group of boys whose existence depends upon her willingness to sacrifice everything to win this war."

Mrs. Henderson's tight-lipped disapproval rankled him as Bartholomew took a last drag on his cigarette and flicked the butt into the fireplace, too. "Not a word of this to the girl."

"You must let her live. You cannot keep her under your thumb forever. If you try, she will tear it off and run fast and far away from you."

He dismissed her warning with a wave of his hand as he returned to the porch.

Where has that girl gone?

His attention stopped at the stable where Matilde sat upon a straw bale, her pink skirt and white petticoats arranged as pretty as could be. Her attention was quite transfixed by Thomas, who stood with his back to the opening of the barn while he juggled three small potatoes.

Bartholomew crossed the yard to the stable. "Mr. Green, I am not paying you to entertain my ward."

The potatoes went astray. Thomas scrambled to retrieve them. Red-faced, he turned to his employer. "I'm sorry, sir. I'm finished with the stalls. And I've refreshed the horses' water and checked their hooves." He produced a piece of paper from his pocket. "And I've got Mr. Vernon's list for the feed store on my way home."

Bartholomew strode into the barn and inspected the stalls. He paused to stroke his horses' soft muzzles and pick green hay from Larissa's black mane.

Matilde said, "I gave Thomas the potatoes for Mrs. Green to cook. Mrs. Henderson approved my request. She said we have more than we can store or eat this year."

Bartholomew scrutinized her. She returned his regard without flinching. He fished three dollars from his pocket and passed them to Thomas. "Your wages for the week. You also may take all the potatoes you can juggle. You may not, however, loiter or squander my time with antics to amuse Matilde."

"Yes, Monsieur. Thank you. I apologize. I won't disappoint you, sir."

Bartholomew pinned him with a hard gaze. "I hope not, Thomas. Good afternoon."

The young man retrieved his coat and the bag of potatoes. He tipped his hat to Matilde, slipped around Bartholomew, and high-tailed it out of the stable.

Matilde looked like she'd sucked a lemon. "That was unnecessary. He'd finished his tasks and then some."

"You're not dressed for fighting." Bartholomew turned and strode across the courtyard toward the house.

She made a small sound of frustration and followed him. "Why are you displeased with me?"

He stopped and pivoted. She squeaked and took a step back. "Because you have lessons to attend. And you should not be diverting Thomas from his tasks. I don't wish to see idleness lead him to wickedness as it has his uncle." He consulted his pocket watch and continued walking. "Go change and return directly. There's time for training before dark."

Matilde trotted to keep apace of him. "Speaking to me does not equate with wickedness and I disagree that a moment of lightness will lead Thomas down his uncle's sinful path. We," her gesture indicated the missing stable boy and herself, "are not the ones hunted by monsters."

Bartholomew stopped. "Non." He looked down at her. "*We*," he tapped his chest then pointed at her, "are the monster *hunters*." He went into the house, Matilde on his heels. As she ran up the stairs, he called after her, "And *you* require training." He returned to the drawing room and dropped into the burgundy velvet wing chair before the fireplace. "Impudent girl."

A few moments later, Mr. Vernon appeared in the doorway, a black umbrella hooked over his arm. "What did you say to Miss Matilde? She's in quite a huff."

"I'm beginning to wonder if having Thomas Green here is creating more challenges than solutions."

"The girl has to have *some* interaction with other children. Best that it occurs where we can monitor it. Don't you agree?" The butler crossed the room with a few long strides.

Bartholomew eyed him. "Mrs. Henderson said something similar not ten minutes ago. Have you been conspiring with her?"

Mr. Vernon chuckled. "Not lately."

Bartholomew stood. "I hadn't expected Matilde to become so attached to the boy. She was remarkably quick to his defense when I criticized him."

"Unfairly," she said as she stomped into the room.

"I see," Mr. Vernon replied as their group returned to the porch and headed into the yard. "What a wicked thing to do, Monsieur."

"*Monstrous*, apparently." Bartholomew smiled to see anger flash in his ward's eyes at the provocation. "He is an altar boy and Matilde's friend and, therefore, above reproach."

Her chin jerked up. "I don't appreciate your sense of humor, Monsieur."

"Non? Very well. I will have it removed."

They reached the side of the yard. Mr. Vernon unlocked and opened a squeaky wrought iron gate. Their small group passed through and followed a worn, wet path into the heavily forested part of Bartholomew's land. They walked in a line, Mr. Vernon in the lead, Matilde in the middle, and Bartholomew at the rear.

"Mr. Vernon, would you care to begin Matilde's instruction?"

"Certainly." The butler gestured at both sides of the trail. "Because you're unlikely to encounter a cadaver in a gymnasium, it's time to move your training into the world around you, Miss. Your environment is a weapon. Look around. How can you utilize it to defend yourself and escape an attack?"

Towering pines filtered the sunlight to cast shadows deep and deceptive. Arching green ferns stooped over the forest floor creating feathery hiding places for rabbits and spies. And blackberry bushes mounded so high in places that neither Bartholomew nor Mr. Vernon could overcome their thorny grasp.

She surveyed the area. "I can shove an attacker into the blackberries."

"Yes," Mr. Vernon nodded. "Thorns from leaf to root, an excellent option. What else?"

"Branches can be weapons." She picked up a fallen bough and wielded it like a staff.

"And?" the butler asked.

"I can hide beneath some of the larger bushes and, maybe, under fallen trees or inside rotten trunks."

"If you can find such a thing before your enemy notices your presence," Mr. Vernon said.

"Or I can climb a tree."

Bartholomew shook his head. "Non. If you can climb, so can a cadaver. Your enemy will take hold of you and throw you to the ground. Much better to run."

"Fine." Matilde crossed her arms and her lips pressed into a thin line.

"I agree with Monsieur." Mr. Vernon pushed an errant blackberry vine from the path with the umbrella's curved handle. "Now, what will reveal an enemy's presence if you can't see him or her approaching?"

"Besides their ghastly stench?"

Mr. Vernon laughed. "Yes, besides that."

Bartholomew slowed to let them move ahead. He slipped from the path where it dipped below the surrounding greenery.

Matilde's voice carried over the soft rustle of leaves and lilting birdsong. "The animals, Mr. Vernon. They fall silent when something's afoot. And any crows will call out a warning. And jays; they're territorial."

"True. What other signs could indicate an approaching threat, Miss?"

Bartholomew ghosted through the underbrush, easily overcoming fallen trees and circumventing blackberry bushes, pink-and-white bleeding hearts, and delicate wild violets.

"Hmm. Rabbits, squirrels, and deer could be startled or at

least become alert. And small birds might take wing as a flock. That's a sure sign of something disturbing the woods."

Bartholomew emerged on the path and caught his ward from behind, his arm crooked around her throat.

She didn't panic. They'd had this lesson. Matilde planted her feet as she seized his forearm. She twisted her body and slipped beneath his grip, turning toward him and ducking beneath his right arm. She clutched his wrist as she torqued his arm around and kicked his knee.

Bartholomew's leg went out from under him and he went to his knees with a curse. "Stop, Matilde. My knee!"

"Did I hurt you?" Her voice was full of concern as she released his arm. She leaned over him and right into his trap.

Bartholomew straightened, seized her arm, and yanked her facedown to the muddy ground in front of him. He pinned her with one knee at her lower back and a hand against her head, his fingers entwined in her hair.

"Non. You're the spider. I'm Mrs. Henderson's assassin bug. Lunch is served."

She groaned, closed her eyes, and began to laugh. "You plucked the strand and I crawled right onto it, didn't I?"

He hopped up and pulled her to her feet with him. "Oui. And there's another lesson to be gained. Do you know it?"

She wiped mud from her face and frowned at the mess covering her clothes. "That not all cadavers will reveal their presence so easily?"

"Good," Bartholomew said. She'd comprehended that quickly. "And your reaction to the attack was admirable. You remained calm and escaped capture." He brushed leaves from his trousers.

"Almost." Matilde wiped her muddy hands on the seat of her britches. "I should have run."

Mr. Vernon shook his head and laughed. "Your guardian is a terrible actor, but you still fell for that old trick."

She scowled and stuck out her tongue. But that just made the butler laugh more, and she grinned at him.

"By any means necessary, my friend." Bartholomew stooped to retrieve a thick, gray branch from the ground.

Matilde scrutinized him as he straightened. "What does that mean?"

He swung the tree limb, testing its strength. "It means we will do whatever we must to defeat Famine and prevent the End of Days." The girl nodded as he added, "Let's fight."

Mr. Vernon tossed the umbrella to Matilde. She caught it then, quick as a blink, snagged the branch from Bartholomew with the hooked handle. The limb sailed away and she jerked her chin at him. "Yes, let's. You must suffer for your treachery." She spun and charged up the path, disappearing around a bend.

The men exchanged glances and Bartholomew said, "So it seems," as they set off after their wayward student.

13

WESTERN UNION TELEGRAM
July 29, 1901
C. Vernon, General Del.

Zurich empty. Bombay reporting?
Max F.

"WHO ARE THEY?" BARTHOLOMEUS LET THE CURTAIN FALL, *shutting out the glow of a lantern coming from the stable. He frowned. The black silhouettes of crows made the wall of his compound an uneven line against the setting sun. Where had all the birds come from?*

"A woman and her adolescent daughter," replied Aemelia as she rinsed grapes in a bowl. "They're traveling on foot without a male companion to protect them. I didn't see any harm in permitting them to rest within the safety of our compound walls. Poor things looked exhausted."

"Where are they going?"

"Antiochia. Traveling from Tyrus."

He grunted. His home in Tripolis put the travelers almost halfway to their destination.

"What harm can a young woman and her child pose?" Aemelia shook her head and touched his cheek as he passed her to sit at the table. "You've been fighting too long. Not everyone is a monster."

"Women can be a threat, too."

She gave him a sidelong look and a soft smile. "Oh, I know that." She came to the table and brushed against him as she set down a plate of cheese, bread, and grapes.

His gaze traveled the curves of his wife's body, pausing on her breasts then her lips, before moving up to her hazel eyes. He growled and snatched her onto his lap.

She laughed. "Beware, Bartholomeus, you're in danger of losing your heart."

"It was cleaved in half when I left you, but I know how you can mend it." He caressed her breasts through her shift and was thrilled by her hardening nipples and the way she squirmed against him.

Aemelia pushed at his hands, but her voice was low and breathy as she said, "You'll wake Lucius."

"No, you will." His mouth found hers and her protests died. But his amorous intentions were interrupted by a knock at the front door.

"Bartholomeus." Aemelia's lips brushed his as she spoke.

"They'll go away."

The knocking continued. She pulled back. "Perhaps, they require assistance."

He cursed beneath his breath then kissed his wife again, long and deep, before standing. "Promise me we'll continue this."

She pressed his palm to her breast and smiled. "On my honor I swear it."

He opened the door to a small woman dressed in a man's tunic and britches, boots, and a heavy cloak. Her head was uncovered and she wore her thick black hair plaited to her waist. She carried a long dagger on her belt, and though she was half his size, she stood straight and faced him like someone who fought often, and won.

Seventeen years of war and training for Rome had taught Bartholomeus how to size up an enemy. He knew what fear and weakness looked like. This woman felt neither. He stepped outside and closed the door. "What do you need?" he asked in Aramaic.

"To speak with you away from your woman," she replied in Latin.

"Why?"

Her dark eyes narrowed. "Because you are Famine's slave."

He squared his shoulders. "I am no one's slave."

"Oh? The hole in your spirit says otherwise."

"Are you the Catcher?"

"Yes." She pivoted. "Come."

Merda. Bartholomeus folded his arms. "You and your companion are neither welcome nor safe here."

She ignored him and strode from the courtyard.

As with Famine, the Catcher had some unseen power over him. Though he grit his teeth and clenched his fists, he was unable to refuse her command. He followed her up a worn dirt path leading to the aquifer above his home. When they reached the pond he said, "You've fulfilled Famine's expectations by coming here, Catcher. She means to ensnare you."

The woman's braid swung across her back as she stopped beside the water. "I'm aware of my enemy's tactics, Centurion."

The moon's reflection rippled across the aquifer's inky surface as she dropped her water skin into the pond. It slowly sank and she looped its leash around her palm. "And she knows that you are irresistible bait."

"What madness drives you willingly into your enemy's trap?"

"This is a risk worth taking. I require a Guardian with the expertise, strength, and will to aid in the destruction of the Four Horsemen. Your knowledge of Famine is invaluable." Her chin lifted. "Bartholomeus Corona Pellis, you will serve me in this war."

He crossed his arms. "I will not. I don't want this from you or Famine." He had a family to protect.

"Want?" She stooped to retrieve the bag. "That implies choice, but there's no choice in these matters. The course of your stars has been set and it cannot be altered." She straightened and tied off the bag's neck.

"I give you my word that I won't aid Famine in your destruction. But neither will I fight at your side. Take your Beacon and leave my family and me in peace." He wanted nothing more than for her to go. "This is not my war."

Her brown eyes narrowed as she looked into the distance. "I cannot change your fate, but I can offer you a fair exchange. Come with me and I will usher your wife and son to safety."

His focus followed hers to his modest house. Aemelia. Lucius. "What if I refuse?"

"*Famine knows of their existence.*" The Catcher turned to him. Her eyes were impassive. "*They will suffer in ways you understand all too well. You were foolish to give her such leverage.*"

His jaw clenched. Since the first moment he knew he loved Aemelia, he'd awakened nightly, shaking and sweating, to peer into the darkness, to listen for her steady breathing, and to stare at his young son's face. It was his greatest fear that Famine would find them. Death wasn't the worst punishment she could inflict.

Bartholomeus's shoulders sagged as he thought, I am a selfish fool. He inhaled and straightened. "*Agreed. An exchange. Their security for my loyalty.*" Sending Aemelia and Lucius away was the only way to protect them.

The Catcher smiled, but pleasure didn't reach her eyes or warm her words. "*You will be the strongest Guardian, Bartholomeus.*" She gripped his arm. "*Together we will conquer the Horsemen.*"

A haze settled upon his mind. He sank to his knees beneath the weight of her will. He couldn't stop the Catcher as she drew her dagger, pressed its point to his chest, and thrust it through his flesh to cleave his heart. He fell back. The world grew dim, black, silent.

Molten light flowed through his brain like lava. He opened his eyes. Her hands were upon his chest where the blade had left a bloody, cavernous wound and split the scars Famine had created when he was a boy. An undulating, orange glow flowed from her fingers, burrowed beneath his flesh, and spidered along his nerves and veins. Fire spread through his body as her spirit writhed beneath his skin. His torn heart stuttered, stopped, stuttered. He arched and twisted. His brain buzzed. His soul roared and fought the Catcher.

But she struggled to pull free of him. Her face contorted with the effort as she finally tore her hands away from his chest. As he writhed amid the dirt and stones, she skittered back, staring.

The Catcher whispered in Aramaic, "Penumbra." She shook her head and gave a short, humorless laugh as she stood. "I should have guessed." She looked toward his house. "Still, I will honor our agreement, Bartholomeus. Your loved ones' souls will be freed from their bodies; Famine will never have them."

She left him on his knees, struggling to retain his humanity, as she descended upon his family.

IT WAS WELL PAST MIDNIGHT. "Fifty-four. Possibly six duplicates." Bartholomew sat at the desk in the library trying to puzzle out how many new cadavers had been spotted since he'd left New York with Matilde. There'd been five active in Zurich but all had left. Recalled, perhaps? And still no word from Shravya, which was worrisome for many reasons. Her son should've contacted someone up the line if something had happened to her; she'd been training him to take her place. Had they been compromised and fled, or worse?

Wood creaked overhead. Floor joists. Bartholomew peered at the white ceiling and snuffed his desk lantern.

The stairs squeaked.

He stood and closed his eyes.

Matilde.

Her soul's song surrounded him in the dark. But it wasn't

the insolent melody of his *Petit Oiseau*; this was sly, darting, like some nocturnal hunter. The house changed as she crept down the wide, wooden staircase. The walls seemed to lean inward, the shadows lengthened, darkened.

Still and silent, he watched from the dark as she crept past the library and stopped at the study. He bit back a reprimand as she produced Mrs. Henderson's keys and unlocked the door.

Like a wraith, he slipped into the hall as she entered the only room forbidden to her. He remained in the shadowy hallway just beyond the open door while Matilde pulled book after book from the shelves of the barrister bookcase. The light of July's full moon streamed into the study, casting long, black crosses upon the floor. She faced each cover to the moonlight and peered inside.

What was she searching for?

Once more, she closed and replaced a book. She paused to listen, then pulled the next volume from the shelf. She made a little noise of frustration and shoved the book back into its space.

Bookplates, he thought, realizing her purpose. *She's seeking my name.* "You won't find it written within any of them."

Matilde gasped and jerked around. A book hit the floor with a resounding thud.

Bartholomew stepped into a shaft of silvery moonlight. He folded his arms and glared down at her. "Explain your disrespect of my privacy and your theft of Mrs. Henderson's property."

She recovered the book and clutched it to her chest. "I had a disturbing dream."

He arched a brow. "Which led you to delinquency?"

She swallowed, pushed the book back into its abandoned space, and faced him. "I want to know your name."

"Non."

She bit her lip and paused, then gazed up at him from beneath her lashes. "Please?" Her whispered word was soft and sensual. It made his ire soar.

Where had she learned to do *that*?

"Do not act like a coquette with *me*. You are not your mother, Matilde Anne Royce."

Her chin jerked up. "My mother worked hard."

"Your mother was a drunk who tortured her children. You are better than that and I will not tolerate you acting like a criminal or a whore."

She gaped at him, then her brows furrowed as astonishment became fury on her face. "How dare you speak to me this way?"

Mr. Vernon appeared in the doorway, pulling a green robe about his large frame. "What's happened, Monsieur?"

"I dare because I am your guardian and I expect better of you." Bartholomew seized Matilde's arm, hauled her out of the room, and shoved her into Mr. Vernon's hands. "Put her in her room lest I do something I will regret."

She was marched upstairs to face the indignity of a locked door. Bartholomew retrieved the governess's keys from atop the bookcase, locked his study, and headed for the drawing room.

Mrs. Henderson's cultured voice mingled with the butler's deep bass as the governess arrived in the drawing room's doorway. "Well, Monsieur, you did not handle that admirably," she announced.

Bartholomew had retreated to smoke a cigarette upon the porch. He looked at her through the open French doors as he exhaled smoke and irritation into the warm night. "You are quite right, but that girl is as mercurial as Seattle's weather."

"Inconstancy is normal for adolescent children." Mrs. Henderson crossed the room and settled upon the white wicker settee beneath the eaves. "A natural consequence of their maturing brains. Miss Matilde requires nothing more than patience from you."

Bartholomew had his doubts. Could Matilde's distrust be caused by some irreparable madness planted in the girl's mind during her dreadful childhood? "I have no patience for nonsense. She needs to focus, train, and grow strong. Our enemy's army is increasing. Famine is steadily making her way west toward the Atlantic. She's hungry and unsettled, and that's what I want."

Mrs. Henderson gaped at him. "You want Famine *here*?"

"Here or somewhere else, Matilde must be ready to spring the trap when Famine steps into it."

The governess sighed and stared into the yard. "I agree that she was in the wrong. But you must not return so soon from your hunts. You come back unreasonable, a fact you cannot deny and that does a disservice both to Miss Matilde and to yourself."

"Humph." Bartholomew hadn't been hunting murderous souls. He'd gone for a long walk in the woods to think. When he'd grown tired of circling his estate, he'd returned to the house and fallen asleep on the library sofa. But, like his ward, he had awakened from a disturbing dream.

Mr. Vernon appeared with a tray holding several glasses

and a decanter. He poured Scotch. They savored their drinks and the warm night.

After a time, Mrs. Henderson said, "We have striven to impart confidence and strength of character in the girl. It shouldn't surprise you that she wishes to unravel the great mystery you present to her."

Mr. Vernon added, "Avoidance was never a winning strategy."

Bartholomew took a long drag on his cigarette. Black shadows and silver light filled the yard. They made the familiar seem foreign.

Everything changes. He blew a thin column of smoke into the eaves. *Perhaps even me.*

"What will you do?" Mr. Vernon's sonorous voice suited the heavy evening.

"Speak to her," Bartholomew replied. "With more patience."

Mrs. Henderson murmured, "I wonder what awakened her."

Bartholomew stubbed out his cigarette in the silver ashtray on the table beside the settee. "Curiosity." He rolled down his white sleeves, straightened his charcoal waistcoat, and fished the governess's keys from his ticket pocket. "Endeavor to keep these under closer watch, please, Mrs. Henderson." A mixture of disappointment and annoyance flickered over her usually-passive face as he handed them to her.

"Yes, Monsieur. I don't know how she absconded with them."

Bartholomew headed for his ward's room. With each stair step he hoped for composure. When he stopped before

Matilde's bedroom door, he considered the key in his hand, hating that his ward was imprisoned.

I do not know what is best here, he thought as he unlocked the door and knocked.

"You may enter."

She sat upon the padded paisley chair beside her open bedroom window. She'd pulled back the curtains and the room glowed with moonlight. She faced him. "I expect you've arrived to offer your apology, which I have not yet decided to accept."

Bartholomew's tenuous patience fled. "Apology? Your nerve astonishes me. Have you learned no respect?"

"Respect? You speak to *me* of respect when I've been locked in my room like a criminal? When you watch my every movement? When you keep your name a secret and force a false one upon me? How dare you accuse *me* of lies, Monsieur Whomever-you-are?"

He held his breath. How could this girl swing so rapidly from rational to irascible? And why did he follow her moods so readily? He exhaled and willed himself to be reasonable. "Matilde, I make your safety my priority, even if that requires a level of discretion and secrecy to which you object. However, I am not required to explain my actions to you and certainly not under my own roof."

"Safety?" she snarled and stood, her hands on her hips. "You mean imprisonment. You treat me like a child when I am almost a woman!"

"I treat you like a child when you act like one."

"I've been with you for six years. *Six.* I'm very nearly fifteen years old." She straightened and folded her arms. "My mother was responsible for a household by my age."

Some of Bartholomew's hard-won patience flagged again. He loomed over her. "And her juvenile choices were reflected in the poverty and filth into which you were born. In no manner did those choices result in a life that was admirable."

Matilde glared at him, tears shimmering in her eyes, her chin aquiver. But she would not relent. She swallowed, marched to the door and jerked it open. "If I am locked behind this door and am denied the mastery of my own self, then I shall at the very least be the master of this room. You are unwelcome here, Monsieur. I demand that you leave."

Her declarations of mastery and maturity were almost comical and Bartholomew's ire lifted as if on a breeze. He suppressed a smile. "I will not be ordered from any room within my own home. And I will not be told how to protect you. Trust my judgment, Matilde. It's motivated by a long lifetime of experience."

Her eyes narrowed. Her expression and her voice hardened. "*Trust* you? I don't even know who you are. For all I know you're one of the Four Horsemen."

Bartholomew's calm dwindled and rage shimmered at the edge of his mind, kept at bay only with a Herculean effort. His fists clenched. He looked down and drew another slow, deep breath. When he responded, his voice was quiet but dark and heavy as a thunderhead. "You insult me?"

As if incapable of sensing danger, Matilde forged ahead. "What else am I to think when you keep secrets and deny me a weapon to protect myself?"

"I am not one of the Horsemen." Bartholomew relaxed his fists. "I am not your enemy." He met his ward's angry gaze. "Matilde, I promise you will master weaponry and learn all my secrets in time. I will not renege upon that agreement." He caught her hand, turned her palm up, and placed the door key upon it. "Moreover, I am not your warden, and this is your home, not your prison."

The anger fled her features leaving behind an innocent girl once again. Her voice was calm when she spoke. "All right. But will you reveal one secret to me?"

He inhaled but didn't release her hand. "We shall see."

She touched his sleeve. "Who gave you the scars on your arm?"

He'd wondered when she would ask. Bartholomew brushed his shirt where her fingers had been. "Famine inflicted these."

Her eyes widened. "Oh." She touched her own arm where she'd been burned as a child.

He released her hand, stepped around her, and went into the hallway.

She followed him to the door. "Monsieur?"

"Oui?"

"I'm sorry."

He faced her. "I accept your apology, Matilde. But don't enter my study without my permission. And don't take things that are not yours. Please."

"I won't."

"Merci." Bartholomew turned away but was stopped once again by the girl.

"You were in my dream tonight. That's why I awoke."

"Was I being cross?"

She hugged herself. "It was like I was someone else—a strange woman. You were dressed like a soldier, and you were suffering." She shivered. "You were dying."

Bartholomew's jaw clenched as a chill crept up his spine and crawled across his scalp.

Matilde rushed forward and threw her arms around him. She pressed her cheek to his chest and whispered, "Please don't die."

For a heartbeat he stared at her, then swallowed dread and returned her embrace, murmuring, "It was just a dream."

She nodded against him. "It felt so real, so awful."

"Just a dream." He caught her shoulders, eased her back, and leaned down to look into her eyes. "I'm fighting fit and too stubborn to die."

She wiped her palm across her eyes. "I'm sorry to be such an irritant."

He smiled. "You're a girl, not an irritant, Petit Oiseau." He straightened and guided her back to her bed.

Matilde's lips curved into a sweet smile as she slid beneath the magenta, cotton blanket and snuggled Bettina to her chest. "I like that nickname."

Bartholomew went to the door. "Well, you certainly are a fierce little bird."

"Good night, Monsieur."

"Good night."

He closed the door and stood outside her bedroom for a long time, staring at the glass doorknob like it was a crystal ball that could reveal their future. Finally, he returned to his sparse white bedroom at the opposite end of the hall but paced a circle once there.

Just a dream.

It was a lie, of course. The same dream had awakened him to peer into the library's dark corners that night—the dream that wasn't a dream but a memory of the Catcher and Bartholomew's death.

He massaged his temples and faced the direction of his ward's room. Nothing like this had ever occurred with the Catcher or Famine. He turned his head to study the enormous map.

"Why are you sharing my memories, Matilde?"

14

WESTERN UNION TELEGRAM
September 7, 1901
C. Vernon, Seattle, WA USA, Gen'l del.

37 men in Rome. Vladimir seen. No Famine to report.

Paolo

THE SWEET NOTES OF *FÜR ELISE* TRAVELED ALONG Bartholomew's nerves and made them sing. The music hung and fragmented in the library, its reverberations dissipating on the air as Matilde brought the piece to its conclusion. She lowered the black Bösendorfer's fallboard over the keys and pivoted on the bench.

"No more?" he asked.

Their household had shared a quiet fall morning. Matilde had received a lesson in Roman battle strategy from her guardian and had taken a long walk with Mrs. Henderson and him. They'd returned to the house and a piano lesson from Mr.

Vernon. The lesson had concluded, but the girl had remained to play for Bartholomew as he sketched.

She shrugged. "I'm tired of Beethoven."

"Hmph." Bartholomew glanced down at the pencil drawing he'd made of her at the piano. "Then this will remain unfinished until the next time you play for me." She slipped off the bench and cocked her head to see the picture, but he closed his sketchbook. "You may not see it until it is complete."

Like a small child, she stuck out her lower lip. "Please?"

"Non. And don't pout. You're not a baby, as you are so fond of reminding me."

She meandered around the room, taking in the pictures, then stopped to stare out the window into the yard. Neither of them spoke for several moments. Afternoon shadows crept across the maple floor toward Bartholomew. The play of light changed the wallpaper. Sweet, blue-and-white French country scenes darkened, turning gray and sinister as shadows swallowed the room. It was dreadful wallpaper.

From the drawing room a bell sounded, summoning them to tea. Matilde clapped her hands and laughed. "I shall play no more this afternoon and your sketch will become a memory." With a flip of her honey-colored curls, she skipped from the room.

Bartholomew shook his head as he returned to his study and placed the sketchbook and pencil in his desk. He paused, his fingers lingering upon another sketchbook. It held memories—acts of fear, rage, regret—impressions he'd inherited from strangers when he'd severed their souls from their bodies. He'd hoped to forget them by committing them to paper.

More than once he'd tried to burn the sketches; he'd stood

before the fireplace, the book clutched in his hand. But reliving their memories was a price he had to pay.

Bartholomew closed and locked the drawer. As he straightened, his focus strayed to a small, oval silhouette hanging over the desk. He reached toward his ward's delicate profile.

Were you sent to bedevil me?

Was the girl's capriciousness caused by her age or her nature? Or was it her proximity to him? And what about the nightmares? He turned away and crossed the room. "By any means necessary," he said beneath his breath before he closed and locked his study door.

Matilde glanced up when he reached the drawing room. "We're going downtown tomorrow."

"Are we?" Bartholomew accepted a cup and saucer from Mrs. Henderson.

Mr. Vernon added cream to his tea. "Have you asked the horses if they wish to go to town in the rain, Miss?"

"They're Seattle horses, Mr. Vernon," she replied. "What's a little rain to them?"

Bartholomew sat beside the cold fireplace. "Obietnica will object. You know that gelding prefers rolling in the mud to being ridden in the rain." He blew steam from his tea.

The room returned to silence broken only by silverware clinking against china and the patter of autumn rain upon the eaves.

Mrs. Henderson placed her cup on its saucer. "This is a gloomy room."

"Monsieur is sour with me." Matilde spooned sugar into her teacup.

"Oh? What manner of treachery have you foisted upon your long-suffering guardian, child?"

"I refused to continue playing the piano for his amusement."

Bartholomew spread sweet cream on a warm scone and attempted not to be baited by his ward's chitchat.

Mrs. Henderson arched a brow. "Is that all?"

"And I pouted because he wouldn't show me his sketch, a portrait of me at the piano. Doubtless he's given me an elephant's nose and donkey ears."

"And the wide, croaking mouth of a bullfrog," Bartholomew added between bites.

"Monsieur!" Mrs. Henderson's protest held all the appearance of being genuine, but Matilde laughed.

"Mrs. Henderson, where is the mosquito jam? You know how Miss Matilde enjoys it with her scones," Mr. Vernon said as he took a scone and even Bartholomew had to laugh.

But when the laughter stopped, Bartholomew sat back. "I'm not sour with you, Matilde. You think too highly of your influence upon my mood." He took a gulp of tea then added, "It is the world which has earned my ire."

"Perhaps our trip into town will cheer you," she replied.

"Perhaps."

Mr. Vernon pulled Bartholomew's dappled gray horses to a stop before Schwab's Grocery and General Store and set the brake on the black rockaway. Inside the carriage, Mrs. Henderson nodded at the crate on the green velvet seat beside Matilde. "Will you not keep even one?"

"No." The girl shook her head. "I'm too old for toys. I want them delivered to the children's home today. There they'll be played with and bring comfort."

"You've kept Bettina." Bartholomew tugged up his gray gloves.

"Of course. She's not a toy. She's special." Matilde tucked a stray blonde lock behind her left ear.

Mr. Vernon climbed down from the driver's seat and put up a black umbrella against the cool September rain. He appeared at the door and opened it for his employer. Bartholomew stepped from the rockaway then helped Mrs. Henderson and Matilde.

Mr. Vernon held the umbrella over the ladies. "I'll fetch all of you after I've stopped at the post office. Miss Matilde can make the delivery to the children's home with me. If that's acceptable to you, Monsieur?"

"How could I deny such a worthy endeavor?" Bartholomew crossed the wet sidewalk. Chimes tinkled as he opened the door to Schwab's. He gestured for the ladies to precede him. Mr. Vernon tipped his black bowler and set off on foot for the post office at First and University, his imposing figure easily a head taller than any man among Seattle's bustling mid-morning crowd.

Orion Schwab stood behind the counter assisting a small woman. "Good day, ladies, Monsieur," he said.

The pungent scents of cinnamon, rosemary, and cloves filled the store.

"Good day, Mr. Schwab." Bartholomew removed his hat and gloves and fished the sestertius from his waistcoat pocket. He flipped it across his knuckles as Matilde headed for the counter and its array of candy jars.

That morning she'd come to breakfast and proclaimed

she'd packed all her dolls, figurines, and games for donation to the Seattle Children's Home. Her decision had caught Bartholomew off guard and plunged him into his past. When Roman girls were engaged, it was their tradition to give away their toys and childhood clothing. Matilde didn't know the custom, but the implication of her maturity in that simple charitable act raised the specter of her death and choices Bartholomew didn't wish to contemplate. The years had passed so quickly and she seemed determined to seize adulthood.

She'd turned fifteen years old the previous month and Bartholomew had agreed to Mrs. Henderson's petition to allow the girl a few "more sophisticated" items for her wardrobe. He regretted the decision still as he rolled the sestertius. Matilde, in emulation of a brazen Gibson Girl, wore a full black skirt, a pin-tucked white shirtwaist, a cream-colored, straw boater, and, of all things, one of his black cravats.

When Bartholomew had confronted her governess about the clothing, Mrs. Henderson had replied, "Seven years ago you chose to allow her to grow up."

"Seven years ago I may not have been in my right mind," he'd said.

"Too late for regrets."

Of course she was correct. If he altered his plans and interrupted Matilde's course, the girl would lose all faith in him and label him a monster. Rightly so.

She's still a girl, even if she doesn't look it. I won't condemn a child to many lifetimes of war, he thought as he watched Matilde peruse Schwab's candy selection.

Mrs. Henderson retrieved a piece of paper from her bag. "Mr. Schwab, I have a list of necessities when you are free."

The grocer pushed his wire-rimmed glasses up the bridge of his thin nose. "Yes, ma'am. That silk you ordered arrived yesterday. I was planning to send one of the boys up with it, but luck has brought you to us. Give me a moment with Mrs. Green, then you'll have my undivided attention."

"Of course."

"David?" Mr. Schwab called toward the store's backroom.

"Yes, sir?"

"Fetch that bundle of packages that came for Mrs. Henderson last evening."

"Yes, sir."

At the mention of Mrs. Green, Bartholomew's focus went to the small woman stooping at the counter. She was Thomas Green's aunt and he'd had in mind to speak with her for several days, after Thomas had arrived for work with a blackened eye. Again.

Mr. Clyde Green had recently returned from the Klondike, worse off than the day he'd left his wife, children, and nephew in Seattle while he sought his fortune. The senior Mr. Green's reputation preceded him, and Thomas's appearance attested to the rumors Bartholomew had heard. Clyde Green's meanness when sober turned to viciousness when inebriated. A state in which, by all reports, he occupied a large part of his days.

Mrs. Green had about her the skittish manner of a dog much abused. Bartholomew recognized her from the train station in San Francisco. Evidently, the woman's temerity wasn't lost to his ward as Matilde's focus, too, was riveted to the woman's face.

A rumble and a crash came from the back room.

"Pardon me, Mrs. Green." Mr. Schwab stepped back from

the counter. "Two dollars, ma'am. I'm sorry. That's the best I can do," he added as he headed for the curtained doorway.

Bartholomew clutched the sestertius as he rounded a shelf stocked with tins and watched Matilde approach the woman. His ward fished several coins from her purse and added them to the small pile of change upon the counter.

"Oh, I—no, miss," Mrs. Green said, but her protest died as Matilde touched her hand.

Bartholomew circled to get a better view of the woman. Purple and black bruises marred the right side of her face from temple to jaw. His own jaw locked as indignation and instinct flared.

Matilde murmured, "I insist."

Mr. Schwab reappeared with his son David in tow and burdened with packages. "All right, Mrs. Green." He glanced from the coins on the counter to the woman to Matilde, who'd returned to perusing the pastilles. He scratched the back of his bald scalp and pushed up his glasses again. "Let me bundle these things for you."

After Thomas's aunt departed, Bartholomew went to the counter. "Mr. Schwab, henceforth, any shortage in Mrs. Green's funds will be applied to Mrs. Henderson's account, please."

The concern that tightened the grocer's face eased as his brows lifted. "Yes, sir, I'll do that. Very generous of you."

Matilde stared at the jar of jelly babies on the shelf. "Someone must do something," she whispered.

The pain returned to Mr. Schwab's face. "Efforts have been made by my Abigail and several of the church ladies to get the children out of the home, but it's nigh impossible without the father's consent. I think Mrs. Green would do it, but she's so tied up with fear that she won't breathe without her husband's direction."

Matilde looked up. "I pray the ladies won't be easily deterred."

Mrs. Henderson joined them at the counter. "Certainly God will come to their aid, Miss Matilde. Prayer has a way of reaching those who can make a difference." Her gaze met Bartholomew's.

"Poor Thomas." Matilde sighed. She stepped back from the shelf and crossed her arms. "I don't feel much like having candy," she murmured as Mrs. Henderson began ordering the grocer and his son about the store.

Bartholomew watched his ward. The ghost of her violent childhood was never at rest. In all the years Matilde had been in his care, she'd rarely mentioned her deceased family. But he saw the way she snuggled her toy cat as she slept. It was so like how she'd held Samuel the first night Bartholomew had encountered her. And it laid guilt upon him. Maybe he should've tried harder to save the boy.

As if she'd read his mind, Matilde's eyes found his. "Thank you for helping the Greens."

He nodded. Had she meant his offer of money? Or did she expect something more *permanent*? The door chimes interrupted his thoughts as Mr. Vernon stepped into the store.

"Monsieur?" The butler handed him a small, rectangular package and an opened envelope. "The letter is from Mr. Sindar."

As Bartholomew took them, Matilde appeared beside him. "May I wait in the rockaway?" she asked.

"If Mr. Vernon accompanies you," he replied, preoccupied by the mystery of *Mister* Sindar.

"Certainly," the butler said and followed her out to the rainy street.

"You've raised a nice young lady, Monsieur," Mr. Schwab remarked as he and David wrapped Mrs. Henderson's packages.

"The credit belongs to her governess." Bartholomew glanced at the return address on the package. It came from his jeweler in New York.

Mrs. Henderson turned to him. "I disagree. It belongs to Miss Matilde. She is naturally kind-hearted, intelligent, and determined."

Bartholomew tucked the box beneath his arm and donned his gloves. "Particularly determined." Indeed, Matilde was trapped between woman and girl. She was not always easy and rarely compliant. Not that Bartholomew wished the future Catcher to be a pushover.

The governess remarked, "Monsieur believes his ward is resolved to vex him at all opportunities."

Mr. Schwab scooped flour onto a scale. "That's the nature of youth."

Bartholomew opened the door but paused before exiting. "Then the fault is mine as I cannot recall what it is to be young."

Mrs. Henderson's cultured laugh followed him out to the sidewalk.

As the door closed behind him, Bartholomew was surprised to find Matilde standing beside the rockaway rather than inside it. She stared across the wide street at four girls who appeared to be her contemporaries. Dressed in fine cotton walking suits, they surrounded a smartly-dressed young man.

They smiled and swished their skirts, touched their hair and hats, and let out nerve-grating giggles.

"Let me help you into the carriage, Miss." Mr. Vernon touched her elbow. The youngsters' spell broke. Matilde turned. The butler took her hand as she climbed into the carriage.

Bartholomew handed her the package. "Will you leave this on the seat for me?"

"Yes, Monsieur."

"Merci."

As he closed the carriage door, Mr. Vernon said, "Shravya Sindar passed away in her sleep four months ago. The letter is from her son, Mr. Chiranjeevi Sindar. He expresses his thanks for your ongoing financial aid and indicates that all cadavers have left India. Seventeen newly made by his count."

"Seventeen? We need to justify our numbers." Bartholomew grimaced and lit a cigarette. "I'm sorry to hear of Shravya's passing, but it's not unexpected; she was in her seventh decade when I last saw her."

Two of the girls had noticed Bartholomew. They whispered and ogled him. He glanced at Matilde. She sat straight and stiff, watching the door of Schwab's.

Mr. Vernon leaned against the rockaway. "I believe we can be confident in Mr. Sindar's discretion."

"Agreed. He's been well trained. Please send my condolences down the line."

The butler nodded. "Already done." Mr. Vernon knew him well.

Bartholomew dragged on the cigarette and gazed up Pike Street. Seattle was awash in black umbrellas. "Shravya had a beautiful voice. Sad to think I will never hear her sing lavani again."

"Lavani, sir?"

"Love songs, Mr. Vernon."

The door to Schwab's opened and Mrs. Henderson emerged from the store followed by the grocer and his son, their arms laden with packages. The butler moved to assist them.

Bartholomew considered Matilde, then glanced at the group of youngsters. Had he made a mistake in distancing her from her peers? A burst of girlish shrieks carried across the street. He took another long drag on his cigarette then snapped the butt into the gutter.

Certainly not, he thought. *The fatuous distractions of youth are a waste of her time.*

He crossed his arms and watched Mrs. Henderson direct the men. He was a pendulum in matters concerning his ward, one moment yearning for her to remain a child and the next encouraging her to adulthood. He exhaled the smoke he'd been holding and smirked.

I'm more frightened of an adolescent girl than a horde of cadavers.

AFTER A SUBDUED STOP at the orphanage and a quiet ride home, Matilde asked, "May I aid Mr. Vernon with the horses, Monsieur?" as their carriage pulled to a stop beneath the portico.

"If he is amenable to your services." Bartholomew opened the rockaway's door.

The butler helped Mrs. Henderson down. "I welcome the company, Miss Matilde."

Bartholomew collected the groceries and followed the governess into the mudroom as the rockaway rolled around to the carriage house.

Moments later rapid footfalls heralded Matilde's hurried approach to the house. She appeared at the kitchen door, her mouth twisting with distress. "Monsieur, please hurry to the stable. Thomas needs help."

Bartholomew put down the last sack of flour and followed her. What he saw when he reached the stable enraged him.

Thomas's right eye was black from cheekbone to eyebrow and swollen nearly shut, his lower lip was scabbed where it had been split, and more scabs and bruises covered his nose, forehead, and chin. The youngster's breathing was shallow, and he winced as he straightened and removed his cap.

As the butler emerged from Larissa's stall, Bartholomew said, "Mr. Vernon, Matilde, I wish to speak privately with Thomas."

"Of course." Mr. Vernon left the barn and crossed to the carriage house.

But Matilde clenched her fists. "I want to help."

"Non."

"But—"

Bartholomew jabbed a finger toward the house. "Don't argue, Matilde Anne Royce."

She bit her lower lip, looked at Thomas with regret, then stomped to the back porch. When the door banged closed behind her, Bartholomew asked, "May I see your hands?"

Tight-lipped and looking anywhere but at him, Thomas pulled off his worn leather work gloves and held out his hands.

Bartholomew turned them and pushed up the boy's sleeves. Bruises and cuts covered his palms, as well as the sides and backs of his hands and arms—defensive wounds. His knuckles, however, were unscathed, indicating he hadn't fought back.

"Who did this?"

"Just a fight with Perry, Monsieur."

Bartholomew studied the boy from beneath his brow. He saw pain and determination on Thomas's beaten face. "What about your torso?"

"Sir?"

"I want to see if your ribs are broken."

The boy hesitated, then removed his jacket and shirt and shrugged out of the top of his dingy union suit, wincing with each movement. A black, diagonal bruise followed the contours of his ribcage on the left side of his body. Boot prints left a clear pattern upon his pale skin. Bartholomew walked around him. More bruises on his shoulders, and scars testified to a history of abuse. But his stomach and kidneys appeared to have been spared this beating.

"Is breathing difficult? Or is there any pain in your stomach or back?"

"It hurts some when I breathe deep." Thomas still didn't look him in the eyes as he tugged his clothes into place. "But no other problems, sir."

"I'll have Mr. Vernon wrap your ribs. If you develop any sharp pain when breathing, or if you cough up or urinate blood, you are to see a physician immediately. I will pay the bill and I'll brook no argument."

Bartholomew pulled two old chairs away from the wall. He gestured for Thomas to sit and settled opposite the boy. "Now. I've fought many men in my lifetime, Thomas, and I recognize defensive wounds. Your young cousin did not do this to you. Your uncle did. I want you to speak with the police."

Thomas finally met his eyes. "I appreciate your concern, but no, Monsieur."

"The authorities—"

"They can't help. I'm strong and I can take a hit. Better than my aunt or my cousins." He stood and added, "If it's all the same to you, sir, I'd rather you just let me do my work and handle these matters on my own."

Bartholomew determined, then and there, to introduce his fists to Clyde Green in the near future. "It's not all the same to me, Thomas."

The boy's eyes widened. He took on the hackles-up appearance of a cornered animal. "With all due respect, this isn't your business."

Bartholomew stood and placed his hand upon Thomas's shoulder. "That is where you are wrong."

15

"Scotch for ya, Monsieur?"

Bartholomew stood at Merchants Saloon's rosewood bar. "Merci." He placed his customary dollar into the man's hand. He didn't have to turn his head to know his target sagged over the end of the bar, fighting to keep his balance and his temper.

Clyde Green had a monstrous soul and when he was intoxicated it made him as savage as a cornered badger and far less reasonable. Since returning to Seattle, Mr. Green had spent more nights in a jail cell than outside of one, and those were the good nights for his family. The man's value lay only in coins for the barkeep and curses for all others.

Misfortune, however, had found Mr. Green; Bartholomew Pelletier's attention, once gained, was not lost. As if on a string, the man swung about on his stool and returned Bartholomew's glare with bloodshot eyes. When his attention failed to flag, the ruddy-faced drunkard stood, offered a middle finger salute, and staggered from the saloon.

Bartholomew savored his neat Scotch and tapped his

fingers on the bar as someone played a ragtime two-step on the piano. When his glass was empty, he slid it across the bar. He tipped his hat to the bartender and sauntered after his belligerent victim.

He didn't take a direct course toward Mr. Green's tiny cottage. Bartholomew had been hunting souls for far too many centuries to make such a mistake. Instead, he strode up James Street toward Second Avenue, then zigzagged northwest to come at the drunkard as the man staggered across the train tracks on Railroad Avenue. The Greens' neighborhood backed up to the tracks.

The earlier rain had ended and a full moon reflected in puddles between the railroad slats as Bartholomew came abreast of the surly fellow.

"I have business with you, Clyde Green."

"Who's there?" Mr. Green swung around and raised his fists. "What? I have no dealings with you, poodle-faker."

"But you do. A matter of justice to be dealt on behalf of your nephew."

"What do you know of that leech?" The man belched a rancid vapor of beer and meat as he squinted toward his home's dim light. "What's the boy done this time?" He returned his watery gaze to Bartholomew and sneered. "Are you a bugger?"

"Don't be vulgar. I'm here in service of my community. Violence begets violence."

A growl escaped the man's throat as he aimed a fist at Bartholomew's face.

The aesir caught Clyde Green's hand in his own. He'd planned to deliver a stupor and a vicious beating, but the bloody memories careening through the drunkard's uninhibited mind turned Bartholomew's intentions murderous. The man had dealt in death many times over.

Bartholomew unleashed his spirit. It rushed forth. It wormed up his victim's nose and plunged down his throat. It crashed through the man's nerves and veins. It sought and captured every wisp of Clyde Green's evil, little soul with relentless fury.

"What are you?" Mr. Green's strangled question was his last. His eyes rolled back. His body convulsed. His bladder failed and added the sharp tang of urine to the stench of tar and coal from the trains.

Bartholomew withdrew his spirit in a violent rush. Like a tidal wave reversing, it dragged Mr. Green's soul from his body. The man toppled. His head struck the iron rails and created a red stain.

Bartholomew inhaled, reveling in the warmth and power filling him as Clyde Green's murky soul slipped through his fingers, seeped from the fallen man's skin, and dissipated into the ether. This was the first total sundering he'd performed since leaving New York, and it was intoxicating.

"Au revoir, Mr. Green." He saluted the dead man, pivoted, and stopped as the back door of the Green's house creaked open. The woman whose need had captured his attention that afternoon stepped into the muddy yard. What had drawn her out? And how much had she seen? He moved toward her. "It's late, Mrs. Green. You should be asleep."

She crept forward, a ragged, yellow robe clutched around her gaunt frame. "Is he dead, sir?" She stared at her fallen husband, her eyes as bright and shiny as the stars.

"Oui, madame. A slip and an iron rail stole his life."

She studied the dark, unmoving mass laying face down in

the dirt. "Good." She looked at Bartholomew. "My prayers were as uncharitable as his fists."

"An eye for an eye." Bartholomew straightened his frock coat.

Mrs. Green took two more steps closer. "A tooth for a tooth."

"What brought you from your bed, madame?"

"Fear of my husband's return. But now I think I'll drift to sleep awaiting him, only to find his body on the tracks tomorrow, felled by his own vice."

"Then I wish you a good evening, Mrs. Green."

"Good evening, sir."

Bartholomew touched the brim of his hat and headed for the Club Stables on Western. He retrieved Larissa and gave the gray mare free rein. She set out on an unerring path northwest toward the pulsing beacon of the West Point Lighthouse. Bartholomew's was the last home before Seattle's undeveloped outskirts.

Puget Sound's inky, moonlight-speckled expanse was a marvel, as was the warm, damp air caressing his face like a lover. His body took up the rhythmic drum of Larissa's hooves, the beat and whoosh of her muscles and blood. The pure, luminous power of the outer darkness coursed through him and filled his damaged spirit.

Famine was not there to steal Bartholomew's pleasure. He smiled. For so long he'd been forced to surrender his soul's power to his enemy. For so long this gift had been extracted from him against his will. He'd forgotten the wonder of it, forgotten that with the pain of becoming an aesir, he'd gained this wondrous connection to the earth and the heavens, the souls and all the living things.

Past Smith's Cove, Larissa took him into a wide track of pines, maples, and alders as the path skirted high bluffs. The trees swayed and groaned. Their leaves chattered as the warm breeze danced amid them and sprinkled Bartholomew and his horse with raindrops.

He reined in the mare and closed his eyes. From the woods around him and the detritus beneath the Hanoverian's feet came the scuttling movements of beetles and mice, frogs, toads, and snakes. From the houses, tenements, and buildings behind him the sweet and sour notes of the chorus of souls ebbed and flowed.

He opened his eyes. He could pick any spirit, feel its fears, know its dreams.

But Bartholomew's smile faded. Perhaps for the first time, he wanted to share his gift not by force but by choice. He dismounted and sat upon a fallen, mossy tree trunk, extracted a cigarette and matches from his case, and began to smoke.

With each passing moment, the stolen fire of Clyde Green's spirit faded. It left behind fear and sorrow, self-loathing and loneliness. Mr. Green's soul had been vicious, weak, pathetic, and...sad. Bartholomew sighed. His shoulders bowed beneath the weight of his target's monstrous memories. Primary among them was a sound—the sobs of children, of women, and of Mr. Green himself.

Bartholomew rubbed his forehead and blew a thin stream of smoke into the night. His attention turned to a stately, gray Craftsman house—visible just beyond the trees—wherein a woman, a man, and a girl slept. He knew its gardens and halls, its stairs and its rooms. His mind lingered on a closed door at the end of a long hall. Behind it slept the girl, her heart beating a steady rhythm that his now slowed to match.

Her soul reached out and ensnared him, its song so familiar yet strange. Haunting, mesmerizing. Beckoning.

The Catcher's soul within him flared bright and hot awakened already by Bartholomew's conquest that evening. She enticed him to do her bidding, to fulfill his responsibility, to make her corporeal, once more.

"Kill the girl and free me," the Catcher whispered within him. *"Together we will stop the Horsemen."*

He stubbed out his cigarette in the moist soil at his feet, stood, and remounted his horse. He encouraged the mare to hurry home. Larissa easily found the well-known path. Once there, Bartholomew stabled her, promising a good brushing in the morning. The French doors were locked at night, so he skirted the house to reach the front porch.

He paused upon the wide, graceful stoop, key in hand. He stared at the ornate carvings covering the door. Hidden within the designs were ancient protective symbols, some of which were inked upon his skin too.

"Use the girl while her trust is strong, Aesir. You must not wait. Our enemy's power grows."

Bartholomew's focus moved from the winged bulls guarding the door's corners to the four shield knots marking north, south, east, and west. He took in the open-palmed khamsa, the Roman eagle above it, and the ten-point circle—the Siamese sip tidt—below. He recalled the burn of each one as the needles split his skin to deposit those marks. He touched the lotus blossom crowning the knocker, spied the eagle tattoo upon his own hand, and the part of him that awaited the Guardian's soul answered the Catcher's call.

"Non. Matilde is not ready."

He pivoted away from his own home and walked back into

the city. He turned up his collar and tugged down his hat to the crows that flew through the night to express the Catcher's wrath with their talons and beaks. More than one received a solid swat that had it shaking its ebony head.

AT WASHINGTON AND THIRD, Bartholomew was let into a four-story, brick building by a short, finely-dressed woman.

"Monsieur, this is a pleasant surprise," she said. "Please permit me to take your coat, hat, and gloves."

"Merci, Georgine." He handed over his things. "I apologize for the lateness of my arrival."

She dismissed his apology with a wave of her hand. "My door is always unlocked to you."

He captured her fingers and brushed his lips across her knuckles. He smiled at the blush that colored her cheeks. "What a lovely shade of rouge."

"Only you could turn these old cheeks pink." The madam turned and led him into a chic sitting room, her body held ramrod straight by corsetry so tightly laced against age and gravity that she creaked as she moved. "Most of the girls have retired, but I'm sure they won't object to being roused by one of their favorites."

"You flatter me."

"A hazard of my position." She stepped behind a tall, mahogany desk, propped a pair of wire spectacles upon her nose, and consulted a book. "Megan, Anne, or—"

"Not fair-haired."

She peered over her glasses at him. "Iona, then. Her father

was Welsh, mother Chinese. She's new to us. Porcelain skin and black silken hair."

"What is her age?"

"Twenty years. Verified by my own eyes upon her certificate of birth and a record in her family *Bible*. You know I'm stringent about hiring girls of legal age."

"Oui. I apologize for asking."

She nodded. "Iona is a sweet-natured girl, though a bit timid. Unless that is a problem?"

"Non. I will treat her kindly."

"Of course you will." She directed him to a blue velvet chair and provided a glass of fine Scotch. "I will explain what is expected of her." She went to awaken Iona.

Bartholomew knocked back the drink, stood, and paced, his eyes roaming the art on the walls. There were small nudes, but also larger works depicting galas, the symphony, boating on Lake Union. Or was it Lake Washington? He looked closer but caught his reflection in the glass and turned away. He didn't want to see the face of a monster. He was unfortunate enough to dwell within its body.

He turned at the groan of the wooden stairs and met the eyes of a dark-haired woman. She wore a pink corset over layers of lacy petticoats, black stockings, and boots. She averted her eyes from his and her décolletage colored to match her corset.

Timid or a fine and fair actress? he wondered.

It mattered. This was sport, but he was paying a premium to set the rules. And Bartholomew's rules were that he be permitted to pleasure Iona. She was not to put on an act. She was not to try to service him. She was being well compensated to give herself to him freely and permit him to enjoy her pleasure. No simple request for a prostitute.

"Good evening, mademoiselle." As he had the madam's, Bartholomew brushed his lips over the back of the young woman's hand.

"Good evening, sir." She tucked a stray lock of black hair behind her ear. "I hope you'll excuse my disarray. I've just awakened."

"The apology is mine to offer. I've arrived very late. Merci for giving me your attention."

She smiled. "My name is Iona. What shall I call you, sir?"

"Monsieur."

"Shall we find some privacy, Monsieur?" She extended her hand. He took it and followed her to the third floor.

An indigo-and-gold canopied bed dominated the room Georgine had prepared. Gaslights glowed, revealing dark, tapestried walls and red wine waiting upon the table beside a crackling fire. Shadows writhed across the floor, enticing Bartholomew to join their macabre dance.

He took it in, then tugged the girl around to face him. "You are beautiful, Iona." He touched her face and trailed his fingers along her jaw, pausing upon a small beauty mark just below its curve. "May I remove the pins from your hair?"

She nodded and turned.

He unfurled each lock, arranged every black, silken strand to cascade down her back. "*Une fille très belle.*" He kissed her bare shoulder, smelled honeyed soap on her clean skin, and knew he could release the power of the outer darkness through this young woman. "Georgine has explained my expectations?"

"Yes, sir."

"Permit me to undress you?" he murmured against her skin as he slid his hands around her corseted waist.

"Very well."

His fingers bumped over the boning, the silk and ribbons, caught and released the frills and lace women thought made them alluring. "Très belle." He flattened his hand against her stomach and pulled her back against his body.

Her breath hitched.

Bartholomew wrapped his other arm around Iona and trailed his lips from her shoulder to her neck to her ear. She hesitated, then permitted him to capture her lips and turn her to face him. His lips parted and his tongue encouraged her mouth open. Their tongues touched, stroked, but when she tried to speed his leisurely pace, he slowed her.

"Non. I wish to enjoy your pleasure," he said against her lips as she inhaled his words.

He ached to be inside her, ached to release the power that had tied him too tightly to the Catcher. But, even more so, Bartholomew wished to control his destiny, and in some small way Iona could help.

He found the white bows holding her petticoats about her waist. With a few quick tugs, they were mounds of silk and lace around her ankles.

Next his hands strayed to her corset's busk even as his lips found her breasts where they mounded over the silken edge of their prison. From the bottom up, Bartholomew released the metal clasps until the garment fell away. His lips moved down to her breasts. Iona moaned and arched against his mouth. He held her hips and back, enjoying the quickening of her breath and the taste of her nipples. Her fingers entwined in his hair, her body trembled, but he would not be hurried.

Her frilly knickers joined her petticoats on the floor and, clad only in boots and black stockings, she gasped as he lifted her and carried her to the bed. He nestled her into the pillows and sheets, perched upon the edge, and unlaced her boots. Each stocking was carefully teased over her knees, over her ankles, and off her feet.

He stood and leaned over her, his fingers slowly sliding up the soft skin of her inner thighs, his mouth returning to hers. Iona gasped and pushed against his fingers as they slipped and slicked and sought to heighten her pleasure. Bartholomew's fingers circled and stroked, his tongue matching the rhythm until the girl's body arched off the bed and she exhaled a long, low moan into his mouth.

Only then, as her chest rose and fell with the need to recover from orgasm, did Bartholomew straighten and remove his frock coat and his tie. He sprang his collar and placed his silver cufflinks upon a table beside the bed, slipped off his boots and opened his waistcoat.

Iona sat up to help him undress, but he stopped her with a shake of his head. He smiled at the childish pout upon her lips until his mind strayed to Matilde mirroring the expression.

Damn you, Catcher.

His tempo changed. Seeking to smother any possible association between this girl and his ward, he shed his remaining clothes, climbed into Iona's open arms, and pushed his hips between her legs. He slid into her warm, mortal body and forged deep, spurred to move in and out by her moans and excited by the smell of lust upon her breath. The woman's body matched the rhythm of his and they slid together and apart, driven by pleasure and a growing need for release.

Bartholomew lapped the sweat from her breasts, trailed his

tongue up her neck to her jaw, to her lips. He kissed Iona deeply as he reached beneath her bottom, lifted her hips, and whispered, "Like that, fille?"

"Oh, yes." She moaned, and the moan became a cry as a quake began in her belly and spread through her body. Her cries soared, and as the girl came Bartholomew released into her all the energy he'd stolen from Mr. Green's conquered soul. His long, low groan was one of both relief and regret as his connection to the outer darkness dimmed and the Catcher's grip upon his spirit eased.

But on his knees, his face pressed to Iona's chest, Bartholomew couldn't escape his creator's last curse. She replaced the scent of his lover's skin with the scent of his young ward's soul. As he inhaled, déjà vu warped his mind and took him back to the night in her family's filthy Sixth Ward tenement when Matilde had exhaled a breath of life into his face and he'd known beyond doubt that she would become the next Catcher.

Mon Dieu.

16

WESTERN UNION TELEGRAM
October 20, 1901
C. Vernon, Seattle, WA, USA P.O. Gen'l Delivery

Paris house F and E and eleven.
Arrived nineteen October. No NB.
Isabeau

THE RAP OF THE BRASS KNOCKER RANG THROUGH THE
house.

Bartholomew straightened from the financial reports he'd
been reviewing all morning. He rubbed his eyes and stood,
stretched, and looked out the window.

Matilde and Mrs. Henderson were harvesting pumpkins
and squash from the flowerbeds.

He liked his gardens laid out in neat and orderly designs,
but within the beds, he approved of a bit of riot and a pell-mell

placement of vegetables and fruits among the blooms. "A healthier garden is grown this way, Mrs. Henderson," Bartholomew said every year when she frowned upon the disarray.

The knocker, again, and the strains of Mozart ceased as Mr. Vernon left off playing the piano in the library. Footfalls echoed on the wood floor.

Bartholomew smiled as Matilde tiptoed between the magenta echinacea and golden chrysanthemums to reach a gnarled cherry tree.

The front door latch clattered and its hinges groaned as the butler received a visitor into the foyer.

Matilde was tall enough to retrieve shiny, red cherries from the tree's lower branches, though not so many years ago she'd cracked her ribs in a fall from it. His smile broadened as his ward, not cowed by the experience, hoisted herself into the tree while Mrs. Henderson protested. He shook his head and turned at the sound of his butler's footfalls.

"The Widow Green and her children are here to see you, Monsieur," Mr. Vernon announced.

Bartholomew returned to his desk. "Merci, Mr. Vernon. Show them into the drawing room, please." He opened a drawer and withdrew two envelopes, one of which was secured with his wax seal.

Mrs. Henderson's favorite sewing scissors sat upon his desk. Bartholomew frowned as he put them in the drawer and locked it. The governess had scoured the house for the shears all spring and summer. Mr. Vernon had finally found them in Matilde's heavy boots when he was retrieving their winter clothing from storage.

When would the girl trust Bartholomew to keep her safe?

He shook his head and locked the study as he left for the drawing room.

In the three weeks since Clyde Green's death, a number of church ladies had come together to discuss what would become of the poor woman and her children. They didn't wish to see the family become destitute through no fault of their own. The sins of Mr. Green should not result in the downfall of the children.

Puget Bank held the deed to the home but was unable to dismiss the debt as it was so deeply in arrears. They'd offered an extension and reduction on the payments, but the woman's income hardly covered that amount and left nothing upon which the family could survive. Someone had suggested an alternative loan could be arranged and the matter was referred to a group of the city's wealthiest, albeit less conventional, businessmen and women. They had addressed the Widow Green's needs. She'd become gainfully employed and her mortgage had come into Bartholomew's possession.

He met the family in his parlor and was introduced to Thomas Green's young cousins—Perry, Adele, and Ulna. "How pleasant to see you again," he said.

"You as well, sir," Perry murmured as the girls gaped up at Bartholomew with wide, blue eyes. All three were courteous and clean, their black clothes as neat as one could expect of children, their manners neater.

After introductions, Bartholomew said, "Mr. Vernon, please show the children out to the garden. Perhaps Matilde can engage them in a game of tag."

"An excellent idea." The butler gestured to them. "Follow me, please."

Bartholomew sat opposite his visitor. "Are you well, Mrs. Green?"

"Yes, Monsieur. And managing better than one could expect considering my circumstances."

"I understand you've found employment."

"Indeed. I've worked four days now as a housemaid at a fine establishment on Washington Street."

"Very good." Bartholomew glanced outside, his attention drawn by the sound of laughter and delighted squeals. A smile tugged at the corner of his mouth. Matilde madly chased the three younger Green children across the lawn. Thomas cheered from the stable as he curried Obietnica's dappled coat.

Bartholomew returned his attention to the matter at hand, removed the envelopes from his coat pocket, and passed them to the widow. She accepted them with a quizzical expression.

"The unsealed envelope holds the deed to your home, Mrs. Green. I purchased the mortgage with the intent to renegotiate terms with you, but I've changed my mind. I don't believe the investment would be profitable enough to trouble with it. So, I've quit you of all debt. The property is yours."

She opened the envelope and examined the papers. "Is it true, sir?"

"Oui. You owe me no payment but one." He paused until certain he had her attention. "The other envelope is not for you to open. Keep it sealed, please. It contains nothing more than a calling card with a name written upon it. At some time in the future you may be called upon to deliver it on my behalf."

She glanced from his face, to the secured letter, to her children beyond the windows as more laughter filtered into the room. "That's all?"

"Oui."

"I hadn't expected your generosity to extend beyond Thomas's needs. But this," she ran her fingers over the front of the open envelope where her name was marked in strong strokes with black ink, "this kindness to my family raises you above disgrace."

Bartholomew sat back. *Disgrace?* It seemed he'd gained a disreputable character through little effort of his own.

She added, "I assure you that I'll guard this sealed envelope as if it is gold, sir."

He inclined his head. He'd left just such items in New York, Paris, and Bombay. Each contained a calling card, and each caretaker owed him a great debt. He stood and offered her his hand. "Good day, Mrs. Green."

She slowly stood and returned his handshake. "Good day and God bless you, Monsieur."

He led her into the garden where she gathered her children. They begged for more time to play, then scuffed their feet in the gravel as their mother shook her head. "No, no. We mustn't trouble Monsieur further." She took Ulna and Adele by the hand. "Lead the way, Perry." The three children waved to Matilde and called goodbye to Thomas as they disappeared around the side of the house.

Bartholomew clasped his hands behind his back and glanced at the stable boy. Thomas had gone back to brushing Obietnica.

Strange that she didn't speak to him.

And equally puzzling that her nephew hadn't said anything to his aunt. Why was there tension between them? He shrugged. Families were strange, his odd little one as much as any other.

Thomas straightened and looked up, not at Bartholomew but at Matilde, who sat on the lawn trying to make a grassblade sing between her thumbs.

"Let us get the pumpkins and squashes inside, Miss Matilde," Mrs. Henderson called.

"All right." The girl pressed her lips to her thumbs and blew across the blade sandwiched between them. A high-pitched, reedy wail sounded. She laughed. "There! I knew I could make music." She hopped up and joined her governess in gathering baskets.

Thomas tracked Matilde as she followed Mrs. Henderson. The boy's eyes didn't avert from her figure until she disappeared around the house to the kitchen's side entrance. Then he noticed he was being observed. He blushed and ducked behind Obietnica.

Bartholomew smiled. Hands still clasped behind his back, he meandered around to the front of the house. More echinacea and chrysanthemums pushed through mounds of white-petaled iberis along the border of the front porch. Bumblebees clambered among the blossoms. His smile widened at their happy droning.

He murmured, "Hurry bees, winter is coming and you'll need lots of honey to carry you through to spring. You don't want to starve."

Starvation.

His amusement faded.

Famine.

"What's keeping you at bay, moecha?"

Bartholomew peered around the manicured front yard. The maples and alders were exchanging their green leaves for golden, crimson, and copper coats. Soon Mr. Vernon and he would spend many hours raking fallen leaves from the curving driveway.

Cadavers gathering in Rome, new recruits from India, Vladimir active again, Famine even closer in Paris, and Barnes missing.

Bartholomew scratched his chin. He needed to consult the map. It was time to plant more misinformation. "Perhaps we should send the rotten bastards running off to Sydney," he muttered. "Or French Guiana. Let them be swallowed by South America's jungles." It was like playing some mad chess game. The pieces moved on the other side of the world while he protected the queen and attempted to decide the optimal moment to send her across the board.

Cover, deflect, attack.

Wind whooshed through the trees and pulled at his coat hem. Soon his world would grow dark and cold.

"Merda."

He crossed the porch and entered the foyer. Conversation filtered down the hallway as he shed his bowler; Matilde and Mrs. Henderson were in the kitchen.

"They're all so sweet, Mrs. Henderson, don't you agree?"

"Yes, Miss. Well behaved and charming children. Mrs. Green has done well with all four of her charges."

"Admirable, considering the struggle she's faced," Matilde added. "I can only hope to be half the mother she appears to be. I certainly don't wish to imitate my own."

Mr. Vernon's deep voice carried beneath the clink and clatter of silverware. "Do you hope to have children, Miss?"

"Oh, yes. Lots of them, so I always have someone to love."

Bartholomew stopped at the foot of the stairs. He gripped the curved, mahogany banister and stared at nothing. Matilde would never have her wish and he was to blame.

"I'm sure you'll be a fine mother," Mrs. Henderson said and added, "Fetch the colander and start rinsing the pumpkin seeds, please, Miss."

"Certainly." Pans rattled. Water splashed in the sink. "I was surprised by Monsieur's aid to the Greens."

Mr. Vernon asked, "How so?"

A cleaver thudded into the wood block counter.

"He owes them no favors and gains little from aiding the family to such an extent."

Mrs. Henderson replied, "I'm a bit surprised, as well."

"Are you?" Mr. Vernon asked.

"Certainly. I suggested helping Thomas would benefit our household. But Monsieur keeps his own counsel and usually ignores my advice."

The butler laughed and Matilde added, "Not that you hesitate to offer it, Mrs. Henderson."

"Watch your mouth, saucy girl." There was humor in the governess's tone.

The butler's voice was muffled as he said, "The severity of Monsieur's manner doesn't negate the generosity of his spirit, Miss."

More pans clattered.

Matilde said, "I know that, sir. His soul is cloaked in darkness, yet if I don't look directly upon it I see its bright light shining through. I often wonder why he buries his goodness."

Silence met that until Mrs. Henderson replied, "Perhaps you should ask Monsieur."

"I don't think so. I don't think he'd appreciate my obser-vations."

Bartholomew ascended the stairs. Matilde was wrong. He appreciated her thoughts very much.

17

WESTERN UNION TELEGRAM
March 18, 1902
C. Vernon, Seattle, WA, USA P.O. Gen'l Delivery

Have reached S.F. No troubles here.
Susanna

"TODAY I'LL TEACH YOU HOW TO FIRE A GUN."

Bartholomew and Matilde stood on a swale not far from a bluff overlooking the sparkling indigo expanse of Puget Sound. Above them crows joined white gulls to ride the breeze, dipping and turning on the wind. Edged by the dark woods beyond his house, the location shimmered with early March sunshine.

"A gun?" she asked.

They sat upon a blue-and-green plaid blanket, a polished wooden box between them.

"Oui. You're almost sixteen, more than old enough to

handle a firearm. You progressed admirably in grappling all winter, but you're better served never getting so near a cadaver that you must use your fists." He opened the box to reveal a charcoal-colored Colt revolver, ammunition, and a spare cylinder. He removed the gun and bullets from the box. "This will prevent them from getting close." Bartholomew checked the cylinder for ammunition then handed the unloaded gun to Matilde.

She held the weapon, muzzle down, and studied it. "Will it destroy them?"

"Non."

She looked up. "Then what good is it?"

He took the gun. "It can give you time and distance." It had been almost a year since she'd hidden a knife, a sign that she finally trusted him and her own training. The little girl who'd beaten a rival with a brick still dwelled within Matilde, but she was harnessed.

Bartholomew laid the weapon down. "Safety first." She sighed and he smiled. He controlled the knowledge, and he controlled her. For now. "This is a single-action, six-shot revolver. Keep it in its holster when it is not in your hand." He pointed out the various parts and explained how the hammer and trigger fired a bullet.

"It holds six forty-five-caliber rounds that are fired singly." He demonstrated how to cock the hammer, use the sites, and eject the spent cases with the ejector rod. He stood and Matilde rose, too. He loaded five bullets into the gun, closed the gate, and pointed the weapon toward the ground. "It's now loaded."

Her focus was intent.

Good.

"This gun will kill an innocent bystander, Matilde. That is why you will not use it unless you cannot escape without its aid. Evasion is always preferable to confrontation if I am not present to protect you."

She nodded. "I understand."

Bartholomew pointed out a wooden target hanging from one of the trees near the cliff. "Cover your ears." She did and he sighted and fired the gun until all the bullets were spent. He lowered the revolver, removed the spent casings, and handed it to her. "Now you."

She took the weapon and loaded it as he'd demonstrated.

"Take your time with the shot. Align the groove with the blade to sight your target. Draw a breath, release it, and pull the trigger. It will kick back hard on you, so be prepared."

She sighted and fired, repeating the process five times. All but one bullet struck the target.

He returned her smile. "Very nice. You have fine control. Now do it until our ammunition is spent or you're too tired to hold the weapon."

When Matilde's hands trembled with fatigue and her aim wavered, Bartholomew called a stop to their session. "You did better than I'd hoped, Petit Oiseau."

She smiled up at him as she massaged her hands. "Thank you. I enjoyed that, though it's terribly loud."

"I should have thought to bring cotton to block your ears. Remember that, eh?"

"I shall. Will we shoot tomorrow?"

They entered the shadowy yard. Bartholomew spied

Thomas through the open carriage house doors. "Weekly will be enough. We'll work on speed and accuracy, then we'll focus on firing while moving and firing upon moving targets."

Her gaze went to the carriage house too. "May I visit with Thomas for a few minutes?"

Bartholomew consulted his pocket watch; it was later than he'd thought. "Oui, but it's almost time for supper. Tell him to go home when he's finished cleaning the rockaway."

"Yes, Monsieur. Thank you."

He watched her stride to where the stable hand washed mud from the carriage wheels. He turned away from the bright greetings his ward and Thomas exchanged, took the porch steps two at a time, and strode into the drawing room. He vacillated between amusement and irritation at Matilde's flirtations with the boy.

It's harmless. But...

He didn't want her heart broken, and he didn't want Thomas to become a casualty of their war. Both youngsters had seen enough troubles.

Mr. Vernon sat at the small teak desk in the drawing room, the house ledger open before him. He looked up as Bartholomew entered. "Good news from San Francisco." He handed a cable to Bartholomew.

The aesir read it. "No troubles. That's a nice change." He folded the paper and returned it to his butler. "We'd be wise to bring a few more associates west."

"I'll make inquiries." Mr. Vernon closed the ledger. "How did Miss Matilde handle the revolver?"

"Admirably."

"I'm not surprised. She has excellent muscle control."

"And the right frame of mind. Finally."

The butler stood. "I'll clean and stow the gun, if you'd like to wash up, sir."

"Merci." Spent casings rattled in their box as Bartholomew passed it and the weapon to Mr. Vernon.

Mrs. Henderson poked her head into the room, her arms laden with china and cutlery. "I thought I heard your voice. Where is Miss Matilde?"

"Speaking with Thomas in the carriage house. She's aware that it's supper time."

"Thank you, sir," Mrs. Henderson said.

She returned to the kitchen as Bartholomew strode down the hall to the first floor washroom. He cleaned his hands but wrinkled his nose at the pungent odor of black powder. A fresh shirt and waistcoat were warranted. The meal chime sounded as he went upstairs to change his clothes.

When he returned to the dining room, Mr. Vernon was pouring wine and Mrs. Henderson was slicing a fresh loaf of bread, but his ward wasn't with them. His stomach rumbled at the aromas of bread, roasted chicken, and steamed spinach. "Has Matilde come in?"

"Not yet." The butler corked the bottle. "Shall I fetch her?"

"I'll do it." Bartholomew waved him off, went through the drawing room, and exited into the rear yard.

As he came off the porch, he spied Thomas's shifting shadow through the narrow opening between the carriage house doors. The young man was polishing one of the glass lamps on the rockaway, but Matilde didn't appear to be with him. Bartholomew surveyed the yard as he crossed to the carriage house, but he paused just outside the doors when Thomas asked, "You've never caught frogs?"

"No," Matilde replied from inside the rockaway.

"But didn't they have them where you—" Thomas broke off. He shoved up the bill of his cap and peered into the carriage. "Where were you before you came to Seattle, Miss?"

"New York City." She shifted and the rockaway squeaked. "Were you born in Chicago?"

"I guess. My aunt's not really my relative, you know. She's paid to foster me."

"Paid? I didn't know that." Matilde sat up. "What became of your parents?"

He shrugged. "Dunno. I remember being in a Catholic orphanage or something before I went to live with the Greens. My aunt writes regularly to the church lady who placed me with them. She's trying to get me admittance and a scholarship for seminary school."

"Seminary? Will you remain in Seattle?"

"I hope so." He ran the rag over the driver's green, goatskin seat. "But it's not up to me. The orphanage is arranging it."

"That's fortunate." She rested her chin on the rockaway's door and dangled her arms over the side. "Do you want to become a priest?"

He glanced up from his work. "Sure. I like the idea of helping people and helping God. I think it's good for a man to have a purpose. My aunt says that was Mr. Green's problem, God rest his soul." Thomas made the sign of the cross then began polishing the rockaway's front window. "I don't have many other prospects." He slid the cloth over the glass, paused, and gazed at her as he added, "A fella's gotta be honest with himself about what he can and can't have, Miss."

"Well, I'm sure you can have peace and success with the Church. You're good at helping people. Just like Monsieur is."

Matilde pulled back into the carriage, knelt upon its front seat, and stuck her tongue out at Thomas from behind the glass.

The stable boy laughed. "He's a gentleman, and you're fortunate, too." He refolded the polishing cloth and ran it around the edges of the window frame. "How'd you become his ward?"

She moved back to sit upon the rear seat. She crossed her arms and stared at the floor. "It doesn't matter."

He shoved the polishing cloth into his trouser pocket. "Of course it matters. You know *my* family history." He rubbed the back of his neck. "Your background can't be worse than mine."

"I can't say, Thomas Green."

Bartholomew nodded. The less Thomas knew, the safer he would be.

The young man hopped down from the driver's seat, moved to the rockaway's door, and leaned into the carriage. "Friends don't keep secrets, Miss. Were you poor? You know that's no matter to me. Money or not, we're friends. Aren't we?"

She met his gaze. "My state of affairs was much worse than yours, but this isn't a matter of money."

"What is it? What are you afraid to tell me? Whatever it is, it won't lessen my esteem for you. Nothing could."

Bartholomew stepped through the doors. "Thomas, have you finished with the rockaway?"

The stable boy jerked around. "Yes, Monsieur. I was just doing a final wipe down. Would you like to look it over, sir?"

"Non. I trust your ability to judge when something is concluded." He held the boy's gaze meaningfully then looked past his shoulder. "Matilde, go inside and change. Supper is waiting."

She climbed from the carriage and nodded to Thomas as Bartholomew gestured for her to precede him into the house. As gravel crunched beneath the retreating girl's feet, he pinned the stable boy with a look that would have frozen fire. "Some matters are private, Thomas. And it is best for everyone if they remain thus."

"I just—"

"If you consider my ward to be your friend, you will abandon this line of questioning. If you cannot, you will become unwelcome on my property and in her life. Is that understood?"

Thomas looked everywhere but at Bartholomew and appeared to chew and swallow some wicked words. Finally, he returned his employer's cold regard. "Yes, Monsieur. I understand."

With a nod, Bartholomew pivoted and strode to the house. Matilde stood just beyond the folds of the drawing room's curtains when he entered. She looked up at him as the French doors clicked shut. She was chewing her lower lip. He touched her face to make her stop. "I know you dislike evading Thomas's questions."

"We need to guard our secrets. Right?"

"Oui. I don't believe he will inquire any further into your past."

She pulled back, her brow furrowed. "Did you threaten him?"

He shrugged. "A little."

Her eyes narrowed. "What does that mean?"

"I told him to cease his questions about your past or face banishment from my property and your presence."

Bartholomew headed for the hallway, Matilde upon his heels. "He covets your affection too much to risk my ire."

"Monsieur!"

He turned at the note of mortification that made her voice strident. "You deny your mutual endearment?" Her discomfiture made him smile. "I suppose a harmless flirtation is healthy for a girl your age."

She flushed. "I was not flirting. I was conversing."

"Is that what you call it?"

She gaped at him, pushed past, and ran up the stairs.

Mrs. Henderson appeared in the kitchen entry, holding a wide platter. "Did you have to embarrass the girl?"

His smile broadened as an upstairs door slammed. "Oui." He took the platter from her.

"I don't understand why." She wiped her hands on her white apron.

"Because it's a small coquetry that threatens to grow."

"You hired him, which must mean you believe he's no menace."

"Menace?" Bartholomew shook his head. "Mrs. Henderson, Thomas Green is harmless to everything but Matilde's heart."

She crossed her arms. "So you will break it before he does? For what my opinion is worth, I believe that is unwise."

"Noted and understood, Mrs. Henderson."

BARTHOLOMEW LIT and turned up the gymnasium's gaslights until their warm glow drove the night's shadows into the corners.

After supper, he and Matilde had sparred until the girl had staggered, too exhausted to continue but too determined to surrender.

He looked around the long, shadowy room. At least she'd learned to harness her anger.

The grandfather clock chimed eleven times and the other house clocks took up the chorus as he sat upon a chair before one of the counters. He balanced a long cloth bundle across his knees and unraveled its fabric. Within, a wood-and-leather scabbard held his gladius. Arrayed before him were mineral oil, a whetstone, beeswax, and a rag.

He slowly drew the sword. The scratch of steel on wood reminded him of long-gone battles and long-dead loves. With a practiced eye, Bartholomew inspected the steel blade and the bone pommel. Not a speck of active corrosion marred the glint of light upon the weapon's ancient surface. He kept it clean and sharp and, as a result, the gladius was one of the finest examples of Roman craftsmanship still surviving outside a museum.

He put the scabbard aside, stood, and tested the weight of the weapon. A few slow slashes and thrusts, and his muscles recalled battle. He picked up speed and power. A low slash to his enemy's kneecaps, a thrust upward beneath a shield into a soldier's belly, a powerful cut to cleave a man's arm or split his skull. Bartholomew recalled the stench of offal and shit, the screams of men and horses, the thud and clang, the mud and blood and suffering that accompanied Rome's might.

"*Such power.*" The Catcher's voice was a seductive whisper in his mind. "*Bartholomeus, do you remember?*"

"I remember my failure," he murmured. His eyes half-closed, Bartholomew struck down their enemies. He cut his way through their ranks, hacked them to pieces, but still the wave of cadavers came on. The rattling of their bones rose above the wind, deafening him like surf crashing upon the rocks so far below Hibernia's towering shale cliffs.

"It isn't over. We can crush Famine with this girl."

Something tugged his nerves. One more pivot brought the gladius around to point at Matilde standing in the doorway.

"Do it now."

The girl didn't flinch.

Non, he replied silently to the Catcher's command. Matilde's trust remained tenuous. He lowered the sword. "You should be asleep."

"I came downstairs for water. I saw the light and thought we'd forgotten to shut off the gas."

He returned the gladius to its scabbard. "Clearly, we did not."

She gestured toward the sword. "Will you teach me?"

"Non." Bartholomew sat again. "Go to bed." He picked up the beeswax.

"Why not?"

"Fists and guns and running. Those are your weapons." He slid his hand down the length of the scabbard. "Not this."

"Because?"

"Because you will never be as accomplished with a sword as some of the cadavers you may face. I don't want you lulled into bravado." He held up the sheathed weapon. "And this is not easily concealed."

Her blue eyes narrowed. "I will concede that last point; the other's an excuse."

He grunted and began waxing the leather scabbard.

"Monsieur?"

"Oui?"

"It's a Roman gladius, correct?"

"It is."

"Genuine?"

He glanced at her from beneath his brows. "Forged more than fifteen centuries ago."

"My. Fifteen hundred years old. How did you come by it?"

"It's a family heirloom."

She moved into the room. "May I see it?"

He slid the sword from its sheath but didn't offer it to her.

She studied the weapon. "It doesn't appear to be as old as you say."

"It's been well cared for."

She cocked her head. "What's engraved on the blade?"

"The owner's name."

"*Bartholomeus Corona Pellis.*" She glanced at him. "Do you know much about him?"

He pushed the gladius home and shrugged. "He was a Gaul and a centurion during the fourth century Anno Domini."

"Amazing." She leaned against the wall. "Is the scabbard as old as the sword?"

Beeswax in hand, Bartholomew returned to preserving the leather. "Only the metal fittings are original."

Silence followed, comfortable and familiar to them after almost a decade of companionship.

"You were a little frightening to watch."

Exasperated, he huffed and stopped cleaning. "Go to bed, Matilde."

She pursed her lips. "I didn't mean to irritate you." He didn't respond, and she added, "Are you expecting trouble?"

He looked at nothing, then at her. "Always. Which is why I practice the art of swordsmanship, and why you should practice the art of *sleep*."

She bit the inside of her lip and studied him. Then, with a little upward jerk of her chin, she pushed away from the wall and left the room. "Good night, Monsieur."

Bartholomew muttered, "Good night," and bent to the task of maintaining the gladius.

18

WESTERN UNION TELEGRAM
March 24, 1902
C. Vernon, Seattle, WA, USA P.O. Gen'l Delivery

London Famine and fifty. Warning sent down line.
C.C.

THE HORSES CANTERED UP A HILL IN WASHINGTON PARK. Once atop the ridge, Bartholomew reined in Obietnica and surveyed the view of Union Bay. Spring had returned to Seattle. The park was lush with yellow daffodils, tulips of every hue, baby blue glory-of-the-snow, and purple crocuses. The sweet scent of hyacinths swirled around them and the air was filled with birdsong as goldfinches, sparrows, and chickadees flitted through the trees.

Larissa tossed her head and champed the bit as Matilde circled her around Obietnica. Bartholomew watched the mare. "Her gait is smooth." It had been a few weeks since the horse had thrown a shoe and bruised her hoof on one of their rides. He'd kept her quiet while she convalesced, but the mare was more than healed now.

Matilde replied, "No trouble at all, Monsieur, aside from being frisky. Doubtless, she's relieved to be out."

"Do you want me to take her?"

"Gracious no." Matilde gave him a sly smile and pulled the dappled mare to a stop. "I enjoy a battle of wills."

He laughed. "That is an understatement."

As Larissa sampled the waving grass surrounding them, Matilde's expression grew serious. "I wish to ask you a personal question."

He tugged up his gray gloves. "All right."

"Why are you unmarried?"

He cocked his head. "That's an unexpected question."

Obietnica pulled on the reins. Bartholomew relaxed his grip. The gelding grazed as the aesir contemplated how to answer his ward. "Why do you ask?"

Matilde shook her head. "I'll say after you've answered me."

"And if I refuse?"

"I hope you won't."

He looked back at the bay. A low-profiled steamer split the emerald water as she ferried passengers across the lake.

"I was married. My wife's name was Aemelia. We had a young son. Lucius." He met her gaze. "They were murdered."

Matilde swallowed and tears appeared in her eyes. "Oh." The tears spilled their banks and trailed down her cheeks. She wiped them away with her gloved hand. "I'm sorry." She looked down. "I shouldn't have asked."

"You have the right to ask me any question." He pulled up

Obietnica's head and turned the gray horse toward the west. "And I have the right to refuse any answer." They were to meet Mr. Vernon and Mrs. Henderson at Produce Row, Seattle's open-air market. "Aemelia and Lucius died a long time ago. I've already mourned them." Larissa came abreast of Obietnica. Bartholomew touched Matilde's arm. "Keep your tears for your own struggles."

She nodded. "Is that why you chose to help me? Did the cadavers wound you, too?"

"It was not the cadavers, though Famine had a role to play in my family's deaths."

As the horses walked beneath the park's maples and pines, Matilde said, "I'm surprised you would make me your ward."

"I couldn't leave you to the cadavers."

"You didn't have to take me in. I know that. You could've left and never thought of me again."

Untrue, but he wasn't ready to tell her that. "You've enlivened my house, Matilde. And brought new challenges to this old man's life."

"You're not old, Monsieur. But I think I understand why you claim to be."

"I've spent too much of my life surrounded by death, child."

She nodded and stared into the woods.

For a time, the only sounds were the creak of their leather saddles and the gentle rustle of leaves overhead. A drop cooled Bartholomew's cheek, and another. He tilted his face to the sky as a gentle rain began to fall.

"I thought it strange that a man such as you would be unmarried," she said.

"Such as me?"

"A man of some means."

"Ah."

Obietnica tossed his head and twitched his black mane.

Matilde inhaled as if to say more, but evidently changed her mind and urged her horse to trot ahead on the trail. Bartholomew wondered what else occupied her mind as Obietnica picked up the pace. He was startled that she would mourn his loss.

Will she still care when she's the Catcher? he wondered. *Or will she become another heartless monster, willing to sacrifice anyone and anything to attain her goal?*

Little differentiated the last Catcher-incarnate from Famine. Both pursued their prey ruthlessly. And both had stolen his freedom.

BARTHOLOMEW FLIPPED his sestertius as he strolled among the carts at the edge of Produce Row. He was waiting for Matilde, Mrs. Henderson, and Mr. Vernon to finish purchasing fruits and vegetables. The rain had stopped, but the sky remained cloudy and gray, which was fortunate as his housekeeper had heard rumors of a grocer selling California lemons. She wouldn't rest until she acquired some or confirmed it was a lie.

"I cannot recall the last time I made lemon tarts," Mrs. Henderson had said and set off on her mission with single-minded focus. Bartholomew could, and relished the thought of enjoying them again.

Now, however, his conversation with Matilde had him

thinking about Famine as he paused in the shadow of a grocer's cart to survey the scene.

Women with baskets over their arms—children and husbands in tow—picked through piles of lettuces and leeks, new potatoes and peas. Carthorses dozed, their tails swishing like lazy pendulums. Merchants hawked and haggled, their wares protected from the elements by awnings and striped umbrellas.

"Fifty in London. And no sign of Barnes," he murmured. He hoped Famine had let the cowboy decay. He scowled. "Fifty. Derr'mo." Fortune had kept Famine at bay, but could his luck hold out the few more years he needed until Matilde reached adulthood?

A young man's voice drew Bartholomew's attention.

"Hey, Thomas! Wait for us."

Palming the sestertius, he peered past the grocer's wide cart and around the crowd.

Thomas Green was fetching a bicycle. "I can't loiter, Micah. I'm making deliveries," he replied.

A different boy called, "Come on. The frog can wait."

"I'm working for Mr. Schwab today, not Monsieur. And don't call him that."

Thomas walked his bicycle along the row of grocers' wagons. Bartholomew paralleled him until he reached the last cart. The aesir paused where he could see without being seen, resting his hand on the appaloosa carthorse's speckled flank and listening.

"Too bad it's not the frog, eh, Jeffrey? Maybe Thomas'd get to ride his pretty filly." Micah and his companion laughed.

Thomas's brow furrowed. "Knock it off."

"Jeffrey!" A younger boy with sandy curls skittered into

view. "You'd best get back to the wharf or Pa's gonna thump you!"

Jeffrey and Micah scrambled past Thomas and ducked into the crowd, a blur of brown hair and ragged clothes. The small boy gave chase.

Bartholomew slipped the Roman coin into his waistcoat pocket, patted the appaloosa, and stepped into his stable hand's path. "Good afternoon, Mr. Green."

The young man stopped, leaned the bicycle against his hip, and doffed his brown herringbone cap. "Good afternoon. What brought you to the market, Monsieur?"

"How are Mrs. Green and your cousins faring?"

"Well enough, sir." He scratched the back of his neck.

Bartholomew nodded. "I trust that all remains quiet in your home?"

"Yes, sir. Mrs. Green is still working, Perry's a Western Union messenger boy, and Adele and Ulna are performing well in school now."

"Hmm." Bartholomew surveyed the market for Thomas's errant friends, but they'd disappeared.

The stable boy dragged his worn brown boot through the damp dirt, making a rut. "Is there anything I can assist you with, sir?"

"Oui. You can tell me the names of the young gentlemen with whom you were conversing about my ward."

"I—ah—Monsieur?"

"Their names, Thomas. I make it my business to know the identities of anyone who demonstrates an interest in Matilde."

Thomas blushed. "You overhead us?"

"I did."

"I hope you didn't get an unfavorable impression, sir." He

worried his cap between his hands, turning it around and around. "I've known those fellas quite a spell now. They're all talk and no intent."

Bartholomew clasped his hands behind his back and inclined toward the young man. "Their names. Please."

"Hello, Thomas." Matilde strolled toward them, her eyes and smile brightening the gray day, her black skirt swaying and swishing with her movement. Mrs. Henderson strode beside her and Mr. Vernon followed leading Larissa and Obietnica.

A pair of men tracked Matilde's passage, elbowing each other and leering until they caught sight of Bartholomew's glare. Suddenly the nearest grocer's cart held far more intrigue than did his small, fair ward.

"Hello, Miss Matilde, Mrs. Henderson, Mr. Vernon." Thomas nodded at each of them in turn and crumpled his hat.

Mrs. Henderson glanced around the Row's crowded stands. "I did not know today is your market day. Is Mrs. Green here?"

"No, ma'am. I was delivering something for Mr. Schwab."

Matilde caught his bicycle's handlebars and leaned toward him. "Where are you off to now?"

"Back to Schwab's, then out to your estate."

She turned to Bartholomew. "May I accompany Thomas?"

"Non."

"But we're going home after this. Thomas and I could meet you on—"

"Non, Matilde."

She opened her mouth to protest, but Bartholomew shot her a look that shut it.

"It's for the best, Miss," Thomas said quickly. He snugged

his cap on, tipped it, and climbed onto his bicycle. "Mr. Schwab may have more work for me anyway."

Bartholomew took Obietnica's reins from Mr. Vernon and swung up into the saddle. "Mr. Vernon, Mrs. Henderson, please excuse Matilde and myself. We'll return to the house now."

His ward watched Thomas disappear into the crowd. Her gaze became a glare as she turned it on Bartholomew. She stalked to Larissa's side, accepted a leg up from Mr. Vernon, and twitched her skirt into place. Every movement was short and sharp and exuded irritation. Larissa tossed her head, skittering beneath Matilde as the girl took the reins.

Bartholomew led the way out of the Row's chaos and toward home. He sat straight and tall in the saddle, waiting for Matilde's anger to erupt as they rode past streets lined with colorful houses and blooming gardens. Some homes stood upright and ornamented, their elaborate finials and scalloped window trim delighting the eye like jewelry on society ladies. Other houses were square and solid with wide sheltering eaves, broad inviting porches, and thick columns.

As the neighborhoods thinned and the woods grew denser around them, Matilde urged Larissa to Obietnica's side. "Thomas Green is good enough to clean your stables but not good enough to be seen with your ward?"

"Thomas Green can't keep you safe."

She tossed her braid over her shoulder. "I can do that for myself."

Bartholomew grabbed her hair and yanked her off the horse. She landed on her bottom. Her bowler was trampled as Larissa shied away. Mud splattered her skirt and white blouse, her hands and face. He kept a firm hand on Obietnica's reins as the dappled gelding tossed his head and danced a circle around Matilde.

She sat for a long moment staring at her knees. Finally, she said, "I suppose this means I'm dinner?"

"Non. Thomas Green is and you are being taken to Famine." Bartholomew halted his horse before her. "Don't underestimate our enemy. And do *not* overestimate yourself."

She inhaled and held the breath before slowly exhaling and glaring up at him. "Fine." She stood, brushed mud and soggy leaves off her hands and skirt, and scowled as she retrieved her mangled hat. "But couldn't you simply have explained that?"

Bartholomew slipped from his own saddle, strode to where Larissa was eating grass, and captured the mare's reins. With both horses in hand, he returned to his ward. "You don't always listen to me."

Matilde considered the state of her clothes then secured her riding skirt up so that it didn't drag on the ground. "I'll walk. There's no sense in coating the saddle with mud." She snatched Larissa's reins from Bartholomew and ran her fingers down the mare's white nose. "I'm sorry. Monsieur is a monster sometimes. He shouldn't have frightened you."

Bartholomew gestured for her to proceed and they continued through a steady drizzle beneath the deep green canopy of trees. "What could you have done to avoid that attack?" he asked.

She glared straight ahead, her mouth pinched into a thin, straight line. "Not trusted *you*."

As MATILDE and Bartholomew exited the stable, Thomas arrived in the back courtyard. He spied her and his eyes widened as he got off his bicycle. "Miss Matilde, did Larissa unseat you? Are you injured?"

"Monsieur is responsible for my state, not my horse, Mr. Green." She glared at Bartholomew, then paused beside the stable boy and placed her hand upon his forearm. "I'm uninjured." Her fingers slid down to Thomas's wrist, over his hand, and lingered as she murmured, "I thank you for your concern. You, *Thomas*, are a gentleman."

The young man swallowed and stared at her hand. "I, uh, I'm relieved to hear you're well, Miss." He looked up and stepped back as Bartholomew came up behind Matilde and seized her elbow.

"Inside the house, Matilde Anne Royce." Bartholomew marched her across the yard and into the drawing room. The glass in the French doors rattled as he slammed them. He loomed over her. "How dare you give that boy false hope? How dare you place him between us? I didn't raised you to be so heartless and manipulative."

She faced him, her eyes narrow and glinting. Her chin jerked up and, hands on hips, she snapped, "What are you inferring? I was thanking him for his kindness and concern. Manners which *you* appear to lack!"

Bartholomew jabbed his finger at her. "Don't lie. That well exceeded innocent flirtation. You pointed that boy down a path he cannot tread, and you know it."

"I know no such thing! I haven't been introduced to any other young woman or man of my station. Thomas Green is the only boy I've known since becoming your ward. I can only assume that, despite all my *learning* and *refinement*, you've concluded my only equal is the stable boy." Bartholomew made to answer, but she continued, "Which I'm quite content with as the men of *your* station, if you are evidence, appear to lack *humanity*!"

He bit back a vicious retort and said behind clenched teeth, "One more word and I will confine you to this house."

She opened her mouth then snapped it shut. She stomped up the stairs past Mr. Vernon and Mrs. Henderson, who'd arrived in the foyer to overhear her tirade. She thudded along the second floor hallway above their heads then shouted, "Tyrant!" and punctuated her outburst by slamming a door.

I am an idiot. Bartholomew bowed his head. To keep her trust, he had to show faith in her. Why had it taken him this long to realize something so obvious? And why couldn't he have realized it an hour sooner?

"Well," Mr. Vernon began, but Bartholomew's upraised hand stopped him.

"I know. I've made a mistake and have torn a hole in a tenuous web of trust."

Mrs. Henderson surveyed the trail of mud and debris Matilde had left in her wake. "Knowing is all well and good, but how are you going to repair the damage?"

Bartholomew ran his hand over his face, down his bearded chin, and away. "I don't know." Another door slammed above. "But I don't believe she's receptive to an apology at this moment."

Mr. Vernon's mouth quirked up on one side. "It doesn't seem so." He gestured toward Bartholomew. "Let me take your coat and gloves, Monsieur."

19

MATILDE'S ROOM WAS DARK WHEN BARTHOLOMEW PASSED it. He paused at her door, his hand on the glass knob. Had he irreparably damaged her faith in him? He stepped back and continued down the stairs. Re-addressing the issue that night would likely worsen things. Best to trust time would bring a new perspective to all of them.

But hours later as he stood in the shadowy dining room watching thin, silvery clouds scud across the full moon's face, something tripped across his instincts. Pebbles hit glass and clattered down the shingles. A door opened on the second floor. The stairs creaked. He closed his eyes and stretched his senses.

Matilde descending. Three souls crossing the front yard. Thomas Green with two strangers. Bartholomew held stone still as Matilde passed the dining room. Then he followed her.

She crept into the drawing room and opened the French doors. The chirp and croak of frogs drifted into the house. "You shouldn't be here, Thomas," she whispered.

"Come with us, Miss Matilde."

"Are you mad? I can't leave the house at night. I'm already in enough trouble with Monsieur today."

"Robert Grus and Micah Kornilov are with me. We're just gonna catch frogs." He raised a bucket and a lantern. "We'll be gone only an hour and have you back before you're ever missed. It'll be fun."

"No. Monsieur will know."

"How could he? The house is dark. Everyone's asleep, right?"

"Well, yes."

The *kree-eek* chorus of frogs filled the night as she weighed her choices. Bartholomew understood her indecision. Thomas was her only friend and defiance was too tantalizing. He hoped she would say no, but expected she would say yes.

"One hour?" she asked.

"Yes. You have my word."

"I don't think this is wise." She glanced over her shoulder into the dark drawing room.

One of the other boys snorted. Bartholomew recognized him and his companion from the market. "That's why we're doing it," the boy said. "My father will skin me if he finds out I was on your property."

"Why?" she asked.

Thomas was quick to answer. "Come along and we'll tell you, Miss."

"One hour, Thomas. I'll get my coat and boots."

Skurwysyn. Bartholomew waited until the drawing room door clicked shut before he slipped out of the house behind the small group. A shadow following shadows, he crossed the rear yard and entered the forest beyond the white wall.

He was irritated with Matilde and more than irritated with Thomas, but there was something furtive and insincere about the other two boys. Both had tarnished reputations and Micah Kornilov's crass comment about Matilde nettled him to no end.

Branches snapped, leaves rattled, and the swaying lantern cast eerie shadows as the youngsters tromped through the black woods like unconcerned elephants.

Alert to threats, Bartholomew followed.

Stupid boy. Foolish risk. All to impress a girl beyond his reach. And damn her for going along. He made a low, guttural sound and muttered, "And damn me for allowing it to come to this." He'd been so cocksure as he'd lectured her about underestimating the enemy. Yet he'd misjudged the boldness of the young men from the market and had failed to warn her about them. "Merda."

As the youngsters entered a moonlit clearing, Matilde stopped. "We're moving away from the closest creek." She folded her arms. "So what's this really about?"

Robert Grus tugged her braid. "We want to know why the frog guards his daughter like she's as good as gold." Thomas's peer was tall, broad, and rough-skinned from working on the docks for many years.

She swatted his hand away. "I am *Monsieur's* ward, not his daughter, Robert Grus. And keep your hands to yourself."

"Show some respect, Robert." Thomas stepped between her and the older boy, though he was half the bully's size.

Micah grabbed Matilde's hair and jerked her back against his body. "Jeffrey McIntyre has offered a day's wages for a lock of this."

The fool had underestimated her bravery and certainly didn't expect her skill. She brought her elbow around and struck his sternum with all her might. Micah fell to his knees gasping for breath, then upon his face as she kicked him in the gut once, twice, and a third time to be certain he remained prone.

Thomas was swatted aside by Robert who produced a folding knife from his coat pocket. Bartholomew's young employee shouted and lunged toward the larger boy's feet. Matilde grabbed a thick tree branch from the ground. Robert kicked Thomas off and lumbered toward her. The stable hand fell back. His head struck the ground with a thud. He slowly got to his hands and knees.

Robert sneered. "Just give me that pretty braid and you can go home, Miss Priss."

"My name is Miss *Matilde* and the only thing I have for you is a bloody nose and broken teeth."

Robert laughed. "And what've you got for Micah?" He jerked his head to indicate his friend who'd regained his unsteady feet.

Her eyes never left her target. "He already got what's coming to him. If he wants more, he can await his turn."

Robert lunged. She moved into the attack. He was blocked. The knife was knocked away. Then he was on the ground clutching his testicles and crying.

She turned on Micah, who gaped at his fallen friend. She stepped toward him, but the young man stumbled backward and scrambled into the thick woods, a frightened deer fleeing a wolf. Matilde pivoted back to her attacker. Robert raised his arms. His high, thin cry ended with a grunt as she cracked his skull with a mighty swing of the branch. The young man collapsed in the dirt and pine needles. He didn't move as she lifted the branch for another blow.

Bartholomew lunged into the clearing. "Stop!" He caught the bough just before it struck the bully again. "Let go, Matilde." The empty look she turned on him disappeared with a shake of her head. She released the branch.

He knelt over Robert. Blood, black and oily in the moonlight, coated the stricken young man's face and fair hair. His heart stuttered. His blue eyes saw nothing. "Derr'mo," Bartholomew muttered.

"What did I do?" she whispered.

"Killed him if I do nothing."

Her cold indifference collapsed into horror. She inhaled a sob. "I'm sorry. I didn't mean to do that. Oh, please don't let him die."

Bartholomew put his hand upon the young man's chest. The ties binding Robert Grus's body and soul were slackening. The bully teetered upon the precipice of death. Wait even a few minutes and his body would die.

What to do?

He glanced at Thomas. Still prone, the stable boy stared at Matilde with wide-eyed reverence.

Damnation.

Matilde knelt beside Bartholomew and grabbed his arm. "Please save him."

He grit his teeth and snapped, "Quippe," as he shrugged out of his coat. Robert Grus was a fool and a ruffian, but he wasn't evil. He didn't deserve death.

Hope brightened her eyes. "You will?"

"Oui, Matilde. But get Thomas away." He stabbed his finger toward their house.

She grabbed the stable boy's arm and pulled him up from the forest floor. "We have to leave."

He stood, but his attention remained on the prone young man. He shook his head. "We can't just go, Miss." Robert's heart stuttered, gave another sluggish beat, and quivered. His body was failing.

"Matilde Anne Royce, get back to the house now!" Bartholomew snarled. No time for discretion, but if Thomas saw his soul—disastrous.

She grabbed the lantern. "Come *on*, Thomas!" She yanked her friend into the woods.

Bartholomew threw his coat over Robert Grus, reached beneath the black fabric, and unfettered his soul. Its shimmering, blue light was muted as he placed his hands upon the fallen young man's shattered skull. His spirit flowed across Robert's skin, sank into his scalp, and cast an eerie hue behind the boy's sightless eyes. But the bully's heartbeat slowed. A tearing sensation traveled up Bartholomew's arms. The boy's flesh and soul were separating.

"Merda."

If Robert died, there'd be no avoiding an inquiry. An elite girl killing a dirt-poor boy would capture the country's attention. Bartholomew's family couldn't afford that kind of scrutiny. Not with Famine's army growing and her web spreading. He hadn't survived all these centuries by attracting unwanted notice, and he certainly didn't want to attract their enemy's eye now. He had to save this boy.

He placed his other hand upon Robert's chest. "You will live, Robert Grus." He forced more of his own soul outward. Instead of burrowing into the boy's flesh, it undulated across the body, becoming a barrier to halt the release of Robert's life force. "I won't allow your death."

Beneath Bartholomew's fingers, the fallen boy's heart

thudded once, then again, and again. Its failing rhythm resolved into a determined beat. His bones and brain regenerated. His body and soul became seamless once more.

Bartholomew exhaled relief. He retracted his luminous spirit, stood, and donned his coat. He watched and waited. After a few minutes, Robert opened his eyes, groaned, and sat upright.

"Get up." Bartholomew seized the young man's collar and yanked him to his feet. "Why are you skulking around my property? You have no business here."

Robert gaped at him. "I-I, sir?"

"Have you been drinking? And fighting? You're a mess." Bartholomew released the bully, crossed his arms, and glared at him. "Answer me. Or I'll call the police and you can explain your circumstances to them."

Robert shook his head and stepped back. "No, sir. That's not necessary. I was just out walking, sir, not drinking. I didn't know I was on your property." He touched his head then squinted at his bloody fingers. "I-I-I think, maybe, I fell. I'll go. I'm sorry. I didn't mean to disturb you."

Bartholomew leaned forward and peered at the boy. "You're injured? Perhaps I *should* call the police."

The young man took two more steps back and shook his head. "No, sir. I'm fine. Just scratched up." He took off like a scared rabbit, white tail flashing and ears flat.

Bartholomew suppressed a laugh, as much relieved as amused to see Robert Grus's flight. The young man had earned his fear.

But Bartholomew's mirth died as he set off for the house. He faced another confrontation and a dire question: Had Thomas seen his soul?

Matilde and the stable hand were waiting in the shadows on the back porch when Bartholomew entered the yard. She came down the steps and ran to him. She resembled a ghost girl in the moonlight with her pale, worried face and her blonde hair freed of its braid to cascade over her shoulders. "How is he?"

"Robert Grus is alive and scurrying home. I don't believe he recalls the blow that felled him. Nor do I expect him or Micah Kornilov to mention the sound beating they received at the hands of a genteel girl tonight."

She covered her face with her hands, bent forward, and began to sob. Bartholomew held her and said nothing. She'd done something monstrous and only fortune had saved all of them from the consequences.

He returned Thomas's grim regard as he continued across the yard, Matilde tucked against his side. "Inside the house, Mr. Green. We have your future to discuss."

Cap in hand, Thomas grimaced. "Yes, sir." He followed them into the drawing room.

"Mrs. Henderson." Bartholomew's voice boomed through the shadowy house.

After a moment, warm yellow light bathed the stairwell.

"What has happened, Monsieur?" The governess's words were slurred by sleep as she padded down the stairs.

"Take charge of Matilde. I want her returned to her bed immediately."

Tight-lipped, Mrs. Henderson surveyed her charge, caught the girl's wrist, and dragged her toward the stairway.

But Matilde pulled away and grabbed Bartholomew's arm. "It was a mistake. *My* mistake." Her frantic gaze went to

Thomas, then returned to her guardian's face. "Please, Monsieur."

Bartholomew caught her shoulders and pushed her back a step. "Go to your room."

Mr. Vernon, who'd joined Mrs. Henderson at the foot of the stairs, captured the girl's arm and steered her toward her bedroom.

Ignoring the plea in her eyes as she craned to see him, Bartholomew donned a frock coat, hat, and gloves. He seized Thomas's collar and the young man grunted. He marched him out to the carriage house and threw him into the black rockaway.

They drove in strained silence through Seattle's empty streets until the carriage clattered to a stop before the boy's tiny house. Bartholomew set the brake and lit a cigarette.

The turn of events was a bitter pill. Thomas would've been an excellent addition to his associates, especially if he attended seminary school. Having a priest in the organization could've proved pivotal. Famine wouldn't suspect subterfuge from a holy man. But now? Bartholomew exhaled. The boy had violated his trust and endangered Matilde. It would be a long time before his faith was restored in Thomas, if ever.

Frogs serenaded from the darkness, an unending song.

Bartholomew flicked his spent cigarette into the gutter and lit another. He smoked, the horses dozed, and the young man fidgeted silently in the carriage behind him.

When his second cigarette was gone, Bartholomew climbed from the driver's seat and opened the door. "What happened tonight? I want the truth, and I want all of it. Do not lie or omit anything because I will question Matilde next. Your stories better match."

"I made the mistake, Monsieur, not Miss Matilde. I wanted her to have fun, so I coaxed her to leave the house with Robert, Micah, and me. But then they threatened to cut her hair. I guess Jeffrey McIntyre put them up to it." He shook his head. "I never woulda thought they'd act like this, sir. It sure is lucky she can fight better than any girl I've ever seen."

"Indeed. Is there any more you need to tell me?"

"Well, only that I was sure Matilde had killed Robert." Regret, fear, and confusion twisted his face. "How could he survive that blow?"

"Even minor head wounds bleed heavily. His injury wasn't as severe as I initially believed." Bartholomew studied the stable boy. There was relief in his slumped shoulders and regret in his hangdog expression.

He saw nothing. "I suggest you reconsider your future and reprioritize your actions, Mr. Green. Endangering my ward is not among them."

Thomas stared at the floorboard. "You're right. It was stupid. Miss Matilde is my dear friend and-and I never meant to cause any trouble to her or to you. Your family has been so good to me." The young man looked at Bartholomew. "I hope you can forgive me, sir."

"I am not a forgiving man. And you have lost my trust."

The young man blinked and his eyes widened. "But— I-I was honest about what happened. I accept full responsibility for my stupidity. Won't you forgive me for my mistake?"

Bartholomew stared the boy down. "Words are worthless. I do not forgive you. I have no reason to do so."

"What can I do to regain your trust?"

"That is for you to decide, Mr. Green. But until you have proved yourself worthy of my faith, you will be unwelcome in my house and I will forbid Matilde from any association with you." Bartholomew turned from the carriage and strode toward the front door where Mrs. Green stood in her bathrobe, silhouetted by pale light from the house. He didn't wait for Thomas; the boy would follow after he'd choked down his first bitter bite of adulthood.

Mrs. Henderson and Mr. Vernon met Bartholomew in the yard when he returned. Before swinging down from the driver's seat, he closed his eyes and pressed his thumb and fingers to his temples. A dull ache thudded against his skull and fatigue pressed down upon him. It would take many months of careful hunting to restore the power he'd spared to Robert Grus. "Koorva."

Mr. Vernon asked, "Monsieur?"

Roused from his thoughts, Bartholomew spied the worried expressions on the faces of his butler and housekeeper. "The boy saw nothing." Tension, like air from a bladder, lifted from their shoulders.

While Mr. Vernon unhitched the horses, Mrs. Henderson brought out the Scotch. "You cannot be surprised by Miss Matilde's defiance. Soon she will be of age. You must begin trusting her if you wish for her to trust you."

"A bit of wisdom I have been too slow to comprehend, Mrs. Henderson," Bartholomew replied.

"She admires you, but she's driven toward independence by her age and nature." The governess handed her employer a glass. "The only shock in her defiance tonight is that it hasn't occurred sooner."

He downed the Scotch as they crossed the porch and entered the drawing room. "Had I not been following, a boy would be dead, Mrs. Henderson, and we would be facing inquiries we can ill afford. Those are the consequences of Matilde's defiance." He handed her the glass and shrugged out of his frock coat, tossing it onto the burgundy wing chair with his top hat and gloves. "We cannot afford a single mistake. The dangers are much greater than losing one bullying boy's soul. Such a mistake could cost every soul dearly."

Mr. Vernon joined them. "Perhaps it's time for you to explain the entire story to the girl."

Bartholomew shook his head. "Not yet. I cannot give her that knowledge until I know she trusts me and is prepared to accept the Catcher. Once she understands her part, there's no undoing what must be done."

"Then we must be ever more vigilant and patient," Mrs. Henderson said.

Bartholomew rotated his head and his muscles and tendons crackled. "Matilde is an unpredictable weapon. And she's too precious to lose." They followed him into the hallway. "I've been too tolerant of her friendship with Thomas. That laxity nearly killed a witless boy this evening." He paused at the stairs. "I've taken steps to prevent another occurrence."

"What have you done?" Matilde spoke from the second floor landing. "Thomas didn't see anything."

"I'm aware of that. But young Mr. Green has broken my trust. I have forbidden him from further contact with you."

Matilde closed her eyes and nodded.

Bartholomew took the stairs two at once until he reached her. "However, I have spoken with him and Mrs. Green about redirecting his current path."

"More threats?" Her eyes were red and puffy, her face pallid.

He caught her elbow and steered her back toward her room. "Non. Your friend expressed only regret over the evening's events and has requested my help in furthering his opportunities. I've agreed to make a loan available for his continued schooling. His chivalry did not go unnoticed by me, even if his regrettable judgment gave root to your endangerment."

"Schooling?" She stopped. "You're paying for his schooling?"

"Oui. I do not wish to see Thomas fail."

"That's very generous of you."

"I'm pleased you feel that way. But you won't feel so charitable toward me after I've determined a suitable punishment for you."

20

WESTERN UNION TELEGRAM
January 7, 1903
C. Vernon, Gen'l Delivery

F and boys plus eight. Manhattan house.
A.M.M.

BARTHOLOMEUS SLUMPED BESIDE THE GRAVE AND FLIPPED HIS *remaining sestertius across his muddy knuckles. He'd had three of the copper coins from Aemelia. One he'd placed in Lucius's lifeless palm and one in hers before he'd climbed from their shared grave and covered them with dirt. He flipped the sestertius from his ring finger to his pinky, over into his palm and clutched it.*

His chest burned where the Catcher had cleaved his heart. His arms, legs, and back were cramped from digging the grave. But his spirit ached the most—the agony of failure and betrayal would never fade. Aemelia and Lucius had been murdered while he'd writhed on the ground like a helpless boy.

His focus swung to the stable. The Catcher and the Beacon were there, and both his horses were saddled and packed with supplies. A lazy, late-afternoon breeze stirred the cypress trees and filled the courtyard with the sweet perfume of jasmine. Bartholomeus peered at wispy clouds softening the sky. Everything felt wrong.

The Catcher had made him an aesir—a halfling—but not the Guardian. "I cannot complete you in this form," she'd said.

Why? Because he was the penumbra? What did that mean? She wouldn't explain.

"Merda."

He stared at the Roman eagle tattooed on his right hand, then stood and went into the house. He emerged carrying his gladius, crossed the small courtyard, and ducked into the stable. He halted at the sight of the young girl—the Beacon—snuggled against her sleeping mistress in one of the empty stalls. Lucius had often curled up with Aemelia in just that way. Bartholomeus swallowed a lump and a curse.

The girl looked at the gladius then up at him. Her wide-set, hazel eyes held more wariness and wisdom than a child's should. "Penumbra or not, you're her aesir. Your duty is to protect her."

His grip tightened on the bone pommel. "Get up. I don't wish you harm, child."

She shook her head. "I can't release my Catcher." She moved her right hand. A ragged, orange scarf bound her to the woman. "I tether her to the realm of man while her spirit travels to the outer darkness. Without me she can't release the damaged souls she's captured. And without her, we can't stop the Four Horsemen from destroying all the souls in this realm."

"Move."

She sat upright. "Do you think you're the only one who's suffered to end this war?"

He pointed the blade at her. "You know nothing of my suffering."

"Your suffering." She snorted and jabbed a finger at him. "You know nothing at all."

The child sat within inches of death and ignored his rage. How could she be so unafraid and so un-childlike? "I know my wife and son shouldn't have died for my loyalty." He raised the gladius.

She shrugged. "Your price was their safety from Famine. That's what the Catcher delivered. If your terms were more specific, you should have defined them clearly."

How could she be so dispassionate? "Defined them? I shouldn't have to tell the Catcher not to murder innocent people."

The Beacon peered past him to the open stable door. She looked down at the prone woman beside her, stroked the Catcher's cheek, and murmured, "Return from your journey. The sun has passed its zenith." She arched her back. "Centurion, your love for your family is a weakness."

"Stop salting my wounds." His shoulders hunched. He lowered the gladius. "The Catcher or Famine—I see little difference between them."

The girl crossed her legs. She had a short body and spindly limbs, her growth frozen between child and adolescent when the Catcher had summoned the Beacon's spirit to possess her.

"You're wrong. The Apocalyptics exist for one purpose—to save this world." Her gesture encompassed the trees, mountains, and sky. "Anything that doesn't serve that goal is an obstacle to be overcome or swept aside." She slashed the air with her hand.

The Catcher stirred.

Swept aside. Bartholomeus scowled. "Shouldn't saving this world include protecting innocent souls? Or is this a contest to see who can murder all the living things first?"

The Beacon replied, "The Catcher will fulfill her duty by any means necessary."

He swallowed that bitter pill as he studied her. "You're not so ruthless as she is."

"I don't have to be."

"And the Guardian?"

She returned his gaze. "He must be the most ruthless of all."

"Well, if my love for my family makes me weak," he jerked his chin toward the Catcher, "your mistress is welcome to release me from this madness."

"Don't put words in my mouth." The girl loosened the scarf as the Catcher's eyes opened. "You're more than capable of fulfilling your duty to protect her. But you must love the one you may give up your existence to save."

"I need to love that?" He stabbed his finger at the Catcher. "A mistake has been made, girl." He would spare no love for anyone or anything ever again.

The Catcher murmured, "That's why all of this came to be."

"How what came to be?" he asked.

She touched the Beacon's hand and her words were slurred as she said, "The Four Horsemen and the Apocalyptics. One of the Horsemen knew love. It was his lover who freed him and his companions from their cells."

The girl smiled down at the woman. "God created the Apocalyptics from souls imprisoned in the outer darkness and sent them where he couldn't go—to the realm of man—to recapture the Horsemen." She stood and stretched. "I'm going to refill my water skin." She left the stable.

Bartholomeus muttered, "How poetic that love could bring the End of Days. I wish Famine and her brothers would speed it along. I'm tired of being a pawn."

The Catcher rose, blinking and bleary. She rolled her blanket. "Individually they're impotent, Bartholomeus. United they're the End of Days. Ally with Famine and you'll have your wish. Then everything will fall before them in a war led by you."

He grimaced and rubbed the back of his neck. "I won't side with the Horsemen, Catcher. The whole world shouldn't suffer for your treachery." He sheathed the gladius.

The horses shifted and nickered.

The Catcher straightened and stumbled toward the stable door.

A cold, nauseating sensation wormed up Bartholomeus's spine and gripped his chest. "What is that?" He strode past her into the courtyard.

Her voice caught. "The Beacon."

"What?" He turned. Something pierced his right shoulder. Pain, sharp and sickening, spread through his chest and radiated down his arm. A bloody arrowhead protruded from his tunic. Merda.

A scream carried down from the aquifer.

The Catcher shrieked, "No!"

Bartholomeus pivoted. Another arrow struck his chest, knocking him back a step. He squinted at the hillside. Scrub, stone, and scattered trees hid the attacker, but he knew who was there. "Famine," he snarled. An arrow whizzed past his head. It thudded into the stable wall.

The trap was closing. If he did nothing, it would be over. If he did nothing, they'd all be destroyed.

"Aesir!" the Catcher shouted and ducked behind him. "You pledged your loyalty to me!"

He grunted as another arrow impaled his left forearm. He looked down at it, aware of distant pain. If he did nothing... His attention went to his family's fresh grave.

Aemelia and Lucius will have died in vain, he thought. The Four Horsemen will enslave their souls.

"Aesir, we must protect the Beacon!"

"To the wall." Bartholomeus ducked as another arrow whizzed past his head. "Stay low and behind me." Rome's training surged within him as he gripped the Catcher's arm. They ran to the shelter of his compound's white stone wall.

With his dagger, Bartholomeus severed the arrow shafts close to their feathers. He turned his back to the Catcher. "Pull them out." He yanked free the one that had bloodied his forearm and split the bone, then stared at the blue glow welling from within him to knit together flesh and bone.

How?

"There's only one all the way through." She removed it.

He grabbed the remaining shaft, and groaning through gritted teeth, shoved the arrow through his body to emerge out his back. "Now there are two." She pulled it out and he drew his gladius. "Stay here until I've drawn out our attackers."

"But my Beacon—"

"Is gone."

He watched the trajectory of the next arrow. Famine had moved down the hill. He stepped into the compound's entry, ducked another arrow, and hurled his dagger.

His aim was true. Wood cracked. Famine cursed. Her bow clattered to the ground, its lower limb splintered by his blade.

But where was Ewan? To draw the cadaver into the open, Bartholomeus strode into the clearing past the wall. "How like you to shoot me in the back, moecha."

Famine emerged from the trees. "You stabbed me in the back first." She hissed and pulled his dagger from between her ribs. She cleaned it with her tongue, spat, and cursed. "She's befouled you."

"No more than you did."

"You dare to betray me after I permitted you to have a wife? And a child, of all the filthy things!" She stabbed her finger at him. "Creating a family was an insult. But that pales compared to this treachery, penumbra. Becoming our enemy's protector to complete God's triumvirate? Do you really believe you can destroy me and seize power? You need me!"

He bared his teeth. She was accusing him of choosing God's power over his family's love. Aemelia and Lucius had died because of her. "All I need is your head severed from your spine."

She sneered and straightened. "All you'll get is suffering." Her hands took on a sickly glow as her soul oozed from her palms and snaked along her fingers. She scuttled forward. He raised the gladius.

Ewan roared and charged down from the aquifer.

Bartholomeus grimaced at the clattering of the Celt's bones. Where was the Catcher? Why wasn't she fighting beside him?

Did she want him dead? He pivoted to intercept Ewan's broadsword before it cleaved him in half. The cadaver maneuvered to cut Bartholomeus off from Famine, even as she clawed at him. He was doomed if she touched him. The world was doomed if she reached the Catcher.

"Stop the centurion," Famine commanded.

Bartholomeus snarled, "If my soul goes, so does yours."

Wailing echoed off the hills; the Catcher had found her Beacon. The clang of steel on steel joined her cries.

Ewan had reach. Bartholomeus had speed. They prowled and tested. Bartholomeus circled like a hound, dodged forward and away, sought weakness. But he was tired and outnumbered. The Celt sliced his right biceps as he was blocking Famine's attack from the left.

He ducked Ewan's next swing and thrust his gladius through the cadaver's hip. As the Celt stumbled back, he slashed at his throat. The blade missed its mark but opened Ewan's face from ear to ear. But Bartholomeus wasn't unscathed. Blood streaked his left leg. A gaping wound revealed muscle and bone.

Famine reached for him, her spidery fingers glimmering with her poisonous spirit. He jerked to the side, swung the gladius back, and sliced her fingers off. She shrieked and clutched her right hand.

He watched his foes with battle-honed eyes.

"You were my weapon. Now you're my enemy. Aesir." She hissed the title like an insult.

"I'll be your executioner," he replied.

Ewan roared and raised his broadsword.

"Guardian!" the Catcher shouted as she emerged from the stable astride Aemelia's mare, his gray gelding in tow.

Bartholomeus ran toward the house and swung into the saddle as she rode past.

They veered away from their attackers, but Famine's laugh chased them. By destroying the Beacon, she'd trapped the Catcher in the earthly realm.

It was only a matter of time before madness consumed Bartholomeus's new mistress.

BARTHOLOMEW OPENED his eyes and listened. There'd been a sound. Famine laughing?

Just the wind.

A winter storm howled inland from Puget Sound. The house's eaves rattled and trees all around the property creaked and whooshed. Sleet peppered the west-facing windows, coating them in a thick, white glaze, and somewhere in the forest there'd been a thunderous crack earlier in the evening. Likely an old tree had succumbed to age, torn free of its roots, and pulled down its companions as it fell.

He yawned, stretched, and caught Dante's *Paradiso* as it slid from his lap. He'd fallen asleep on the couch in the library. He opened the book to straighten the telegram he'd used as a bookmark. Famine, Ewan, Barnes and eight cadavers were in Manhattan.

"But where are the others?" he muttered. He rubbed his scruffy chin and scanned the book's page:

> You shall leave everything you love most
>   dearly: this is the arrow that the bow of
> exile

shoots first. You are to know the bitter taste
of others' bread, how salt it is, and know how
hard a path it is for one who goes
descending and ascending others' stairs.

He grimaced. That was where he'd drifted off? No wonder he'd had another nightmare. "'This uncouth dream of evil sprung.'" Another grimace and he closed the book. "That's no more helpful to me than it was to Eve when Adam said it."

"Monsieur?"

He glanced up. Mrs. Henderson stood in the library doorway, concern twisting her expression. He thought she'd gone to bed hours ago.

"Oui?"

"I think you should see this."

He closed the book and glanced at the mantle clock. Half past ten. The house groaned and shuddered as he followed the governess up the stairs.

Mrs. Henderson said, "I heard Miss Matilde speaking when she should have been asleep, so I paused at her room, believing you were with her. But, clearly, that was not the case."

They reached his ward's bedroom. The girl's voice carried to Bartholomew. With it came dread. She was crying and repeating two words *in Aramaic*.

"Mar Parwanqa." My Beacon.

He eased open the door. Hunched in the middle of the room, Matilde rocked to and fro, a pillow clutched to her chest. She turned unfocused eyes to him. "They sundered my Beacon," she said in Aramaic.

Mon Dieu. He gestured for Mrs. Henderson to remain in

the doorway as he crossed the room and crouched beside his ward. "Petit Oiseau, you're dreaming. You don't know the Beacon," he said in English.

"You let her die, Centurion. She wasn't supposed to die."

"Let me help you into bed, Matilde."

The pillow rolled from her arms to the floor. She stepped back from it. "Now I can't go to the outer darkness, I can't fulfill my duty, and I can't be free of this burden. I should not have believed in you!"

"You're having an unpleasant dream." He touched her elbow. "Please return to bed."

"Bed?" she asked in English as he steered her away from the pillow.

"You should be in bed now."

Still asleep on her feet, she followed him, slid between the sheets, and settled into quiet slumber.

He retrieved Bettina and the pillow from the floor, and tucked the little cat beneath Matilde's hand. She sighed and snuggled the toy close. He dropped her pillow onto the end of the bed and left the room. He ushered Mrs. Henderson to the top of the stairs. "She should be restful for the remainder of the night."

"How could she speak that foreign tongue?"

"Perhaps she heard it in the Sixth Ward."

The governess looked hard at him and folded her arms. "I am not an unobservant fool. Miss Matilde spoke of someone whom she has never met, in a language she has no basis for speaking."

He returned her gaze. "I know and respect your intellect, Mrs. Henderson. It's best if you assume Matilde heard that language spoken in the Sixth Ward."

Her lips pursed. "Is she in danger?"

"From a dream? Non." He touched her arm. "It's late. Go to bed. Only you and I will recall these events in the morning."

"All right, Monsieur. Good night."

"Good night."

As she retired to her bedroom, Bartholomew returned to the library. But Dante no longer held his interest.

The Catcher's voice knifed him. *"The distortion of her dreams will not cease."*

"Stop this harassment," Bartholomew demanded, knowing he was impotent to prevent the Catcher from haunting his ward. His connection to the outer darkness had been strengthened by a brief encounter with a pair of thugs the previous evening. They'd wanted his wallet, his pocket watch, and his cigarette case. They'd emerged from the encounter empty-handed, stupefied, and with an inexplicable pattern of silvery scars around their necks.

"You can end her nightmares, Aesir."

"By cursing her with an eternal, nightmarish existence?"

"That existence will come to all in the earthly realm. Soon Famine will have the strength to summon the others."

"Matilde is not ready. Her training isn't complete." Six months had passed since the incident with Robert and Micah. Matilde was sixteen years old, but Bartholomew had learned to tread more carefully with his adolescent ward. "She's still too volatile and vulnerable."

"What horror should I share from your memories next?"

"Get out of her dreams." He stalked to the mudroom and donned his heavy coat, boots, gloves, scarf, and bowler. He couldn't go to bed now. The Catcher's connection was too strong. She would torture him and Matilde all night if he remained in the house.

He awakened Mr. Vernon. "Keep them safe until I return." Ignoring the butler's protests about the weather, Bartholomew set off on foot into the frigid January night.

21

"Georgine says you're scrupulous."

"Does she?" His pencil sketched a flowing line across the paper—a lock of Iona's black hair.

She sat in a pale-blue damask wing chair beside the room's only window. "I told her that was a lie and you're in perfect health." He laughed. She smiled with him and added, "Gwendolyn told me it means 'honorable,' and I forgave Georgine."

"That was generous of you," he said around his cigarette. Iona shifted and he murmured, "Don't slouch, please. I'm almost finished."

"Sorry. I forgot." She straightened her shoulders and lifted her chin again. "Like this?"

He glanced from his drawing to her. "Drop your left shoulder just a bit and tilt your chin away from me just—stop. There." He sat cross-legged on the floor clad in his trousers and union suit. Iona wore nothing but a sheet around her waist and draped down her legs. Her hair cascaded over her shoulders to cover her breasts and give only a hint of their fullness.

"Will I get to see it?"

"Oui." He sketched a fold of the fabric. "It's for you. A birthday gift."

She laughed. "It's not my birthday."

He shaded the curve below her left breast and added a few strokes to give depth to her hair. "Then you decide if it's an early or late present." He took a long drag on his cigarette and looked from the girl to the sketch. He nodded, exhaled, and turned the paper to her. "Finished."

Delight widened her eyes and her smile. "Is that how you see me?"

"That is how you appear."

She whispered, "I'm beautiful?"

He made a small noise in the back of his throat. "So I've told you." He stood and gave her the drawing then stubbed out his cigarette in the bedside ashtray. "Now do you believe me?"

Her eyes lingering on the picture, Iona let the sheet fall as she crossed the room and retrieved a hair ribbon from a low dresser. She rolled the sketch and tied it with the ribbon. Turning away from him, she pulled on her white, frilly knickers and camisole, and retrieved her red corset from the bed. In a hushed voice she said, "That's the nicest gift a man's ever given me."

He almost dismissed her sentiment as a trifle but thought better of it. "You're welcome," he replied and donned his white shirt.

She closed the front busk of the corset, encasing her body in steel and red silk. With the snap of each hook, her spine straightened and a wall grew between them. "I hope you won't be angry if I am unavailable for your next visit." Her voice had flattened. She'd turned him from 'lover' to 'client.'

Bartholomew secured a silver cufflink on his left sleeve. "I won't."

"Why do you defy me, Bartholomeus?"

He'd hoped to silence the Catcher's voice when he'd reached Georgine's house. With Iona he'd found release, but their dalliance had brought only temporary relief.

The prostitute slid her feet into her unlaced boots and sighed. "It's difficult, you see." She peered at him from the corners of her eyes. "You do understand what I'm saying, don't you?" Her wall was fragile.

"Oui." He rolled down his right sleeve. "I've heard this many times, Iona. It's why you've been well compensated for my demands."

"I know, but it's become—difficult." She plucked pilled fabric from the blanket. Her black hair snaked forward to hide her face.

"You will condemn us all, Aesir."

Bartholomew donned his waistcoat and went around the bed.

Why is our connection so damnably strong tonight? Always before, sexual release had quieted the Catcher.

"Emotion is the most troublesome enemy to conquer." He stroked Iona's cheek. She pressed her lips against his palm and nodded. "You'll be fine." He knelt and tugged the laces tight on her left boot. "Let me help you."

"Thank you."

He tied a neat bow and lifted her right foot. "For lacing your boots?"

"That. And your generosity." She sucked in a breath and her wall straightened, strengthened. "Because of you I've been able to help my family far more than I ever expected."

"I'm pleased to hear it." He looped the laces around her boot's eye-hooks. "How is your mother's health?"

Iona's father had died in a foundry accident when she was twelve. Eight years later her mother had developed heart problems after a bout with rheumatic fever. She couldn't work, so Iona's income supported the family while her brother completed school.

"Much improved. Keith wrote just last week that Mam's able to climb the stairs and even spends time in the garden every day now." Her smile was sad.

"You miss them." He tied a neat bow.

"I do, but it's good they're not here. He wouldn't approve of this." She gestured around the room. "Wouldn't even take the money if he knew. I told him I'm an artist's model. Maybe I'll send your drawing to Mam."

"Had I known, I would've made something more discreet." Bartholomew stood. "Next time we'll include clothing."

There was a tap on the door. "I should go." Iona stood and crossed the room. "There are other men."

"Of course."

She cracked the door. Georgine's husky voice carried in from the hall. "The Red Room. The quiet one you saw last Wednesday. He's been waiting. Are you clean?"

"Yes, ma'am." Iona left the room.

Bartholomew watched the door close. "*Adieu.*" He grimaced. Iona had proven to be the inexperienced girl Georgine had promised him that first night. But with her innocence came a heart that was not well armored. She'd fallen in love with him and could ill afford the emotional turmoil that accompanied unrequited love.

Bartholomew kept his heart encased in concrete. His

demand of the women he paid to be his lovers was the cruelest sort—the sacrifice of their emotional dispassion with the full knowledge that, should they open their hearts to him, their affection would never be returned. That Iona had endured nearly two years with him was a testament to her tenacity and her financial need.

He smoothed down his mustache. Now where was his tie? Not on the bedside table. He checked the wing chair beside the bed, but it wasn't there with his coat, hat, and gloves either. He scanned the room and pushed aside the bed's blue sheets and pillows. Not there. Finally, a hint of black fabric gave it away. He pulled the duvet off the floor to find the tie.

"I will not allow you to bring the Apocalypse, Bartholomeus."

He knotted the tie around his collar, muttering, "Go away," in response to the Catcher. He shrugged into his frock coat and picked up his gloves.

He stopped and stared at nothing.

Fear had come to Georgine's house. It slunk down the hall and slithered beneath the door. It wrapped around his nerves and clawed up his spine.

One of the women was terrified.

Merda. "Catcher, what have you done now?"

Bartholomew reached the hall as a strangled wail raised the hair on the nape of his neck and silenced the brothel's customary chorus of sighs and moans.

The would-be Guardian strode down the hall until a suffering soul beckoned from behind the locked door of the Red Room. Another scream accompanied the percussion of feet upon the stairs. He barreled through the wooden door like it was made of twigs.

There was Iona. Her pale breasts were bloody. There was a serrated knife. There was a man with white hair and dead eyes. Bartholomew loathed the ones with dead eyes. He inhaled Iona's fear and exhaled rage.

Without a word, the man produced a second knife from his waistband and lunged off the bed.

Bartholomew dodged the blades, kicked the bastard's legs out from beneath him, and followed through with a solid punch to the side of his head as he hit the floor. He stomped on the man's left hand, sneering at the crunch of bones beneath his boot. He intercepted the other knife as it plunged toward his thigh and wrenched it from the madman's grasp.

He flipped the bastard facedown and impaled his left palm to the floor. He retrieved the other blade and crucified the man's other hand too. The attacker struggled to break free, yet no sound escaped him.

Two ladies had come to Iona's aid while Georgine ushered patrons downstairs. Bartholomew turned to offer assistance. What he saw made his blood boil. The bastard had carved up Iona's breasts. She writhed and moaned as the other prostitutes tried to aid her.

"Where's Miriam?" one of the women shouted down the stairs. "Iona needs stitches or she'll bleed to death!"

Snatching a sheet from the bed, Bartholomew bound the attacker's feet and ran the fabric up to wrap around the man's throat. If the bastard lowered his legs, he'd strangle. Bartholomew grabbed the man's hair and yanked his head back. "Don't choke. I'm far from finished with you."

Miriam pushed past the huddled girls in the doorway, gasped at the damage done to her friend's flesh, and got to work stitching the wounds. Someone produced a bottle of sherry and Iona choked down half of it.

"Shouldn't someone call the police?" asked a new girl who trembled in the doorway still wearing nothing but a white cotton blanket.

Georgine's eyes met Bartholomew's as she replied, "We don't exist to the police, child, and they don't exist to us."

Iona moaned and sobbed as Miriam pieced her chest together. They all knew she would look like a rag doll. If she survived blood loss and infection, the only people who would pay to touch her were perverts and freaks.

When the stitching was finished, Bartholomew carried her to the attic bedroom the ladies shared. Pale and shaking, Iona gasped with every small motion as he settled her into bed. He stepped back and let the ladies fuss over her. He pushed his fingers through his hair. If only there weren't witnesses. He could relieve her suffering and heal the wounds. But the other girls were here and helping. He could do nothing. Iona wasn't the first person he'd had to turn his back on in an hour of need, but he wanted her to be the last.

Bartholomew's hands curled into fists as he left the room. While he was helpless to ease her pain, there was something he could give the girl: Revenge.

He returned to fetch his belongings and speak with the madam outside the room that still held the attacker.

"I will dispose of this filth, Georgine."

She shook her head. "There's no reason for you to become entangled in this mess, Monsieur."

"I already am and this is something at which I excel."

It was the first time he'd ever seen shock widen the madam's eyes.

"So that's how you earn your living."

"Protection and revenge are my specialties. Let me do this for Iona."

She eyed him and nodded. "What do you need from me?"

"A horse cart and secrecy."

"I've sent all the customers away. I'll have the wagon drawn around to the alley. I guarantee the girls will say nothing." She turned as Bartholomew opened the door. "Be certain that he suffers greatly, Monsieur."

"That is guaranteed." He closed the door behind him and approached the monster.

The man's rotten soul panicked. His eyes were no longer dead; they'd come alive with fear like a horse facing a pack of hounds. He kicked out and gagged himself, snuffling and drooling.

Bartholomew watched for a moment before producing the thin, sharp blade he always carried in his coat. He sliced through the sheet. The man's face struck the floor and left a red smear behind.

"Do you feel that fear?" Bartholomew pulled the madman's head up by his hair. "That's your soul's terror." He shoved a pair of dirty socks into the bastard's gaping mouth. "It knows what I am and what is coming."

He yanked the knives from the madman's palms leaving behind holes and blood. He bound the man's wrists behind his back and wrapped him like a cigar in the bloody blanket from the bed. He dragged the attacker to the top of the wooden stairs and pushed, lighting a cigarette and enjoying the bastard's grunts and cries as the roll bumped and tumbled down to the first floor.

The mere proximity to the malevolent spirit had started

the Catcher humming within him. Sixteen months had passed since he'd taken Clyde Green's vicious soul. Though he'd siphoned spirits here and there, he'd been cautious and conservative, and this was the first deserving soul he'd encountered since killing Mr. Green. This one's power crackled like lightning inside a thunderhead.

BARTHOLOMEW DROVE the wagon into the wilderness at the northern end of Lake Washington until he found an isolated, wooded area. He hobbled and blanketed the horse then dragged the squirming body off the back of the cart.

"You smell worse than the tide flats." He yanked the blanket away, sending the bound man tumbling across the dank ground until he smacked into a fallen log.

"I don't want your loathsome spirit, but I am forced to take it." He grabbed the attacker's lapels and yanked him to a sitting position. "The price I'll pay is grossly unfair." He gestured at the man with his boning knife. "Your victims' suffering has strengthened your soul. When I sever it from your body all of their final moments will congeal within *my* mind." He tapped his temple with the blade. "Like a moldering residue."

The attacker's watery eyes tracked Bartholomew's hands. The rotten bastard's face crumpled like an old, burlap bag and he began to sob.

Bartholomew sneered and shook his head. "Don't cry. Don't beg. It's a waste of time." He gestured at the man and added, "Don't pray, either. Another waste, that. God doesn't care." His jaw tightened. His heart hardened. "Which is something your victims know."

Stowing the knife, his raised his hand and unfettered his soul. He inhaled as its nebulous blue light rose from his skin, slipping and sliding like mercury. "You relished Iona's fear. Now you will feel her suffering." He reached toward the man's face. "I'll do this slowly to avenge that beautiful, sweet girl."

The man toppled and tried to squirm away, but Bartholomew pinned him to the ground with a knee upon his chest. He grabbed the madman's face. His soul burrowed into the bastard's eyes, slid up his nostrils, and oozed down his throat. Bartholomew slowed the movement of his spirit and smiled as the man arched and gagged. "Horrible, isn't it? But not as bad as Iona's terror." The blue light spread, flickering beneath the bastard's skin, lighting and burning his insides as it rooted out the power of the soul dwelling within each cell. "If she has to live with what you've done, I want her to know your last moments were long and horrible."

He unleashed his spirit when it reached the man's thundering heart. It raced through the remainder of the body, rending and burning any resistance it encountered. It shot up his spine into his brain. It hunted down the malignant soul in every fiber.

When the murderer stopped twitching, Bartholomew retracted his own soul and tore the evil little spirit from the body. It slid from his hands, turbid and oily, thick with madness and villainy. Too congested to dissipate into the ether, the soul seeped into the ground.

Bartholomew slumped upon the fallen tree, covered his face with his hands, and groaned. So much suffering. So many victims. All women and children. This was one of the worst souls he'd ever encountered. It was a fetid and stinking thing, like the putrid ooze of a rotting corpse. This was death and violence, mindless brutality that came from no cause and brought the killer no relief.

If only he was the Guardian, then Bartholomew could've destroyed the monstrous soul. But he wasn't and it was free to occupy a new body, while Bartholomew endured Iona's screams in his mind endlessly.

"Merda."

"*Release me Bartholomeus. I will help you.*" The Catcher's voice was clear and commanding, strengthened by the power Bartholomew had just stolen.

"Damn you!" He took his boning knife to the body and went to work releasing the violence he'd inherited from it, trying to weaken his connection to the outer darkness. When he stopped hours later, he was covered in gore and there was little left that resembled a man.

"*This is only the beginning. I will have my freedom. I will have the girl's body.*"

Cursing the Catcher with every slipping step, Bartholomew found an icy creek, forded in, and lay down. Silvery stars winked overhead in a cold, black sky. He groaned and grit his teeth against the burning pain of frozen skin and cramped muscles. The burbling water washed blood away, but he'd never be clean.

He left the carcass for the animals and insects, climbed onto the wagon, and returned to Georgine's house hunched and shivering, his clothes stiff with ice. He struggled to tie the horse to a post in the alley as his body fought frostbite and death. He pounded on the brothel's back door.

After a moment, the madam peered out, spied him, and opened it. "Good god! You're frozen, Monsieur! Come inside."

Bartholomew kept his eyes down. "Non." He wanted to

take her hand, enter her house, and seek release. But the soul's residue was too dark, too dangerous. "The task is done. Stable the horse."

"Yes, of course."

"How is Iona?"

Georgine's heavy silence answered his question. He squeezed his eyes shut and swallowed regret as she replied, "The physician said an aorta had been nicked."

"Have the police come?"

"No. He's reporting it as heart failure due to defect." She shivered. "Come inside."

He shook his head and stepped back as she reached for him. Their eyes met. The madam's widened. She retreated as her soul cringed.

He closed the door between them. He would walk until his rage was reduced to a roar. His matches and cigarettes were frozen, his hands too cramped and shaky to light one anyway. He scrubbed his palms over his face, knocking frost from his beard.

Iona. Her suffering was palpable. He still tasted her terror and felt the attacker's mania.

Frostbite numbed his fingers and face. Blisters knifed his feet with every step. They were welcome agonies, yet they couldn't block the flood of atrocities spilling through Bartholomew's brain. Even Seattle's sleeping populace tortured him. Dark and violent nightmares, visions of suffering, fear, and loneliness drifted from the minds of desperate and dispossessed people.

He wandered past downtown's brick and stone buildings, through neighborhoods lined with Victorian and craftsman homes, and followed the snowy shores of Lake Union until he reached a low promontory where an enormous gasworks plant was being erected. There he sat upon the frigid brown grass and held his face in his cramped hands.

Mon Dieu, Iona. Bartholomew couldn't escape her suffocating terror. It was foremost of the memories he'd inherited from her attacker.

But the Catcher had other intentions for her troubled aesir. *"Don't stop, Bartholomeus. You must return home."* She set him on a direct course toward a large, gray manor surrounded by woods and occupied by a butler, a governess, and a sleeping girl.

He knew its rooms, its furnishings, and its occupants. His mind lingered on the closed door at the end of a long hallway. Behind it slept Matilde. Once again, his heart slowed to match the steady rhythm of hers as her soul reached out to ensnare him, its sweet song so familiar, so powerful. It tuned his discordant spirit and quieted his rage.

Home. Matilde.

The Catcher's soul within him surged, discontent to lose her domination and this opportunity. *"Bartholomeus, free me now. Help me capture that deranged soul before it attacks again."*

Compelled by his ancient mistress, Bartholomew ran. The Catcher's fire warmed his soul. His soul warmed his muscles. He gained speed and power as he neared the house.

He charged up the gravel driveway, onto the front porch, and stopped before the carved front door. He pressed his palms to its cold wood. He stared at the Roman eagle marking him as a warrior and a fallen hero. Too afraid of himself to go inside and too driven by the Catcher to retreat, he pushed away from the door. He circled to the back yard and threw a rock through Mr. Vernon's third-floor bedroom window.

After a moment, the butler opened an unbroken pane. "Have you gone mad, Monsieur?"

"Get down here and fight me!" Bartholomew's hands formed trembling fists.

A light came on in two other windows. The screech of wood on wood filled the night as Matilde opened one. "Monsieur? What's happened?"

Bartholomew snarled, "Shut that window and stay in your damned room!"

Her eyes widened. She slammed down the sash as Mr. Vernon stalked around the corner of the house from the kitchen door wearing trousers and wrapping his hands.

"You should not have returned home."

"Don't tell me what I can't do, you mouthy bastard."

"Mrs. Henderson is armed and has barred Matilde's door." Mr. Vernon pointed at Bartholomew. "This is the worst I've ever seen you, sir." His expression was grim as he added, "So let's beat the devil out of you." He threw the first vicious punch.

The two pugilists fought like madmen. They crashed through hedges, tore up the wintered flowerbeds, and shattered ceramic planters. They slipped on icy cobblestones, bloodied each other from fist to face, and stained the snow red. Every blow eased the blackness in Bartholomew's mind, but it wasn't enough. And when he finally knocked out Mr. Vernon with a right hook to the man's jaw, Bartholomew straightened, wiped blood from his nose with the back of his hand, and charged toward the house.

The drawing room doors yielded to his shoulder. Something shattered on the floor as he thundered into the hallway and up the stairs. He stopped upon the second floor landing to straighten his tie and suck the blood from his teeth.

"Matilde, if you don't come out now I will drag you out by your hair." *Whose venomous voice is this?* he wondered.

"You may converse *civilly* with your ward from behind this locked door," Mrs. Henderson replied from the girl's bedroom. "If you attempt to come through it, I will shoot you, Monsieur."

"Shut your mouth or I'll shut it for you, woman."

"How dare you speak to her in this manner?" Matilde snapped. "How dare you come to the house and injure Mr. Vernon?"

For the third time that night, Bartholomew broke through a door. He was stopped upon the threshold by the muzzle of Mrs. Henderson's rifle. He forced it upward as she pulled the trigger. Ceiling plaster rained down upon them. He wrenched the weapon from her hands. The gun shattered the window on its way into the rear yard.

Mrs. Henderson stepped back to shelter Matilde.

The girl shouted, "You promised to protect me, but now you're threatening all of us! You monster! If you want a fight, I'll give you one!"

The governess held her arms out. "Do not provoke him! You cannot win!"

"Yes, I can. I know how he fights." Matilde pushed past her governess and brandished a filleting knife.

Bartholomew stepped back and stared at his ward, at the blade in her hand. *Merda.* He'd been so certain she'd stopped hiding weapons.

"*Give me the girl's form,*" the Catcher commanded. "*We must stop Famine and her monsters.*"

"Monsters," he muttered.

Matilde had called him a monster.

A monster had hacked apart Iona.

"*Kill her, Bartholomeus.*"

He looked down at his shaking fists. "Non-non-non." It was the Catcher. She was using the murderer's power to drive his frenzy.

Something struck the back of his skull. There was blinding pain. He turned. Mr. Vernon held the Winchester like a bat. The butler swung again. More pain followed, and the floor and unconsciousness came at Bartholomew.

22

WESTERN UNION TELEGRAM
January 9, 1903
C. Vernon, Gen'l Delivery

Barnes and two men in Chicago. Maybe more.
Will confirm.
JHB

Obietnica thundered past Thomas as the young man strode up the white gravel driveway. Bartholomew had given his gelding free rein and encouraged him to go full-tilt all the way home from Iona's burial. It had been a short, horrible event full of lies and half-truths for the sake of her mother and brother. The weather mirrored the solemnity of the affair with a slate sky and a pissing sort of drizzle. And the telegram in his pocket did nothing to improve the day.

Like a jockey, Bartholomew rode low over the saddle, crop in hand, indifferent to the splatter of mud coating the horse and himself. As he passed Thomas, he straightened, reined Obietnica back to a canter, and circled across the wide lawn, slowing the snorting gelding to a walk. He slipped from the saddle as he came abreast of the young man.

Thomas doffed his wet black cap. "Good afternoon, Monsieur." He wore a gray sack suit.

Ten months had passed since the night he was banished from Bartholomew's property. Gone was all the softness from the young man's features, and though he didn't match Bartholomew in height, he was as broad across the chest, and his hands and face were weathered by long days spent loading and unloading ships on Seattle's wharves.

"What brings you back to us, Thomas Green?" Bartholomew fell in stride with him and they passed into the shadows of the side portico.

Mr. Vernon emerged from the mudroom as they reached the stairs. He took Obietnica and accepted the telegram from Chicago. Reading and frowning, he nodded at Thomas then led the horse around the house to the stable.

"I came to thank you for helping me stay on the right path, sir. I've been granted admission into St. Joseph's Seminary School in New York."

"I know." Bartholomew opened the mudroom door and fetched the bootjack. "I've already paid for your housing and tuition." He wedged his heel into the jack and slipped his right boot off, followed by the left one.

Thomas cleared his throat. "I'd almost given up hoping for the opportunity. I didn't really think you'd take the chance on me." He twisted his hat around his right hand but didn't shy away from Bartholomew's scrutiny. "I wish I had more to offer than just my gratitude, sir."

"I have faith you will do all within your power to not disappoint any of us, Mr. Green."

"That's my intention. I cannot see how following God's ways can mislead me."

Bartholomew nodded. He wouldn't say anything to ruin the young man's resolve, though he couldn't agree with that assessment of God. "I wish you great success in this new endeavor." He descended the three steps and proffered his hand. The young man took it in a firm grip.

"Thank you, Monsieur." Thomas donned his wool cap to block the January rain. "Will you give my regards to Mr. Vernon, Mrs. Henderson, and Miss Matilde?"

"Of course." Bartholomew studied his wide back as the young man turned away. He glanced into the house. "Wait. Will you come in? I'm certain Matilde will wish to say farewell in person."

Thomas faced him and ducked his head. "Yes, sir. I'd like that."

"Go around to the front door. Mrs. Henderson will let you in." Bartholomew closed the door and took in the state of his clothes. Mud everywhere. "Mrs. Henderson?" he called.

A moment later she appeared in the kitchen. "Gracious, you are a site, Monsieur."

"Oui, and we have a guest. Thomas Green is waiting at the front door. Please show him into the parlor."

"Thomas? I— Yes, sir."

"Where's Matilde? I'll change clothes then will bring her to visit with him."

"She's in the sewing room."

"Merci." He stripped off his gloves.

Mrs. Henderson surveyed him. "Do try not to get mud all over the house."

He shrugged out of his black frock coat. "Shall I undress here for you?"

Her expression soured. She threw her towel at him. "Honestly, Monsieur!" She pivoted and marched from the room.

He looked around and scowled. Where were his house shoes? He'd left them in the mudroom before departing for the funeral. Barefoot, he retreated up the back stairs to his bedroom. Perhaps Mrs. Henderson had put them away.

He washed his hands and face, and dressed while the housekeeper settled Thomas. He checked his closet. Still no sign of the black leather shoes.

Matilde was hemming a dark blue skirt when he paused in the sewing room's doorway.

Without interrupting her stitching, she glanced up. "I thought I heard you stomping up the stairs."

He stepped into the room. "You have a visitor."

Her brows arched. "*I* do?"

"Thomas Green is in the parlor."

She stopped, her hand in mid-stitch. "Thomas is here? You let him in?"

"Oui. And you're keeping him waiting."

"I—? Yes, you're right." She set the skirt aside, stood, and glanced down at herself. "But I'm not dressed for a visitor."

"It's Thomas, not the President. You look fine." She did look quite presentable in a magenta day dress over a high-collared, moss-hued shirtwaist.

She huffed a sigh and fussed with her hair as she followed him to the foyer. Once there, however, she paused and stared at his feet. "Where are your shoes?"

"Not where I left them this morning." He strode across the foyer and opened the parlor door for her.

Thomas popped up from the cream-colored velvet sofa. "Miss Matilde, how have you been? Well, I hope."

"Hello, Thomas." She strode into the room and offered her hand. "I've been well. Thank you."

He clasped her hand with both of his. His face relaxed into the wide grin that had become so familiar, and he was a boy again; the one who'd befriended her by discussing crows and juggling potatoes.

Her smiled matched his. "Please sit." She gestured to the sofa. "Will you stay and visit for a few minutes?"

"A few. If I'm not keeping you and Monsieur from anything?" Thomas looked at Bartholomew.

"Non, but I hope you will excuse me for a moment. I've misplaced my house shoes. I don't mean to be unsociable."

"Of course, sir."

He stepped from the room, leaving the door open behind him. He paused in the foyer, not intending to eavesdrop but unwilling to go far. He considered his feet.

Where are those damnable shoes?

Matilde's voice carried to him. "I'm surprised to see you here."

"I'm surprised to still be here," Thomas replied. "I more than expected your guardian to run me down when he came charging up the driveway on Obietnica."

She laughed. "He knows how to instill fear in a man's heart."

There was a pause. "What happened to your cheek, Miss Matilde?"

"My cheek? Oh, that. I was sparring with Monsieur. He caught me with a wicked left hook. I forget he's ambidextrous."

"Sparring? He *struck* you?"

"Yes, of course. How do you think I learned to fight?"

Mrs. Henderson appeared in the hallway from the kitchen. "Are you searching for these, Monsieur?" She held his shoes.

"Oui. Where were they?" He slipped them on. "I thought I left them in the mudroom this morning."

"You did. I brought them into the kitchen so they would not be cold when you returned."

He scrunched his toes. The shoes were warm and cozy. "That was good of you. Merci." As her attention strayed to the open door behind him, Bartholomew murmured, "Remain close. He's been accepted into the seminary and is off to New York."

She met his gaze. "Oh, dear."

He pivoted and returned to the parlor as Matilde asked, "Where are you going?" to Thomas. Bartholomew stopped in the doorway and clasped his hands behind his back. If they noticed his presence, they didn't care as neither of them acknowledged him.

"New York City, Miss."

"I see." She looked down at her hands. They were folded together in her lap, her fingers interlaced, her knuckles white against her skin. "Did you receive your acceptance?"

"Yes. St. Joseph's Seminary School. I'll be a priest when we meet again."

She looked out the window. "A priest. I'll have to call you 'Father.' That's a strange thought." Her attention returned to her friend. "Will you write to me?"

"Sure." He cleared his throat. "I, ah, I never apologized for what happened."

"There's no need."

The young man's voice rose and he leaned toward her. "There is, Miss. There is. I made a mistake. I shouldn't have pressured you to leave the house that night."

She bit her lip. "Thomas—"

He shook his head. "Please let me say this, Miss Matilde."

"All right."

He wrung his cap like a wet towel. "You don't have to forgive me. I'm quite certain Monsieur never will. I frightened and endangered you and I don't think that deserves to be dismissed so easily. I need to make amends, though I'm not sure how. But, someday, I hope to make it up to you."

Her chin lifted and her shoulders squared. "Thomas, I was more frightened of myself than I was of those boys. And I'm responsible for my own actions. You credit yourself with too much influence over me. I wanted to defy Monsieur. You simply provided the opportunity." She stood and he rose as well. "So I, too, owe *you* an apology and a promise to make amends in the future." Matilde stepped away from him and her tone dropped as she added, "But I believe this separation is for the best."

"Oh. Maybe so." Thomas retrieved his cap from the sofa. He cleared his throat and proffered his hand. "Well, goodbye, Miss Matilde. I'll let myself out."

She stared at his hand then returned his handshake. "Goodbye, Thomas. Study hard and do well."

Bartholomew stepped from the room and let the young man out of the house. He offered Thomas his hand. "Goodbye, Mr. Green. I wish you success."

Thomas shook his hand. "Thank you, Monsieur. Goodbye."

The patter of rain accompanied the crunch of gravel as Thomas Green trudged up the long driveway toward the road. Matilde's sobs carried into the foyer. Bartholomew kneaded the back of his neck as Mrs. Henderson closed the parlor door.

PART THREE

23

WESTERN UNION TELEGRAM
February 10, 1903
C. Vernon, Gen'l Delivery

Twelve men travel west from Chicago.
F and E in NYC.
JHB

IN THE SMALL, STONE TOWER'S DIM LIGHT, THE CATCHER'S *soul flared orange beneath her olive skin. "My fate ends today, but yours carries onward, Bartholomeus."*

"You cannot surrender to Famine." He blinked dust from his eyes and glared at her. "If your fate ends, so too does the world's."

"I am not surrendering. Draw your gladius and free my soul from this body, Aesir."

"Suicide? To what end?"

"Within you dwells a fragment of my spirit. It will guide

you to my next vessel. Find that body and imbue it with my soul."

"Give up your power?" He shook his head. *"Summon the Guardian into me, so I can protect you."*

"Not in this form. It is too dangerous."

"If my form is so objectionable, why didn't you kill me a fortnight ago?" He crossed his arms. *"Why make me your aesir?"*

Realization dawned on the Catcher's face. "Not your form, Bartholomeus. Mine. You are the penumbra. To summon the Guardian now would be to condemn all of the world."

He clenched his fists. *"The penumbra bears great weight with you and Famine, yet I still know nothing of it."*

She studied his face as if searing his visage in her mind. Just when he thought she would offer no explanation, she said, "Penumbra means almost shadow. The point at which shadow and light blend."

The ground rumbled beneath their feet. Dust rained down from the tower's ancient walls. "Three of the Horsemen are unrepentant evil," she continued, *"but the fourth, Conquest, bears another name—Righteousness. The penumbra is the vessel meant to contain him. The fourth Horseman will become either the world's conqueror or the world's hero."*

Bartholomeus clutched the stone wall. Cold seeped through his tunic and wrapped around his rib cage to seize his lungs. He shook his head. "You are mistaken."

"Should Famine gain the power to summon her brothers, Conquest will possess you. But if your Catcher summons the Guardian into you, he will arise as Righteousness and bring an end to this war."

He seized her arm. "So summon the Guardian!"

She shook her head. "I am the Catcher, but I am not your Catcher. She must be of your making, and she must willingly bind you to her."

More dust rained down upon them. The rattle of bones carried above the howling wind beyond the tower's crumbling walls. Famine's army of cadavers was upon them.

Bartholomeus groaned and seized the Catcher's wrist. "We're out of time." He yanked open the rickety door and pulled her toward Hibernia's ragged cliffs.

The vibration of the army's thunderous approach rattled his bones. A thick fog enveloped the black shale cliffs, hiding their enemy's approach and settling a dank blanket about him. The wind whistled around and past the inlets, an eerie tune that set his teeth on edge. He dragged the Catcher headlong toward an unseen doom. The fog hid the cliff's edge, but he moved with unerring steps.

"Why are you running?" She fought his grip. "I've told you what you must do."

"Not yet. I have too many unanswered questions."

A mass of dark gray silhouettes thundered through the fog toward them. He jerked her to a run.

The clatter and clack of a thousand bones became percussion to the whistling wind. Famine's soulless army had them because the Catcher had embraced this trap and ignored his warning. The enemy charged behind them, their figures distorted by curling morning mist, their line reaching out to ensnare its prey.

Bartholomeus held the Catcher's wrist as they ran along the cliff edge. He hoped to slip around the cadavers' closing ranks.

But it was impossible.

Pale sun broke through the fog. He stopped. They stood

mere feet from the ledge. "We should not have come here." Steel scratched wood as he drew his gladius. He stepped between his mistress and Famine's undead army, the sword raised and ready.

The Catcher gripped his arm. "Aesir, all souls are lost if she consumes my spirit. You must destroy this body!"

At their heels, a dizzying precipice plunged to the grey ocean below. Before them stood a horde of insatiate cadavers.

Famine pushed through the ranks, triumph ringing in her voice. "Bind the Catcher. I want her soul."

Bartholomeus turned his head toward the Catcher. "Forgive me. I will summon you, again. I promise."

She touched his cheek. "There is no wrong to forgive, Aesir."

He pivoted. He swung his sword. Sunlight glinted on steel. His mistress, head severed from spine, plunged down, down to the crushing gray Atlantic.

Bloody gladius striking like an asp, Bartholomeus charged into the swarm of cadavers as Famine bellowed her rage. His blade cleaved heads and limbs as he cut a wide, unerring swath through the inhuman horde. He was bent upon the destruction of the creature at its center, the monster who'd brought him a lifetime of suffering.

The rattle and clack of cadaver bones couldn't overcome her shrill commands. "Stop him! Catch him! Bring me the aesir!"

His ferocity was not enough to turn aside the enemy wave as they trampled their fallen brothers and sisters to reach him, overwhelm him, capture and hold him for their mistress.

They dragged him through the mud and blood. They made him stand before her. His hands, arms, and feet were bound, and still they kept their claws upon him as she circled.

"*There's a piece of you within me, Bartholomeus.*" She stopped before him and wielded a small, thin blade. "*And I promise I will never let you go.*" She gestured to her offspring. "*Put him on his knees and hold him fast.*"

The weight and power of the cadavers forced him down. They grabbed his hair, arched his head back, and held him as her knife danced closer and closer to his face.

"*Now you will see the error of your ways. Aesir.*"

Bartholomeus roared as she carved out his left eye. He strained to escape. Tears and blood coursed down his cheeks. The cadavers forced open his other eye, so he could not avoid seeing as she placed the orb upon her tongue and savored her prize.

Afterward, tender as a mare with a newborn colt, she stroked his head and licked his face clean. "*Hush, Bartholomeus. Your immortal body will reconstruct your eye.*" She pressed her forehead to his and whispered, "*But you will never forget this pain.*"

"MONSIEUR!" A voice that didn't belong was calling through the haze of agony and horror. "Monsieur, please! You must awaken."

Bartholomew opened his eyes to his dark room and Mrs. Henderson shaking his shoulder. "Oui, oui. I'm awake." He grimaced and pushed her hand away. "What is it?"

"Miss Matilde has left the house."

Tendrils of nightmare clung to his mind and slowed his comprehension as the governess spoke.

"She had another night terror, walking the room and arguing with someone in that foreign tongue again."

Now he was awake. "Where is she?"

"Mr. Vernon has gone after her. She ran into the woods."

Koorva. "Fetch my trousers."

She obeyed and brought his heavy boots, as well, then followed her master as he descended the stairs. "Out the kitchen door and into the woods through the—"

Bartholomew's raised hand silenced her.

He stepped into the yard. Pale, frosted lawn crunched beneath his boots. February's frigid wind stung his face and scrubbed away his ward's tracks. "Stay here. Prepare coffee for Mr. Vernon and a warm bath for Matilde. I will retrieve her." His words steamed, billowed, and were stolen by a hard gust.

"Wait, sir, let me fetch you a lantern."

Ignoring her, Bartholomew crossed the yard, went through the open gate, and disappeared into the woods. He didn't need light to find Matilde.

"Miss Matilde, where are you?" Mr. Vernon had headed straight into the copse that paralleled the property. But that wasn't where she'd gone. Matilde was following the footsteps of memory—Bartholomew's memory—and taking an arching path to the west toward the bluffs.

Ignoring the bite and scratch of alder branches and pine needles, Bartholomew plunged into the dark forest. The sweet song of Matilde's soul led him. He knew it almost as well as his own. In a crowd of hundreds, hers sang the purest notes to harmonize with the Catcher's song and tune its discordant strains within him. With the previous Catcher-incarnate, the song had never been so pure. And when he was away from his ward, dissonance returned to his soul.

He dodged trees and logs. He skirted a frozen marsh and struggled up an icy rise, spurred on by Matilde's frightened, fluttering heart.

When he finally spied her white gown against the dark night, she was walking not two feet from a wind-scrubbed ledge.

He charged down the slope and yanked the sleeping girl away from danger. They tumbled to the ground. Matilde gasped awake. Bartholomew's body slid across the icy brown grass toward the cliff. He scrabbled to stop his momentum. Roots yielded. Leaves slipped through his fingers. At the last moment, he snagged a bare, woody bush and jerked to a stop. His right foot found purchase. His left foot found air. He breathed out relief.

"M-m-m-ons-s-s-ieur?" As if her body suddenly realized its circumstances, Matilde began to shiver and her teeth chattered. "W-w-where are w-w-we?"

He crawled back from the cliff as she scooted away from the icy edge. They reached safer ground and he stood and shed his coat. "You went for a stroll in your sleep, Petit Oiseau." He helped her stand, wrapped the wool coat around her, and picked her up.

"I w-w-what?" She rubbed her eyes. "I d-d-don't remem-m-m-ber d-d-dreaming."

"That's for the best."

***

BARTHOLOMEW STOOD in the kitchen doorway, blowing steam from a cup of coffee and watching Matilde. She sat in the rose garden, bundled in a red blanket and basking in unexpected morning sun. Crows perched around her upon the low stacked-stone wall that hemmed the garden. He sipped, hissed cool air across his singed tongue, and glowered at the offending liquid. "Mrs. Henderson, did you go to Hades itself to brew this morning's coffee?"

"I'm sorry, Monsieur. It sat on the fire longer than is customary. I find that I'm a little fatigued and forgetful this morning."

"Understandable." His attention returned to his ward.

Her feet were the only victims of her early morning wandering. Once they'd begun to warm up, the pain of lacerated skin and nerves had brought her to tears.

Poor girl. Bartholomew blew on the coffee. He was familiar with the unique torture of wounded feet.

After he'd concluded she'd sustained no permanent injuries, he'd extracted thorns and splinters, applied salve, and bandaged her. She'd be an invalid for a week or two.

The girl held a crow's plume up to the sun and studied it, turning the feather this way and that to catch its variegated blacks. She saw a beauty in the creatures that Bartholomew had never appreciated. They'd only ever been his bane. Yet with her they were the most attentive companions. Two perched upon the back of the stone bench where she sat, intently watching her and ducking their heads as if in agreement with her observations as she maintained a lopsided conversation.

Even more astounding was the one sitting at her right shoulder, diligently plucking twigs and pine needles from her tangled, golden hair. Matilde insisted the bird was Edgar, the crow from the *Overland Flyer*. Its unusual white wing certainly supported her claim.

Mr. Vernon limped into the kitchen. "I've always thought those birds were thieves at best, harbingers of doom at worst."

"They're quite like humans, but I've never known them to display such affection toward anyone." Bartholomew sipped his coffee. More of the black birds winged into the yard. "Did last night's foray into the cold aggravate your rheumatism?"

The old fighter shrugged. "Nothing a warm Epsom bath won't relieve."

Mrs. Henderson, coffee cup in hand, peered out the window. "Another night terror. They're occurring more frequently."

"Oui."

"And the crows' numbers tripled last year," she added.

Mr. Vernon joined them at the window. "You're running out of time, sir." He nodded toward Matilde. "Both of you."

Bartholomew took a gulp of coffee. He'd dismissed the connection between his dreams and Matilde's as more an irritant than a danger, but the last four hours—no, four *weeks*—proved neither of them had the luxury of ignorance.

The Catcher would not be denied.

His cup clunked on the windowsill. He looked from Mr. Vernon to Mrs. Henderson. "I need you to be strong for her, as you were last night. That was merely a skirmish. This war will grow far more savage before it's won."

Mrs. Henderson replied, "We are dedicated to your cause, Monsieur."

Mr. Vernon gripped his arm. "We will remain strong for both of you."

Bartholomew bowed his head. "Merci."

Mrs. Henderson considered Matilde. "Poor thing. If only you could heal her feet."

"Regrettably, I cannot." His soul would sever Matilde's spirit from her body and open her to the Catcher. Bartholomew wasn't prepared to sacrifice his ward's life. Not yet. "Mr. Vernon, have our associates settled in Los Angeles and Vancouver?"

"Yes, sir. And San Francisco reported all's quiet."

Bartholomew said, "But Famine's troops are moving westward."

Mrs. Henderson eyed him. "Soon your mad mistress will follow?"

The governess was worried. Understandably. Bartholomew retrieved his coffee cup. "Oui. The leash restraining Famine is fraying."

"What leash?" the governess asked.

"Matilde."

"What?" his companions asked in unison.

"Famine knew I'd never condemn a child. She, too, waits for Matilde to reach adulthood. She intends to be present when I summon the Catcher." He sipped his coffee. "Time loves no one."

Mrs. Henderson topped off her cup. "But Chicago. She tried to stop you."

"Of course. I'm easier to control when I'm shackled at her side. Because she failed to capture me that day, our escape and the Catcher's freedom remains a possibility. That is something Famine cannot abide."

"Should we leave?" the governess asked.

"Only if they come to Seattle. Only if Matilde isn't ready."

Mr. Vernon said, "You should tell her, Monsieur."

"I agree." Mrs. Henderson nodded.

"Perhaps." Bartholomew crossed the kitchen to the mudroom and went outside to join his ward.

A late winter sunrise painted the horizon fuchsia. But night's purple shadows clung to the far end of the yard and stars still littered the western sky. The stone wall stood out in stark contrast to the dark woods beyond it. Crows perched upon its length and it resembled a line of broken teeth in a black maw.

Hissing and grumbling as he approached, the birds arched their wings and hopped out of his path. One snapped at his trousers. It was only his respect for Matilde that prevented him from punting the menace across the yard.

"Be polite," Matilde scolded them. "Monsieur is my particular friend."

"Merci, for coming to my rescue. Your guards are fierce."

As he sat beside her the birds left the back of the bench. They winged into the trees and the rest of the murder opened a space around Bartholomew and Matilde. In their wake was a scattering of feathers.

"Monsieur, may I impose upon you to gather the fallen feathers?"

"Certainly." When finished, he handed her a dozen quills.

"Thank you." She fanned them out on her lap, sorting by size.

"What do you plan for them?"

"A mask. Don't you think that would be lovely?"

He pulled his sestertius from his waistcoat pocket and watched her as he flipped it across his knuckles. "Not a hat?"

"No," she murmured, her focus intent on the plumage. "A disguise."

He palmed the coin and lit a cigarette.

She picked a white quill from her assortment. "Last night was another one for the devil."

He nodded. "The devil, indeed."

They sat in quiet companionship as he rolled the coin and smoked. A few of the braver crows ventured closer, led by Edgar, who settled upon the back of the bench beside Matilde's shoulder.

The Catcher's crows were displaying great wisdom in keeping their distance. It was as if they knew Bartholomew would wring their scrawny, black necks if doing so would avenge his ward and himself. More glided across the lawn and dozens squabbled in the apple trees, making the limbs dance and sway.

"I'm sorry about your feet, Petit Oiseau."

She ran her fingers along the edge of the white feather. "Why? You're not at fault."

"It pains me to see you suffer." He glanced at her face and was rewarded with the most beautiful smile.

"Your concern puts me in the right mind to heal."

"Hmm." He stood. "Rest and do not catch a chill out here."

"I'm quite comfortable," Matilde replied. He took a few steps toward the house, pausing as she asked, "Do you suppose Mrs. Henderson would bring my lessons outside today?"

"I will ask."

"Thank you."

Edgar rasped and raised his wings. Bartholomew glanced at the bird. Its focus was on him. The crow ducked its head and sidestepped along the bench toward Bartholomew. It croaked and chattered as if lecturing him.

Matilde laughed. "He wants you to linger."

Edgar's companion crows took up his dialog. Bartholomew

surveyed the yard. They were addressing him, and they numbered in the hundreds. The white-winged crow snagged his sleeve with its beak and gave several tugs, then regarded him with unblinking eyes.

Bartholomew returned its scrutiny. "Whom do you serve?"

"What do you mean?" Matilde asked.

Bartholomew shook his head. A bare maple tree loomed over her. Its scraggly, gray branches reached down like boney fingers as an icy breeze swirled through the courtyard.

She would soon be an adult.

He frowned. *I can't delay this much longer.*

He pulled another cigarette from his case and cupped his hands around a match to light it. He inhaled the smoke and peered up at the tree for a few long moments then scanned the yard. Broken black branches littered the ground and served as makeshift perches for the massive murder of crows.

"There's a reason for the crows' interest in you, Matilde."

"Aside from the crackers I share?"

He gave a fleet smile. "Oui, aside from them." He sat beside her once more. "They led me to you."

"This morning?" Her brows rose.

He exhaled smoke. Wind carried it away in a blink. "Eight years ago."

Her eyes widened.

"I first saw you the evening before we spoke. I watched from a roof as you took a brick to Catherine Connelly's face because she had stolen Samuel's bread. It didn't matter that she was older and bigger and two boys stood with her. It didn't matter that she had blackened your eye and split your skull. You were determined to have your revenge."

She gaped at him. "You *saw* that?"

"I did. The crows that accompany you," he gestured around the yard with his cigarette, "are the eyes and ears of the Catcher."

"Who?" She stroked Edgar's glistening feathers.

"A hunter from the outer darkness. She's been tasked with capturing and imprisoning the Four Horsemen." Bartholomew took a long drag on his cigarette before continuing. "For centuries the Catcher has been unable to fulfill her duty for lack of a body in which to walk the earth."

"If she doesn't have a body, how can she be a hunter?" Matilde asked. Edgar nudged her hand. "How can she even exist?"

"She is a soul. Her last body was destroyed to prevent her power from going to Famine. It's my responsibility to furnish her with a new vessel."

Matilde stared at him. "I don't think I want to hear what you're about to say."

He squared his shoulders and looked at the sestertius. It was a token of his wife's faith in him. He pocketed the coin and faced his ward. "Matilde, you will become the next Catcher."

Wind whistled past the house and around the bare trees.

"All the training. All the lessons on strategy. All your scrutiny, demands, and caution." Her voice was hushed and halting. "All because *I'm* expected to catch the Four Horsemen of the Apocalypse?"

"With my help."

She stared into the distance. "How am I to do that?" She looked down at her hands. "I'm a girl, not a god." She opened her fingers. The white feather lay mangled upon her palm. "Why me? Why did you choose *me*?"

"I didn't." He flicked his cigarette into a pile of slushy snow and nodded at the crows. "They did. *She* did."

Matilde scanned the yard. "You mean the Catcher?"

"You were not a random choice. You sense souls." He held her gaze. "Do you know what a rarity that is?" She shook her head and he continued. "The search for you took fifteen hundred years." He caught her hands between his. "You *can* do this. You won't be alone. The Catcher exists to hunt the Horsemen. The Guardian," he touched his chest, "exists to protect her, and the Beacon is her guide. They are God's Apocalyptics. They were created to prevent the End of Days."

She looked from their hands to his face. "Do you want me to do this?"

How could he answer that? Bartholomew released her and stood. He scratched his chin and squinted into the dark woods beyond the wall. "When you were young, it was easier for me. This conversation was a distant eventuality. I told myself you were my responsibility but not my child." He'd grown fond of her when he'd vowed that he would not. "I don't wish for you to be unhappy, but I won't lie to you. You face suffering and struggle. There will be terrible choices for you to make. You will know fear. Pain. Brutality."

She swallowed. "You make it sound like a garden party."

"I've been to some terrible garden parties."

She smiled and gave a little laugh, though there was no gaiety in her eyes and the smile faded as quickly as it had arrived. "How will the Catcher stop the Horsemen?"

"She captures souls." Edgar cocked his head and Bartholomew returned the crow's regard. "Given the opportunity, she will capture theirs and return them to the outer darkness."

Matilde's fingers played across the fanned feathers on her lap as she watched him. "And how do I become the Catcher?"

"She will possess your body."

Her fingers stopped. "Possess? Like a demon?"

He gave her another fleeting smile. "Non. Such creatures are figments. The Catcher will act through you when evil is near."

She hugged herself. "But what will happen to *my* soul?"

"It will become part of the Catcher."

Her shoulders hunched as her hug tightened. "But will it find salvation? When I'm dead."

"There is no salvation. You know that."

"Will it be reborn then?" She bit her lower lip.

"After the Catcher has succeeded in returning the Horsemen?"

"Yes."

He hated seeing her distress, even more so because he had no way of easing it. "I don't know."

She shivered.

"Let's go inside," he said. There was so much more she needed to hear, but he was loath to share it. She wasn't ready to know the whole truth of her transformation. She wasn't ready to become the Catcher. The hardest part lay ahead and Bartholomew was content to leave it in the future, companion to his own terrible struggle.

Matilde shook her head. "Not yet. Please?"

The morning brightened and fuchsia turned blue as the sun rose. She studied the sky. Was she searching for God? "How do you know Famine?"

He lit another cigarette and filled his lungs with heat. He didn't want to discuss Famine or his childhood, but if not now, eventually. Matilde would persist until she extracted the information she wanted. Her tenacity was marvelous even if often it was his bane. He pushed up his sleeves and rubbed his thumb down the ladder of scars. "I was a boy when she made these. After my family was murdered I became her traveling companion and a ready snack when she was denied a full meal."

Matilde made a sad little "ugh," and stared at him. "Did she keep others that way?"

"Non."

The kitchen window squealed. Mrs. Henderson called to them. "It's cold, Miss, and you have not slept enough. Monsieur, please bring her inside."

"Oui, madame." He ground the cigarette beneath his heel and lifted her from the bench.

"Must I go inside?"

"Your governess has spoken. Some monsters even I will not face."

She sighed and put her arms around his neck. "Do Mrs. Henderson and Mr. Vernon know all of this?"

"They know what they need to know. They know you are meant to become the Catcher and I your Guardian."

"I see." She rested her chin upon his shoulder. "How long have you been separated from Famine?"

He crossed the porch. "Since I met you. She nearly caught us in Chicago."

"I know."

He carried her into the sitting room.

"Do you think she's vexed that you've been gone so long?"

He quirked a small smile at her as he settled her upon the wide forest-green sofa, taking care to not bump her feet. "I hope so." Bartholomew spread a peacock blue blanket over her lap, then regarded her with dark solemnity. "Matilde, by any means necessary we must defeat Famine and her cadavers. To lose is *unthinkable*. I've raised and trained you for this purpose. But I have not done so without regret for what you've lost."

"I understand."

Mrs. Henderson entered the room with tea, books, and paper.

Bartholomew left Matilde to her lessons. The replacement windowpanes and new French doors had been delivered and he helped Mr. Vernon install them. They repainted where they'd previously patched the bullet hole in the bedroom ceiling and Bartholomew climbed into the attic to pry the Winchester's bullet from the heavy beam in which it had lodged.

"I'm going to rest in my room, Mr. Vernon," he said as they descended the steep attic stairs hours later.

"Shall I fetch you for tea, Monsieur?"

Bartholomew shook his head. "Supper, please, unless Matilde needs me." He closed the door to his room, stripped off his waistcoat and tie, and toed off his shoes. He lay back on his bed and studied the gray shadows slashing across the map of the world.

Howling wind. An icy cliff. Matilde had come so close to death. "Derr'mo." He groaned and pressed his palms against his eyelids. "You love that girl, you damned fool." He had to accept it. She was the first person he'd loved since losing Aemelia and Lucius.

Lucius. Holding his infant son for the first time, Bartholomew had marveled at all the potential of the boy's future, all the wonder of the world yet to be discovered. Being a father had given him the strength to defy Famine's control when the Catcher had come to his home in Tripolis. Loving his wife and son had compelled him to reveal Famine's subterfuge.

He scrubbed his palms over his face.

His love would doom Matilde just as surely as it had destroyed his family.

"There must be a way to save her."

24

WESTERN UNION TELEGRAM
March 27, 1906
C. Vernon, Gen'l Delivery

Chicago unchanged.

MARCH TWENTY-SEVENTH BROUGHT BLUE, DAZZLING days. Content to escape the house after winter's long confinement, Bartholomew sat on the porch's top step. He stretched out his legs and tilted his face to the rising sun while Matilde slogged about the muddy yard, knocking slush from the twiggy bushes with a broom.

As if being reunited after many years absent, the resident crow family swooped the length of the lawn. They landed in the garden and hopped along with Matilde, poking at the bushes, burring, and clicking their pleasure, but she didn't chat with them.

Mr. Vernon had ventured downtown to fetch the mail and

any overnight telegrams, so Bartholomew stood and set to mucking out the barn and scrubbing the floor and walls. Many hands made lighter work as Matilde arrived and silently curried dried mud from the horses' coats and brushed their manes and tails. In the house, Mrs. Henderson beat the rugs and swept and dusted from top to bottom.

Upon the butler's return, they opened the windows, bundled up in sweaters and blankets, and settled in the warm kitchen while the house aired out.

"For you, Monsieur." Mr. Vernon handed Bartholomew a letter and two telegrams.

"Merci." Bartholomew scanned the first of them. "Good news. The last two of the twelve missing cadavers have finally been located in Quebec. Four remain in residence in Los Angeles, the two who crossed into Mexico haven't returned, and three were seen in Houston. The remaining three continue to trek through the Deep South."

"Misinformation wins again," Mr. Vernon remarked and turned away.

Bartholomew scanned the telegram from Chicago. "Wait."

"Sir?"

He displayed the piece of paper. "This is unsigned." The butler frowned. Bartholomew said, "Send a request for identification. Roll it down the line, all associates to report within forty-eight hours." He handed the cable back to Mr. Vernon. "It's likely operator error, but I want confirmation."

"I'll call it in immediately," Mr. Vernon said and passed Matilde a white envelope. "For you, Miss, from Thomas Green."

Her attention shifted from Bartholomew to her mail.

"Thank you." She ran her fingers over the address, extracted the letter, and scanned both pages.

Mr. Vernon's deep voice rumbled in from the hallway as he spoke with the telephone operator. "Put me through to the Western Union office in the Boston Block, please."

Bartholomew folded and unfolded the other telegram. Was there a problem in Chicago?

Mrs. Henderson's attention strayed from the fossils she'd arrayed upon a tray to Matilde's letter. "What does Thomas say of his third year?"

"He continues to enjoy Dunwoodie and is still teaching Latin through one of the local churches." Matilde read on silently, sipped tea, and gave a scant laugh. "It seems the interest in learning Latin among young ladies in Yonkers has grown rather significantly year over year since he began instructing."

Mrs. Henderson smiled. "Wishful thinking on their part." She separated a fossil into one of three groups on the tray and added, "I suppose that's one of God's strange ways."

Mr. Vernon strode past the kitchen doorway with an outgoing telegram in hand. The floorboards in the front hallway squeaked and the door latch clattered as the butler went out to wait on the road for a Western Union messenger.

Bartholomew's attention returned to Matilde. Thomas Green's unsecured knowledge of their location was galling, but he couldn't deny the pleasure she gained from their friendship. It was one of the few things that lifted the burden of knowledge from her shoulders now. In any case, the young man had no reason to connect *Matilde Anne Royce* to *Bartholomew Etienne Pelletier*. Indeed, Thomas had no knowledge of Bartholomew's identity, and that would have to ease his mind.

Matilde peered at her governess's tray. "Are those more shark teeth, Mrs. Henderson?"

"Yes. I now have a rare complete set from a sand tiger shark." She gestured toward the note as Matilde murmured her approval. "What else does the letter contain? Did he receive his Christmas gift?"

Turning to the second page, Matilde replied, "Yes. He says, 'Please give my thanks to Mrs. Henderson for the excellent gloves and scarf. They arrived with a bitterly cold ice storm. I was quite warm even as Deacon Campbell and I took our usual morning campus stroll.'" Matilde looked at her governess. "That's devotion, a stroll in an ice storm. Can you imagine?"

Bartholomew muttered, "Devotion or self-mortification?" as he opened the letter Mr. Vernon had given him.

"You're a beastly man, Monsieur." Matilde crumpled her envelope and threw it at him.

He swatted it away without glancing up. "Incorrect, Miss Royce. I am not a man at all."

She gave him a thin smile. "Well, Beast, Thomas Green sends you his regards and his thanks, once again."

"As he should," Mrs. Henderson murmured.

"Very good," Bartholomew replied. "When you write to him, Matilde, please ask that he not freeze to death before I have recouped my investment."

She shook her head. "I shall write to him of your pleasure at his success in his studies."

"Hmph." Bartholomew held up the letter. "Ladies, I am of the mind to take possession of my new automobile today."

That got their attention and questions filled the room.

"I purchased a Sunset Tonneau and it was delivered

yesterday from San Francisco. I think this is an excellent day to learn how to drive."

"Really?" Matilde leaned forward.

"Oui."

"Can we go now?"

"I'll hitch the team while you and Mrs. Henderson change your clothes. We'll leave when Mr. Vernon returns." Bartholomew pushed back from the table. "Adventure awaits."

AFTER A STOP at the Western Union office to fetch reply telegrams, Mr. Vernon drove them home, though not without a great deal of jouncing and skidding and some pushing from behind on the hills. Still, the butler had become an automobile enthusiast from the moment he'd settled into the driver's seat. Bartholomew, however, was not convinced yet, and Matilde pronounced Larissa's gait to be "far less bone rattling than this mechanical contraption."

The Sunset was parked in the carriage house and they hiked out to the bluff with a loaded picnic basket. A heavy bank of dark gray clouds filled the horizon, but there was time yet for food and relaxation. Their group settled in a small swale that afforded a view of the Sound but blocked the worst of the wind.

As they spread a blanket and unpacked a light lunch, Mr. Vernon protested Matilde's condemnation of the car. "It's not the vehicle, Miss, it's the lack of smooth roads."

"That may be so," Bartholomew conceded. "I foresee an age of automobiles and long stretches of fine roadways, Mr.

Vernon. Then, perhaps, Matilde will not judge the Sunset so harshly."

The butler nodded. "Where horse and carriage cannot go, soon the motor coach will."

"Mountains will fall," Bartholomew murmured and lit a cigarette. "History is trampled by progress without fail."

Matilde plucked a blade of grass and sandwiched it between her thumbs. "No one values the old things."

Bartholomew let a cloud of smoke drift from between his lips. "Indeed." He lay back on the blanket, tilted his bowler over his eyes, and rested his hands on his stomach, the cigarette smoldering between his fingers. Beside him, Matilde blew gently against her thumbs to make the grass sing as Mrs. Henderson set out the picnic.

After they'd dined on cheese, cold meats, and scones smeared with the last of Mrs. Henderson's excellent strawberry rhubarb sauce, the men hung paper targets at various distances.

Bartholomew produced his newly acquired Colt semi-automatic. "Come, Matilde." He pulled her up from the blanket. "Let's have some practice before that storm chases us back to the house." He waved his hand toward the patchwork of gray clouds that had swallowed the horizon and now battled the sun.

"We'll have to compensate for the breeze." She shoved golden wisps of hair back from her face. The wind had tugged them free from their pins and plaits.

"Ladies first." He handed her the pistol and a loaded magazine.

She curtsied. "Merci." She accepted the weapon as Mr. Vernon came to stand beside them. "I think I'll try for distance." She blew another stray lock of hair off her face. "And moving targets, evidently." She checked her grip, sighted, and fired. When she'd emptied the gun, she lowered it and frowned at the swaying target. "Curse the breeze. I don't believe those shots are well-placed."

"I'm sure it's a fine grouping, Miss." The butler eyed the distant paper.

"Thank you, sir. I've had the benefit of an obstinate though capable instructor."

"Some day you will thank me." Bartholomew accepted the gun and checked that its chamber and port were empty. He removed the magazine, returned the pistol to its holster, and gestured for Matilde to accompany him to the distant paper target.

"You handle guns as well as anyone, Petit Oiseau."

"Thank you. I enjoy target practice."

"That's evident. You're unafraid of weapons, which is good."

They retrieved the paper, hung a new one, and discussed the spread of Matilde's shots as they returned to the blanket. Once there, Bartholomew offered the gun to Mr. Vernon, whose speed and accuracy caused Matilde fits of jealousy.

"I will best you, sir, though it may take many years. But I am determined," she insisted as he laughed.

Mrs. Henderson took a turn but proclaimed her continuing preference for her Winchester rifle. "It makes a particularly fine bludgeon," she said and smiled to see Bartholomew's dour expression.

Sunlight winked and failed as the clouds swallowed the sky. Bartholomew squinted at them. "It seems our pleasant weather is fleeing."

"And so shall we," the governess said and began repacking their picnic. Bartholomew and Mr. Vernon fought the wind as it snatched at the blanket they were folding.

"I suppose so," Matilde agreed. "But now we are buoyed to endure April's caprice with the memory of these few beautiful days. May will bring flowers not a moment too soon."

"Brought by April showers?" Mr. Vernon asked as he fetched the picnic basket.

"Don't forget March, February, and January rains," Bartholomew said.

Matilde tugged her guardian's sleeve. "Thank you, Monsieur Mope."

He cocked his brow at her. "It wasn't *I* who played Mozart's *Requiem* all winter long, Mademoiselle Melancholy. That dirge isn't suitable for the winter months." He bent to stub out a cigarette in the dirt. When he straightened, she was watching him. He gestured for her to follow the butler and the governess toward the house, but she shook her head and asked, "May I have a few moments with you?"

"Certainly." He called, "Mr. Vernon, go ahead with Mrs. Henderson. Matilde and I will be along shortly." The butler nodded and followed the governess into the woods. Bartholomew offered his arm to Matilde. "We may get soaked if we linger."

She hooked her arm through his. "Neither of us is sweet enough to melt in the rain."

Bartholomew laughed.

They set off at a leisurely pace beneath the trees, branches chattering and swaying above them.

"Can we climb down to the beach?" she asked.

"Oui. But let's mind the tide." Bartholomew led her to a

path that wound down to the rocky shore alongside a small creek.

They crossed railroad tracks to reach the sand and Matilde found a smooth driftwood log upon which to perch. "I owe you an apology."

"Oh?" The log resembled the giant, curved rib of some long-extinct beast, and Bartholomew mused, *Extinct. That's something I should be.*

"I don't know that I offered a proper one after sneaking out with Thomas Green."

He shrugged. "I hadn't placed myself within your good graces that day, so I wasn't surprised when you left with him."

"But you were disappointed."

He studied her. "Perhaps."

"I was disappointed, too." She hugged herself. "I thought it would be a grand adventure, so I put Thomas's interests first. That was a mistake."

Bartholomew slipped his silver cigarette case from his pocket and lit another cigarette. He held a lungful of smoke for a moment then exhaled. "We all make mistakes, Matilde. What matters is that you've learned from yours." He considered the cigarette and added, "That's more than I can credit myself with."

She gave a little laugh, but it quickly died. "Thank you for saving Robert Grus."

He nodded. "It appears he and Micah learned from their mistake, as well." On the few occasions he'd encountered the young men downtown, they'd averted their eyes and hastened across the street. Robert's inexplicable shock of white hair called him out in a crowd.

The familiar sounds of crashing surf and crying gulls

replaced their conversation. Bartholomew stooped to dig a brown-and-white shell from the sand and gave her his find. "I've made mistakes with you, as well. I'm sorry for the times I've frightened you, and most particularly for every time I've struck you."

"But that's training, Monsieur. You owe no apology for teaching me how to defend myself."

"I feel that I do."

She shook her head. "How can I work with the Catcher and destroy cadavers if I'm not prepared to fight?"

Work with. He frowned. "Why have you avoided asking me about her?"

"I'm...not ready to know more." She shifted the shell between her fingers. "Strange turn. I've always pestered you for information and opportunity, haven't I?"

"What's changed?"

She scanned the horizon. "Perhaps, I've learned to trust your judgment." He stared at her long enough to make her laugh and repeat, *"Perhaps."*

A crow swooped down from atop the bluff, a black shadow against a charcoal sky. It circled them and gave a harsh alarm call. Another crow appeared, then another followed to swoop, circle, and caw.

Matilde watched them. "The crows are disturbed."

Bartholomew stood and surveyed the beach. "Something's amiss."

A steamship paralleled the shore close enough to identify passengers on her deck. A locomotive's whistle split the sky.

He grabbed her hand and pulled her behind a pile of fallen boulders at the foot of the cliff. "Cadavers." He stubbed out his cigarette, pressed his finger to his lips, and whispered, "Don't move." She obeyed, even as the birds' din grew and rain speckled the boulders.

His shoulders hunched. He swallowed a curse. Either the steamship or the locomotive carried a cadaver, possibly more than one. Matilde's hand tightened on his. Damn providence and slipshod judgment; he'd sent the guns with Mr. Vernon. He would've breathed easier if she'd been armed. But the art of evasion often was more desirable than confrontation—certainly so in this case as he had no confirmation of their enemy's whereabouts or numbers.

The train thundered past, its wind blasting them and its whistle piercing the air once more. Matilde released Bartholomew's hand and covered her ears. The steamer's horn answered as passengers waved at the passing locomotive.

Bartholomew sheltered her even after the train had disappeared around the curve of the bluffs and the steamer had rounded the shoreline. The weight of her tension and the growing cold of their rain-soaked clothes marked time's slow passage. Only after the crows' agitation had eased did he pull her up the path toward home.

"I thought cadavers couldn't travel in daylight." She trotted to keep up with his long stride.

"Hats, gloves, cloaks, hoods—all are adequate protection from the revealing sun." He gripped her hand and scanned the woods and beyond. "It's not their preference, but they will risk it if adequately compelled."

"Compelled? You think Famine has found us?"

They reached the stone wall. "If that was the case, we'd have a soulless army on our heels." The black iron gate squealed as he yanked it open.

Mr. Vernon emerged from the stable. "You took your time,"

he remarked as they reached him. "Mrs. Henderson's put out because supper's gone cold."

Bartholomew said, "A cadaver has arrived in Seattle."

The butler's expression darkened and his chin rose. "Where?"

"Via steamer or train. Fortunately, Matilde's crows warned us and I believe we avoided detection." Bartholomew clenched his right fist. "I dislike the proximity."

Mr. Vernon asked, "Shall I begin packing?"

Bartholomew considered the manicured grounds. His gaze came to rest on Matilde. He brushed his fingers down her cheek. A decade had passed. He nodded. "Time to leave, Mr. Vernon. Tell Mrs. Henderson and telephone for another Western Union messenger."

25

"Cold or not, the meal was quite good, Mrs. Henderson." Bartholomew set aside his fork.

The housekeeper inclined her head. She placed the evening newspaper beside Matilde and tapped an article. "Caruso will be singing on the Fifth of April, Miss."

"That's next Thursday." She scanned the paper. "But in San Francisco."

Mrs. Henderson collected their dirty plates. "Enrico Caruso. How wonderful it would be to hear that man's voice on stage."

"San Francisco?" Bartholomew asked.

Matilde passed him the paper and sighed. "Not Seattle. They get Caruso. We get cadavers."

He skimmed the article. "Then we shall go south to see *Carmen*."

She looked up, spoon poised as she handed it to her governess. "You jest."

"Never."

"How? I thought we were leaving."

"Oui. Steamer to San Francisco. But our overseas passage doesn't depart until next Friday, the Sixth of April. There's time to enjoy the opera before a long sail."

She smiled brightly and dropped the spoon onto the stack of dishes. "Thank you."

"You'll need a proper gown," he said. "Mrs. Henderson, you as well. If you ladies don't have something fitting, dresses will have to be obtained in California."

"Me?" the governess asked.

Bartholomew feigned surprise. "You do wish to hear Caruso, do you not?"

"Well, yes, of course. But I never dreamed of attending." She scanned the room and added, "There's so much to be done in such a short time."

He replied, "Much of it can wait until you return from San Francisco. We'll only take necessities, of course, but I'm relying upon you to settle this home's caretakers while Mr. Vernon and I relocate Matilde. I expect you'll rejoin us by the end of the summer."

Mr. Vernon asked, "You hope to return to Seattle in the future?"

"I do. We've a lot invested here." Bartholomew looked at his ward. "This is Matilde's home. I'm unwilling to abandon it as I did the Rye house."

Mrs. Henderson replied, "A good plan. And thank you for the opportunity to hear Caruso."

"Of course." He passed the newspaper to his butler. "Four tickets for *Carmen*, Mr. Vernon, the best available seating. And a suite at the Palace Hotel, please, with adjoining rooms for yourself and Mrs. Henderson."

The butler folded the paper. "And return travel for Mrs. Henderson. Will you be in contact with business associates while in the city?"

"Oui. I've some affairs to put in order before we leave America. Always wise to remind my representatives that I still exist. Please notify Susanna to expect us." He touched Matilde's hand. "You will accompany me on those calls. It's time that you become familiar with some of my business associates."

With a wide and wary gaze, she nodded. "Yes, Monsieur."

"Mrs. Henderson, be certain to assess Mr. Vernon's clothing needs. And I would like a new tuxedo."

"Not a frock coat?"

"Non. Perhaps it is time to dress *à la mode du jour*."

"Twenty years too late for *du jour*," she murmured.

He arched a brow at her. "You know I dislike change."

Matilde, who was looking from her guardian to the staff, cocked her head and asked, "What occasions such lavishness?"

Bartholomew turned to her. "Did you suppose I'd lost track of time? It's April. Eleven years ago you and I first spoke."

Mr. Vernon nodded. "I remember the night Monsieur brought you to our home in Rye. You were such a tiny thing."

"And filthy from head to toe," Mrs. Henderson added.

Matilde smiled. "It seems so long ago yet like yesterday." She faced her guardian and the smile disappeared. "Once again cadavers threaten us. And once again we're running. Why?"

Bartholomew's mood gained a sudden, sickening weight. "Because you're not ready to face Famine."

Mr. Vernon asked, "You believe this isn't a coincidence?"

"I don't believe in coincidences. The crows' numbers increase. The Catcher's sway strengthens. Now Famine's scout is here."

Matilde asked, "The Catcher's sway?"

"She may not occupy a body, but that doesn't make her helpless, Petit Oiseau. Her influence has caused my boorish behavior on more than one unfortunate occasion."

Matilde hugged herself. "Why didn't you tell me she's so monstrous?"

"Because you will command her." He touched her arm. "I will help you."

She poked her fork at the slice of opera cake Mr. Vernon set down before her. "I'll control her? But she's powerful, isn't she?"

"Quite." Bartholomew sat back. "That's why the strength of your soul is significant. It's another reason why it took fifteen centuries to find the right vessel for her."

She murmured, "The right vessel," and began to eat.

Bartholomew studied his ward. She was an ever-changing puzzle.

"Where's our next home?" she asked as Mrs. Henderson poured tea.

Bartholomew shook his head to the governess's offer to fill his teacup. "You'll learn that when we depart."

"Why the secrecy?"

A knock at the door summoned Mr. Vernon.

"Your safety comes first. Always," Bartholomew replied.

"Because the Catcher chose me."

"Because she *needs* you. We all do."

The butler returned and handed a note to Bartholomew. He read it. "Bon. Mrs. Green has agreed to become the caretaker of this house. She'll meet with you at ten o'clock tomorrow morning, Mrs. Henderson."

"Very good, sir."

Matilde said, "What great fortune for her."

"The fortune is mine." Bartholomew folded the note. "It's not a simple task to find someone I can trust to care for my property. But I believe Mrs. Green and her family will do a fine job and will benefit from the opportunity."

Matilde put down her fork. "I imagine they're quite cramped in that little house."

Bartholomew pushed his chair back from the table. "Are you finished, Matilde?"

She wiped her lips with her white napkin. "Yes."

"Dress for easy movement and secure your hair in a tight bun. You'll come with me tonight."

"Where?"

"To destroy the cadaver before he harms anyone or discovers us and confirms our location to his mistress."

Her chair screeched against the wood floor and she was gone from the room before he could complain about the sound.

Bartholomew deposited his napkin upon the table and pushed back his own chair. "We'll be gone much of the night, Mr. Vernon."

The butler nodded. "Tomorrow I'll finalize our international passage, as well as arrange for the opera and the hotel."

"Must you take her tonight?" Mrs. Henderson's voice was heavy. She pressed her hand to her throat.

Bartholomew stood. "She'll be safest with me."

"You know I've never approved of you using the girl."

"Using?" Unexpected ire threatened Bartholomew's reason. "Select your words more carefully."

"Mrs. Henderson." Warning deepened Mr. Vernon's voice.

"Keep my own counsel?" She looked from one man to the other. "I will not. You're endangering Matilde for your own benefit, Monsieur. This can only end poorly for her, just as it did for the last Catcher. Bringing that child into this affair was shameful."

"Tell that to the Catcher." Bartholomew grabbed the pile of dishes from his housekeeper's hands and stalked to the kitchen. The plates and silverware clattered into the sink. He flattened his palms against the gray slate counter and released irritation as the stone's coldness seeped into him. It wasn't Mrs. Henderson's attitude that provoked him so, it was everything. "Stinking, damnable cadavers and their bitch mistress."

Matilde appeared in the doorway, clad in a black dress, britches, and boots. Her green-plaid coat hung over her arm. "Who's Susanna?"

He straightened, smoothed his cravat and waistcoat, and faced her. "My associate in San Francisco."

"Yes, but who is she?"

He cocked his head. What exactly did she want to know? "The daughter of a woman who worked for me in Philadelphia. Many of my associates are from families that have aided this struggle for generations."

"Generations? I forget it's lasted so long."

"Because it's new to you."

She chewed her lip and glanced down the hall. "Mrs. Henderson still disapproves?"

"Of course and understandably. I appreciate her concern,

but she risks overstepping her place in this matter." Bartholomew gripped Matilde's shoulders. He held her gaze. "Are you ready to face a monster again, Petit Oiseau?"

Her regard was stolid. "More than ready."

"Très bien. Let's catch a cadaver."

ON BOREN AVENUE, Bartholomew and Matilde hid behind a dogwood hedge opposite a large, yellow boarding house. He was like a statue, watching, waiting, listening, silent. She alternated between spying upon the house and studying him. She shivered and shifted from foot to foot but didn't complain. Cadaver catching was tedious work, but patience and focus had kept Bartholomew alive for a very long time.

They'd walked downtown's streets for several hours before they'd sensed the cadaver's movements. But it hadn't been just one. Two cadavers had come to Seattle and led them to this location.

Rough, braided hemp scratched Bartholomew's fingers as he tucked his hand into his pocket. A Balearic sling was coiled there with several smooth, oval stones and a few rolled socks. He also carried a heavy, wedge-shaped boning knife in a sheath strapped to his belt.

Matilde pulled up her coat collar against the evening's relentless drizzle. "Are we catching and questioning them?"

"Interrogation is wasted on creatures that feel no pain. You're observing. I'm dispatching." He caught her wrist. "You will not engage them in any way. Is that understood?"

She held his gaze for a heartbeat then nodded.

The boarding house door opened and masculine laughter

filled the night as both cadavers emerged onto the porch, tugging on gloves. They weren't alone. Five mortals accompanied them, doubtless residents of the home. A deep noise escaped Bartholomew's throat. Now he had more than just Matilde to protect.

"Who are those men?" she asked.

"Innocents and inconvenience."

"What will you do?"

"Follow and figure out how to cull the cadavers from the herd."

They trailed the boisterous group into downtown, past brick and stone buildings. The only witnesses to their passage were their own reflections watching from the blackened windows of closed businesses. Falling rain shimmered in the glow of gaslights. The wet sidewalks reflected the light like black mirrors. When the men entered a tavern, Bartholomew and Matilde paused in the gray marble entryway of a neighboring building.

"What will happen if the cadavers see you?" Her voice echoed in the two-story, arched entry.

"They'll flee if they have any wits."

She eyed him. "Cadavers fear you?"

"You're the only creature who doesn't." He leaned against the cold wall and crossed his arms. "Stubborn or stupid?"

"You're not as scary as you think." She mirrored his posture. "What makes you such a threat to Famine's soulless killers?"

"Stubbornness and stupidity." He gave her a grim smile. "I've made it my life's work to destroy all of them."

"And I'm to understand you're quite accomplished at that?"

"I've had a great deal of experience."

"But you haven't done it while I've been with you."

"You don't know that." He reached out and pushed her wet blonde hair back from her face. "Matilde, this decade raising you has been a pleasant change for me. A break from the evil that marred my life for so long."

"For me as well, Monsieur," she murmured.

Suddenly, he needed her to know how much she meant to him. Bartholomew cradled her face between his hands and kissed her forehead. She smelled of honey and lavender. Everything was changing. She didn't realize to what extent, but he did. They stood upon the precipice once again, and he was determined not to lose her.

He stepped back. "Tonight we begin ridding the world of the cadavers that seek to ruin our pleasant existence."

She nodded. Her eyes narrowed and she turned toward the tavern. "Do you remember Mrs. Henderson's assassin bug?"

"Oui. Why?"

She glanced up at him. "Let's pluck the spiders' web." She slipped from their hiding place.

"Matilde," Bartholomew hissed. He grabbed for her, but her wool coat evaded his fingers as she hurried across the damp sidewalk.

She disappeared into the tavern as he reached its entrance. However, she re-emerged as he opened its door. Ignoring him, she scanned the street and crossed it. He stepped out of the doorway, leaned against the brick building, and hunched over as if lighting a cigarette. She paused on the corner. A moment later, the cadavers exited the tavern, spiders chasing a false fly. They strolled after as she skittered up James Street.

Bartholomew pulled the sling from his pocket and loaded a stone as he trailed them.

Koorva.

At mid-block Matilde ducked into a narrow alley. One cadaver followed her, but the other turned at the *crack* of Bartholomew's sling. A stone shattered the front of the man's skull and he toppled like a tower.

Bartholomew passed the fallen cadaver and strode into the alley as Famine's man reached Matilde. She stopped the bastard with the muzzle of her pistol.

"Don't fire," Bartholomew ordered her.

"What? Why?"

The cadaver knocked the gun away. He grabbed Matilde's throat and arm, yanked her against him, and faced Bartholomew. "This yours?"

Though the scarred brute towered over her, Matilde seized her attacker's wrist and pulled down, locking her elbows to her sides to prevent him from choking her.

"Release her." Bartholomew stalked toward them. He dropped the sling.

The cadaver sneered. "I don't know what your gambit is, but you've got the wrong muggins."

Bartholomew kept coming. He pulled the boning knife from its sheath. "Release her."

"I've got the jump here, mate. Back down or I'll slit her throat."

As the cadaver produced a jackknife, Matilde slipped beneath his arm, pivoted toward him, and twisted free.

Their enemy turned.

She leaped away.

Bartholomew thrust his knife into the cadaver's throat

until it scraped bone. The man grabbed his wrist, but Bartholomew didn't release the blade. "Wrong, *mate*. No one gets the jump on me." He intercepted the cadaver's jackknife even as he yanked his own blade across the soulless bastard's throat, cutting him from ear to ear. Like his companion, the cadaver collapsed. Bartholomew hogtied him with the long sling and stuffed a rolled sock in his gaping mouth.

He dragged the first cadaver into the dark alley. The body twitched as it began to reanimate. Bartholomew dropped it like a sack of rubbish. He glared at Matilde and snarled, "Keep watch."

"Why? You don't think I can stomach what happens next?"

Behind him fabric scratched fabric, leather scraped concrete.

"I *think* you need to watch the street while I behead these fools."

A bubbling breath.

Matilde's focus went past his shoulder.

Bartholomew pivoted and buried his knife in the standing cadaver's forehead. Once again the body toppled. "These bastards smell worse on the inside than on the outside." He yanked off his kidskin gloves and shoved them into his coat pocket.

Matilde swallowed. "Fine." She returned to the sidewalk and loitered just inside the alley.

Stupid.

Bartholomew flipped the cadaver facedown and repeatedly smashed the metal pommel of his knife against its vertebrae close to the skull.

Unnecessary.

He cut through the tendons, ligaments, and muscles that secured the skull to the spine, working his knife around and past the shattered vertebrae to free the head.

Risk.

The *crack* of brittle bones and *snap* of dried cartilage bounced off the wet alley walls.

The cadaver's existence ended when a dim spark shocked Bartholomew's hand. "*Zut,*" he cursed the sting. It was the fragment of Famine's power that had animated her soldier.

Smoking had dulled his sense of smell, an advantage when it came to beheading cadavers. But Matilde wasn't so fortunate. She gagged and covered her face with a blue handkerchief. "Merciful God, it stinks worse that the Five Points on a midsummer day."

Bartholomew snorted. His anger eased, marginally. He paused, gory knife in hand. "Rotting from the inside out since the day they died." He wiped the blade on the cadaver's waistcoat and returned the knife to its sheath. He straightened, stepped upon the cadaver's back, then grasped the head and twisted until it tore away from the shattered spine. "By sunrise they'll be dust and a stain." He tossed the head into a pile of rubbish then set to work on the second cadaver.

"Why do you behead them?"

"To be certain they cannot rise again." A bone cracked beneath his blade. "And I gain a sizable measure of satisfaction from the procedure."

When he was finished and the bodies were fairly disintegrated, he set off with Matilde toward the dark neighborhood where they'd left the car. Seattle slumbered and dreams swirled out from its populace. Love, hate, lust, fear, joy—so many emotions twisted, tumbled, and pulled him in every direction. It was impossible to block them. Impossible not to be poisoned by the cadavers' dark energy. Impossible to deny the sweet melody of his ward's powerful spirit as it danced around him and skipped across his soul.

Bartholomew stared ahead and swallowed anger and confusion. He needed a distraction. "You handled their dismemberment well."

"Foul monsters. I'll do that to every one I encounter."

He stopped. "Non. You will leave the cadavers to me." He raised his right fist. "And if you meet one with a mark like mine upon his right hand, you will run."

She looked from his tattoo to his face. "Who is he?"

"Ewan. Famine's right-hand man and the most dangerous cadaver. Do not provoke him. Run."

Her lips tightened into a straight line.

"Promise me, Matilde."

She nodded. "I promise."

They climbed First Hill in search of their white car, a strange tension between them. It crept up Bartholomew's spine and nestled between his shoulder blades.

"Do you think more are coming here?"

"I won't hazard a guess." He lit a cigarette and took a drag, held the smoke, and looked uphill at the rows of unlit houses. "Matilde, that unwarranted risk nearly cost your life."

She turned a steady gaze on him. "But it didn't."

"It was foolish."

"I would've shot him if you hadn't distracted me."

"You would've brought a crowd to that alley, forcing us to flee and leave the cadavers to return to Famine with news of our whereabouts."

"But—"

"You knowingly faced them without your guardian." His ire was growing again; the cadavers' foul energy didn't help.

"You said they needed to be separated from the innocents." Her tone hardened to match his.

"Which would have happened with time." He stopped and loomed over her. "I haven't protected you all these years so you can be reckless."

Her chin jerked upward. "I didn't think it was."

"You didn't *think*." He threw down the cigarette and ground it beneath his boot.

They reached the car and headed north toward a home they soon would abandon. Matilde kept her arms folded. Bartholomew ignored every daggered look she shot his way.

When they reached home and he'd parked the car in the carriage house, he faced her. "You are important to me, Matilde. Please remember that the next time you plan to risk your life."

Her eyes tracked him as he climbed from the car, came around the front, and opened her door. But she didn't move. "You care about me?"

He frowned. "Of course. Why would you think I don't?"

She looked down at her lap, smoothed the cotton fabric of her black skirt, and swallowed. "I thought...you were just raising me for the Catcher."

He rested his foot on the running board and studied her. Gone from her face was little girl softness, but vulnerability remained in the gaze she turned upon him. There was a plea within the blue depths of her eyes, a plea to give her connection and a reason for existing beyond just becoming a vessel for God's vengeance.

He took her hands. "You are my family, Petit Oiseau. I don't want to lose you."

"Family?"

"Oui." Bartholomew helped Matilde down from the car and steered her to the house. "Time for bed. It has been a long day for both of us."

26

THE GLOVE SHOP'S SALESGIRL SMILED. "THERE. I THINK that's much better, Miss, don't you?"

"Yes, much. Thank you." Matilde inspected the pale-pink silk opera gloves encasing her arms.

Bartholomew and Mr. Vernon sat in chairs beside the fitting counter as she and Mrs. Henderson tried on altered gloves.

April Fifth in San Francisco had dawned unseasonably warm and clear. They'd enjoyed Golden Gate Park, lingering in the Japanese Tea Garden and marveling at the Dutch windmill that rotated with the Pacific Ocean's breeze. They'd retrieved gowns, hats, shoes, and tuxedos that had been purchased the previous day and hastily altered overnight. Gloves were the last necessary item.

Bartholomew blew steam from a cup of coffee the salesgirl had brought him. "Did the concierge send a man to Susanna's apartment?" he murmured to Mr. Vernon.

"Yes, sir. I'll check for a message when we return to the

Palace." The butler picked lint from his dark-blue cutaway. "It's possible she's visiting her brother in Sacramento."

A pair of young ladies in wide, feathered Merry Widows circled the displays eyeing Bartholomew as thoroughly as the gloves, but he found no amusement in their insipid fawning. His attention hovered between the mystery of Susanna's silence, his ward's presence, and any possible threat.

"You may be right, Mr. Vernon. I'd forgotten her brother lives so close. Still, her silence is a sliver beneath my skin. She's always so reliable." He added, "I find it difficult to anticipate the opera's splendor with this question hanging over me."

"I understand, sir."

As the salesgirl boxed the gloves, Matilde turned in her chair. She considered the fawning ladies then her guardian. "I never realized how handsome you are, Monsieur."

Bartholomew nearly choked on his coffee. He swallowed and replied, "Beauty is in the eye of the beholder."

"Well, my eye finds you to be very attractive." With a sly smile she added, "As do many of San Francisco's women, I've noticed."

He opened his mouth to answer, but words escaped him. He took a gulp of coffee instead.

Mr. Vernon chuckled. "Cruel girl, you've left your guardian speechless."

She laughed with the butler then pointed toward the wide store window and a passing carriage beyond it. "Mrs. Henderson, look at those beautiful blood bays."

"A lovely matched pair." The governess wasn't watching the horses. She was eyeing Bartholomew. There was something in her expression, some cryptic message.

"You have something to say, Mrs. Henderson?" he asked.

She smiled and pushed her chair back from the counter. "Miss Matilde, have you decided how you wish me to style your hair for this evening?"

The girl stood and caught her governess's arm. "Yes, indeed."

Mr. Vernon settled the bill and they headed for the Palace Hotel. The flirtatious ladies stayed behind, evidently discouraged by their subject's disinterest.

As they strolled, Matilde described the elaborate hairstyle she had in mind for the opera. Bartholomew and Mr. Vernon followed, twine-tied boxes and brown-paper packages in hand.

For a woman who never hesitated to offer opinions and advice, the governess's smile had been downright cagey. Bartholomew wondered was was on her mind as they reached the hotel. He disliked that he couldn't decipher her expression.

As their party entered the Palace's lobby, Matilde craned to see every detail in its painted arches, ornate marble flooring, and glossy woodwork. "I'd forgotten the beauty of this hotel."

Mrs. Henderson smiled. "I don't believe you noticed when we last visited, Miss. Every one of us was exhausted from cross-country train travel."

"You're likely right." Matilde nodded. "And it's filled with interesting people."

Bartholomew gave her a sidelong glance. "Don't mistake rich for interesting."

With another shrewd smile, she said, "I suppose I've been spoiled living with a man who's both."

He shook his head. Whether it stemmed from the cadavers' defeat, his professed affection, or both, Matilde had lost the melancholia possessing her for the last three years. Rather than distressed by the prospect of leaving Seattle and becoming the Catcher, the girl flourished with the change, unmercifully so with the élan of youth driving her. Bartholomew didn't relish the prospect of trans-Pacific travel with a shipload of sailors and his spirited ward. This promised to be an arduous trip.

They waited near the elevators as Mr. Vernon checked for messages with the front desk. He rejoined them, shaking his head. He leaned close to Bartholomew and murmured, "Still no news of the missing Chicago associate and nothing from Susanna. I instructed the concierge to keep trying her."

Bartholomew grimaced. "Once we're settled again, we must investigate our man in Chicago. I want contact with his family."

"Yes, Monsieur."

A sleek-haired man with two women upon his arms glanced at Mr. Vernon as they strode past and remarked, "It appears that the Palace will permit any Jim Crow through their doors."

Mr. Vernon's hard expression said he'd heard the affront. Bartholomew set down his packages. "Sir? Do you expect I will tolerate the great insult which you have given to my friend?"

The man stopped and turned. He was trim, stylish, and appeared to be in his mid-thirties. He returned Bartholomew's glare with nary a blink. "A man may be judged with great accuracy by the contents of his billfold and the makeup of his ancestry. *Sir.*"

"And what is your ancestry? Did your kin hail from the Land of Imbeciles?"

The man sputtered. The lobby fell into an awkward silence as guests craned to see who would utter such abuse. His face in high color, the man pointed a finger at Bartholomew. "Look here, you cannot offer up such slander and not expect repercussions. I have in mind to trounce you right onto your foreign derrière."

That elicited chuckles from some, whispers from others.

Bartholomew addressed his butler. "Mr. Vernon, am I mistaken or were you not born to American parents?"

"In New York City. My mother was a school teacher. My father was a practicing attorney and a professor of law."

"And do you not hold a doctorate degree from Yale?"

"Two of them. I studied business and medicine."

"Well, I will not insult you by requesting that you reveal the contents of your billfold. But as you are in my employ, I don't doubt it holds far more currency than does this scurrilous gentleman's."

"How dare you speak to me with such disrespect?" the man snarled.

"I dare because I know a *gentleman's* mettle is determined not by the color of his skin nor the wealth of his holdings but by his character. And you have revealed your quality to be unworthy of Mr. Vernon's attention." The man stepped back as Bartholomew came forward. "As for trouncing, I don't recommend such an endeavor, sir. Unless you enjoy the taste of your own blood."

The elevator arrived. Bartholomew turned his back. "Good. Day." It took all his self-control not to beat the man senseless then and there as he retrieved the packages.

Matilde tucked her arm over the butler's forearm. "Come,

Mr. Vernon. Let's leave before that man's ignorance corrupts us all."

When the elevator door had hidden the reddened face of the man and the astonished expressions of his female companions, Mr. Vernon turned to Bartholomew. "Thank you, Monsieur."

"I detest that it had to be said. Racialism demonstrates an inexcusable lack of intelligence."

"Dolts," Mrs. Henderson remarked.

Matilde rested her hand upon Bartholomew's, covering his tattoo. "You're a good man, Monsieur."

He contemplated her slender fingers. "I'm pleased you think so, but Mr. Vernon's is the superior character."

Once in their suite, Matilde and Mrs. Henderson disappeared to spend the remainder of the afternoon primping and preparing.

Mr. Vernon produced a deck of red-and-white playing cards. "Poker?"

"What are the stakes?"

"Ironing, of course."

Bartholomew smirked. He went to the bar and poured two drinks. "A fool's bet that I'll take."

The cards clacked as the butler shuffled them. "Five-card. Suicide king's wild."

"Deal, Mr. Vernon."

By the time the blue sky was black, Bartholomew had earned a week's worth of shirts to iron and Mr. Vernon was jovial with anticipated freedom from the odious task. But the price was worth paying; the butler's good humor was infectious.

After cards, Bartholomew enjoyed a leisurely bath and was

dressing for the opera when Mr. Vernon returned to the suite with his own tuxedo jacket over his arm. The harsh white light of arc lamps illuminated the streets below as the butler straightened Bartholomew's white bowtie.

"I'm facing a heavy prospect, Mr. Vernon." Bartholomew clipped his watch fob to his waistcoat.

"Yes, Monsieur. I see its weight on your shoulders."

Bartholomew turned the pocket watch between his fingers and light winked off its silver surface. "I didn't realize it was so evident."

"I've known you a long time."

Bartholomew slipped the watch into his waistcoat's watch pocket as the butler fetched a small box from the travel trunk. "Which links, sir?" He held out several sets of cufflinks on his palm. Diamonds, pearls, gold.

"Did you bring the moss agates?"

"Of course." Mr. Vernon returned the selection and gave his employer a set of rectangular gold links the centers of which were creamy agate with green moss rampant within. They resembled an Oriental landscape on a misty morning. "They'll match nicely with Miss Matilde's gown."

The links weren't as conspicuous as the others, but they were Bartholomew's favorites. "Merci." As the butler secured the right cuff, Bartholomew considered the eagle tattooed upon his hand. Then Mr. Vernon attached the left link and held open Bartholomew's tuxedo jacket. He slipped it on.

The butler brushed the back of the jacket. "A nice fit."

Bartholomew closed the front of the tuxedo. "I want more control in the matter of Matilde and the Catcher. I'm carefully considering the possibility of defiance."

Mr. Vernon paused, Bartholomew's cigarette case in his hand. "I didn't realize that was an option."

Bartholomew slipped the silver case into his jacket pocket and added a matchbox from the bedside table. "It may not be. But I must try. For Matilde."

"Yes, for Matilde." Mr. Vernon nodded. "Which reminds me; you wanted to give her this before the opera." He took from the trunk a green gift box tied with a wide magenta bow.

"Ah. Merci."

There was a knock at the suite's door as the men entered the sitting room. The butler opened it to unexpected visitors—the ignorant gentleman from the lobby and the Palace's manager.

"I want a word with your master." The bigot stepped forward as if to push through the doorway.

Mr. Vernon stood his ground, barring the man from the suite. "I am my own master." Even in his fifth decade, he had an imposing presence.

"I'm not speaking to *you*."

"Yes, you are. And we'll have this conversation in the hall."

Bartholomew left the gift on the table beside the door and stepped from the suite with his butler.

"Have your say then leave," Mr. Vernon said to the racialist.

Bartholomew added, "This interruption isn't appreciated."

One hand on his hip and the other jabbing a finger into Bartholomew's chest, the man sneered. "What's *not appreciated* is your man's presence here."

Bartholomew glanced down at the finger then up at the bastard. Behind the bigot, the hotel manager fiddled with his jacket cuffs and looked at everything but the aesir and the butler. Bartholomew addressed him. "Why are you here, sir?"

The racialist answered, "Mr. Guthrie is my witness."

Bartholomew cocked an eyebrow. "You require a neutral party to witness your idiocy?"

The man's hand became a fist. "You and your man need to learn respect." He raised that fist. "I promised a trouncing and now's the time. Mr. Guthrie will allow a fight in the basement."

Mr. Vernon eyed the manager. "He must have paid you quite a lot of cash to secure that space, Mr. Guthrie. What other part do you play in this?"

"I've agreed to provide two referees for the bout, sir. They'll even attest to its fairness in a court of law, if necessary."

Bartholomew folded his arms. "Quite a bit of cash, indeed. Which makes you a biased party to this lunacy."

Mr. Guthrie shook his head. "I'm only providing the connections and location. I'm not one of the witnesses."

"Who are?" Mr. Vernon asked.

"A physician from Tennessee, sir, and his wife. Level-headed, *unbiased* folks."

Bartholomew addressed his butler. "This is your decision."

Mr. Vernon glowered at the challenger. "We will meet you in the basement, Mr.—?"

The bigot's face warped into a self-satisfied smile. "White." He strode to the elevator. The tight-lipped Mr. Guthrie ducked his head to Bartholomew and Mr. Vernon then followed on the fool's heels.

Bartholomew glanced at his pocket watch as they stepped

back into the suite. It was almost time to depart for the opera house. "What are your intentions, my friend?"

Mr. Vernon donned his black evening coat. "I intend to enjoy the opera, Monsieur." He settled his top hat upon his head. "I didn't indicate *when* we would arrive in the basement."

Bartholomew laughed and clapped his friend on the shoulder. "Well played, Mr. Vernon."

Matilde's bedroom door opened.

Bartholomew smiled. "Petit Oiseau. I have a gift for you."

Such a scene it was at the Mission Opera House, though Bartholomew found more bemusement in his ward's wide-eyed excitement than in the pomp and glitter of San Francisco's elite.

Silk and lace, velvet and fur vied with diamonds and pearls for attention. The city's wealth was on full display for Caruso's performance in *Carmen*. A kaleidoscope of color and sparkle filled the lobby. The women were at their fairest, the men in their finest, and the music promised to be a touch of rapture colored by the basest emotions of man.

"Have you ever seen such spectacle?" Matilde held his arm and peered in every direction.

Beside her, Mrs. Henderson looked quite elegant in a gown of dark-blue silk. "And the opera has yet to begin."

Matilde smiled at her governess. "I think this must be a dream. How can I be standing amid so much beauty awaiting the most enchanting voice? It seems impossible."

Bartholomew covered her hand with his own. "Perhaps,

next we will attend the opera in Paris. You'll be astounded by the beauty of that city's opera house."

"That would be wonderful, Monsieur."

The finery around them was dull compared to Matilde. Not for the first time during their stay, Bartholomew saw that his ward was no longer a child. She'd selected a soft shade of green lace for her overdress, in contrast with her pale pink slip, cape, and gloves. The effect was one of sweet, youthful beauty and *joie de vivre*. His gift, which he'd obtained many years prior, she wore around her neck—a wide, scalloped collar of lustrous pink and white pearls.

Enthusiasm heightened the flush of her cheeks and the brilliance of her blue eyes. Her confidence—born from years of fitness, fighting, and respect for her intelligence—gave her a grace and presence that caught many admiring glances as Bartholomew led her through the crowd. Matilde was a beauty. Men watched her and turned critical eyes upon him. Was he father or lover? Could she be tempted away from him? Would he go to battle for her?

Worse than their regard, however, was Matilde's reaction. Her eyes lingered when she returned the interest of strangers. She touched her golden hair. She stroked the pearls at her throat.

Her awareness of her effect upon men was blossoming. She still clung to him—her source of security. But for how long? This power was a weapon she would wield to lure predators into her deadly embrace when she became the Catcher.

Bartholomew frowned and looked down. Her future weighed heavily on his conscience.

She noticed and asked, "What's wrong, Monsieur?"

"Nothing. What could be wrong on such a glorious night?"

She pressed her cheek against his arm and smiled up at him. "Good. You mustn't be so serious. We're surrounded by glittering finery. It's as if the stars themselves have come to earth to listen to Caruso's heavenly voice. Don't you agree?"

Her smile hammered his dead heart and made it ring, like steel striking stone. Bartholomew touched her cheek and nodded as the doors to the hall were thrown open and they were invited to revel in the beauty and death that was *Carmen*.

27

"Prepare to be knocked down to your proper place, Jim Crow." Mr. White, bound knuckles up and pumping, danced about Mr. Vernon like an irksome flea. Bartholomew stifled the urge to swat the man flat; his butler required no aid to quash the contemptible idiot.

The bigot hopped forward and his fist connected with his towering opponent's jaw. However, it didn't have the anticipated effect. Mr. Vernon's stony expression didn't waver. But Mr. White's did.

The butler's bare-knuckled right fist put the racialist down with a solid blow. Knocked quite literally off his feet, the challenger looked up at his opponent with unfocused eyes.

The Tennessee doctor bent over the stunned fool as the doctor's wife stepped forward to address Mr. Vernon. "Is your honor satisfied, sir?"

"An apology would have satisfied me, ma'am. But as that's not been offered, I'll make due with knocking down the disparaging gentleman."

"Excellent," her husband said, "because this fight is finished. Mr. White is incapable of continuing."

"I can. I'm not through." The fool attempted to stand, but fell back on his ass.

Bartholomew proffered a handkerchief. Mr. Vernon wiped blood from his knuckles.

"Mr. White, had you asked," Bartholomew said, "I would have informed you that this match was grossly unfair. The Gentleman Giant never lost a bout in half-a-dozen years." He received the handkerchief back from his butler and tossed it onto the bigot's lap. He didn't want the man's blood on his hands, either.

He held open Mr. Vernon's coat. The butler inclined his head as he slipped his arms into it. "Thank you, Monsieur." Matilde offered up his bowler. Mr. Vernon accepted it. He nodded to the doctor, his wife, and the hotel manager. "Good evening."

Mrs. Henderson led them back through the gray bowels of the hotel.

"That was most gratifying to witness, Mr. Vernon." Matilde's voice and their footsteps echoed in the long concrete corridor.

The butler flexed his fingers. "It was unnecessary violence. But I've lived long enough to know that some people are incapable of avoiding harm."

They emerged into the lobby and continued up to the fifth floor via elevator with a Negro operator who couldn't keep a slight smile from curving his lips.

Back in the suite, Mrs. Henderson fetched ice for Mr. Vernon's knuckles and for drinks. Bartholomew poured three glasses of Scotch.

Matilde laughed and twirled about the room. "What a numbskull!" She grinned at her guardian and some wicked light glinted in her eyes. "Is that the sort of reprobate the Catcher seeks?"

He scrutinized her. She was entirely too excited by the violence she'd just witnessed.

Mr. Vernon settled an ice-filled towel upon his right hand. "Miss, while I won't deny gaining a certain satisfaction from putting down Mr. White, my preference would be to live in a world that didn't require fisticuffs to shut the mouths of ignorant racialists."

She grew still and her expression cooled. She faced Bartholomew. "That man deserved well more than he received. As do so many others. Ours is a world filled with inequality and vice. I am quite ready and willing to mete out justice."

He grimaced and pinched the bridge of his nose. She had no idea what consequences she faced for such an assertion.

Mrs. Henderson touched Matilde's hand. "This is not the time for that discussion."

Bartholomew turned to the suite's tall windows and stared into the night without seeing the city spread out before him. He kneaded the back of his neck. A knot had settled into the muscles, radiating pain through his skull.

Matilde asked, "Are you unwell, Monsieur?"

"The whole damned affair has given me a headache." He focused on her reflection in the glass. "Don't fret. It will pass with rest."

She went to the bar, filled a glass with ice and water, and brought it to him. "Water, rather than Scotch, may be some help, as well."

"Now you're caring for me?"

"Someone must. You deny Mrs. Henderson's excellent advice at all opportunities and Mr. Vernon only encourages you." She waved toward the butler who chuckled and raised his drink.

Bartholomew looked from his glass to his ward. "I prefer Scotch."

"And I prefer you in a jovial mood, which is being obstructed by your headache." She took the Scotch from him and replaced it with the water.

Bartholomew appealed to Mr. Vernon. "God, help me."

"You know he will not," Mrs. Henderson said and turned to Matilde. "Bed beckons, Miss. You've had an exciting evening and there's much to do tomorrow."

The young woman looked to her guardian. "Monsieur, am I or am I not legally an adult?"

He looked up from contemplating the water. "You are."

She laughed and clapped her hands. "Good. I'm old enough to determine my own bedtime, freeing Mrs. Henderson to hound *you*." She pointed at him.

The governess's expression didn't waver. "I shall make Monsieur's keep primary of my responsibilities. You, however, cannot mother your guardian one moment and ignore your own needs the next. Off to bed, young woman."

Matilde huffed. "But, Monsieur said—"

"Good night," Bartholomew finished for her.

"But—"

"Good night," he repeated.

With a lift of her chin, Matilde said, "Fine. I'll be the only one who's well-rested tomorrow and I'll mock your woes when we're enduring the crowds upon the Embarcadero."

Bartholomew saluted her with his glass. "I have my water and have been assured that I'll be quite well as a result."

Matilde stuck her tongue out at him, turned, and took Mrs. Henderson's hands. "I'll miss you every moment you're not with us."

"I do doubt that. You'll be too busy learning from Monsieur and reveling in the freedom away from my watchful eye."

She shook her head. "Not true."

Mrs. Henderson smiled and stroked her cheek. "The months will be fleeting. Don't fret, Miss." She embraced Matilde then stepped back. "Now, off to bed."

Matilde bit her lower lip, nodded, and retired to her room.

Bartholomew pressed his hand against the window and peered the five stories down to the quiet street. The city's lights were going out. The hectic pace of its populace had ebbed. Night and slumber beckoned all the souls to dream.

Mr. Vernon left his empty glass on the bar. "Mrs. Henderson, if you'll excuse me, I'll take your case down to the lobby and arrange for a carriage to the train depot."

"Thank you, Mr. Vernon. I'm most appreciative of your assistance. I'll meet you downstairs momentarily."

He picked up her travel bag. "Monsieur, if it's no trouble, I'd like to accompany Mrs. Henderson to the depot. Once I've seen her onto the train, I'll return to the Palace."

Bartholomew inclined his head. "An excellent notion."

The butler's departure left Mrs. Henderson standing in the middle of the room, watching her employer.

Bartholomew returned her unflinching scrutiny. "There's something on your mind. It's been there for quite some time. What is it?"

Ice clinked against glass. Humanity murmured all around.

"Miss Matilde is not a girl," Mrs. Henderson said. "She is a beautiful, vivacious, and intelligent woman."

"I've noticed."

"Yes, you have. As have a great many men. And so has she."

"And?"

She went to the mirror and desk near the door. "And you would have to be dead not to find her attractive."

"I am dead. What's your point?"

She pinned and adjusted her wide-brimmed, mauve hat. "Your avoidance of the obvious." She caught his gaze in the mirror. "If you do not make her your lover, another man will. And you'll be forced to make an unsavory decision affecting *his* well-being for which she may not forgive you."

A *crack* broke the room's silence as the water glass broke in Bartholomew's hand. "Merda," he muttered. He hadn't realized how tightly he'd been gripping it.

She started across the room. "Oh, sir."

He stopped her with a shake of his head. He dropped the pieces of the glass into the waste can then took a rag from the bar and mopped water from the floor and blood from his fingers. "I'm one hundred times Matilde's age. And I've done a great many things that I've lived so very long to regret. I will not add what you insinuate to that list."

She returned to the desk and donned her gray gloves. "I don't insinuate anything. I'm stating the obvious. You care about Miss Matilde; we all do. But if you don't take your mastery of her to the next stage and summon the Catcher soon, you'll lose the opportunity you've so carefully manipulated. Then it will be by force that you make her your mistress and she will hate you the way you hated the previous Catcher."

He scowled.

Mrs. Henderson continued. "Today Matilde regarded you as a woman does a man, rather than the way a child does her father."

Ice clinked as he retrieved his glass of Scotch.

"Soon she will be the Catcher, Monsieur. And we all know the Catcher commands you." She picked up her slate-colored coat. "Becoming her lover is an eventuality you've avoided considering. Better that *you* control that timing. Don't you agree?"

It was true. Matilde's notice, her maturity, the Catcher's control, and the growing urgency to summon her that he struggled to keep at bay; all of it hung over him. But he felt certain he could avoid the entanglement Mrs. Henderson viewed as inescapable, confident that Matilde would have lovers and still fight by his side.

Bartholomew squared his shoulders. "Matilde is not her mother. Nor is she the Catcher yet. She has a strong moral compass. I trust it to guide us both away from the inevitable misery you predict, Mrs. Henderson." He turned back to the window and looked past his own reflection to take in the city and the dark, expansive bay. "To this day, I cherish my memory of the little girl who held her baby brother to keep him warm and safe against a cold, cruel life."

The ice in his glass settled with a clatter. He left it on a table beside the couch as he crossed the room to the governess. "I won't think of Matilde differently." He took the coat from her hands. "I won't subject her to the corruption that marred *my* youth. I am not one of the Horsemen."

She returned his steady regard. Her voice softened as she replied, "Other men will not see her that way, and you cannot afford to lose her affection."

"No. I cannot." He opened the coat. As she slipped her arms into it he said, "Your wisdom and forthrightness will be missed in the coming months, Mrs. Henderson."

She buttoned her coat then touched his arm. "As I told Matilde, the time will pass more quickly than you think." She followed him to the suite's door. As he opened it for her, she added, "Farewell, Monsieur. I'm confident you'll do what's best—for everyone."

"Adieu."

She strode to the elevator. Bartholomew closed the suite's door when her thin frame disappeared from sight. With a grimace, he dropped to the couch and ran his hands through his hair. Time certainly had passed more quickly than he'd expected, a decade gone in a blink.

Matilde's bedroom door opened. She stood in the dark doorway, clad in a lavender robe, her honey-blonde hair in a long braid over her shoulder. The distress and confusion upon her face made Bartholomew's gut twist.

She'd overheard the conversation his conversation with her governess.

"I've long known you're not an ordinary man. I've learned prying into your affairs will bring me no satisfaction, while patience rewards me with information. But," she swallowed and pressed her hand to her chest. "But I never suspected my governess to be capable of such a perverse notion. And here you stand before me speaking and breathing, yet you asserted only moments ago that you're *dead and one hundred times my senior*. What am I to believe?"

He downed his watery Scotch and put the glass on the coffee table. He removed a cigarette from his silver case, lit it, and inhaled deeply. "Will you sit?"

"No."

Smoke hovered between them like a spirit. He looked through it to her face. "I died over fifteen hundred years ago, Matilde."

Her brow furrowed. "That's ridiculous."

"Apparently not." He turned his right hand to her. "This mark was made when I served Rome in the Third Gallic Legion. I was a centurion. You've seen the sword I carried when I was called Bartholomeus Corona Pellis." Her eyes widened as he added, "Now I'm known as Bartholomew Etienne Pelletier."

She mouthed his name—*Bartholomew*—then shook her head. "This is madness. I'm no longer that ignorant, little girl from the Sixth Ward."

"I've never believed you were ignorant."

"You can't be so old. You can't be dead. You *can't* be. There's nothing cold, lifeless, or decrepit about you." As if to prove it to herself, she strode to him, grasped his biceps, then let go. "See? The epitome of vitality."

He stood. This was the culmination of his efforts. Now was the time to lay bare history and hope her trust was absolute.

"I told you about the Horsemen and the Apocalyptics. I explained that you are to become the Catcher and I your Guardian. But, as you have deduced, there's a great deal I have not said." He stuck the cigarette between his lips and combed his fingers through his hair. "And I don't know where to begin."

She folded her arms. "Just start."

He squinted at her. *Just start.* It was good advice. "Oui." He dropped the cigarette into his empty glass. "Robert Grus and Edgar. You know both would have died without my aid."

She nodded. "I felt certain that Robert's condition was far worse than you said. You used that rare medicine to heal him?"

He considered the eagle on the back of his hand. Showing would be more effective than telling. "One of many deceptions I've told you. There's no medicine that grows feather, heals bone, and restores flesh in minutes." He extended his palm. "What you saw in that bottle was this."

He released his soul and watched her. The blue glow, like liquid flame, seeped from the center of his palm, spread across his skin, and wrapped around his fingers. As he slowly moved his hand, it undulated across his flesh, and he willed it to form an orb, then tilted his palm to let it slide into his other hand.

Confusion and wonder vied for dominance upon her face.

"This is my soul." He willed it to retreat as he clenched his fist. "It is your beginning and your end, Matilde."

"My end?"

"My soul is the means to ready you for the Catcher, Petit Oiseau. Before she can possess you, you must die."

Her head jerked up. "You're going to—"

The weight of his task pulled Bartholomew down. He sat heavily upon the couch and rubbed his forehead; his headache had intensified. "When I was in my third, mortal decade, the Catcher-incarnate stole me from Famine. She ended my life then animated me with a piece of her soul. It has imbued me with the power of the outer darkness and immortality."

Matilde stared at him. "I think I will sit." He stood as she settled upon the couch. He brought her a glass of water. She stared at his hand, hesitated, then accepted the drink. She took several quick gulps as he moved a chair and sat opposite her. Wariness had crept back into her eyes; something he'd hoped never to see again. "I thought the Guardian is supposed to protect me."

How could he cement her trust? Bartholomew sighed. "The Guardian's responsibility is the Catcher's safety, Matilde. Not yours. She reminds me daily that while I delay your transformation, Famine grows stronger."

"She speaks to you?"

He tapped his temple. "Up here."

The ticking of the mantle clock filled the space as he fell silent.

"This all seems a mad story."

"I wish it was a fiction."

She traced a wavy line through the condensation on her glass. "I understand why you didn't tell me." Her hand trembled. "About my death, I mean." She put down the glass and whispered, "No one wants to hear their savior is also their executioner." She covered her face and started to cry.

Bartholomew swallowed a lump. He moved to the couch and held her. Matilde didn't push him away. When her tears were spent, she slumped against him and wiped her face and nose with his handkerchief.

"I'm sorry for all the lies, half-truths, and untold confessions." He held her hand. So delicate and small compared to his. "I'm sorry for all your nightmares."

She looked up. "Why?"

"Because they were my memories."

She jerked upright. "They were *real*?"

"Oui."

"How awful." Her tears began anew and he held her tighter.

After a time, her horror eased and Matilde whispered, "What will happen now?" She sat beside him, her feet tucked beneath her and her head resting against his arm.

"Nothing for as long as possible."

"Nothing?"

"You're my only family, Matilde. I cannot abide the thought of you suffering. You've come to mean a great deal to me, though that wasn't my expectation when I took you in."

Her finger traced the Roman eagle's outstretched wings on his hand. "But what about the Catcher and Famine?" She looked at him, fear in her eyes. "What about the End of Days?"

"Your fate is unavoidable. My search for you lasted fifteen centuries. It would be lunacy to think that another acceptable candidate can be found before Famine gains enough power to summon her brothers." He turned his hand and held hers between his palms. "The time will arrive when I can no longer delay my responsibilities. But you are not ready to die tonight." He kissed the top of her head. "And I'm certainly not prepared to end your life." A band of misery loosened from his chest with that confession.

She released a long, slow breath. "What must I do?"

"What you've been doing. Train, study, and learn from me. Though I cannot change the Catcher's choice," Bartholomew looked into her eyes, "I can dictate *when* this transformation will occur."

"But waiting is a risk."

"A risk worth taking if it means you can live a normal life for a few more years." He released her hands and tucked a stray curl behind her left ear. "The previous Catcher was barely older than you when she was possessed. And she claimed my loyalty through deception."

"She lied to you?" Matilde retrieved his sestertius from the coffee table. She slowly flipped the coin over her knuckles.

"By omission. I was trained for combat by Rome. I knew warfare. And I'd spent over two decades subjected to Famine's bloody appetite and brutal whims. But I didn't know the consequences of the Catcher's actions that day, nor was I given the opportunity to understand what lay ahead."

She handed him the coin. "You've suffered."

Bartholomew shrugged. "That's inconsequential." He slipped the sestertius into his waistcoat's ticket pocket. "What matters is that I've already condemned you without your knowledge. The least I can do is offer you my guidance, my guardianship, and inclusion in every decision henceforth. Most particularly, the timing of your transformation."

Matilde gaped at him. "You're trusting me as an equal?"

"We're partners in this undertaking. As you said to Mrs. Henderson, you are an adult. However," he raised a finger, "I ask you to respect my *centuries* of experience."

A tentative smile lifted her expression. "All right, Monsieur." She proffered her hand. "Partners."

Bartholomew smiled back and grasped her palm. "Against the Apocalypse."

The clock chimed once. Matilde released his hand to cover a yawn. "I wonder if I'll awaken to find that this was just another disturbing dream."

"I hope that comes to be," Bartholomew murmured as they stood. "I would embrace a dull life with all my heart."

She paused in her bedroom doorway. "Regarding Mrs.

Henderson's insinuation, Monsieur. I trust your moral compass too."

He ducked his head. "Merci."

After her bedroom door closed, Bartholomew lay back on the couch and closed his eyes. His shoes hit the carpet with a muffled thump as he toed them off.

"My love for that girl has made me selfish and stupid," he whispered. Was he condemning the whole world by not seizing this moment? The Catcher would object. He lit another cigarette and laughed. *Object* was a gross minimization.

He recalled the time on the *Overland Flyer* when Matilde had learned his presence had resulted in her family's annihilation.

"I hate you and I will forever!"

Her disapproval hadn't troubled him then. Now, however, he cringed at the thought of it.

"Partners." *Someone with whom to share the burden.* He took a drag on the cigarette and smiled. How she'd changed him over the brief span of a decade.

28

MOONLIGHT WINKED OFF THE THIN BLADE AS FAMINE *pressed it to his skin. Bartholomew closed his eyes. The sharp bite of the knife against his throat, the scrape of her tongue across the wound. She moaned and moved atop him, her cold body slick with his sweat. He smelled the musk of sex and excitement. His low murmur and groans echoed hers. His hands slid down her hips, beneath her buttocks. His fingers slipped inside her. Famine pushed against them, against him. She moaned into his mouth, teased his tongue with hers.*

"Open your mouth," she whispered. "Give me your tongue." He obeyed. She bit down upon its tip, crunching through muscle and sinew. She held his tongue captive and pierced it from the underside with his own knife. Bartholomew cursed and swatted her off his hips. Famine hit the floor laughing.

The knife skittered beneath the bed.

BARTHOLOMEW SAT UPRIGHT in the dark room. He swallowed blood. He'd bitten his tongue. "Merda." He scratched his bearded chin then planted his feet on the floor and dug his toes into the plush Oriental rug. He hadn't meant to fall asleep on the couch.

The dark sitting room's air was heavy. He stood to open a window but spied the Catcher's crows beyond the glass. The black sentinels were perched upon the window ledges, watching, waiting.

"Bartholomeus, the vessel is ready. She will follow you."

The Catcher. She'd sent the memory to haunt him in that twilight time between waking and sleep.

"You will keep your promise to me." The Catcher's patience had come to an end.

"Koorva." Bartholomew massaged his temples then buttoned his waistcoat, straightened his tie, and scanned the room for his frock coat. A quick stroll around the fifth floor veranda to clear his head and escape the oppressive room, that was what he needed.

He slipped on his shoes and spied his coat draped over the desk chair. Before he reached it, he stopped in the middle of the room and turned back, transfixed by the soft, legato song of Matilde's quiet soul behind her bedroom door.

As if in a waking dream, he entered her room.

His ward slept on her left side, her right hand atop the covers, and her velveteen cat tucked to her chest. A golden lock had escaped her braid. It curled upon her cheek and jaw to frame her face.

A porcelain doll with a steel spine. That was how she'd always seemed to him. Would she hold together after the

Catcher possessed her soul? If not, could he piece her back together and make her stronger than ever?

"Aesir, your delay will destroy the girl and everyone whom you hold dear."

The Catcher's accusation snaked through his thoughts, heated his soul, and possessed his mind. She knew his worst fears.

He removed the narrow, leather sheath from his coat pocket. From that he slid the thin, sharp boning knife. He shifted the blade this way and that. Dim light winked off its old surface.

"Summon me for the girl's sake. Don't let Famine take her."

He crouched beside the bed and rested his arms on his thighs, his hands hanging loose as he studied Matilde's face.

His duty was to the Catcher. He was to become the Guardian. He needed to become Righteousness. But if he had to sacrifice Matilde, why must it be now?

In fifteen hundred years Famine hasn't gained the strength to begin the Apocalypse, he thought. *What's changed?*

"You have, Aesir."

He whispered, "For better or for worse?"

"That's a matter of perspective."

The headache had returned. "Whose?"

The Catcher answered with silence. He rubbed the back of his neck and sighed. And, like a night so many years before, Matilde stirred in her sleep. She echoed his sigh and her breath caressed his face.

Bartholomew stood and stepped back. He shook his head, spied the knife in his hand, and retreated from her room, their suite, and the Palace Hotel, fleeing his mistress's powerful will and his own weakness.

Damnable, old fool. He reached Market Street and strode downhill toward the Embarcadero smoking, thinking, and trying to ignore the crows that circled and swooped and made the Catcher's impatience evident. How could he ever hope to dictate the timing of Matilde's transformation?

She's more than just a means to an end. She's all I have.

The Ferry Building's towering white clock beckoned, its face glowing gold against the dark gray morning. It was a few minutes past five o'clock and the wharf vendors were preparing for the day.

Bartholomew headed southeast from Market, zigzagging through the neighborhoods and not really seeing anything around him. He smoked and covered a good distance with each long stride, knowing he had to turn back. He couldn't leave Matilde for long.

Baying and barking dogs broke the morning calm.

He scanned the quiet street. Crows still circled, but other birds now joined them. The sky was changing shades of gray, the stars were fading. What had spooked the animals?

"I will wait no longer, Aesir."

Bartholomew stopped and muttered through clenched teeth, "I gave you choice after choice after choice. I gave you my loyalty and lost my family. I surrendered my freedom for centuries. Yet now when I find the *one* living person whose life is worth these sacrifices, you deny me?" He looked up. The crows were gone. His hand became a fist. "Well, now I deny *you*, Catcher. Matilde and I will decide when this happens. *Not you.*"

There was no response, just a heavy, unnatural silence. No barking. No birds. No crows.

The sidewalk heaved.

Bartholomew staggered as if his feet and the ground were waltzing. The earth slipped and swayed, the waltz became a drunken reel, and he lost his balance. He tried to stand, but it was impossible to counter the rolling waves of the massive earthquake.

The street and sidewalks fractured. Water sloshed upward where there'd been dry bricks only seconds before.

From all quarters came the roar of destruction. Bricks and mortar plunged from great heights to smash against the sidewalks and streets. Windows exploded. Wooden beams groaned, twisted, cracked. Screams, cries, shouts—some cut off unnaturally—accompanied the destruction to create a din so enormous that not one sound could be distinguished as all built to a cacophony of death and ruination.

Even after the shaking stopped, the roaring, cracking, and crashing continued. A great, choking dust cloud enveloped Bartholomew as he regained his feet. The Catcher momentarily forgotten, he beheld destruction in every direction.

The city had fallen to an eerie silence, as if holding for the next cataclysm. And in that moment of waiting, a dark void moved, spread, reached toward Bartholomew and away.

Cadavers. Did they follow us?

"Matilde."

Bartholomew ran.

Survivors poured into the streets around him and the chaos of unleashed souls overwhelmed him. So many bodies had been crushed, their lungs filled with dust and blood. He lost the subtle sign of the cadavers in the madness. Even worse, he couldn't sense Matilde's soul.

At every block, obstacles stopped, slowed, or redirected him. San Francisco was inundated with a sea of people in their nightclothes—white cotton and ashen faces. Gaping sinkholes waited to swallow the careless and scared. Electrical poles leaned like inebriated gents. In some places, the streets and walks jutted at impossible angles two, three, even four feet above their former paths. Water mains flooded some streets. Entire buildings blocked others.

Aftershocks rattled the city. Gas lines failed. Explosions concussed the air and more bricks and concrete plummeted from buildings. More windows shattered.

Smoke made the rising sun a demon's fiery eye as Bartholomew fought the tide of refugees fleeing the obliterated areas south of Market Street. Many plumes originated from the direction where he'd left his ward. It was as if Lucifer himself had smashed the city and, being unsatisfied with his efforts, had opened his Inferno to blast the remains of San Francisco off the face of the earth.

Matilde, please be safe.

Finally reaching Montgomery Street, he spied the elegant edifice of the Palace. The hotel stood unbowed, debris scattered at its feet and patrons milling about the sidewalk. He calmed his mind and focused. He still couldn't sense his ward, but neither did he sense any cadavers nearby. As he shoved through the crowd, another temblor rattled the ground and sent people scurrying.

Displacing people and ignoring protests, he pushed through the hotel's front doors into a broken and chaotic lobby. Eschewing the elevators and the beleaguered hotel staff, he charged up the cracked marble stairs, dodging plaster, glass, and the detritus of hastily retreating patrons to reach the fifth floor.

The door to their suite stood wide. The splintered remains

of a writing desk and a chair were scattered across the floor. They mingled with shattered glassware and white goose feathers from torn pillows.

"Non-non-non."

The stench of decay lingered.

"Matilde!" He called her, knowing she wasn't in the room or the hotel, knowing she'd been taken, knowing he'd failed her.

Matilde's bedroom door was smashed inward. He found more splintered furniture, more broken glass. More feathers drifted and swirled in the wake of his footsteps. He saw blood on the wall, on the floor, on his ward's bedding. He stopped in the middle of her room to catch his breath and gather his wits. The stench of cadavers was strongest in the small room.

"Merda!"

Fists clenched and shaking, Bartholomew scanned the bedroom. Seven bullets were lodged in the wall beside the door, high up and closely clustered. He retrieved her automatic from the floor. Its slide was open and locked, the magazine was empty. She hadn't been taken without a fight.

Tapping came from the window. He drew the curtains. Crows blackened the wide sills. Their beady eyes beckoned. Matilde's white-winged bird perched in their midst.

"Edgar." The crows would lead him. The cadavers had invaded the suite and taken Matilde from all of them.

Bartholomew inhaled and looked at her bed. Bettina sat amid the tangled covers. He retrieved the worn velveteen cat. She regarded him with her shiny black eyes. He nodded.

"By any means necessary, Petit Oiseau."

Back in his room, he stripped off his coat and upended his travel trunk. He pulled away its false bottom and extracted two gun holsters and eight full magazines, his Balearic sling, the large boning knife, and his gladius. The metallic *clack* of a magazine sliding home filled the silent room as he reloaded Matilde's Colt.

There was movement in the sitting room. He stretched forth his senses. Not a cadaver. "Mr. Vernon?"

"Sir?" A bellhop appeared in the bedroom doorway, a key in his hand.

"Oui?"

"Um—" The young man gawked at the weaponry arrayed upon the bed, swallowed, and held out an envelope marked with their room number. "I, um, this came just before the earthquake, sir."

Bartholomew chambered a bullet and loaded Matilde's gun into a holster on his right hip then took the envelope. "Merci." Inside was a telegram from Susanna that had been forwarded from Seattle to the Palace. The message read: *Famine in SF. Go east.* Bartholomew crumpled the paper in his fist.

"The manager has ordered the hotel evacuated, sir. We've been told the Palace will burn."

He followed the young man's focus to the suite's windows. A ruddy glow against black smoke filled the view. The conflagration was mere blocks away and showed no sign of stopping. "Doubtless."

"Guests may keep their keys, sir."

Bartholomew nodded. As the young man turned away, he asked, "Is your home safe?"

"No, sir. It was down there." The bellhop nodded toward the window.

"What will you do?"

"The Palace will be rebuilt, sir. I'll stay on to help." His chin lifted. "Maybe this is a chance to remake ourselves and our city. Make it even better." The young man tugged down his dirty cuffs and scanned the damaged room. "Can I help you take anything down to the lobby, sir?"

Bartholomew shook his head. He strapped a holster to his left side and loaded his gun. The bellhop stepped back. "Wait." He removed one hundred dollars from his billfold and gave the money to the young man. "You never saw me."

"I-I can't take that."

"I insist. Tell your manager you left the telegram with my butler."

The bellhop stared at the money then slowly accepted the tip. "Thank you for visiting us at the Palace Hotel, sir."

When the young man was gone, Bartholomew dug an old haversack from his possessions. In went his, Matilde's, and Mr. Vernon's passports, their boarding passes for the *Siberia*, a black leather wallet bulging with cash, Matilde's jewelry, and Bettina. He shrugged into a clean frock coat then slung the sack over one shoulder and across his back. The large boning knife slid into a sheath he belted on his right side. The small boning knife went on his left thigh. Bartholomew sheathed the gladius, attached it to his belt, and adjusted it to carry on his left. Finally, he pocketed the spare magazines.

He worried for Mr. Vernon's safety, too, wondered if his good friend had escaped, been murdered, or taken. But the butler could care for himself. Matilde had to be Bartholomew's only concern.

He went to the window where Edgar perched and pressed his hand to the glass. Flames blazed from the windows and eaves of the building across the street. "Come, bird. Let us rescue Matilde."

Bartholomew smoothed down his hair and donned his black bowler. He would spare Matilde from Famine's savagery by any means necessary.

"Peccatum meum contra me est semper." *My sin is ever before me.*

29

FIGHTING THE HOWLING, FIRE-BORN WIND, EDGAR circled as Bartholomew left the Palace, surprising him by lighting upon his shoulder. The bird kept a keen eye on its airborne kin. When he received clues as to a new direction Bartholomew should take, the bird dropped off his shoulder, flew ahead to land upon some signpost or standard, and stared pointedly down that path.

Bartholomew climbed San Francisco's hills and wound through her crowds, sometimes pushing an overloaded cart for a beleaguered family or hefting a trunk from a weary man's back.

It seemed the whole of the city's populace flowed uphill in an exodus away from Armageddon. Being much accustomed to hard work and long hours, the laborers had a better time of it than did the middle class, whose reliance upon their lesser neighbors' backs had become a cause of regrets and blisters. But that morning all people were equally destitute as they climbed toward the refuge of Golden Gate Park.

A tremendous explosion concussed the air, accompanied by cries from the surrounding crowd. Rising smoke made it impossible to determine the cause. Like some great, nervous beast, the refugees skittered and cringed as explosions continued at irregular intervals. Finally, they encountered soldiers from the Presidio who explained that without water to douse the flames, the San Francisco Fire Department had turned to army explosives to create firebreaks. Judging by the wicked, red blaze consuming the city, they were failing.

Reaching Golden Gate Park at last, Bartholomew surveyed the scene and stretched his senses for any trace of Matilde or cadavers. Weary refugees wandered about, dirty and dazed. Police and soldiers oversaw a food line, gathered supplies, and directed people to aid tents. Here a toddler girl, her red curls disarrayed, sucked her thumb and watched Bartholomew. There a small boy scuttled through the crowd with a black-and-white terrier cradled in his arms. But nowhere did Bartholomew see his towering butler or petite ward.

He moved to the park's perimeter and leaned against a tree, lit a cigarette and closed his eyes. There were so many chaotic souls in the park and around city that it was impossible to pinpoint Matilde. He strained to sense her soul, waited for the Catcher to direct him, and searched for the harmony that came when his spirit tuned to Matilde's. But there was nothing.

Bartholomew ground his spent cigarette beneath his heel and stared at the dirt. *Where are you, Petit Oiseau?*

Edgar landed on his shoulder. The crow cocked his head this way and that as he contemplated Bartholomew. As if understanding the aesir's despair, the bird cooed and rubbed his head against Bartholomew's jaw. The crow dropped off his shoulder, hovered before him for a moment, then flew to a distant tree and exhorted him to follow with a raucous *caw-caw-caw.*

Bartholomew watched Edgar then pushed away from his resting spot. He slapped ash and dust from his frock coat and straightened his bowler. "I will find you, Matilde. I promise." He turned northwest and plunged into the crowd.

The murder of crows grew as the birds led him away from Golden Gate Park. Their strident calls added to the stricken city's bedlam as they circled and dove. Like doddering old men, some hopped ahead of him across the park's trampled grass. Others flew from tree to post to structure, swooping, turning, and performing acrobatics to avoid collisions.

As Bartholomew reached the edge of the park, the chaos of souls was replaced by the cold void of cadavers. He spied three approaching from the south. He frowned. Ash darkened the sky, which meant no sunlight to keep the monsters inside. Doubtless they were drawn by death and fear, but why had they come to a populated area? Cadavers hunted by stealth, lurking in dark alleys to pounce upon their unsuspecting prey. Golden Gate Park was full of refugees, soldiers, and police. It offered little cover for those with evil intentions.

He skirted Spreckels Lake, left the park, and paused beneath a tall cypress tree on Fulton Street. Wings rustled overhead. A large flock of crows returned his regard from the tree's branches. More perched upon benches, occupied other trees, bushes, even the belongings of San Francisco's newly homeless.

It's the crows. Of course. Their unusual numbers had captured the cadavers' attention.

He glanced back. Famine's trio of bastard offspring were

running. They'd recognized him. Bartholomew tensed to fight, but the birds rose as one black mass. Screeching defiance and calling encouragement, they attacked the monsters. Claws and beaks gouged and tore, pulled hair and clothing, scratched eyes and faces. Mortal men, women, and children dove for cover. They screamed and crouched as the birds shed feathers and blood in their mad onslaught against Famine's soldiers. Bartholomew watched the unfolding battle with rapt fascination, his admiration for the birds growing exponentially.

He looked around. He could escape or lead the cadavers away from the park and into a deadly fight.

If he chose to fight, it would mean a further delay in locating Matilde. But doing nothing meant trusting fate. Like roaches, where there were a few cadavers, soon there would be many. And Bartholomew never trusted fate. Sooner or later he would be facing this trio. Better to take them now, rather than when they had support.

Edgar returned to perch upon his shoulder, croaking and chortling as he cocked his head and took in the chaos cause by his family and friends.

"I need to dispatch these enemies, bird. Call off your kin."

The crow considered him for a moment then launched into the air, circled, and called the other crows. The birds broke off their attack.

Bartholomew crossed the street and waited for the cadavers. Two of the bastards were strangers to him, but the third, Vladimir, was a Russian brute who enjoyed killing old women and horses. Bartholomew had narrowly missed an opportunity to dispatch him in Warsaw several centuries past. He hadn't forgotten the cadaver's prowess with the *shashka*, a wicked, curved blade.

"Time to rid the world of you, Vladimir," he called. The cadavers paralleled him on the opposite side of the street. "Who are your pups?" Bartholomew lit another cigarette and smiled at the curses his insult garnered. "Their manners are atrocious." He gestured with his cigarette toward the scratched and bloodied group. "All of you are a mess. Doesn't your mother care for you anymore?"

"Running away, Centurion?" Vladimir replied. "You have a standing invitation for dinner. Lady Staniak has caught a Catcher."

Bartholomew dragged on his cigarette. "I would ask you to deliver my regrets, but you won't be seeing Famine again."

The Russian replied, "Your confidence will be your undoing." The two lackeys laughed, but Vladimir scowled. "Shut the hell up," he snarled in Russian. "Don't underestimate the aesir."

"Vladimir is right." Bartholomew spied an abandoned, damaged house. "Come, moechae. Your graves await." He took a last drag then flicked his cigarette at the cadavers as they charged across the street. He ducked into the house, crossed a front room that had been demolished by a fallen chimney, and wrenched the radiator from the wall. His strength grew as the traces of the Catcher's fiery spirit surged through his nerves and muscles.

The radiator crushed the first cadaver's skull and torso. His equally foolish friend met an equally abrupt ending when he leaped over the first cadaver's twitching body and Bartholomew's gladius sliced his head from his spine.

Too easy.

Vladimir watched the swift demise of his companions

from the crooked doorway. He shrugged. "Idiots." Brains and blood covered the floor.

"Famine's become less discriminate, I see." Bartholomew picked up his bowler and placed it on a chair.

"You have a way, Bartholomeus. It's admirable when you kill."

"Keep your compliments."

The first cadaver was twitching. One swift blow with the gladius beheaded him. Bartholomew's nerves burned as he captured Famine's fleeing pallid spark. He tasted something putrid—the bastard's last meal—and swallowed bile even as Famine's tainted power filled him with swaggering confidence.

Vladimir shook his head. "You'll regret absorbing Pierre's energy, Bartholomeus. It will make you stupid. He was incompetent at best. I cannot comprehend Famine's choice of him." He smirked. "Perhaps it was his French accent."

Bartholomew sneered. "Famine is a whore and you are a cockchafer."

"Such disrespect." Vladimir drew the long, curved shashka from its scabbard and pointed it at Bartholomew. "Because I admire you, Aesir, I will kill you quickly."

"You've said that before, yet here I remain."

The Russian leaped across the room, swinging the blade toward Bartholomew's face.

He parried the blow and returned the favor.

The crash and crack of furnishings filled the room as the aesir and the cadaver battled with unbridled ferocity. The clang of steel upon steel was deafening. They lunged at one another. They slashed and stabbed, backed away, circled, studied. They sought weaknesses, kicked and punched, cursed, taunted, and tested.

Bartholomew lowered his guard, luring Vladimir in, and redirected the shashka into the wall with a furious parry. Masonry dust showered fallen books and raised more motes to join the ones already swirling around the two combatants.

He bloodied the cadaver's nose with a quick jab. But Vladimir's meaty fist slammed into his skull. Bartholomew's face struck the corner of an oak bookcase. His ears rang and his vision blurred as blood filled his left eye. He staggered back shaking his head.

Vladimir wrenched the shashka from the wall and charged his half-blind opponent. Bartholomew straightened. He moved into the attack and deflected the curved sword with a fat, leather-bound book. He slammed the tome into the Russian's head and thrust his gladius through the man's throat. Bones twisted and cracked, cartilage tore. The sword shattered the cadaver's vertebrae.

Vladimir gagged but clamped his fingers around Bartholomew's wrist, his hand like a vice. The Russian raised the shashka. Once again, the book blocked a powerful blow. This time its cover split. Bartholomew twisted free. Ragged pages fluttered about the wounded combatants as they withdrew and faced off.

Drooling blood, Vladimir wheezed, "I'd forgotten your speed and strength."

Bartholomew blinked. His vision was clearing and something alerted his instincts, something that was cold, empty, and moving toward him en masse. "And I'd forgotten you're a strategist, Vladimir."

He raised the gladius. *This ends now.*

Faster than a heartbeat, Bartholomew lunged forward and removed his opponent's head. The cadaver blinked and toppled. The aesir claimed the small spark of power from the outer darkness that had animated his enemy for too long.

Then Bartholomew ran. He took an unerring course and gave little mind to the black cloud of crows descending upon the mass of cadavers in his wake. Singing through the silence was Matilde's soul. He was close enough to hear and feel her spirit, and he was determined to free her.

Bartholomew climbed onto the roof of the Sutro Baths entrance. Staying low, he ran across the peak and dropped to the lower roof of the long building that enclosed a museum and pools. Three acres of glass panels stretched before him. The baths housed an expanse of saltwater swimming pools. Astonishingly, they'd escaped harm in the earthquake.

The lower roof was solid and he slipped down to the edge where metal met glass. He peered past the first truss into the bathhouse below. The setting sun's ruddy light filled the building, turning the water into macabre, bloody pools.

Movement drew his attention. Famine paced and gestured, herky-jerky, frenetic.

Where was Matilde?

Six cadavers stood in a group. Ewan stepped forward to say something to his mistress and Bartholomew spied the girl on the deck at their feet. Her hands were bound behind her back. Her hair had come loose of its braid.

"I'm here, Matilde," Bartholomew murmured. She lay on her side and her head slowly moved as she surveyed her surroundings. Likely she was searching for a weapon or a way out. "Look up."

Famine strode to her and bent over. She grabbed the girl's face, forcing Matilde to look at her. There was an exchange of words. Famine slapped Bartholomew's ward, straightened, and stomped away.

Matilde bit her lip and blinked repeatedly. She turned her head and looked upward.

Their eyes met.

Bartholomew pressed his finger to his lips. Rage burned his nerves. Black bruises marred her face from temple to jaw. Her nose was bloody. Her left eye was swollen. She nodded once, slowly. He placed a gun against the glass, pointed at the surrounding windows, and gestured for her to move away from the pool. Finally, he counted down on five fingers.

Matilde nodded again. She gathered her legs beneath her and got to her knees. One of the cadavers glanced at her, then returned his attention to his raving mistress.

Bartholomew edged as close to Famine as possible. He had bullets for his rotten mistress and her six guards but needed to inflict maximum damage before hitting the deck. The four-story fall would hurt, and if he went into the water his ammunition would be ruined. This way he could land on his feet, get a good trajectory for clean shots, and cover Matilde.

Bartholomew stood.

He aimed.

Famine lunged at Matilde, catching her hair just as she rocked back onto her heels.

Bartholomew sucked a breath, waited, and watched. Famine yanked Matilde to her feet, pulled her around, and shoved her into the pool.

"Skurwysyn."

Matilde surfaced, kicking to stay above water as the

cadavers laughed and jostled each other. She wouldn't last long with her hands tied behind her back.

Two great strides put Bartholomew over the pool. He drew a breath, aimed for Famine, exhaled and fired as he crashed through the windows. Thirteen bullets struck their targets before Bartholomew and a rain of glass hit the water. One gun clattered to the deck. The other was lost to the pool. That left one dry bullet.

He reached Matilde as she went under again. He pulled her to a deck ladder and cut the ropes binding her hands. He swallowed a curse at the sight of the rope burns encircling her wrists. She clung to the ladder, coughed, and vomited water. He drew his gladius and climbed to the first deck.

Fallen cadavers littered the area, but Famine and Ewan were missing. His first shot had struck his mistress, but it wasn't enough to drop her. His second shot had hit the Celtic cadaver in the chest but had missed his heart.

Bartholomew surveyed the building. A large, L-shaped pool bracketed three short lap pools. He and Matilde clung to a ladder leading from the largest pool. To their left was the main deck with two observation decks above that. To their right, a wide staircase exited upward from the pool area. The main deck and first observation deck were lined with long rows of doors—changing rooms for swimmers and hiding places for cadavers.

He descended to Matilde. He brushed dripping hair back from her bruised face. "Can you run?"

Her voice was ragged but steady. "Yes."

"Do they have weapons?"

"One. A tongue-less cadaver she called Cowboy has a revolver, but he wasn't with the others on the deck."

Bartholomew closed his eyes and focused on the bastards. Three twitched on the deck. Two had taken refuge in the changing rooms. Another group was crossing the museum level above. "The main exit is blocked. We'll go up and left. Stay on my heels and do as I instruct."

Matilde nodded. "Give me a knife."

"Head for the doors at the north end of the building." Bartholomew passed her the large boning knife. "I'll get you a gun too, but there's only one bullet."

She snagged his sleeve. "Monsieur?"

"Oui?"

"I think you're right. I'm not ready for any of this."

"Nor am I." He squeezed her fingers. "So let's go."

They hit the deck running. Cadavers rose and gave chase. Bartholomew scooped up the gun and passed it to her. The rattle and clack of bones joined crunching glass, a cacophony of echoes.

"Four are up," she reported.

Two more lunged from a changing room. Bartholomew's gladius was ready. They lost their heads and gave up their energy to empower him. He never broke his stride. Matilde stayed with him. "How many now?" he asked.

"Five. And four on the stairs."

They'd almost reached the far doors when instinct warned him. Bartholomew yanked Matilde forward and shoved her against the wall as a shot ricocheted off a steel column beside his head. Its boom echoed through the building. Another shot followed and a third brought the sound of shattering glass. A fourth bullet struck his left biceps. He cursed but didn't drop his sword. Matilde opened a door and pulled him into a cramped changing room.

Nash Barnes appeared behind him and delivered a vicious kidney punch. Bartholomew dropped to one knee. Matilde plunged the boning knife through the cadaver's right eye. The cowboy staggered back, yanked the blade from his skull, and shook his head. But his snarl was bisected by the gladius. Bartholomew grabbed the doorframe and kicked out with both feet. Barnes staggered back. But the bastard recovered again. He straightened and gave a gurgling, bloody roar.

The boom of Matilde's pistol echoed throughout the building. The bullet tore through the cadaver's chest. He tumbled over the rail and into the saltwater pool. "Stinking, rotten bastard," she said. "Why won't you just die?"

Bartholomew stepped from the changing room and took on the next wave of cadavers. The gladius stabbed and hacked. It grew slick in his hand. But the cadavers fell quickly. They surrendered their stolen power easily.

Too damned easy. Famine's soldiers were falling too quickly. Was her power weakening? No time to wonder. Bartholomew grabbed Matilde's hand.

"Wait!" She retrieved Barnes's gun from the deck.

They charged through the doors at the north end of the glass building.

"Merda!" Bartholomew cursed as the doors closed behind them. They stood in a huge, white-walled laundry facility. "This is a trap." He pulled a long table away from the wall and wedged it against the doors. "This whole situation."

Matilde wiped blood from her hands with a towel. "And I'm the bait?"

"Oui."

She threw the towel on the floor, scanned the area, and pointed. "Windows."

They ran through the maze of rooms, dodging carts and racks to reach another long table furthest from the entrance. Thudding echoed in the room as the cadavers hammered on the door. She climbed atop the table and unlatched a tall multi-paned window. Bartholomew joined her. Spying no cadavers, he slipped through and dropped to the ground. She clambered after him. They eased around the square building and made a run for the nearest corner of the long bathhouse.

Matilde peered around the corner. "Nothing's moving."

"That doesn't mean they aren't waiting and watching." Bartholomew surveyed the hill rising above them. "Do you have any idea of their numbers?"

"Not exact, but I'd guess about a dozen were here. She mentioned more waiting at a house."

"A house? Where?" Famine was rebuilding her army, which meant she was stretching her soul thin.

Something winked from the hillside, a reflection. It returned, remained, disappeared.

Matilde shook her head. "That's all she said."

The reflection was a warning. *Mr. Vernon?*

"Which way, Monsieur?"

Bartholomew sensed movement on the roof. *Ewan.* Then searing pain cut through him. He looked down. They'd lost the boning knife when Barnes had attacked. "Derr'mo." Mr. Vernon's warning had come too late.

"What's wrong?" Matilde turned and screamed.

Famine had come up behind them and run the knife through Bartholomew's heart. He stared at the bloody blade protruding from his chest. How had she gotten the better of him so easily? Had the Catcher abandoned them?

Matilde pointed the cowboy's gun at Famine.

She sneered. "Shoot me and I will remove your dear guardian's head. Trust me, that's not a wound from which he can recover."

The gun wavered, but Matilde didn't lower it. "You won't. You need him to summon the Catcher."

Ewan dropped from the roof to land behind the girl as cadavers swarmed them. The gladius was yanked from Bartholomew's grip. There were far more than a dozen of the undead bastards; too many for him to overcome alone. He'd tried that once before and lost the Catcher and his eye.

Famine slid two fingers along the boning knife's blade then sucked the blood off them. She exhaled and shivered against Bartholomew's back. "You've seen through my bluff, little girl." She yanked the blade from his body and shoved him to his knees. Ewan seized Matilde. Another cadaver bound Bartholomew's hands.

He hated that he couldn't ease the fear in Matilde's eyes. He could still save her with Mr. Vernon's help and the Catcher's power, but first he had to endure and wait for an opportunity to escape.

"Bring them to the house," Famine said. "This is far from finished."

30

"Do you have any notion of the depths of my hunger, Bartholomeus?"

Bartholomew squinted out the window at the dark hulk of the Sutro Baths far below. They were inside the neighboring Cliff House's tower, and the bed and furnishings told him Famine had bribed someone to let her take up residence. She'd been there for weeks, possibly months, judging by the clothes and dishes, bones and rotting entrails piled in the corners and covering the floor. Black ants swarmed a crow carcass on a small table and roaches crunched beneath Famine's feet as she prowled the room. She'd never been neat, but this level of filth was shocking. And the stench of decay, death, and evil intentions had made Matilde dry heave when they'd reached the room.

Matilde. Mon Dieu.

She lay on her side facing away from him, unmoving but alive where Ewan had dropped her. They'd made her watch while the Celt and Barnes had traded opportunities to avenge themselves upon him. Bartholomew had known suffering for centuries, but his ward had never witnessed barbarity like this, even living in the Five Points. Her sobs and pleas had hurt him far more than had the cadavers' knives and fists.

Not an inch of him was pain-free. His hands and face had taken the brunt of the abuse. Ewan relished breaking small bones, and it seemed Barnes harbored resentment about the tongue incident; he'd sliced Bartholomew's from tip to root more than once. Famine had encouraged her soldiers' depravity, directing them to stop and laughing once Bartholomew had healed and they started anew.

The abuse had lasted into the early morning hours until Famine had grown tired, impatient, and jittery. "Get off him," she'd snarled. Now she was a slathering dog circling a baited bear and not as beautiful as Bartholomew remembered from his nightmares.

"Look at me!"

His mistress's rage hammered him. Her will clawed at his. But Bartholomew finally had a choice. He looked away from his ward. Despite their proximity, his connection to Matilde still outweighed Famine's influence, which meant the Catcher hadn't abandoned them.

Miraculous.

Gaunt and wan, Famine prowled, his small boning knife in her hand. Wild auburn ringlets cascaded around her shoulders. Her eyes were sunken, made to appear more so by the smeared kohl ringing them. And a rusty bloodstain marred the ivory Chantilly lace of her gown, right where her heart should have been. She stopped, stroked his cheek from temple to jaw, and murmured, "My darling brother." Then she punched him in the nose.

Bartholomew's eyes watered and he shook his head at the stinging pain. "I'm not your brother," he slurred then swallowed blood. He breathed through his mouth as a wave of nausea surged through his stomach. It was astonishing how much blood his body held and how much he'd swallowed. He opened his jaw wide, and with a loud *crack*, it reseated. "Koorva." Bartholomew looked back at his ward.

Her eyes were open. Their gazes met. There was iron behind those reddened eyes. He gained strength as she mouthed, "By any means necessary."

He glared at Famine. "We're not family." The longer he kept her occupied, the more time Mr. Vernon had to maneuver, and the longer Matilde would remain unharmed.

His hands were cuffed in front of him. Famine seized them, yanked him forward, and kissed him hard. When he wouldn't open his mouth to her prying tongue, she grabbed his crotch. Nothing but revulsion stirred within him. Famine sank her teeth into his lower lip, crunching through muscle and sinew. He held still lest she tear off his entire lip. She moaned as she drew blood and sucked his flesh. She pulled back and brandished the boning knife.

He straightened. "You will not cut me."

"Yes I will, Bartholomeus. You seem to have forgotten you're the penumbra—*my* penumbra—and you belong with me, not that whore's girl."

He spat in her face.

Famine laughed and licked his spittle from her lips. "I understand, you know. I can't compare. She's so young and sweet, and must be such fun in your bed."

They'd been idiots not to restrain him better. The chair

clattered away as he lunged to his feet and backhanded her to the floor. Four towering cadavers grabbed him.

Famine stood. She laughed as blood and mucus bubbled from her nose. "Damnation, Bartholomeus, that blow was sincere." She retrieved his knife from the floor, sheathed it, and slipped it into her cleavage. She grabbed the wooden chair and dragged it across the room. "Take your seat. It's time for supper."

He was shoved into the chair. The cuffs were removed. His left arm was bound to the chair with rope, his right was held by the cadavers. Ewan slipped a noose around his neck then stood behind him and pulled until Bartholomew gagged.

Famine held up his frock coat and robbed the pockets. She grinned as she extracted a box of matches. "See what I've found?" She rattled it in one hand and held up his silver cigarette case with the other. "Let's smoke and fornicate and eat, Bartholomeus. Just like old times." She surveyed the room and muttered, "Someone should clean up before supper." She opened the window and tossed out Bartholomew's coat, his haversack and gladius, and some dead, feathered thing. "That's better."

She lit a cigarette, then another, and straddled his lap. "We wouldn't want our guest to think we're ill-mannered." Buttons careened around the room as she tore open his wet waistcoat, his bloodied linen shirt, and the top of his union suit. She purred as her fingers traced the winged bull tattoo on his chest. "No, indeed. She should know that we specialize in *legendary* soirées."

Famine took a deep drag on one of the cigarettes then blew the smoke in his face. "Remember all the laughs we so often shared?" She smirked and added, "Well, not you so much. I don't recall you having much humor. But we," she gestured to her cadavers, "have had grand times."

Famine passed the other lit cigarette to Barnes. "Cowboy, hold this." She continued, "Truthfully, I've missed you, Penumbra. Nobody," she gestured for emphasis toward his face with the lit cigarette, "I do mean *nobody*, can make me moan like you." She took another drag then blew smoke across the burning end of the cigarette. It flared red and wicked. "Which is why I'm so angry with you for being away. It's been a very long time, Bartholomeus." She ground the lit cigarette into the eye of the bull tattoo. Bartholomew grit his teeth and groaned.

"No-no-no!" Matilde cried.

Famine took a drag from the other cigarette as Barnes held it to her lips then she yanked the knife from its sheath. "Give me his arm." She flicked the blade across Bartholomew's cheek. He jerked away and hissed. She echoed the sound as she licked the blood that ran from the wound.

"Stop it!" Matilde lunged toward them, but was yanked back by a cadaver.

"Don't spoil my fun, little girl." Famine pointed the blade at her. "You're next."

Fighting Bartholomew every inch of the way, the cadavers brought his right arm to within Famine's reach. She cut away his sleeves, sliced the first scar from his arm, and place it upon her tongue. She sighed as she chewed. Her eyes closed. Her face relaxed with pleasure as if she was tasting the most exotic delicacy.

"I am no longer yours to *torture*," he growled.

She peered at him through slitted eyelids. A malicious

smile lit her face. "I wonder..." Her oily gaze slid to Matilde. "Who tastes better?"

Cold seized Bartholomew's chest, but it brought the lull before a storm. "Do not."

She smirked. "Barnes, bring her."

Matilde struggled against the cadaver as he pulled her up. But her hands were bound. Escape was impossible. He dragged her to Famine's side.

Bartholomew's calm deepened as the Catcher's power swelled with his rage. "Do. Not. Touch. Her."

She yanked Matilde forward and shoved up her gown's sleeve to reveal the old fork burn on her forearm. "I thought I spied a manmade flaw." With a practiced hand, she sliced the silvery scars from Matilde's flesh, so quickly the girl only gasped.

Finding some impossible well of strength, Bartholomew yanked free of the cadavers' grip and seized Famine's throat before she could consume her prize. "I *warned* you!"

Barnes shoved Matilde aside. She stumbled and fell.

"Release me or I will eat your eyelids, your ears, and your nose." Famine's voice was pinched, but her anger filled the room and the walls creaked. "I'll flay all the skin from your darling girl's body, starting and ending with her palms and her feet!"

Ewan pulled back on the rope. The other cadavers tore at his fingers, but Bartholomew's grip tightened. Famine's vertebrae popped and crackled. Gagging and gasping, she struck out. She stabbed him in the chest again and again and again. Still he didn't release her.

Bartholomew's left arm strained against the rope holding it. That rope strained against the chair. The chair's leg snapped. They tumbled to the side and he came up straddling Famine, both hands around her neck.

Barnes snatched the dropped knife from the floor, grabbed Bartholomew's hair, and pressed the blade to his throat.

A gun *boomed*. The cowboy flew sideways, a large hole in his head. Brains and blood marred the white wall.

Mr. Vernon had arrived just in time.

Ewan seized his mistress and dove behind the bed with her.

Staying low as his butler obliterated cadavers, Bartholomew retrieved his small knife and reached Matilde. He cut her bonds and held her as she cried. "Shhh. We're all right, Petit Oiseau." He tore a strip of fabric from her night-gown and wrapped her wounded arm.

The room fell silent. Of their enemies, only Ewan and Famine remained intact. A picture frame swung to and fro, scraping the wall. Water from an upended glass dribbled off the bedside table onto an Oriental rug.

"Kill them!" Matilde ordered.

Bartholomew stood and pulled her up. "Save the ammunition. Barnes is already stirring." He gestured toward the cowboy's twitching body. "I hear the rattle and clack of more cadavers. Time to run."

She grabbed his arm. "But now is our chance to destroy her."

"Non, not now. You cannot kill Famine with bullets," he said and pulled her through the doorway. They ran down the hall toward the stairwell. "Are you coming, Mr. Vernon?"

Another rifle shot answered him. Ewan must have moved.

Four stories down they were blocked by a group of cadavers charging up the stairs. Bartholomew dodged through a large banquet room and out a door to the balcony. Thudding feet announced another group of cadavers coming for them. He pulled Matilde to a run. They circled the white Victorian building, rounded the corner, but reversed course as a phalanx of cadavers appeared from that direction.

He pulled her back to the ocean-side of the Cliff House and looked through the windows. A cluster of enemy soldiers waited inside.

He retreated and leaned over the balcony. "Merda!" Below were jagged rocks, slick and inky in the moonlight, and foaming, swirling surf. He could climb down, and even survive the pounding waves, but Matilde would never make it.

He needed a gun, his gladius, a damned fountain pen, anything that could be a weapon against their over- whelming enemy. And he needed the Catcher's will.

Help us, damn you.

The cadavers closed ranks to block all possibility of retreat. Famine's voice rang out as they parted to let her pass. "Bring that little shit to me and secure Bartholomeus before he does something stupid."

Bartholomew fought them back. He bloodied faces, broke bones, and threw bodies into the Pacific Ocean to be smashed against the rocks. But he couldn't dismantle the wall of cadavers. Matilde screamed and fought. More than one cadaver learned her strength belied her size. But their enemy was too numerous. She was torn from his arms and he was forced to kneel.

"*Ty chory suka!*" Bartholomew cursed Famine in Polish.

"I'm a sick bitch?" She sneered. "Indeed, I'll show you how sick I am. Where's dear Mr. Vernon?"

The throng parted. Bartholomew's butler was dragged

before Famine and dropped at her feet. He was bloody and beaten but alive. The cadavers pulled him to his knees and forced him to look up at their mistress. She pointed at a large, bald brute. "You. Hack off the butler's fists."

"No!" Matilde twisted in her captor's grasp. She struck his throat with her elbow and kicked into the side of his knee. He released her and she lunged in front of Mr. Vernon. "Don't touch him!"

"Wait." Their mistress's command stopped the cadavers as they moved toward Matilde. "Gracious, Bartholomeus." She caught his chin and forced his face up. "I see why you've chosen her. Your little bird is a marvel." She put her lips to his ear and whispered, "You should've summoned the Catcher when you had the chance." She whirled and plunged his boning knife into Matilde's chest.

"Non!" Bartholomew strained against his captors.

Matilde gasped, staggered, and seized her attacker's wrist with both hands. Famine tried to withdraw the blade, but the girl had a death grip on her.

Mr. Vernon drew two automatics from his coat pockets and fired point blank into the two-dozen cadavers surrounding them.

Bartholomew tackled Ewan as the Celt lunged toward the butler. The cadaver landed on his face. He rolled over and kicked out, catching Bartholomew in the chest and knocking him back. Bartholomew recovered and yanked Ewan away from Mr. Vernon once more.

He met the cadaver blow-for-blow, turned aside an unexpected knife, and disarmed his opponent. But he was forced to bury the blade in another attacker's throat. Ewan took the opening. Bartholomew received a blow to the head that had him seeing triple. He blocked a kick with his shin then delivered one to Ewan's stomach.

The cadaver staggered back. Bartholomew charged. He closed with the Celt, kicked him in the face, punched his skull again and again. Ewan doubled over and grabbed Bartholomew's waist. But the aesir slammed his elbow into his opponent's neck and brought his knee up into the cadaver's jaw. Ewan stumbled backwards. Bartholomew's next kick sent him over the balcony wall and into the crashing surf.

Bartholomew turned.

Famine finally yanked the knife free from Matilde's grip. Hissing like an asp, she raised it to strike again.

Mr. Vernon tackled her. Famine shrieked. The butler shouted. Both tumbled over the balcony wall.

Bartholomew stared at the spot where Mr. Vernon had been then caught Matilde as her legs buckled.

"Monsieur." Blood pumped from her chest with each weakening heartbeat staining her lavender nightgown scarlet. "Don't let me go."

"Never, never." He cradled her. "I promise."

"Summon me now, Bartholomeus, or you will lose her forever."

"Merde."

The Catcher was right. Her power was the only way to save Matilde. He unfettered his luminous, blue soul and whispered, "Mea culpa," as it rose and pooled in his palms.

But as Bartholomew reached for her, a strained voice carried over the surf.

"Monsieur? A hand up would be most appreciated."

Bartholomew snapped his soul back. He lunged to the balcony wall and looked over it. His butler clung to a drain spout. "Mr. Vernon, so good of you to remain alive." He helped him to safety. "I need your soul to save Matilde."

"Of course." The butler kneeled beside the girl and reached toward Bartholomew. "Though I'd be grateful to have it back when you're done, sir."

Bartholomew clasped his butler's outstretched hand. "This will be painful, my friend." Once again he released his soul. Mr. Vernon grit his teeth and trembled as it burrowed beneath his skin and captured the smallest fragment of his soul.

Matilde's heart stuttered. Her breathing grew shallow and rapid.

Bartholomew withdrew his spirit, released his butler's hand, and gazed in wonder at the glorious, silvery fragment nestled upon his palm. "Like holding lightning, Mr. Vernon," he murmured. "You have the most beautiful soul."

"Thank you, sir." Pain tightened the man's voice.

"I thank *you*." Bartholomew placed his hand upon Matilde's chest.

Let this work. Please.

Mr. Vernon's spirit reached hungrily for the gaping wound and plunged into her heart. It knit together her porcelain skin and spread throughout the torn muscle.

Bartholomew held his breath and lifted her into his arms. "I'm still here, Matilde." His grip tightened. "I won't leave you." He pressed his cheek to her temple. Her skin was cold, pallid.

For a long, agonizing moment there was only the surf, the wind, and the cry of seagulls.

Bartholomew closed his eyes. *Please, Petit Oiseau.*

Mr. Vernon whispered, "Monsieur?"

"Shh." He shook his head. Between that moment and the

next, he heard it; Matilde's soul hadn't stopped singing. What had fallen to a murmur beneath the wind now rose, a dolce aria that wrapped around him to harmonize with his soul once more. He lifted his head, saw his butler's distressed face, and whispered, "I hear her." He stood with Matilde in his arms and turned.

Edgar was perched on the balcony wall, watching them with black, unblinking eyes.

"Look." Mr. Vernon pointed over the railing.

Below the Cliff House, a massive murder of crows circled and dived at an auburn-haired figure clinging to the rocks.

Matilde inhaled and opened her eyes. With a cry, she threw her arms around Bartholomew's neck. "I knew you wouldn't let me go."

"Never, my child. I'll never leave you." He smiled and held her close. "I'll protect you forever."

The crows appeared from below and circled them, a maelstrom of black feathers and beady eyes. Edgar launched into their center. Once again, the Catcher's spies were showing her objection to Bartholomew's continuing defiance.

But, like it or not, the Catcher would have to wait. He no longer bowed to her, just as he no longer bowed to Famine. Matilde was his future, his family, his champion and his child. And he would guard her until the end of his days.

THANK YOU
FOR READING *FAMINE*

———◆—◆—◆———

Please consider sharing your thoughts and reactions with other readers everywhere books are reviewed and sold.

It's all about the details, and many people contributed many details to this novel.

Thanks to Ric and Gwen Colgan for not saying I'm crazy, even though we all know the truth of it. Thank you to Mike Garrett, Nicole LaDonne, Jacob Cartwright, and EFP for lending me your lovely faces, to Lily Talamaivao and Miguel Vigil for making those models look even better, and to Belle of Boring Sidney Hats and Kim of Kimmi Designs for your gorgeous clothing. Thank you to Melanie Bonadore, John Bianchi, and Angie Benson for letting us invade the kitchen and to Vintage Costumers in Seattle for permitting me to browse like a kid in a candy shop.

My gratitude also extends to Jennifer Singleton of the Carriage Association of America and Mindy Groff from the Carriage Museum of America for suggesting the proper gentleman's carriage. And to Ben Brooks, thank you for helping me get Bartholomew and friends got off on the right (train) track. Also, I couldn't have done without Paul Dorpat's *Seattle Now & Then*, an excellent compendium of historical photos and essays.

Thank you to Maia Driver, my outstanding editor; you made a good book so much better. And thank you Jennifer Munswami/J.M. Rising Horse Creations for giving it such a stunning cover!

Again and always, to my family, thank you for your support, enthusiasm, and undying patience.

Monica Enderle Pierce and her characters have been kicking the crap out of evil since 2012. Her first novel, *Girl Under Glass*, was an Amazon Breakthrough Novel Award semi-finalist and a multi-category sci-fi bestseller. Of her dark fantasy novel, *Famine*, reviewers have said, "Jeez. Effing heck. I need more now!" and of her epic fantasy romance, *The Shadow & The Sun*, they've written, "One of the best fantasies I've read in quite some time." Her stories are filled with intrigue, love, adventure, powerful heroines, and intelligent heroes. Monica has an English literature degree from the University of California, Los Angeles. She lives in Seattle, Washington, USA, with her husband, their daughter, a neurotic dog, and two crazy tomcats.

Where you can find Monica online:
www.monicaenderlepierce.com
monicaenderlepierce@gmail.com

.

www.ingramcontent.com/pod-product-compliance
Lightning Source LLC
Chambersburg PA
CBHW030545260626
47157CB00006B/2197